WRITERS

HARVEST

SOS

WRITERS
HARVEST

●

Edited by

W I L L I A M   H .   S H O R E

A Harvest Original

Harcourt Brace & Company

San Diego   New York   London

Requests for permission to make copies
of any part of the work should be mailed to:
Permissions Department, Harcourt Brace & Company,
6277 Sea Harbor Drive,
Orlando, Florida 32887-6772.

"Auggie Wren's Christmas Story" was originally published in the *New York Times.*
"Fault Lines" was originally published in *Frontiers: A Journal of
Women's Studies.*
"Ironwood" was originally published in the *Antioch Review.*
"Lady's Dream" was originally published in *Harper's.*
"Three Mothers" was originally published in the *Boston Review.*

Library of Congress Cataloging-in-Publication Data
Writers Harvest / edited by William H. Shore.—1st ed.
p.   cm.
"A Harvest Original"
ISBN 0-15-600117-9
1. Short stories, American. 2. American fiction—20th century.
I. Shore, William H.
PS648.S5L693   1994
813'.010805—dc20   94-20156

Printed in the United States of America

First edition

A B C D E

CONTENTS

ACKNOWLEDGMENTS

I wish I had the opportunity to thank in person each of the twenty-two writers who donated their stories to make this book a reality. The honor of working with artists of their caliber and generosity is a rare one, and I am grateful for it.

The entire staff of Share Our Strength also deserves credit for their unrelenting efforts to build a national and international network of supporters, whose donated work continues to have a major impact on the fight against hunger. Three SOS staff members have been especially instrumental in establishing and maintaining our ties to America's literary community: editorial assistant Meg Russell, who led the effort to produce this volume, and National Reading coordinators Beth Webb Jelks and Rob Corwin. Their passion for connecting writers to community has enlightened and inspired all of us.

The relationship between SOS and Harcourt Brace has evolved into a truly special one, and this book is one of five already created from our partnership. Our editor, Alane Mason, and her assistant, Celia Wren, have demonstrated an enthusiasm for great literature and good causes. Flip Brophy at Sterling Lord Literistic, our agent and my dear friend, is a familiar name on the acknowledgment pages of all SOS books. She has given more than five years of pro bono work to SOS and has become an integral part of all our book projects.

Thoreau said "To affect the quality of the day, that is the highest of the arts." Everyone associated with this book, all artists in their own right, has done just that. Each person's contribution, along with our readers' support, affects "the quality of the day" for so many people, especially children, in need. For that only two words remain: Thank you.

INTRODUCTION

•

William H. Shore

A STORY BY A GIFTED writer is a gift in
itself. And when, as in the case of this collection, a story is
literally given—donated to support the ongoing nationwide
relief efforts of Share Our Strength—it is doubly so.

This is SOS's third collection of short fiction. As with
the previous two, we asked each writer for his or her best
new work. The response was enthusiastic: in addition to
sending in their stories, the authors recommended potential
contributors and asked to help in other ways. Their eagerness
affirmed the central premise upon which SOS was founded
in 1984: creative individuals can contribute in ways that
go beyond financial support—they can contribute through
their craft. Only rarely is genuine talent matched by this
kind of generosity. But when it is, readers aren't the only
ones to benefit.

We did not require that the stories address hunger, homelessness, or poverty, only that they be good stories, previously unpublished, that the authors wanted to share. The writers' job was to produce their best stories; ours was to worry about using the proceeds to make an impact on hunger and poverty.

But what can be the impact of a few dozen stories, of another fifty thousand or one hundred thousand dollars raised in the seemingly endless battle against poverty in America? The answer might surprise you because the effect has been profound.

On one level we know that even twenty-five thousand dollars, depending upon how they are used, can directly affect the lives of thousands of needy people. A food bank can use that funding, for example, to cover the costs of collecting, preserving, and distributing close to one hundred thousand meals. A school district can take the steps necessary to participate in the federal government's school breakfast program, providing a free or reduced-price breakfast to young children from low-income families, who are at nutritional risk. And a Failure to Thrive medical clinic, which treats young victims of malnutrition, can hire a community outreach worker to ensure that no family falls between the cracks.

But the impact doesn't end there; it is felt, too, on another broader level. Our own experience with collaborative creative efforts like this one has shown that one such effort leads to another. Even if it's not planned that way at the outset, such, inevitably, is the result. One contributor to our first fiction anthology went on to edit two similar books for children on behalf of SOS. Another contributor conceived and organized an annual reading called Writers Harvest, for which this volume is named, in which hundreds of writers around the country read from their works to raise funds and awareness for SOS's antihunger programs.

In many cases the eloquence of writers speaking out

against hunger and poverty can be as influential as the dollars that are raised. There is still much misunderstanding about hunger—and who is hungry—in America. The most common assumption is that hunger is confined to the many homeless people we see on the streets or in the parks or panhandling for spare change at subway stops. But this assumption is contradicted by government statistics that show 27.5 million Americans on food stamps: more than 10 percent of our population for the first time in our history. We know that almost none of these people are homeless since homelessness makes it difficult to receive food stamps. And surveys find that more than twenty-five million Americans a year are going to food banks and soup kitchens because they don't have enough food in their homes to get them through each month. Most are young families with children.

To the many pleasures that come from reading the well-crafted contemporary fiction in this volume, you can now add one more: the satisfaction of helping someone who is hungry.

There are many ways in which writers help to build community. The author Terry Tempest Williams said in a recent interview that "what I found in sharing . . . and in giving readings was the yearning we have to belong to a community, the yearning we have to share our stories. We are told a story and then we tell our own. . . . We can transform the world through story."

Stories, of course, can transform us as well, taking us somewhere we've never been, or taking us back to someone we once were, inspiring us to peer around the corners of our lives. Whether the world will be transformed by this or any other collection—well, only time will tell. But the generosity represented here will certainly result in lives that change, children who are fed and who will grow, all of them uniquely touched by a body of literature they've not yet read.

F A U L T   L I N E S

●

Barbara Kingsolver

Randall is moving away from his living wife. With the reckless, innocent grace of a liberated animal he scrambles toes-and-hands up the face of a huge rock; this must be Africa because none of the trees look right. The two boys are little and hold onto her hands, watching their father. When he straddles the top, Randall turns around to wave at the three of them. She's about to tell him to be careful, but then he jumps off, just jumps on purpose, as if he means to amuse the boys. It's much too high. His body bounces several times with a dull energy like an old tennis ball. He lies still, and then looks up at her sorrowfully because he knows he's going to die.

Grace wakes up with her breath quick in her throat. It's exactly 5:00 A.M. She gets up to check on the boys, who are breathing, as they've been doing steadily for more than a decade and will surely continue to do. She wishes she could believe it. Her new friends in California tell her to "trust the universe," but Grace sees nothing trustworthy about the universe; it's full of exploding stars. Randall didn't die in Africa but in Louisville, two miles from home, when a drill bit broke in the machine shop where he worked. His employer called it a freak accident. Grace considers it a freak accident that anyone ever makes it through life in one piece. When the life insurance came through she thought it would help her mind-set to get away from Kentucky, so they moved to Oakland. Now she has earthquakes to consider.

She goes back to bed but sits up against the headboard waiting for the sun to come up and the boys to stir and another day to happen. The blue shirt she hugs around herself is Randall's, going threadbare at the elbows, wearing out without him. Maybe she dreamed of Randall out of guilt, because she's going on her first date tonight. A blind date—the term alone sounds hazardous. A redhead named Fiona in her grieving group is setting Grace up with her brother. Grace would rather pass, but Fiona has that California air of calling everything between here and New York "the Midwest," in a pitying way, and organizing your whole life for you over the phone before you know what's hit you. Fiona also likes to brag that her apartment is located exactly on the San Andreas Fault.

Grace's relatives have reminded her that Kentucky gets earthquakes too—in 1812 one hit that made the Mississippi run backward. "There's nothing new under the sun to worry about," her cousin Rita declared. Grace is amazed at the things people will say, supposedly to be helpful. When she was pregnant, both times, women would stop her in the grocery to describe their own pregnancies, always disastrous. "Don't do what I did," someone actually told her once in frozen foods at Kroger's. "I went into labor in the fifth month and had a boy that's blind and retarded. He's at the Lexington Shriner's home." Grace was exactly five months along with Jacob then. It was Christmas Eve. She went straight home to bed, not daring to carry in the groceries from the car. When Randall got home the ice cream had melted into a huge puddle in the bottom of the trunk and then refrozen. He tried to make her laugh about it: he called it the Neapolitan skating rink. Randall always trusted the universe. And he ended up with a drill bit in his femoral artery. Grace wipes her eyes on his shirtsleeve. The people in her grieving group say she's in the denial phase, but she's not denying anything. She knows he's dead. She just wishes she could go back and start life over. She'd meet Randall again and they'd move into a safe-deposit box.

In the parking lot after work Grace has an attack of despair. Her job is not the cause. It's a position she secured with the help of her former boss, before moving here: she's a secretary for a company that sells high-pressure liquid chromatography systems to scientists everywhere. She's not clear on what high-pressure liquid chromatography is, but Kareema, the cheeky receptionist who shares the front office, has even less of an idea, and she's been there over a year. "Do I look like a rocket scientist?" she asks Grace.

She doesn't. She looks like an exotic paintbrush. She wears black tights and has dyed her hair fuchsia on the ends and somehow persuades it to reach for the stars. She gives Grace wardrobe tips and tells her she envies her petite figure and undamaged hair. This is one more concern Grace hasn't much considered before: hair damage. When she confided this afternoon that she had a date after work, Kareema offered the loan of her lucky earrings.

So Grace has a pair of little silver snakes biting her earlobes now, but she has no idea what good luck would bring her, if she came into any. She doesn't want to drive to U.C. Berkeley and fall in love tonight. She wants to go home and find Randall in the driveway shooting baskets, missing on purpose so Jacob can win a round of Horse. Puberty is turning Matthew's face into an exact replica of his father's. He'll never even know what they look like, she thinks. When he died they still had preteen baby faces, no jawbones, no real noses yet, just stamped-out cookie-dough faces like all kids have till they've lived long enough to reveal their family secrets. She pulls the car off the street and crumples around the pain in her stomach. She thinks of Randall's face in her dream, so pleased, before he jumped. Why Africa? Where is he trying to take her? How can she hold back what happens next? She lies curled on the front seat, staring up at the darkening sky and a neon fish blinking its way to no particular reward. People have told her she's taking his death too personally. She wonders what options she has; if she were a plant, she'd take it like a plant. She sits up again, fixes her eyes, and drives.

Fiona's brother Loren turns out to be fortyish and tall, with long black hair and pale blue eyes and a blue tattoo in Chinese that curls around his wrist like a suicide scar. If you saw this guy on the street, Grace thinks, you'd expect him to ask for a quarter or steal your purse, but now here he is, her date.

Parking is a problem so they leave her car in his reserved space at the university and walk to the restaurant. Grace never knows what to make of Berkeley's cleverness: a stationer's shop called Avant Card; a coffeehouse called Sufficient Grounds.

"In the town where I grew up," she confesses, "nobody would even get these jokes." It's true. Grace barely remembers what she once expected to find here: trolley cars and the ocean. Now she isn't sure whether she's come up in the world or just moved to a city of pretenders. If these people have the answers, why are they living on a fault line? Also, they're dying like crazy: a great, sad wave of them. Loren touches her arm and they both stop to let a blind young man pass by—his sight taken, Grace now understands, by AIDS. She's learned about retinitis and pneumocystis and the other devastations from three different people in her grieving group; she often feels she's being introduced to her new home through the tragedy channel.

They arrive at their destination, the China Doll. The menu is printed in Chinese with hesitant-looking translations in pencil. Grace laughs at an item called "Funny-Tasting Eggplant." "Who'd order that?" she asks Loren. "It sounds like you'd get salmonella."

He smiles. "My sister forced you into this, didn't she?"

"No, it's okay. She's trying to help me take charge of my life. She thinks I'm lonely."

"Are you?" Loren watches her. Up close he's going a little gray and seems more respectable than she'd first thought.

"No. I've got two boys. Did she tell you that? Teenagers in the house are like living in a buffalo herd." His face registers a tiny shock. People here always do that, she's noticed. It's one more backward thing she's done with her life, had kids before she was twenty.

"I'm envious," he says. "My life is too quiet. Nothing ever happens. Maybe one of my books might fall off the shelf."

Grace doesn't believe for a minute that this man's life is too quiet. It dawns on her that the envies people claim on her—undamaged hair, rowdy teenagers—are stretching it; they're being nice to a widow from East Jesus Nowhere. She looks around the restaurant and wonders if everybody has already guessed this is a first date going on here. She and Loren are both practically glowing with miserable goodwill. "What kind of, what are you at the university?" she asks. "Fiona said an associate professor."

"Of Chinese history," he says, and her eyes inadvertently

go to the tattoo on his wrist. He looks down too, then draws up his sleeve and displays it for her. "It says, Beware of funny-tasting eggplant."

Grace laughs, feeling grateful. Even if she never sees him again, she'll remember that he helped her get through this day. "So can you read this whole menu?" she asks.

They're interrupted by a peppy blond waiter wearing checked pants and a moppy haircut something like Dennis the Menace. "Can I answer any questions for you tonight?" he asks.

"Sure," says Loren. "What is the meaning of life?"

"Enjoy it. You don't die with your assets; you die with your memories."

Grace is amazed. She doesn't think she'll ever be witty enough to live here. When the waiter is gone, she asks, "What does it really say? Your tattoo. I'll bet it's some girl."

"Worse than that. It's a quote from the I Ching that I considered momentous when I was seventeen."

"You don't die with your assets; you die with your memories?"

"Something along those lines. Never get a tattoo."

The waiter brings their wine and they stare into their glasses. Then they both glance up as the blind man who passed them earlier comes into the restaurant with a companion and is seated at a far table. "Everything that happens to you is like a tattoo," Grace says quietly. "It might not show on the outside, but it's permanent."

"Or it shows up later," Loren says.

Grace wonders if he's thinking of AIDS. "You know what I keep imagining? Whenever I come over here to Berkeley I see all these guys blinded, in wheelchairs, and I think they're home from some war nobody knows about."

"Everybody knows about it; they just wish they didn't."

"No, I don't think so. There's lots of little towns like the one I grew up in where they're still in the dark."

"They haven't heard?"

"Oh, they've *heard*. But they scrub behind their ears and go to church and count on being saved. My cousin told me somebody I used to know was back there visiting his mother and went swimming at the Country Club pool. After he'd left, the city council found out he was HIV positive. They revoked his mother's membership and drained the swimming pool."

Loren appears to choke, or laugh. "Drained the pool?"

"Yes. Can you imagine? They don't have any idea of how big a disaster it is. I guess they figure they had a near miss, but it's all under control now."

"People don't believe in disasters."

"I do," Grace vows.

"No, I mean real Cecil B. DeMille natural disasters, epidemics and floods and locust plagues. People believe in individual will. They think they can control what happens to them. Drain the pool, hell, drain the ocean. Uncontrollable pestilence and boils are things that happened a million years ago, to Moses, not to people who possess microchip technology."

"Right. Here's to pestilence and boils," Grace says, raising her glass. She's aware that this may be the unsexiest conversation in the history of dating.

Matthew is asleep when she gets home, but Jacob is still up working on an experiment with goldfish he's conducting for a science fair. Grace is amazed at the difference between Kentucky and California school systems. Last year Jacob pasted photos of endangered species on a poster and won first prize; this year he's worked every night for weeks to make something Grace thinks ought to go on *Nova*, and he says it's terrible—a lot of kids have better projects. It stuns her to realize she's brought her sons to a place where they'll grow up feeling second-rate, as she does. So many things in life she has failed to predict.

Jacob's experiment involves electricity, but he swears it doesn't hurt the goldfish. Grace believes it, because he's named them: Madonna and Goldilocks. Jacob has the softest heart of any fourteen-year-old she's ever heard of. He's been obsessed with endangered species all his life. *Jacob believes in disasters*, Grace knows. Adults walk around making jokes about the hole in the ozone, even Johnny Carson does, but Jacob looks up at the sky and chews the skin around his cuticles.

"They do this in Germany to test the drinking water," he explained to her on the day he brought home the fish and a box of electrodes. "They keep all these goldfish in a tank of city water downtown and they monitor the current. The fish give off so many electrical impulses per minute when the water's pure. If there's too much zinc or cadmium or stuff like that in it, then they give off less. It makes a power shortage, and that sets off an alarm at the headquarters."

Jacob's experiment only shows the electrical emissions from happy fish. His teacher told him he would need to show both control and polluted conditions for a chance at the prize, but Jacob said no. His room is papered with endangered cheetahs and great dying whales. He's not going to poison Madonna and Goldilocks with zinc.

On Saturday morning Grace feels an unsteadiness in her kitchen she suspects of being a tremor. Two minutes later the phone rings and she's pretty sure it will be Fiona telling her to go stand under a doorway. It's Fiona, all right, but she just wants a report on the date. Grace runs down the details, including the menu of China Doll; there's not a lot more to tell.

"No electricity," Fiona concludes, and Grace laughs,

thinking of Jacob's goldfish. Maybe we're swimming through too much pollution, she thinks, and then on impulse decides to tell Fiona about her dream. "Your brother's sweet, but I'm still too attached to Randall to see another man," she says, describing how her heart was pounding, how she woke up feeling guilty.

"He *bounced* when he fell? That sounds almost whimsical."

"It wasn't whimsical," Grace says, shocked. "It was awful. He looked down at us and then he just jumped. On purpose."

"Sounds like you're holding him responsible for his death," Fiona says. Fiona has been through so much therapy she feels qualified to say things that normal people would consider extremely none of their business. She and her husband got a no-fault divorce and lived for one year as best friends before he died of a drug overdose. But this grieving group is only the latest of a long series of groups for Fiona.

"I don't hold him responsible," Grace says. "It was an industrial accident. I blame OSHA."

"But you blame him for being there. You've told me yourself you wished he'd finished his night courses and been a CPA."

Grace regrets bringing up the dream. She knows Fiona could be partly right. "I just feel abandoned sometimes. Not that it's his fault. Just mad that we got left behind."

"It's natural to want to blame somebody."

"I know. Your brother said people don't believe in disasters, they believe in individual will."

Fiona laughs. "Loren's a little intense. But it's true, it's the modern age—Grace, we all act like we were born with some certificate saying we're going to have perfect, happy lives, guaranteed. So if you slip on a bar of soap, you sue Procter and Gamble."

"I saw a show about that on *Oprah*," Grace says, hoping to change the subject. "This woman got window cleaner in her eye and went blind. She sued the window-cleaner company, and then she turned around and sued her maid for taking the day off."

"It's a totally American phenomenon," Fiona says. "We refuse to accept bad luck."

After work on Monday, Grace drives into San Francisco to pick up Jacob from the science fair. Matthew will come home on the bus alone and log in a few more hours as a Latchkey Child. He's thirteen and seems tough beyond his years, with his spiked haircut and heavy high-topped sneakers, but Grace still worries.

"Mom, I think there's going to be an earthquake today," Jacob reports from the backseat as they're transporting Goldilocks and Madonna home. They won third prize.

"Why's that?" Grace asks, not doubting it a bit.

"All the experiments with white rats messed up today. They wouldn't go through the mazes or anything; they all just huddled up together in their boxes. It was lucky for me—that's the only reason I won a prize."

"You think white rats know when an earthquake's coming?"

"All mammals do. Except people. They can smell the positive ions that get released into the air."

"If that's so," Grace says, "they ought to have a big cage of rats downtown at the fire station, like your German goldfish."

"They do have rats downtown," Jacob says. "But nobody's keeping an eye on them."

Grace smiles. She believes Jacob is a near-genius, something she always felt about Randall too, even though he worked in an auto plant. He didn't want to be a CPA, he wanted to make cars. He just had his own crazy way of looking at the world. "So how come we can't smell the positive ions like other animals do?"

"I don't know," he says, and Grace can tell he's looking out the window thinking about this. They're approaching the eastbound on-ramp to the Bay Bridge. The double-decker traffic makes her nervous, with all those westbound commuters whizzing by above them, but both boys love crossing the water. She tries to relax and see the bridge as they do: an intricate forest of I-beams.

Finally he says, "I guess we're tracking so many other stimuli that we don't notice the positive ions. We're too busy doing our own stuff."

Isn't that the truth, Grace thinks, and then suddenly her car is out of control. "Oh God," she says. "Oh my God, I've got a flat tire. I've got *two* flat tires." She pulls as hard as she can on the steering wheel and the car sways less and less violently and finally comes to a stop as far over to the right as she can get on the cramped bridge. She jumps out and looks under the car. She can't see a thing wrong with the tires on this side. She walks around to the other side, and then sees Jacob getting out of the car, laughing. He points behind Grace and she turns around.

A hundred other cars are pulled over, a hundred other drivers all bent over staring at their tires. It's taking everybody quite a while to realize this isn't a personal problem.

She finds the scene hilarious. She thinks again of Randall, catching her eye, spreading his arms wide to embrace the air. It *is* whimsical; nobody knows what's going to happen next. That's where he's trying to take her—that far and no farther. There are only two choices in the "what happens next" department: to pretend it's your job to know or to admit you don't have a clue.

The steel cables over Grace's head hum strangely and then suddenly go slack. Somewhere the structure has broken.

Lots of drivers have raised their hoods and are waiting for a tow truck, civilized salvation, hoping they still might make their appointments. For once Grace feels like the only person around who's getting the joke. It will be hours, if not tomorrow, before they're all off the bridge. "Forget it!" she says aloud. "Nobody's coming. This is the mess we're in."

The concrete is still trembling under her shoes and Grace laughs so hard she can't stop. There are stalled cars over her head and the dancing bay below and Jacob is hugging her. She decides to trust the universe.

HOBBITS AND HOBGOBLINS

•

Randall Kenan

THE WORLD WHISPERS TO those who listen. Secrets collide in the air with visions of truth and particles of fancy. *Listen.* Hear the murmurs of owls speaking of buried treasures, the sparrows conversing over great battles of yore, the squirrels telling tales in hushed voices of the time an angel lighted on the shoulders of a young girl and allowed her to see the ghosts of her future. The voices canter about unceasing, sibilant and silken and silvery in the ether, containing all the wisdom of the great world; all the knowledge ever needed floats about in the air simply to be heeded, contained in faint hummings slightly louder than the chiming of the spheres. Any boy can hear. If he only listens.

Malcolm sits in his grandmother's chair, a great chair it is. In truth, a throne once owned by an Egyptian empress.

Malcolm knows. She sat here, as he does, nibbling peacock's brain and honey-covered hippopotamus eyes, fanned from behind by a Nubian, naked but for a blindingly white turban and gold bracelets. He fans Malcolm now, an idle coloring book in Malcolm's lap while the gossamer plumes create an imperial breeze. Malcolm sighs.

"Brandon, I'm really tired of discussing it."

"Don't call me Brandon again, Denise. It's Fetasha. Fetasha Yakob."

"Jesus, Brandon—"

"Denise!"

Malcolm's father cannot see it, but a cobra slithers about his feet. Malcolm can see it. He does not worry. Malcolm knows it will not harm his father. The snake has a bright red hood and is striped like a barber's pole in orange and black. It has no venom; but it can breathe fire when it is angry.

"You have no respect for me or my beliefs."

"Brandon, *you* have no respect for you or your beliefs. You've changed your damn mind so much you don't even know what you believe."

"Don't use language like that in front of the kid."

"Jesus, Brandon. He's six."

"Exactly. Set an example."

"Mother, can you believe this?"

"Hm."

Malcolm grins when he sees that his grandmother, who sits ignoring his quarreling parents, trying to read a magazine, has a hobbit on her lap. The hobbit's name is Fidor. He winks at Malcolm. Fidor's orange hair is pulled back in a long ponytail and he wiggles his big toes in contentment, enjoying the grown-ups' argument.

"*You* are the one who hasn't held a job in ten fucking years."

"Denise. The boy."

"Don't come into my house and lecture me on how I should raise my son, Brandon. My god, you haven't seen him in three months and suddenly you've decided you can't live without him."

"He's my son, Denise."

"You noticed. Finally. Took you six years."

"Don't be mean, Denise. There's no reason."

Malcolm is pleased to see that the blue cockatoo—a very rare creature, with the ability to fly through walls—is perched atop his mother's head. The blue cockatoo sings in a Tibetan dialect taught to it by the great pirate Yeheman, a friend of Malcolm's who invited him onto his flying pirate ship, the galleon *Celestial,* once. Yeheman wanted to take Malcolm on an expedition to the other side of the sun. But Malcolm had to go to school. Yeheman left the blue cockatoo with Malcolm as a bond of friendship. The cockatoo is named Qwnpft.

"The answer is no, Brandon. No."

"The name is Fetasha, Denise. It means 'search' in Amharic, the Ethiopian tongue."

"I don't care. No. You can't take him."

"Only for a month, Denise."

"Not for a day."

"I have rights, you know."

"Sue me."

"Denise. I am his father."

"Brandon, I was there. For both events. The conception and the delivery. I know who the father is."

"You're trying to be funny, Denise. This is not productive."

"You're being flaky, Brandon. This is not sane."

The curtains are covered with speckled lizards, they chirp like birds and create melodies in eight-part harmony; gifts from the Maharajah of Zamzeer. He keeps sending gifts to Malcolm to gain his hand in marriage for his royal daughter, the ugly Princess Zamaha. Malcolm plans to hold out.

"Mother, do you hear what your *former* son-in-law pro-
poses to do?"

"Hm."

Fidor giggles and slaps his knees; Qwnpft trills in Tibetan. Yamor, the black winged horse, another gift from
the Maharajah, wanders into the room, up to Malcolm, and
nuzzles him softly behind the ear. Yamor is lonely and wants
to go for a fly. But Malcolm can't right now. His parents
are arguing.

"Denise, I know how to take care of him. He'll be well
looked after."

"Brandon—"

"*Fetasha!*"

"*What*ever. You can't even look after yourself. How on
earth do you expect me to allow you to take my son to
Jamaica for a month? Has this Rastafarian bullshit really
messed your mind up that much?"

"Denise. Your language."

"I cussed like a sailor when you met me, remember? That's
what you liked about me, or so you said."

A green orangutan hangs from the ceiling lamp; giant
fire-red Amazonian toads play leapfrog in the thick carpet;
a yerple sea turtle swims the length of the room, turning
somersaults as he completes laps over everyone's head. Underneath the coffee table perch three demons, Ksiel, Lahatiel,
and Shaftiel, whom Malcolm caught a week ago trying to
punish a knight. He has made them his slaves. They smoke
long pipes of blue tobacco, which puffs up in pungent clouds
of pink.

Today is Malcolm's sixth birthday. Jerome, Sheniqua,
Perry, William, Davenport, Clarise, Sheryl, Tameka, Yuko,
Bharati, John, Björn, Ali, Federica, Francesca, and Kwame
came to his party. School will be over in three weeks, his
grandmother says, and he will be taken from his Kingdom

in the Land of New Jersey to his summer residence in the Land of the Carolinas, to rule with his Imperial cousins at the Imperial Palace at Tims-on-the-Creek. But now his father, who used to be a sorcerer named Mahammet al-Saddin and has now become this Prince Fetasha Yakob, plans to steal him away to the island principality of Jamaica, where rules, Malcolm has heard tell, the sinister Lord Jam-Ka. His father must need him to do serious battle. But Prince Fetasha must convince the Empress, his mother. Malcolm is worried.

"Just stop asking, Brandon. You are not going to let my son smoke ganja and commune with Ja and fiddle with some crystal around his neck. And what on earth are you wearing anyhow, Brandon? You look like . . . Jesus, what does he look like, Mama?"

"Hm."

"What's that around your neck?"

"Cowrie shells. And the name is Bran—I mean Fetasha."

"Your name is Brandon Church Harrington, okay? And that's what I'm going to call you."

"You continue to disrespect me, just as you always did. That's what ruined our marriage."

"O Lord, here we go. How dare you—"

Prince Fetasha came to Malcolm's party as a surprise. He tiptoed around back, in through the wood, and made a grand entrance in the backyard, coming through the hedges. He scared Malcolm's friends. Malcolm was surprised and happy. Malcolm's mother was angry. They fail to "commu-niticate," his mother once told him. They're just from different worlds, child, his grandmother said. His grandmother likes Prince Fetasha. He likes Prince Fetasha too.

"How can a man, a black man, with your background, with a degree from Morehouse with Honors, no less, with a J.D. from fucking Yale, *fucking Yale,* go around with his head twigged up like a reggae singer, wearing—what the hell is it you have on, Brandon? I liked last year's get-up much better—Do you know how much you'd be pulling down now if . . . ? I have to take a Valium every time I think about it—"

"It's always money with you."

"*You* were the one born with a trust fund, okay? Don't talk to me about money. I worked my way through med school, fool. *You* don't even pay alimony, which I could still contest."

"I don't *caaarre* about money, Denise. Can't you get that through—"

"You don't *caaarre* about anything. Except your hair."

Malcolm's mother, the Empress of the Kingdom of Orange, in the Land of New Jersey, is a baby doctor, a pediatrician. Her office has walls of tangerine and licorice and lime and lemon and blueberry. Grandmother, the Queen Mother, takes him there sometimes. All their subjects, waiting for an audience, sit in the candy-flavored room playing with blocks and trucks and rainbow-assorted animals—toys Malcolm now finds boring. The Empress doesn't have any video games there.

"Okay, for the last time—now I'm going to say this slowly, Mr. Rasta, so you can possibly, perhaps, maybe, understand me: Under. No. Circumstance. Will. I. Allow. You. To. Take. My. Son—the one who's sitting over there in that chair. With. You. Any. Where. Not Jamaica. Not Ethiopia. Not Newark. Not New York. Not to the convenience store down the road. After your last escapade, Mr. 'I'll-have-him-back-Sunday-night,' Malcolm is OFF LIMITS. If you want to see him, you do it *here*. There he is. Now look."

"Denise. You're being unreasonable again."

"Unreasonable? Again? Need I remind you that you kidnapped—"

"Kidnapped is unfa—"

"You were gone for a week—"

"Should we really be arguing in fron—"

"—instead of a weekend."

"—of him?"

Malcolm likes to go to the Savage Land with Prince Fetasha. He likes the caverns and the canyons, the mountains of steel and glass. They speak in loud booming voices. Sometimes they scream. The roads are wide and black with strange hieroglyphics painted about them, and the inhabitants rush about, surely chased by some monster like Godzilla or Smaug or Bigfoot. Prince Fetasha, when he was Mahammet al-Saddin, carried Malcolm on his shoulders when they were in the Savage Land. He could smell the scent on his father called M-cents. Malcolm liked the smell. Prince Fetasha's hair is in long black snakes like Medusa's. He says they are called deadlocks. Malcolm likes to play with his father's deadlocks. They feel spongy and soft, and they smell of M-cents. Once Fetasha, who was then Mahammet al-Saddin, gave Malcolm a necklace of shells like the one he's wearing now. The shells told Malcolm where a magic amulet, long lost, lay in Africa. But when he got home his mother, the Empress, tore the shells from his neck and said he might get a funjus from them and threw them into the trash compactor. The amulet will never be found.

"Denise."

"No."

Yamor, the black winged horse, is getting antsy, and the floating yerple turtle seems to be slowing down. A mask on the wall winks at Malcolm, and the hobbit is climbing down off his grandmother's lap. Malcolm stands up, and his wing'd sandals take him across the room to his mother and father.

"Mom, can I get some deadlocks like Daddy's?"

His mother, the Empress, raises her hands in the air and rolls her eyes—the look she has when his grandmother says his mother is "disgusted with the world again." His father, Prince Fetasha, pats him on the head. But before either of them say anything, his grandmother pops her magazine shut.

"Okay, Boo"—his grandmother always calls him Boo—"time for your bath and bed, birthday boy. It's been a big day."

Malcolm's grandmother, the Queen Mother of the Empress, sells castles and palaces when she's not being Queen Mother. They call her a Real Tor and she wears a man's jacket with a house decal on the breast just like his F-16 decal. Each day she meets people looking for a new castle. Sometimes she takes him with her. People make very strange noises when they look about and ask the Queen Mother weird questions. Malcolm likes to explore the castles, looking for ghosts and lost elves, always on the lookout for hobgoblins, his sworn enemies.

Sometimes his grandmother, the Queen Mother, takes him to the movies and gives him candy and makes him swear he won't tell his mother, the Empress, since she'd be "disgusted with the world." Malcolm isn't allowed to have candy. But he sneaks plenty.

In the bathroom his grandmother helps him undress. He lifts his arms to get his shirt off. The water sloshes into the tub with a river's rush. The Queen Mother sprinkles the secret magic special potion into the water and it begins to bubble like a witch's cauldron.

"Okay, soldier. In you go."

"Gramma?"

"Hmmm?"

"Am I going to go to Jamaica with Daddy?"

"I doubt it very seriously."

"Will I get to go to New York with him?"

"I don't think so baby. Not for a while."

"Can I get deadlocks like his?"

"Hell no."

"Why?"

"Into the water."

The silly octopus with the glasses caresses Malcolm's ankle as he steps into the water; the bubbles tickle his hind parts as he eases down. When each one pops it says a magic word. The water is warm and heavy and fun.

"Now don't forget to wash behind your ears."

The Queen Mother leaves, and Malcolm closes his eyes and says the magic words and—Qwiza!—he is a merman with a fishtail wide as the dining-room table, its scales diamond-shaped and sparkling and the color of oil on water, and it flops gracefully in the air like a sail in the wind. When Malcolm is in the water he is transformed into the Lord of the Sea (a part-time job), and he must save his Dominion from the evil sea-wizard Nptananan who takes on many forms, his favorite being that of a merwolf with fangs like a viper.

Malcolm knows when it is about time for his grandmother to come to fetch him out of the water, "so your skin won't wrinkle," she says, so in a flash he turns back into a boy. He lathers himself with the secret magic special potion soap that will make him invincible to arrows and bullets and swords and hexes. He remembers to wash behind his ears.

Grandmother, the Queen Mother, dries him off in the huge towel that could eat him whole—yet another gift from the Maharajah. In times of trouble, with the right magic words, it becomes a flying towel.

After saying good night to the Empress and the former Prince-Consort Fetasha, who once was the Crown Prince Mahammet al-Saddin, Malcolm is tucked into bed, the Nubian still fanning him. The yerple turtle sleeps bobbing in the air current; the lizards are aligned on the curtain in the pattern of the family coat-of-arms; the flying horse, Yamor, is ZZZZZZing on the floor, his wings fluttering ever so gently with each breath; Fidor, the hobbit, is curled underneath the covers with Malcolm; Qwnpft, the blue cockatoo, nestles in Malcolm's hair; and the barber-pole–striped cobra coils into a perfect O at Malcolm's feet. The demons, Ksiel, Lahtiel, and Shaftiel, are secure in the closet and Malcolm can smell the pink smoke as it wafts up from underneath the door.

"Sweet dreams, Boo. Happy birthday."

" 'Night."

The Archangel Rafael, right on schedule, appears in the corner when the lights go out, his blazing sword at the ready.

Voices drift up through the ventilation shaft.

"Denise, you know it would really be a good experience for him at his age."

"I've already paid for his trip down South with Mama."

"Money, money, money."

"I know, I know. I was the Marxist once, remember? I still . . . well, you know . . ."

"Oh yeah, the occasional freebie at the clinic, the volunteer work at the soup kitchen, the checks to Amnesty and the NAACP and Klanwatch and Greenpeace. You mean the payoffs for the guilt ghosts?"

"Now who's being mean? I'm not going to be a hypocrite, Bran—Fe—I can't. Mr. Dreadlocks. I've worked hard for this life. If you don't like it, fuck you and the horse you rode in on. It's my life, okay? I'm the one going to Capitalist Hell."

"But do you have to take Malcolm with you? I just don't want my son to grow up to be a vain, pampered, spoiled, over-educated, suburbanite airhead with no sense of history and no sense of self."

"Like you, you mean?"

"Hey, I'm trying, okay? At least I'm—"

"Well, so am I."

"   . . ."

"   . . ."

"Look. I don't want to take the bus to the PATH to the subway to home."

"Brandon? I don't know why you won't just buy a car."

"Can I . . . ? Well . . . you know . . ."

"Oh, you're such a baby, Brandon; a cute baby, but a thirty-six-year-old baby just the same."

"Please, Dr. Harrington, ma'am, *please.* I'll wash your turbo-engined-diesel-guzzling-air-polluting-whatever-the-hell-it-is in the morning. Please . . ."

"Stop that. You know . . . I'm . . . oooooh . . . Now quit that. Brandon. *Brandon.* You . . ."

" . . ."

" . . ."

"Remember the time we got ourselves holed up for a whole weekend and listened to nothing but Carmen MacRae and ate nothing but fruit and did it till we were sore?"

"Hmmmmmmm . . . Where do you plan to sleep?"

"Right here."

"But Mama'll . . ."

"She *is* a grown woman, you know."

" . . ."

" . . ."

"I do like the way those feel."

Through the open window Malcolm can see four red eyes aflame. He knows they belong to the hobgoblins, Gog and Magog, on the lookout for him, lurking in the whispering New Jersey night. But the Archangel will protect him and there is no cause for worry. The castle is secure. The drawbridge is drawn. The Imperial Family is one. And he is six years old.

Once in a great while, now and again, deep within dreams of dreams of dreams, we may chance to hear our true selves speak, and in those words are kept the keys to ourselves; but we must listen softly, listen soundly, listen silently, or we may never hear our voices telling tales of who we are.

A CHRISTMAS IN ROME

●

Reynolds Price

I WAS TWENTY-TWO YEARS old and still hadn't spent a Christmas away from home and family. That day, though, I was half laid back in unmarred sun on a bench in the one true Colosseum—Italy, Rome, December 25th, 1955. Europe had only begun to believe that the devastation of Hitler's war might be survived, and even in Rome the sight of a winter tourist was rare as a failure of courtesy.

I'd left my room and made my way down through the city past ruins posing in vain for their picture—today they were empty of all but cats and the ghosts of assorted psychotic Caesars, woolly Vandals and Visigoths. I'd even walked the length of the Forum and on across to the Colosseum with no sure glimpse of anybody as lost and foreign to the place as I and not a sign of holly and gifts.

I'd passed a few couples, sporting that brand of Italian child who easily seems the world's most loved, and some of the parents had bowed at my greeting. But the Colosseum was likewise empty of all but me and one of the bent old ladies who then sold tickets to everything Roman, toilets included.

So there, lone as Robinson Crusoe, I had one question— was I *lonely* in this grand place on such a high love feast? It seemed the right question for a journeyman writer. I shut my eyes to the broad arena that drank the blood of so many thousands and let the Mediterranean sun burn its health deep into my bones.

The answer was no. I was happy. I'd got the gene from both my parents and, despite a normally bleak adolescence, had been sheepishly happy most of my days—*sheepish* because I wondered still if smiles were the kit for an artist's life. Even if I was here today on one of the world's great magnets alone, I knew I was backed with a travel grant; my first short stories were down on paper; more ideas were ticking in me; and—best—in only three more weeks I'd join my first requited love who was skiing in Austria.

What but love had I ever wanted more than the freedom I tasted now? So I sat for the better part of an hour in those two lights—the sun and the fierce shine that leaked from my triumph. I was already well down the road to my work and my free choice of love. If another human entered the Colosseum with me, I failed to see. So the place itself, for all its gore, conspired to keep my joy pure as radium, fueling my life with dangerous rays.

High as I was, I managed to nod awhile, and when I woke a half hour later, I knew the sound of a distant bell had brought me back; its toll had triggered the chill I felt. The light in the midst of the arena was dimming, and my mind spoke out, strong as the bell: *What are you up to this far from home on this day, of all days, and lonesome as any hawk on a thermal? What can you learn here that you don't already know in your bones? Get the hell on home.*

If I'd seen or heard in the next two minutes the least reminder of the day at home—an indoor tree, some merciful laughter—I might have hailed the nearest cab and tried to board a westbound plane. But the guts of the Colosseum dimmed further till all I saw was purple murk—the locker rooms of gladiators, holding pens for the beasts and martyrs. And I knew I needed this strange lone time in whole new worlds; so when I stood to enter the day, I turned, not due north back to my room, but south toward the Circus Maximus, flat on a plain below the devastated mansions of the Palatine Hill.

The film *Ben-Hur* with its chariot race was still four years ahead in time; but my high-school Latin book had shown the racecourse at its clamorous pitch—the oval track, the island around which the horses had turned, the ranks of seats. I stepped across one strand of wire and walked to where the island had stood—no visible remnant of marble or horseflesh, brawn or fury. The ground was littered with modern paper, though there were signs of recent digging— the earth was freshly turned and spongy.

Again no other human in sight. By now I was well into midafternoon. Surely Christmas mass was over; shouldn't some of the family meals be ending? What *was* the local Christmas schedule?—dinner at my pensione was not till eight and would feature salt fish. Even the beggars that walked the streets as late as midnight were under cover, real shepherds from the country who'd brought real lambs and homemade bagpipes with weird music more Arab than western—a firm recall of the shepherds' role in the birth at the heart of this darkest month.

It wasn't all self-pity then when I thought, *I'm the one lone man in Rome for the birth that turns the wheel of the year.* I'd better aim back toward my room. I could write this day down anyhow and save some piece of an hour that sud-

denly threatened to down me. At the third step, my foot
stubbed hard.

I leaned and dug up a piece of marble the size of my
palm with a perfect vine leaf carved on its edge, plainly
ancient. I looked around me—still nobody, a few fast cars
half a block beyond. I hid the marble deep in my pocket and
walked ahead, my first real robbery. Before I'd gone another
ten steps, I drowned the guilt by thinking, *It's all you'll get
today, ace.*

That was only the truth; and I'd got near the rim of the
Circus before I saw two people blocking my path. Before
I halfway understood, my first thought was, *Well, Christmas in jail;* and I froze in place. But then I took their presence in.

A young woman maybe my age in a tan dress, a coarse
brown shawl on her hair and shoulders, one hand on the
child beside her—a boy with filthy knees and a coat so tattered it hung in comical strips. Was he five years old or older
and stunted? They were beggars, surely, but—no—their
hands didn't reach out toward me, though their black eyes
never flinched from my face.

I knew I had a handful of change, the featherweight coins
worth almost nothing; and I dug in another pocket to find
them.

Before I'd brought them to daylight though, the woman
shook her head once—no. She gave the boy a gentle push
forward.

He came to me, solemn but sure, and when he stopped
two yards away, he held his hand out clenched as if he offered
a game.

I asked what he had.

He thought a moment, opened his fist, and brought it
toward me—a dark disk, half-dollar size, that was meant to
look old.

They were selling souvenirs, likely fakes. I smiled a "No, *grazie*," holding both my hands out empty.

But the boy reached up and laid the coin in my right palm.

I'd spent hours with a boyhood coin box; and when I turned the bronze coin over, I knew it was real with the profile of one of the saner Caesars, Hadrian—worth maybe fifteen dollars. I still didn't need it and offered it back.

But the child wasn't selling. He turned and trotted to join his mother, never facing me and not returning to take the marble vine leaf I offered.

His mother's voice, though, gave me the first real news of the day. She stooped to the ground and scratched in the dirt to show where they'd just found the coin; then she launched a smile of amazing light and said what amounted to "You, for *you*."

I have it still—a useful gift.

HOLD TIGHT

●

Amy Bloom

MY SENIOR YEAR IN high school, I was in two car accidents, neither of them my fault, and I was arrested twice, also not my fault. I couldn't keep my hands on the wheel and the guardrails flew right at me.

I found myself on emergency-room examining tables, looking into slow-moving penlights, counting backward from forty to demonstrate consciousness and calling my mother terrible names. I hate hospitals, nursing homes, places like that. That smell makes me sick and the slick floors trip me up. When I visited my four dying grandparents, who dropped like dominoes the winter I was ten, I had to leave their rooms and go throw up. By the time February came, I had a favorite stall. With my mother, I could never even get that far; before I even saw her I'd throw up from the thick, green smell cloaking the pain and stink and helpless-

ness. When there was no reason to keep her, they let her
come home.

My mother painted about forty pictures every year and
her hands smelled of turpentine, even when she'd just gotten
out of the shower. This past year, she started five or six
paintings, but only finished one. She couldn't do her big
canvases anymore, couldn't hang off her stepladder to reach
the upper corners, and this last one was small, kept on an
easel near her bed. After December, she didn't leave the bed.
My mother, who used to stand for hours in her cool, white
studio, shifting her weight from foot to foot, moving in on
the canvas and backing off again, like a smart boxer waiting
for the perfect opening. And then, in two months, she shrank
down to an ancient little girl, loose skin and bones so light
they seemed hollow. Friends suggested scarves for her bald
head, but they slipped down constantly, half-covering her
eyes and ears, making her look more like a bag lady than a
soap-opera star. For a while she wore a white fisherman's
hat with a button that said Don't Get Me Mad and then she
just gave up. I got used to the baldness and to the shadowy
fuzz that grew back, but the puffiness in her face drove me
crazy. Her true face, with cheekbones so high and sharp
people didn't think she spoke English, was hidden from me,
kidnapped.

When I got angry at her, I'd leave the house, throwing
rocks against the neighbors' fences, hoping to hit a neighbor,
someone's healthy mother—who wasn't as smart or as
beautiful or as talented as mine. My friends bickered with
their mothers over clothes or the phone or parties and I
wanted to stab them to death for their stupidity. I didn't
return calls and they all stopped calling, except for Kay,
who left a jar of hollyhocks or snapdragons on the front
porch every few weeks. When I can talk again, I'll talk
to her.

I could hardly see the painting my mother was still working on, since I became blind and deaf as soon as I'd put my hand on the doorknob. I stared at the dust motes until my vision blurred and I could look toward the bed. My mother held my hand, weakly, and her weakness made me so angry and sick, I'd have to leave the room, pretending I had homework. And she knew everything and I couldn't, and cannot, forgive myself for letting her know.

It was June, like it is now, and everything outside was bright green and pale pink and our house was dark and thick with dust. My father was hiding out in his study, emerging only to entertain my mother and then lumber back to his den. He'd come out, blinking in the light, putting his hands before him, as if he'd never been in our front hall before. We barely spoke, avoiding dinner conversation by investing heavily in frozen foods. He'd chat with my mother from five to six, reading to her from the *National Enquirer*, all the Elvis stories, and then I'd take over while he drank bourbon-and-soda and nuked a Healthy Choice dinner. The nurse's aide went home at five and we saved money by not getting another aide until the night shift. Six terrifying hours every night. While my mother rested a little, if the pain wasn't too bad, I'd go down to the empty kitchen and toast a couple of Pop-Tarts. Sometimes, I'd smoke a joint and eat the whole box. If my father's door was open, I'd sit in the hall outside his door, waiting until the sharp, woody smell brought him roaring out of the study; we didn't have the energy to really fight. More often than not, I'd end up taking a last puff in his study, my legs thrown over his big leather armchair, my father sipping his bourbon and staring out at the twilight. I think I ate Cheez Doodles most of the night, leaving oval, orange prints all over the house. We'd take turns sitting with my mother until the next aide came at eleven. I'd watch the clock. One night, I woke up on the floor of my mother's room, my feet tangled with the dust ruffle. I could see my father's shoes sticking out on the other side of the bed. He'd fallen asleep on the floor, too, his arms wrapped around one of my mother's cross-stitch pillows. I don't know what happened to the aide that night but in the morning, I was under an old wool bathrobe, my father gone.

On her good days, I'd help my mother paint a little. She always said I had a great eye, but no hand. But my hands were all she had then, and she'd guide me for the bigger strokes. It was like being very young again, sitting down at the dining-room table, covered over with endless sheets of smooth-surfaced drawing paper.

And I said "Mommy, I can't make a fish, not a really *fishy* one." And she told me to see it, to think it, to feel its movements in my hand. In my mind it glistened and flipped its adorable lavender tail through bubbling rainbows (I think I'd just seen *Fantasia*), but on paper all I had were two big purple marks and some smaller scribbles where I wanted fins. She took my hand and rested her own big, square one over mine, very lightly like a magic cloak, and the crayons glided over the paper and the fish flipped its tail and even blew me a kiss, from hot pink Betty Boop lips. And I was so happy that her hand could do what my mind could see.

By the end of June, though, she wasn't even trying to have me do the same for her. We just sat and sometimes I'd bring in paintings from the year before, or even five years before, to give her something new to look at. And we looked hard, for hours, at the last painting, done on her own, not a sketch or an exercise, a finished piece. She called it *Lot's Wife*. The sky was grays and blues, beginning to storm and in the foreground, in the barren landscape, was a shrouded figure. Or it could have been just an upright shroud, or a mass, or a woman in a full-length muslin wrap. But the body was no longer alive; it had set into something dense and immobile. And far off to the right, bright and grim, were the little sticky flames of the destroyed city, not even rubble around it.

"It's so sad," I complained to my mother.

"Is it?" She hardly talked anymore; she never argued; she never commanded. A few requests, mostly silence. She took a deep breath. "Look again. The sky is so full and there is so much happening." She looked cross and disappointed in my perception until she closed her eyes and she just looked tired.

My graduation was the next day and it went about the way I expected. I overslept and didn't even open my eyes until the phone rang. Kay called me from school. I told her I didn't know if I could get there on time. I didn't know if I wanted to. I asked my father, who shrugged.

"I don't know if you want to go, Dell. I suppose you should. I could come, if you want."

My father was, and is, a very quiet man, but he wasn't always like *that*. This past year, she took the life right out of him. I have spent one whole year of my life with a dying woman and a ghost.

I went, not even noticing my shorts and ratty T-shirt until I saw all the girls in off-the-shoulder clouds of pink and white, slipping the blue robes down over their party dresses. Kay stuck my mortarboard on my head and elbowed me into my section. In the class picture, there are rows of dyed-to-match silk shoes and polished loafers and my ten dirty toes, sticking through my sandals. I didn't win any prizes, which I might have, if I hadn't been absent for fifty-seven days my senior year.

Kay's parents, who are extremely normal, dropped me off, on their way home to a graduation picnic for Kay. Her mother showed me the napkins, with Kay's name flowing across in deep blue script.

"Send our . . . tell your father we're thinking of you

all," Mrs. Greene said. Our parents didn't know each other.

My father made room for me on the porch swing. He ran one finger over the back of my hand, and then he folded his arms back around his chest.

"How'd it go?"

"Okay. Mr. Switzer says 'hi.' " Mr. Switzer used to play chess with my father, when we had people over.

"That's nice. You were a hell of a chess player a few years ago. Eight years ago."

I didn't even remember playing chess; my father hadn't taken the board out for ages and when he did, he didn't ask me to play.

"When? When was I a chess player?"

My father shut his eyes. "I taught you when you were five. Your mother thought I was crazy, but she was wrong. You were good, you got the structure immediately. We played for a few years, until you were in fourth grade."

"What happened?" I could see him, thinner, with more brown hair, sitting across from me. We sat on the living-room floor, a little bowl of lemon drops between us.

"Mommy got sick, the first time. You don't remember?"

I didn't say anything.

"You don't have to remember. Dell, we don't even have to talk about this now. But, car accidents or no, she's going to die. She is going to leave us and even if I am blind drunk and you are dead in a ditch, she is still going."

The swing creaked and I watched our feet, both long skinny feet, like our hands, flip back and forth.

"Mrs. Mason's leaving, let's go upstairs. It'll be a treat for your mother. Two for the price of one."

"I'll stay here."

His fingers left five red marks on my arm, which, honestly, bruises up at nothing.

"Please come."

The swing rocked forward, free of us, and I followed him.

When she died that night, I wrapped the painting of Lot's wife in an old sheet and hid it in the closet, behind my winter boots. I guess I thought the lawyers might take it from me. I still don't know where to hang it. No room in the house is right for it and I cannot bear for it to be in a museum. I unwrap it at night and keep looking.

LADY'S DREAM

●

Tobias Wolff

Lady's suffocating. Robert can't stand to have the windows down because the air blowing into the car bothers his eyes. The fan is on but only at the lowest speed, as the sound distracts him from driving. Lady's head is getting heavy and when she blinks she has to raise her eyelids by an effort of will. The heat and dampness of her skin give her the sensation of a fever. She's beginning to see things in the lengthening moments when her eyes are closed, things more distinct and familiar than the dipping wires and blur of trees and the silent staring man she sees when they're open.

"Lady?" Robert's voice calls her back, but she keeps her eyes closed.

That's him to the life. Can't stand her sleeping when he's not. But he'd have some good reason to wake her. Never a mean motive. Never. When he's going to ask somebody for a favor he always calls first and just passes the time, then calls back the next day and says how great it was to talk to them, he enjoyed it so much he forgot to ask if they would mind doing something for him. Has no idea he does this. She's never heard him tell a lie, not even to make a story better. Tells the most boring stories. Just lethal. Considers every word. Considers everything. Early January he buys twelve vacuum-cleaner bags and writes a different month on each one so she'll remember to change them. Of course she goes as long as she can on every bag and throws away the extras at the end of the year, otherwise he'd find them and know. Not say anything—just know. Once she threw away seven. Sneaked them outside through the snow and stuffed them in the garbage can.

Considerate. Everything a matter of principle. Justice for all, yellow brown black or white they are precious in his sight. Polite as a Chinaman. Can't say no to any charity but forgets to send the money. Asks her questions about his own self. *Who's that actress I like so much? What's my favorite fish?* Is calm in every circumstance. Polishes his glasses all the time. They gleam so you can hardly see his eyes. Has to sleep on the right side of the bed. The sheets have to be white. Any other color gives him nightmares, forget about patterns. Patterns would kill him. Wears a hard hat when he works around the house. Says her name a hundred times a day. Always has. Any excuse.

He loves her name. Lady. Married her name. Shut her up in her name. Shut her up.

"Lady?"

Sorry, sir. Lady's gone.

She knows where she is. She's back home. Her father's away but her mother's home and her sister Jo. Lady hears their voices. She's in the kitchen running water into a glass, letting it overflow and pour down her fingers until it's good and cold. She lifts the glass and drinks her fill and sets the glass down, then walks slow as a cat across the kitchen and down the long dim hall to the bright doorway that opens onto the porch where her mother and sister are sitting. Her mother straightens up and settles back again as Lady goes to the railing and leans on her elbows and looks down the street and then out to the fields beyond.

Lordalmighty it's hot.

Isn't it hot, though.

Jo is slouched in her chair, rolling a bottle of Coke on her forehead. I could just die.

Late again, Lady?

He'll be here.

Must have missed his bus again.

I suppose.

I bet those stupid cornpones were messing with him like they do. I wouldn't be a soldier.

He'll be here. Else he'd call.

I wouldn't be a soldier.

Nobody asked you.

Now, girls.

I'd like to see you a soldier anyway, sleeping all day and laying in bed eating candy. Mooning around. Oh, general, don't make me march, that just wears me out. Oh, do I have to wear that old green thing, green just makes me look sick, haven't you got one of those in red? Why I can't eat lima beans, don't you know about me and lima beans?

Now, Lady . . .

But her mother is laughing and so is Jo in spite of herself. Oh, the goodness of that sound. And of her own voice. Just like singing. General, honey, you know I can't shoot that nasty thing, how about you ask one of those old boys to shoot it for me, they just love to shoot off their guns for Jo Kay.

Lady!

The three of them on the porch, waiting but not waiting. Sufficient unto themselves. Nobody has to come.

But Robert is on his way. He's leaning his head against the window of the bus and trying to catch his breath. He missed the first bus and had to run to catch this one because his sergeant found fault with him during inspection and stuck him on a clean-up detail. The sergeant hates his guts. He's ignorant trash and Robert is an educated man from Vermont, an engineer just out of college, quit Shell Oil in Louisiana to enlist the day North Korea crossed the parallel. The only northern boy in his company. Robert says when they get overseas there won't be any more Yankees and Southerners, just Americans. Lady likes him for believing that, but she gives him the needle because she knows it isn't true.

He changed uniforms in a hurry and didn't check the mirror before he left the barracks. There's a smudge on his right cheek. Shoe polish, maybe. His face is flushed and sweaty, his blouse soaked through. He's watching out the window and reciting a poem to himself. He's a great one for poems, this Robert. He has poems for running and poems for drill and poems for going to sleep, and poems for when the cornpones start getting him down.

> *Out of the night that covers me*
> *Black as the Pit from Pole to Pole*
> *I thank whatever Gods may be*
> *For my unconquerable Soul.*

That's the poem he uses to fortify himself. He thinks it over and over even when they're yelling in his face. It keeps him strong. Lady laughs when he tells her things like this, and he always looks at her a little surprised and then he laughs too, to show he likes her sass, though he doesn't. He thinks it's just her being young and spoiled and that it'll go away if he can get her out of that house and away from her family and among sensible people who don't think everything's a joke. In time it'll wear off and leave her quiet and dignified and respectful of life's seriousness—leave her pure Lady.

That's what he thinks some days. Most days he sees no hope at all. He thinks of taking her home, into the house of his father, and when he imagines what she might say to his father he starts hearing his own excuses and apologies. Then he knows that it's impossible. Robert has picked up some psychology here and there, and he believes he understands how he got himself into this mess. It's rebellion. Subconscious, of course. A subconscious rebellion against his father, falling in love with a girl like Lady. Because you don't fall in love. No. Life isn't a song. You choose to fall in love. And there is a reason for that choice, as there is a reason for every choice, if you can get to the bottom of it. Once you figure out your reasons then you control your choices. It's as simple as that.

Robert is looking out the window but he's not really seeing anything. He's repeating to himself a verse from Longfellow's "Hymn to the Night," and every time he says *the cool cisterns of the midnight air,* it's like a breeze blowing through him.

It's impossible. Lady is just a kid, she doesn't know anything about life. There's a rawness to her that will take years to correct. She's spoiled and willful and half-wild, except for her tongue, which is all wild. And she's southern, not that there's anything wrong with that per se, but a particular kind of southern. Not trash, as she would put it, but too proud of not being trash. Irrational. Superstitious. Clannish.

And what a clan it is, clan Cobb. Mr. Cobb a suspender-snapping paint salesman always on the road, full of drummer's banter and jokes about Nigras and watermelon. Mrs. Cobb a morning-to-night gossip, weepily religious, content to live on her daughters' terms rather than raise them to woman's estate with discipline and right example. And the sister. Jo Kay. You can write that sad story before it happens.

All in all, Robert can't imagine a better family than the Cobbs to beat his father over the head with. That must be why he's chosen them, and why he has to undo that choice. He's made up his mind. He meant to tell her last time, but there was no chance. Today. No matter what. She won't understand. She'll cry. He will be gentle about it. He'll say she's a fine girl but too young. He'll say that it isn't fair to ask her to wait for him when who knows what might happen, and then to follow him to a place she's never been, far from family and friends.

He'll tell Lady anything but the truth, which is that he's ashamed to have picked her to use against his father. That's his own fight. He's been running from it for as long as he can remember, and he knows he has to stop. He has to face the man.

He will, too. He will, after he gets home from overseas, from this war. His father will have to listen to him then. Robert will make him listen. He will tell him, he will face his father and tell him . . .

Robert's throat tightens and he sits up straight. He hears himself breathing in quick shallow gasps and wonders if anyone else has noticed. His heart is kicking. His mouth is dry. He closes his eyes and forces himself to breathe more slowly and deeply, imitating calm until it becomes almost real.

They pass the power company and the Greyhound station. Red-faced soldiers in shiny shoes stand around out front smoking. The bus stops on a street lined with bars and the other men get off, hooting and pushing each other. There's just Robert and four women left on board. They turn off Jackson and bump across the railroad tracks and head east past the lumberyard. Black men are stacking planks, their shirts off, skin gleaming in the hazy light. Robert pulls the cord for his stop, waits behind a wide woman in a flowered dress. The flesh swings like hammocks under her arms. She takes forever going down the steps.

The sun dazzles his eyes. He pulls down the visor of his cap and walks to the corner and turns right. This is Arsenal Street. Lady lives two blocks down where the street gives out into fields. There's no plan to the way it ends—it just gives out. From here on there's nothing but farms for miles. At night Lady and Jo Kay steal strawberries from the field behind their house, dish them up with thick fresh cream and grated chocolate. The strawberries have been stewing in the heat all day and burst open at the first pressure of the teeth. Robert disapproves of reaping the harvest of another man's labor, but he eats his share and then some. The season's about over. He'll be lucky if he gets any tonight.

He's thinking about strawberries when he sees Lady on the porch, and just then the sweetness of that taste fills his mouth. It surprises him. He stops as if he's remembered something, then comes toward her again. Her lips are moving, but he can't hear her; he's aware of nothing but the taste in his mouth, and the closer he comes the stronger it gets. His pace quickens, his hand goes out for the railing. He takes the steps as if he means to devour her.

No, she's saying, no. She's talking to him and to the girl whose life he seeks. She knows what will befall her if she lets him have it. Stay here on this porch with your mother and your sister. They will soon have need of you. Gladden your father's eye yet a while. This man is not for you. He will patiently school you half to death. He will kindly take you among unbending strangers to watch him fail to be brave. To suffer his carefulness, and to see your children writhe under it until they flee the house, one by one. To be changed. To hear yourself, and not know who is speaking. Wait, young Lady. Bide your time.

"Lady?"

It's no good. She won't hear. Even now she's bending toward him as he comes up the steps. She reaches for his cheek, to brush away the smudge he doesn't know is there. He thinks it's something else that makes her do it, and his fine lean face confesses everything, his fear, his kindness, his need. There's no turning back from this touch. But she can't be stopped. She has a mind of her own, and she knows something. She knows how to love him.

Lady hears her name again.

Wait, sir. She blesses the girl. She turns to the far-rolling fields she used to dream an ocean, this house the ship that ruled it. She takes a last good look and opens her eyes.

A RIDER TO HIS END

●

Richard Currey

It was late afternoon when the woman took the seat next to Calder Lux.

She was heavy, sandbagged into her late fifties and wearing a plain sack dress above a pair of black cowboy boots, a smudged Atlanta Braves ball cap pressed to her eyebrows. "Afternoon," she said to Calder.

He nodded, returned the greeting.

"Waiting on a bus?"

Calder glanced around the station, wondering if anyone was there for a different reason. "Yes, I am," he said. "Yourself?"

"Headed up to Grimsby. They're tearing down the church up there and I want to watch."

"You don't like churches?"

"Not that at all," she said. Her voice was a forthright

rasp. "More a form of entertainment. I'll watch it come down brick by brick, plank by plank. Might be a souvenir to take away."

She gave full attention to Calder for the first time, studying his face a moment before she spoke. "You know, it's a strange thing—I mean, if you don't mind my saying so, you look just like my brother who died with his boots on and got buried the same way, sitting straight up in his Cadillac."

Calder hesitated, afraid to speak.

"Embalmed and dressed in his Sunday best," the woman continued, "and sitting up behind the wheel of his Cadillac."

"You buried the entire car? With your brother's body *inside?*"

The woman nodded in the affirmative. "I'm aware it's a tad unusual, and it wasn't as if he wanted it that way, wrote it in his will or anything. I mean, Harlon didn't even *have* a will, which of course offered me a bit of leeway in the funeral planning. And it's only me anymore, what with Mother and Daddy gone themselves, so the arrangements fell to yours truly. And I thought, well, the way Harlon positively adored that automobile—the one earthly possession which I felt he should carry with him into the beyond."

It was the first time Calder had seen a woman of this vintage wearing cowboy boots with a dress. It left him uneasy.

"The thing is, I probably wouldn't have been reminded of any of this if I hadn't sat down next to you and took note of the fact that you are something very close to a dead ringer for brother Harlon. When he was younger, of course."

"How old was your brother when he died?"

"About ten years older than you are right now."

Calder calculated. Thirty-two years old, early in life. "He was young, then."

"It was a youthful passing, make no mistake. It was a

death of sin and liquor and all that sort of thing. But to
each his own."

"That's what I always say."

"What?"

"To each his own."

"Oh, right." She settled back on the wooden chair and
centered her huge black purse on her lap. "It was the middle
of a windy April when we set him in his final resting place.
The eleventh of April, 1973. God I recall it like a nearby
yesterday. The bulldozer to one side, resting after a hard
day's work. Sycamores bursting into new leaf. The comfort-
ing sound of the river nearby. The Goodhope River, east
fork, which of course I pretended was the River Jordan
during the ceremony. The roof of Harlon's Cadillac barely
showing over the lip of the grave. The sky on the verge of
a fresh spring rain."

"Perfect day for a funeral."

"Oh my, yes. As it happened the rain did let go there for
a few minutes, really came down. We climbed into the car
to get out of the wet."

"Into your brother's car?"

"We thought it fitting. Another small way to say farewell."

"You got inside the car? Everybody at the funeral? *With*
the body?"

"There was just me and the preacher. We took the back,
so as not to disturb anything going on between Harlon and
his ghost up in the front seat. Lucky that big yellow thing's
a four-door!"

"The Cadillac was yellow?"

"What's wrong with that?"

"Nothing's wrong with it, I just . . . well, that's a bright
color to send a man off with. That should keep things bounc-
ing in the afterlife."

"One would hope so," she said plainly.

Calder looked out onto the open bay of the station. "I'm just out of the Army," he said. "Going home, I guess."

If the woman heard she gave no sign, tipping her head back and closing her eyes.

"Not much to go home to is what I was thinking." He glanced at her, unsure if he should continue. It seemed she was going to sleep and Calder assumed the conversation was ended. He finished the last of his cold coffee from a vending machine cup.

A minute passed and she spoke again, startling Calder, her voice slower and softer than before, emanating from behind the closed eyes. "You know, Harlon and I had a lovely childhood. Out near Gentry. Daddy had a fruit tree ranch, pretty as you please. A dream upon a dream, I must say, even in the hard days."

"The hard days?"

She opened her eyes and focused into the light, still speaking at a measured pace. "Well, there was that sordid business surrounding fornication with farm animals, none of which either I or my mother believed for an instant. But that's the thing with this country—you're poor and out of the way and there'll be people take a stab at undermining what little you do have, try to cut the rug out from under you. Make up stories. Tall tales."

"Sounds like a very tall tale."

She pushed her ball cap high on her forehead. Calder was surprised by her green eyes, lambent and opening toward him. "You may be assured, my young friend, that there are gents in this neck of Texas who engage in carnal relations out in the barn at midnight, but to make the passing suggestion that my father and brother were two of those is the height of God's nonsense. Let me tell you."

"That's what I figured."

She fixed her gaze on the center of the vast Confederate flag filling the station's west wall and concentrated on the swerving vistas of her past.

"So," Calder said, "I guess this nasty rumor did some damage to your family?"

"That it did. Make no mistake. What it also did was cut down on Daddy's markets for his fruit. He ended up having to drive as far away as Houston and San Antonio, or going out on a roadside somewhere fifty miles from home to sell right there on the shoulder." She shook her head, disapproving. "Eating dust and all. All for the so-called love of a cow."

Calder looked down into his paper cup. "Could I get you a coffee?"

"How very fine of you to ask," she said, "but no, I've sworn off the brown stuff. Just one more of the many drugs in this life. Look what happened to Harl."

"I guess your brother must have had trouble with more than coffee."

She razored a hostile stare into Calder's forehead. "Starting with that dirty gossip about the cow, is that what you're getting at?"

"No, no, I mean, you know, of the *drugs* in this world . . . he must have had more and worse than coffee."

"Oh," she said, releasing him from the stare. "Yeah, it's safe to say he experimented with more than coffee. Dumb ass."

"I'm sorry?"

"I said he was a *dumb ass,* my brother. Sweet-hearted sad sack of a dumb ass."

Calder nodded.

"Well," she said, purging a sigh, "life does go on, doesn't it?"

"That it does," Calder said.

"That's a fact Harlon had difficulty getting a grasp on.

He seemed to think life was standing still, that it was a big room you found yourself in and you could carry on with this and that, and then when you were ready just go out the other side none the worse for wear. Well, ho boy, I'm here to tell you it is not that way."

"No, ma'am."

"And life isn't like a river, either, although that's another comparison you often hear. No sir, a river's wild and prancing if you know what I mean, it drives and sulks around and buries itself and bursts out into the sun and you never know what's next with a river. Now that's not much like the life of any human being I ever knew. The only person to use such a comparison would have to be a poet or some sort of damned fool."

"I guess that must be correct."

She turned quickly to appraise Calder, this time taking in the cleft of his small chin. "You don't happen to be a poet, do you?"

He shook his head, refusing the job. "Army clerk," he said. "Up until a few days ago. We never had to write any poetry."

Her eyes moved up to his nose, evaluating.

Calder said, "What I meant is that I follow what you're saying. About how life isn't quite the same as the things it gets compared to."

She shifted her attention away, lifting her head up, back down. "There you go."

Calder sat quietly, watching movement in the station. There was an announcement for the departing Galveston bus. Across from where they sat an old man stood and dropped his trousers in order to rearrange his shirttail.

"I'll tell you what life is like," she said, taking no notice of the old man with trousers bunched below his knees. "It's like riding one of these Greyhound buses. You get on board—that's like being born—and find yourself a seat.

That's childhood. And you see that you're on board with a slew of other folks, some older than you are, some younger, some richer, some poorer, some prettier, some uglier. The bus takes off, and then you're on the highway and that, you see, would be the highway of life. Well, directly you decide the seat you're in is a bit uncomfortable and get up and find another available seat. Your choice of course is decided by how and where other people are sitting and this is how it is moving through life, you have to make way for others and figure how you're going to make a place for yourself at any given time and in the teeth of whatever situation presents itself. So now anyway you've found this new seat and lo and behold it's next to a reasonable-looking man"—she glanced at Calder—"or woman who takes a quick shine to you, and you dip right into the old honeypot, which in turn lifts the skirt on a whole host of troubles. But now when you're looking around for a new seat, you're looking around together, as a couple, you follow me?"

Calder was uncertain he was following her at all but said that he was.

"Good, because where a couple goes is likely to develop into three, four, Lord knows how many. Now of a sudden you're in need of more than just the two seats. The die has been tossed, as it were."

"Absolutely."

"But the funny thing is, you threw the die without thinking too clearly about it beforehand. You were simply allowing soul and passion its natural motion, right?"

"Right."

"That aside, the deed is done, and now you need more seats on the bus."

"And this bus is still moving?"

"The bus never *stopped* moving! Hell, how could it? This is the bus of life we're talking about here."

"That's right," Calder said, "of course."

"My point is that what was once a lonely child has become a family and when that's a cool fact of nature you're in need of more space on the bus and you take more time in the bathroom, use more chairs around the table, leave a bigger mess in the wake. So what you've ended up doing is changing the lives of all those people around you, people who are also riding the bus but don't necessarily know you and never even thought they'd have a place in your life. They don't know how your life—one little thing darting through this big night of a universe—could have any appreciable effect in their lives which are off on their *own* whirligig rides."

Calder ran a hand through his hair, took a long breath.

"And hang on to your thing because the ride's just begun."

"Excuse me?"

"You heard me, young friend."

"I guess I did. You don't by any chance have an aspirin tablet?"

"Why should I?"

"Just a question."

"Lay your questions aside on this bus of life!" she said, nearly shouting, fervent, religious. She paused then for breath, and when she continued her voice was quieter. "Once aboard, you don't get off—well, not until the end."

"Which was the case with your brother."

"Indeed it was. Dear sweet Harlon. A rider to his end." She smiled affectionately, looking into a corner near the ticket counter as if the ghost of Harlon was there and waving out to his sister. "You know, there's so much fuss made over self-destruction, don't you think?"

"Well—"

"I mean, take my brother. We all know Harl killed himself. It's a given—cigarettes, whiskey, pills, too many strange women. Suicide as certain as if he'd put a gun to his temple. But it was his own damn business, wasn't it? There's nothing

I could have done anyway. I suppose it might have been something in his childhood but, sweet Jesus, I was there right with him all along and look at me. I came out fine."

Calder nodded, looking again at the bottom of his paper cup.

"You know, I recall the day brother beat a man senseless with a pumpkin." She chuckled. "What a day! Harl wasn't more than thirteen years old. Matter of fact, I think he was just thirteen."

Calder said, "Your brother . . . injured somebody with a pumpkin?"

She was still giggling. "Damn near killed him! Wouldn't that've been a hoot, if he *had* killed him. I'll wager it would've been the first murder in this nation's history committed with a ripe pumpkin!"

"I'm sure of that."

"You remember I mentioned that Daddy had to sell his goods out of town after the rumor spread? Well, one fall— an October it was, 1953 if memory serves—Daddy took us with him up north of some little scratch-town in the flats, and he had along a pickup load of some very nice pumpkins. He'd planted them on an impulse, having never before grown pumpkins, but they came out fine, every one of them big as the moon. So, anyway, we're along for the ride and whatever labor two kids might be able to provide. When we got to where Daddy wanted to set up shop, Harlon and I laid the pumpkins out in a pretty marching line and in pulls this touring car big as the Queen Mary. This extra-tall son-of-a-gun steps out looking like a deep-fried version of LBJ and pokes about in the apples and what all, and then he stops and gives Daddy the eye. After a second or two he says, 'Now aren't you the fella from down south that broke his wife's heart with a milkcow?' And this man cuts loose in a big steamboat hee-haw laugh, shake-your-shoulders, slap-your-knee kind of laughing, and I swear Daddy simply lost his mind. Daddy came at that big guy, flailing around and trying to punch him and the two of them went down in the dust, rolling over and over and raising a billow right there where the cars were passing. Which is precisely when Harlon did what any sensible boy would do upon seeing his father in trouble and perhaps in mortal danger—he hefted about the biggest pumpkin we had and smashed it down on that stranger's head. Bombs away! What a damned mess. That pumpkin split over the man's skull and juiced out in the dirt and the seeds plastered all over his cheeks and eyes and hair."

"Jesus," Calder said.

"Well, that immediately brought the struggle to a flaming halt. The stranger could have been killed for all we knew—he just lay there in the dirt. Trouble was, Harlon—child being father to the man and all that—Harlon got another pumpkin and proceeded to smash *that* one into the stranger's chest. That's when Daddy had recovered wits enough to call off brother. Which is I'm sure the thing that saved that stranger's life."

"I don't doubt it."

"Hell of a note, isn't it? Defending your old man's honor with a couple oversize pumpkins." She shrugged. "You do what's necessary in this life."

Calder eased out a breath and set his cup on the floor. When the jukebox caught his attention, shining ocean-blue next to the gum machine, he recognized his need for a change in pace and asked if she'd like to hear some music.

"Aren't you the sweetest thing," she said. "That would be nice."

He stood and felt in his pockets for change.

"Harlon loved Porter Wagoner. He loved those clothes Porter wears. All that piping and sequins and doodads. But who he really loved was Hank Williams. The Reverend Hank, he used to call him. You know, after we sang 'Shall

We Gather at the River' at brother's funeral, we did our best with 'I'm So Lonesome I Could Cry.' I thought it fitting. I wrote the words on a slip of paper so the preacher could sing along. Of course he knew the tune. Who wouldn't?"

Calder waited for a moment to move off to the jukebox.

"It's like I said—a tad unusual but if you think about it there was a certain wisdom in the whole thing, putting brother to rest in his own cherished automobile. And that sky just full of a spring rain. You know how a spring rain falls at a slant, you look out at it and it's slicing down at an angle across your eyes and peppering the leaves everywhere, thunder booming and striding along the sky as if there's a floor over your head?" She was gazing at Calder, plaintive, distant, nearly secretive.

"Yeah," he said, "I've seen rains like that."

She was disappeared into the reverential moment, a meditation of April rain that broke cleanly as she swept a heavy arm through the air. "All in the past now," she announced, her voice regaining its ample volume. "Sweep it away. What's one to say? A way of life gone as buffalo or the whistling wind. How about that music?"

Calder stepped to the jukebox to scan the selections. He found a Creedence Clearwater Revival tune, and "Sixteen Tons" by Tennessee Ernie Ford, dropped two quarters and made the selections. The loudspeaker scraped alive: "*Now departing gate four, the Odessa Express with intermediate stops in Cornudas, Salt Flat, Grimsby, Nickel Creek. Now boarding gate four. All aboard, please.*" The Creedence Clearwater record dropped onto the turntable. Big drums punched into the room.

She was standing when he returned, ball cap repositioned on her head, pulled low, travel-ready. "That's my bus," she said. "Back on that old highway of life."

"Right," he said. "Like you talked about."

"I had a thought," she said.

"What's that?"

"Perhaps you'd care to come along with me. Pay a visit to brother's grave."

Calder swallowed. "Well, I—"

"Pay your respects. See for yourself that lovely place beside the river where Harlon sleeps sitting up."

Calder glanced around the station. It was true he had no sense of destination.

She smiled. "What with you being a dead ringer for brother. That can't be a coincidence."

"Why not?"

"I don't believe in coincidence," she said flatly. "Everything in life has a meaning. That's my medicine."

Calder stared at the woman.

She extended a manly hand for shaking. "Lenore Hartnett. Forgive me for not saying so sooner."

Calder took the outstretched hand. "I was on my way home," he said.

"And where is that anyway, young friend, except where you find it? Brother's grave is right on the road to Grimsby. The driver'll let us out along the highway. It's a short walk back into the willows. So damn pretty it'll break your heart."

"I guess . . . I suppose I'm not expected anywhere," Calder said. "Not actually expected." He shifted his face to one side and worked his jaw a moment without speaking. "I suppose nobody's looking for me."

Lenore was all beatific smile.

"I'd have to trade in my ticket."

"I won't leave without you," Lenore told him.

Calder Lux collected his duffel and exchanged tickets, taking the $1.26 refund that came to him. A thought flickered out on the rim of his mind, an avowal, a vagrant confession. It had the quality of fleeting desire, a pressing confidence that rose in the dark and stood speechless, waiting. Lenore was beside him. "All set there, young friend?"

"Yes, ma'am."

"I asked the driver to wait," she said. "Let's hurry along."

Calder followed after her, out the door, and onto the bus. As soon as they were seated, the bus was in motion, quickly gaining the two-lane at the eastern edge of town. Lenore patted Calder's left knee. "You'll be glad you came along," she said. "Brother'll be glad, too."

Calder nodded, looking out the window. The endless western sky seemed venerable with its threat of freedom. Never before had he given vent to wild impulse or the simple echo of a nameless thought, and he turned from the window to see Lenore sitting beside him as she had in the station, hugging the black purse against her chest. Her eyes were closed and her head rested on the seat back, and he thought of his waiting double, brother Harlon driving underground and blind, a fine new Stetson sitting square atop that vacant skull. The notion that their meeting was necessary—fated even—cheered Calder. He sensed a salutation in the flat-handed landscape of thistle and dry wash and gawking fencepost vultures, a growing welcome from the still, distant grave on the Goodhope River, east fork, which Calder could pretend was the River Jordan when he finally and firmly stood on its beautiful shore.

MR. QUINN

•

David Michael Kaplan

I WOKE UP THIS MORNING thinking of Mr. Quinn. This was strange, since I hadn't thought of him more than once or twice in nearly fifty years, yet here was his face before me as clear as when I was eight years old and had seen him last. And I felt uneasy—why, I had no idea. In the years he'd lived next door to us, I'd barely known him, had only occasionally spoken to him, and had hardly missed him when he was gone. He'd seemed a kindly enough man, quiet, a bit remote. Certainly nothing about him had been threatening. Yet now, remembering him, I felt uneasy. It seemed as if a grayness had leached into the bright April morning, a spice pulled from the air, and everywhere a withered fairness.

"You're awfully quiet this morning," Sarah, my wife, told me as I drank my juice and ate my cereal.

"I've been thinking about someone I haven't thought

about in years," I said. She didn't ask who, and I didn't say anything more.

When I was a child, we lived in Tyler, a small town in western Pennsylvania. Mrs. Adcock, the tall, nervous woman who lived next door, took in a few boarders, and one of these was Mr. Quinn. He seemed very old to me then, with a face sallow as old candle wax. He was as tall as Mrs. Adcock— seeing them together, you might have mistaken them for brother and sister. He was a heavy smoker, and in summer would sit hour after hour on Mrs. Adcock's porch, legs crossed, cigarette held delicately between his fingers, listening to the Pirates ball games on the radio. He had a habit of puckering his lips when looking at you, as if quietly amused by something. "How's the boy?" he'd call, and I'd mumble, "Fine," and walk on by. Other than that, and the occasional pleasantry like "Hot today, huh?" he hardly spoke to me at all. I didn't mind him, nor he me. More than anything, he was just *there.*

Once he beckoned for me to come up on the porch. "Are you being a good boy?" he asked.

I nodded dutifully.

He knocked ash off his cigarette. It landed on his shoe, but he didn't seem to notice. He studied me hard. "No trouble to your folks?"

I shook my head.

"You go to church? You love Jesus?"

"Yes."

He squinched his lips and nodded approvingly. He reached in his back pocket, pulled out his wallet, and took out a dollar bill. "Here." He handed it to me. I looked at it, then stuffed it in my pocket. "You keep it up now," he said.

I didn't know what to say. I shifted my feet. He was staring at me, as if expecting something else, and then I realized he was waiting for me to go. At the bottom of the steps I turned and said, "Thanks." He made a small wave.

That was the longest conversation we ever had, and the depth, I thought, to which I knew him. Or he me.

"Mr. Quinn," I murmured.

I shaved and dressed quickly. Because I still felt uneasy, I decided to drop by St. Anne's for early mass before going to the office. When I go there on days other than Sunday, Sarah worries, convinced I'm becoming excessively pious. But I don't think I'm really that religious. The church comforts me, is all. Its damp chill on these early spring mornings, the hardness of the pews, the smell of varnish and old wool, comfort me more than observances and rituals. When I look at a crease in the pages of the hymnal, or a fissure in the smoky wood of the pew in front of me, I sometimes feel my life become as simple and real as coffee or apples or the dew on my neighbor's grass.

"I think I'll go to early mass," I told Sarah as I left. I could see her lips tighten.

"We're going to the Durnans' buffet tonight," she said. And then stared at me oddly, as if I were going away for a long time and she wanted to fix me in her mind.

Something has happened, I thought. Somehow, in a way not yet known to me, I've changed. And for the first time that morning, I felt afraid.

As I drove toward St. Anne's, I thought more about Mr. Quinn. My parents said once that he was from Oklahoma, and that he had no family. I couldn't remember—if indeed I'd ever known—when he'd come to Tyler, or why. He'd just always been there. And then one morning, he wasn't. When I went down for breakfast before school, my parents seemed sober, and I knew something had happened. "Well, he's gone," my mother said, as she wiped a dish. "He died last night."

"Who?" I said, even though I already knew. She told me about the ambulance coming in the night, its orange light flashing like a knife through the tree branches; the quick step onto Mrs. Adcock's porch; the muffled opening and clos-ing of doors; the gurney rolled out, then carried down the steps, my mother and father watching from the window, already knowing what had happened since the sheet was over his face and Mrs. Adcock was standing in her bathrobe, her mouth working soundlessly, like a nun at prayer. It seemed I'd seen it all myself, that I had dreamed it almost, or if not dreamed, then foreseen it with the ghostly predestined imag-ination of children.

"Such a shame," my mother said. "Such a nice man."

"Real quiet," my father added. And then, in one of his highest tributes, "He was no trouble at all."

I looked at Mrs. Adcock's porch when I walked to school that morning, and thought, Death has been here. I wondered where Mr. Quinn was now. With Jesus in heaven? Could he see me? Could he read my thoughts? I suddenly realized I could never ask him, he was *gone,* after all, and that fright-ened me even more than death—it *was* Death, somehow—and I skedaddled down the street to school.

Now, almost fifty years later, he seemed close, somewhere just off my shoulder, so that if I turned I might see him looking at me, cigarette held like a pencil in his fingers. What did he want? Why had he come back? I was suddenly overwhelmed by a feeling of darkness, as if a scrim had been thrown over the sun. Behind the cicadas' murmur, the smell of fresh azalea bloom in the air, I felt that darkness almost as a pressure against my skull, squeezing it softly. I pulled over to the side of the street. The steering wheel was sticky in my hands. Two children carrying school packs went by. I thought, Something is going to happen. I breathed deeply. A dog scampered after a squirrel. A woman pulled weeds from her lawn and threw them in a plastic sack. I swallowed hard and waited, hands clutching the wheel, and then the feeling passed, like a wave sliding along a beach, and I was restored to sunlight.

I took stock. There was no reason to be feeling this . . . dread. For that's what it was—dread, sticky as a spiderweb against your face. I was in good health, as was Sarah. My daughter, happily married as far as I knew, lived in Colorado, where she was a land rights lawyer. My insurance business, while small, was doing reasonably well. Our house was almost paid for; we had a little money in the bank. I'd lost hair, put on some middle-aged pounds, and had stiff knees in the morning, but otherwise was in good health. I was, I thought, modestly respected and valued in my community. I served on the planning committee at St. Anne's and helped organize the drive for neighborhood park renovations. Twice a week I swam thirty laps—no more—at the YMCA. While Sarah and I no longer embraced with quite the passion of before, we were reasonably affectionate and gave one another space, which might be the better thing at our age anyway. While we weren't overly social, we could count on going to dinner once a week with one or several of the couples we knew.

All right, I told myself. Enough. I took another deep breath and rubbed my cheeks. I decided to go straight to the office and begin the day in earnest. St. Anne's could wait. At Rumsey Avenue I turned the corner and looked up at the window of my office. The blinds were already open— Betty, my secretary, must have arrived. I stopped and parked but didn't get out. Betty would be making coffee and setting the postage meter. Sometime during the morning she'd tell me the latest installment in her daughter's latest separation, and I would listen, half curious, half impatient. I'd begin making my phone calls, the daily rounds of checking and chatting. I stared up at my office window as someone who'd been away a long time might stare at the window of a house he'd lived in long ago.

And somehow I just couldn't get out of the car and go up. I imagined myself doing it, I *wanted* to do it, but I couldn't. Instead, I pulled away, drove down Rumsey, and some miles later turned onto Bay Boulevard toward the shore. I sometimes go there at lunch or after work to watch the waves and gulls. Like the church, it calms me. I'd stay there awhile, I thought, maybe take a walk until I was myself again. I stopped at a pay phone and called Betty. I told her I wasn't feeling well and might take the morning off. She sounded solicitous, but I knew she was glad: she could take an early lunch, and talk with her daughter on the phone.

"Are you at home?" she asked.

"Yes," I lied.

"Should I call you if something comes up?"

"No. I mean—I might be sleeping. I'll call you later. I'm sure I'll be in this afternoon."

When I pulled into the parking area at the beach, the tide was out, the surf a gentle lapping, barely audible. Except for a blue Dodge parked at the far end, mine was the only car there. Gulls scratched for food in the sand channels; occasionally one flapped and struck another, setting off a chain of screeches and peckings. A fishing boat trawled offshore; far beyond it, a tanker was pasted on the horizon. I stared at the water, and all of a sudden the old syllogism from my college logic course came to me: *All men are mortal, Socrates is a man, therefore, Socrates is mortal.* It seemed reassuring that mortality could be contained by logic.

I thought again about Mr. Quinn. I remembered, for the first time in years, something that happened soon after he died. I had just come home from school, was in the kitchen taking off my jacket, when I heard my parents talking in the dining room. Their voices were low, almost conspiratorial, and I tiptoed to listen. They were talking about Mr. Quinn, but I couldn't remember now what they said, except for my mother's words, "He seemed like such a nice man." Then my father saw me and said, "What are you doing skulking around there?"

Why had he been so irritated? I didn't know.

The air in the car seemed close. I got out. The morning had gotten a bit chilly. I closed my eyes and breathed deeply. There was a rotting smell to the sea. I walked to the water-line, then along the shore. The tide had left a jumble of broken shells and glass, beer cans and plastic bottles, kelp and rockweed. I saw a dead jellyfish, a woman's mascara case, a child's sneaker heavy with mud. I remembered a line from a poem, or a hymn—I wasn't sure—"the sea will give over its dead." Again I felt the morning's dread surge within me, like an inner tide, lapping, lapping. I thrust my hands deep in my jacket pockets. The gulls flew farther downshore.

Maybe I am going crazy. I'd never thought anything like that before. I turned and walked hurriedly back up the beach to the parking area, as if to run away from the thought. As I passed the blue Dodge, I glanced inside—and started. In the backseat a human head and arm extended from under a blanket. My skin went cold. A corpse. But just as I thought that, the arm moved. I stared, and saw there were two of them, a man and a woman, moving slowly under the blanket. The woman's hands fluttered against the man's back. She arched, and a part of the blanket fell away. I could see her bare leg rubbing against his thigh, the curve of her rump. She opened her eyes, turned her head, and saw me through the windshield. She smiled slightly, as if amused, then reached for the blanket and re-covered them. Flushed, I walked quickly back to my car. I drove away, back toward town. My thoughts were churning. I tried to imagine who the man and woman might be, what exigencies of passion drove them here so early in the morning. Did they do it often? Had they been here before, and I'd never noticed? I saw her hand reaching for the blanket, her white leg brushing her lover's darker skin. I imagined them making love, naked and unashamed, while teenagers played their boom boxes from the backs of pickup trucks and early sunbathers unfolded their beach towels and rubbed on creams. I realized after a while that I was driving aimlessly. I have to collect myself, I thought. I have to go somewhere. I decided once more to go to St. Anne's.

No one was in the church except a cleaning lady—Mrs. Galati, I thought her name was—who was mopping the floor. Mass was long over. A sign in the aisle announced evening confessions from seven until nine-thirty. I sat down in a pew, folded my hands in my lap, and bowed my head slightly, as if to pray, although I didn't. I found myself glancing at Mrs. Galati as she mopped. She was a stocky woman in her early fifties, heavy and thick-waisted, but with a face that was sweet and yeasty. I watched her dip the mop's thick coils into the pail, watched the milky water splash over the cool tile. She languidly moved the mop back and forth, a small smile on her lips, and I saw her thighs swell against the thin cloth of her dress. They seemed of one motion, like a hammock rocking, her thighs and her arms, thighs and arms, and I imagined hugging those thighs, kissing them, rubbing my groin against them. I imagined cupping my hands around her breasts while she bent over her task. I felt an erection pressing against my pants. I was suddenly ashamed to be having these thoughts here in church. I stood up and walked hurriedly down the aisle and out the door.

I got back in my car and sat. I kept seeing Mrs. Galati, the woman in the Dodge, even my secretary, Betty, beckoning, their lips nuzzling me, their legs parting and winding around me in a salty ocean of sex. I pressed my groin and shivered. The images whirled and swirled, and I couldn't get them out of my mind.

All right, I thought. I'd give in to it all. I knew where I would go.

I drove to a phone, called Betty, and told her I was very sick and wouldn't be in at all. I felt like a child playing hooky. Then I drove across town to the Swinging Pussycat, an adult bookstore I'd sometimes passed by and, although tempted, had never entered. I parked in a lot a few blocks away and cut through an alley to the street. Most of the stores here were vacant and boarded over. My heart raced faster as I approached the Swinging Pussycat. I stopped in front of the shuttered thrift shop next to it. A sign on the door announced the shop was open only on Wednesdays. I looked at its dirty window display of toasters, old TVs, globe-less lamps.

I walked past the Swinging Pussycat. All I could see through the opaque lettering on the window was a cash register and the back of someone's head—the clerk's, I supposed. I walked to the end of the block, looked around, then doubled back, head down. I was afraid someone might recognize me, even though I was the only person on the street. I didn't know whether I would really go in or not. Maybe I'll just walk by and go back to my car, I told myself, and I might've if the clerk hadn't glanced out the window just as I passed. His eyes briefly met mine, and I knew if I was ever going to go in, it had to be now. I reached for the knob and entered, feeling much as I had as a child when I'd stood on the edge of the high dive at the swimming pool, hesitant before the leap into air, the abandonment to water.

It was fluorescently bright inside, and I blinked. The store smelled piney, astringent, as if it had just been scrubbed. All along the walls, magazines and books were displayed in sections marked Hard Core, Bondage, Lesbian, Men. At the rear was a dark curtained-off area, with a sign saying Video Booths. Except for the clerk, who glanced up from the soap opera he was watching on a small TV under the cash register and then never looked at me again, I was alone.

From the magazine covers, picture after picture of women and men in all the various postures of copulation greeted me. It was like walking through a grand gallery of sexual possibility. I opened up *Maneaters,* in "Sexational Color," and stared at one photograph after another of women fellating men. Time seemed both to slow down and open up, and I felt a hollowness in my stomach, as if I had just gone down a very fast elevator. I opened *Forbidden Fantasies.* The pictures here were glossier and made token efforts to tell stories. One depicted a blond man and an even blonder woman on their "first date" as they quickly proceeded to undress and then couple on the living-room table beneath a poster of the Swiss Alps; another featured an orgy at a "Roman bath"—looking suspiciously like the steam room in some health club—the celebrants' togas held in place, but not for long, by highly visible safety pins. In still another, a "cowboy" was seduced by two bargirls in Gay Nineties dress, which they more or less kept on for the entire sequence, though he was quickly stripped to boots and chaps.

Penises and vaginas and breasts. Semen on lips and stomachs and backs. The people in the photos strained and bucked and cavorted. I stared and stared, and the images passed before me like water. I looked at them avidly, hungrily. It was as if they were all there for me. I wanted to stay in that room and look at them forever.

"Look at this," someone behind me said, and I started. A young man with a shaved head and an earring was holding a magazine open to show me. His T-shirt said *Bundeswehr* and his jeans were greasy. He must have come from the darkened room where the video booths were. He was pointing to a picture of a woman simultaneously servicing two men. She was dressed only in a silver choker and black high heels. Her hair was wild and tousled and her mouth wet with saliva and smudged lipstick as she sucked their engorged penises.

"She really knows how to take care of a man, don't she?" the man said. He grinned. One of his teeth was blackened, dead.

I grunted, put *Forbidden Fantasies* back, and moved

away from him down the rack. To be spoken to here, where I only wanted the sweetness of anonymity, was disturbing. I picked up another magazine and glanced back. The man was leering at me. I flipped through the magazine, unaware of what I was seeing, conscious only of his eyes on me. I put it back and moved closer to the door. I picked up a tabloid, a singles newsletter of some sort, and opened it, just to do something. The man was still staring at me. I put down the newsletter and walked quickly out the door. In my nervousness I turned in the opposite direction from my car and walked almost to the corner before realizing my mistake. I was backtracking when the man with the shaved head stepped out of the bookstore. He saw me and grinned again.

The moment I stopped, I knew I'd made a mistake: I'd telegraphed fear. But it was too late. I turned and walked in the direction I'd just come from, away from my car. At the corner I looked back, hoping he'd gone in the other direction, but he hadn't. He was following me! I turned the corner and walked faster along a warehouse which ran the length of the block: at the next street, I could cut back and reach the parking lot. I looked back. He too had turned the corner. As far down the street as I could see, I was alone. I walked faster. When I reach the parking lot, I told myself, there will be people. But there weren't. The lot was empty, and the man with the shaved head had closed distance. He yelled something. Like a flushed grouse, I panicked, and started running across the lot. And suddenly I was falling, tripped over a buckle in the asphalt. My hands scraped hard, and I grunted in pain; when I stood up, I saw I'd torn an elbow of my jacket. I ran again, not looking back, sure that he was almost upon me. And then I was at my car. Blessedly, I'd left it unlocked. I jumped in, slammed the door, and looked, sure that the man was only a few steps behind. But he'd vanished. I rested my head on the steering wheel for a moment, then started the car and eased into the street. A minivan passed me, honking wildly. The man with the shaved head leaned out the passenger window and banged madly on the side, grinning and leering. A second man— where had he been?—was driving. They honked and honked until they were out of sight.

I drove until my breathing quieted. I drove in a daze, my hands raw and stinging. I passed my office. It looked empty, the lights already off. I scrunched low in the seat in case Betty might be looking out the window. There was nowhere else to go, and I hurt, so I went home. Sarah was out. I washed my scraped palms and applied antiseptic. I lay on the bed, fully clothed. My throat ached, as if I'd been crying. I closed my eyes and saw naked men and women clutching and clawing one another, tearing flesh, biting and gouging in a passion much like death. I saw the man with the shaved head laughing at me. All the sweet innocence of the world seemed spoiled, and I was its despoiler. I was a coward and a lecher and a fool.

I lay in the gray afternoon light, and that's how Sarah found me when she returned. "What are you doing home so early?" she asked.

"I'm sick," I said.

"What did you *do* to your hands?" She lifted them gently, turned them over. I saw her nose wrinkle, and I wondered if they'd putrefied, if all of me, soul on out, was rotting.

"I fell," I said.

She touched my forehead, and I flinched slightly. I wanted her to comfort me. I wanted her to go away. I'm not the man you think I am, I almost said, but I didn't.

"You feel flushed," she said, as if my shame were a fever. "Do you feel like going to the Durnans'? We don't have to—"

"Just let me rest awhile," I said. She turned off the light and left. And with the darkness came once more the face of Mr. Quinn. He looked bemused, quizzical. *Have you been a good boy?* he seemed to be asking. And at last I knew why he'd come: he'd come to judge me.

We did go to the buffet, and I performed very well. I laughed on cue, frowned when necessary, said things that I immediately forgot. I praised Amelia Durnan's centerpiece. My friends smiled and talked to me as if they knew me, which they did not. I felt unclean, as if in no way did I belong with these people among whom only the day before I had walked with confidence. After a while, I had to get away. I went upstairs to Amelia Durnan's sewing room and sat in a chair by the window. Conversation swirled below me. On the end table was a Wedgewood vase with a relief of two sea nymphs embracing on a large shell. I stared at it. One nymph swam down to meet the upraised lips and arms of its lover, who reached out tenderly. Above them, Poseidon gazed with an indulgent smile. Their love seemed so chaste, so innocent, that I had to look away. I pressed my fingers hard to my forehead so that I wouldn't cry.

I closed my eyes. And felt a last shy hope rise within me. It was late confession night at St. Anne's.

Stealthily, without saying anything to anyone, I went down the back stairs, through the sun porch, and out the back door to my car.

The streets were dark and wet with a light drizzle. St. Anne's looked dark too—had I misread the sign for evening confession? As I walked up the steps, however, I saw light under the door—the portico light had simply burned out. I went inside. Only the chancery and nave lights were on—an economy measure, I now remembered, my buildings-and-grounds committee had recommended. I smelled candles, the coldness of stone, umbrellas, and wet shoes. Two old women were shuffling up the aisle, arm in arm. I recognized one of them from Sunday masses. I didn't know her name, but she smiled at me as she passed. I sat in a pew near the confessional. Someone was in the booth—a man. I could see his scuffed shoes below the curtain. I heard the wooden seat in the booth creak, and a cough, a mumbling. And I felt despair. Could I really confess to what had happened today? Or would my tongue thicken, my words turn to ash? Always before when I confessed, I knew what I'd done, had in effect understood and forgiven myself even before the priest's benediction. Now I felt not only guilt and shame, but confusion, the impossibility of saying why any of it had happened, why the day had slipped from uneasiness to dread to despair. *And?* the priest would say. *What happened?*

I woke up, I would say, *thinking of Mr. Quinn.*

I stared at the scuffed shoes of the man inside the confessional. The soles were thick and old-fashioned, the cuffs of his flannel pants slightly frayed. And I had the strangest feeling that it was he inside the booth, Mr. Quinn, risen not only in memory and dream, but here, real, now. The curtain would part and he'd step out, his fingers tobacco-stained, his face even sallower in the dim light. He would look at me appraisingly, lips slightly puckered. *How's the boy?* he'd say.

I will tell him, I thought. *I don't love Jesus, and I'm not a good boy at all.*

I felt the church grow even dimmer, what light there was seeping away as had the sunlight earlier that morning. *Is it happening here too?* I thought. Was there no refuge anywhere? And then it was not the church's darkness around me at all, but that of another time. Again I'm eight years old: it is only a few days after Mr. Quinn has died; my parents are talking in the dining room. They do not hear or see me as I stand there in the shadows and listen.

The filth Mrs. Adcock found in his room, my mother says. *Disgusting.*

What did she do with it all? my father asks.

Oh, she burned them all right. Every last one of them.

It's a shame an old lady like Mrs. Adcock had to find that.

He seemed *like such a nice man,* my mother says. After all these years, I heard now the true inflection of her words.

My father turns and sees me. *What are you doing skulking around there?*

What? I ask. *What did they find?*

Never mind.

But what?

It's nothing, my mother says, *for little boys to know.*

A shuffling in the confessional, another cough. I imagined the curtain parting and Mr. Quinn stepping out. He would grin at me, and wink, as if to say, *Now you know about me, about my secret which you'd forgotten: we are not ourselves at all.*

He had come across time and memory this morning not to judge, but to show me this. And I realized I must be as old now as he had been then—it was strange I'd never thought of it before.

But I couldn't know, I told him. *I was just a little boy.*

But now you do.

Yes, I said. *But I'm also no longer a little boy.*

A lightness like birds' wings settled over me. I rose and left St. Anne's and drove back to the Durnans', coming in again through the back door. No one seemed to have missed me. I talked with people awhile, smiling, nodding like a fool or a freshly minted man. Sarah came up beside me and touched my arm. "Where have you been hiding all this time?" she asked, and I told her I'd been gone for a while, but I was back.

LISTEN TO ME

•

Margot Livesey

ONE OCTOBER DAY WHEN the sky above the city of Edinburgh seemed grayer and more solid than the buildings, Morag met Marcel shoplifting. She caught his gaze just as he was sliding a bottle of perfume into the pocket of his raincoat. He stared at her steadily, a man of about thirty whose hair equivocated between fair and brown. Morag thought he might put the bottle back, but instead, without taking his eyes off her, he picked up a second bottle and walked, unhurriedly, out of the shop. When Morag emerged onto Princes Street a few minutes later with her bottle of vitamins and tube of handcream, paid for and in a bag, she found him loitering outside the bookshop a few doors down.

"What rubbish," he said, gesturing toward the window filled with books about the royal family. "As if there were an inside story; as if we'd know it, if there were. Do you have time for coffee?"

Morag hesitated, taking in his shiny blue eyes and clean shoes. When she first came to Edinburgh University she had had a wild patch, picking up boys on the street, but the overworked angel who looks after young people had taken care of her until she met James. A friend had introduced them because they both liked fishing. On their first date they had caught three mackerel apiece and had gone on to live together for eight fairly happy years. Morag had moved out last spring, her departure fueled not by any quarrel but by a pervasive sense of staleness. Outside the other window of the bookshop a man in a kilt began to play the bagpipes. Morag looked at Marcel and thought, Why not. "Coffee would be nice," she said.

"I'm Marcel Dunbar," he said and held out his hand.

The formal gesture surprised Morag into responding with her full name: Morag Findlayson.

At a café on Rose Street they ordered coffee and sat down. Marcel, as had been obvious from his first syllable, was Irish. He came from the town of Bray about thirty miles from Dublin. His older brother was often mistaken for the poet Seamus Heaney. "Sometimes he goes along with it," Marcel said. "He's memorized a couple of poems. My younger brother doesn't look like anyone." His was a small family, only three children. His aunt Veronica, with thirteen, was the pride of the parish.

Morag listened, happily caught in the web of his voice. His nose had a slight bump on the bridge, as if it had once been broken, and there was something odd about his blue eyes. Were they too close together? Or slightly crossed? The uncertainty drew her back, again and again. Each time, it seemed Marcel was watching her, daring her to say something about the perfume until, finally, she blurted out, "Why did you do that?"

"Why didn't you turn me in?"

"I don't know," Morag said, although several reasons

came to mind: fear of embarrassment, that she did not consider shoplifting from large shops a crime, that she liked his looks.

"Perhaps you think sins of omission are all right but not sins of commission."

"No, I don't think that," said Morag. "I almost admire those who commit rather than simply stand around."

"So what was your last sin?"

It was a women's magazine question but Marcel's expression of interest made Morag want to answer honestly, or at least to know what an honest answer would be before she lied. Was it something she had done at work? With James? Probably the latter.

A few weeks ago they had arranged to meet for a drink at a pub near the hospital where he worked as an administrator. Morag had arrived early, for once, and installed herself in an alcove. When James came in, on the dot of six, he had failed to see her. As she watched him cast around the crowded room, Morag had been assailed by a sudden sharp distaste for the evening that lay ahead. The moment he turned to the bar, she slipped out the back door. She might have gone straight home, save for a picture of Loch Lomond in the window of a nearby travel agent. The sight of the calm water, a reminder of their many fishing expeditions, had made her return to the pub and greet James as if newly arrived. Now she thought her secret watching had been as much a theft as anything Marcel might put in his pocket.

This was not, however, the story she told Marcel. Instead she described the accident she had had with her parents' car, a minor collision resulting in five hundred pounds of damage. She had still been fretting about how to pay for repairs when someone reversed out of a driveway and hit the car in exactly the same place. "So the insurance paid for everything. I gave the car back in better condition than I borrowed it."

She expected Marcel to exclaim admiringly, but a look of disappointment came over his face. "Well," he said, "that was clever, but I'd been thinking of something a little less conventional? Something you're ashamed of? And you tell me about your erratic driving."

Morag watched his hands. There was a mark on the back of one, a smudge or a bruise perhaps. She finished her coffee and stood up. "I'd better get going," she said awkwardly.

"You can't just leave," he exclaimed. "Where are you going? Can I come?"

Morag started to laugh. "No, but you can give me your phone number."

At work Morag was absentminded. Twice she brought a customer the wrong size of clothing and once she gave the wrong change. She and her two partners, Yvonne and Lucy, ran a shop called Poppies, which sold clothes and jewelry and expensive knickknacks. It kept the three of them afloat although they each did something else as well. Lucy, who was sturdy and down-to-earth, gave yoga lessons. Yvonne, the artistic one, made jewelry. She had a workbench at the back of the shop, and the effect of her sitting there, bending the silver wire into intricate shapes, spread like a mantle over the other merchandise, making people feel that everything they saw was the result of the same care and attention. Morag used to teach English to Vietnamese women but the grant that paid her salary had been cut. More recently she had been bartending two nights a week. The hours were long, but the job suited her need to meet new people in a new way.

She was pressing a blue blouse, when suddenly she wondered if Marcel had given her his real phone number. She set the iron on end and went to try it. An answering machine with his unmistakable Irish voice responded. She hung up and turned back to the second sleeve. Only a few people she knew had answering machines at home; it made her think Marcel must be well-off or have some kind of job that required it. She put the blouse on a hanger and did up the buttons. Or perhaps he had stolen it.

Every day Morag considered calling Marcel and found a reason not to. The first day was too soon. The second day she went round to see Steve and Janet; they had both recently joined AA and did not want to stray too far from their fridge full of soft drinks. The third day she was working at the pub. At quarter to nine the next morning her phone rang. "Aren't you ever going to call me?" said Marcel. He had got her number from directory enquiries.

They had supper at Kalpna's. When Morag announced she was a vegetarian, it turned out that Marcel was too. Simultaneously they named Kalpna's as their favorite restaurant. After they ordered, Marcel held out his fists to her. "Left or right?"

She saw that the mark on his hand was still there, a faint maroon birthmark, shaped like a cloud, and that was the hand she chose.

"Got it in one," Marcel said, uncurling his fingers to reveal an earring, blue-and-gold flowers, dangling. His other hand held the mate.

"They're lovely," said Morag.

"Try them on."

There was a mirror on the wall beside their table and she pulled back her hair and slipped them in. The earrings were exquisite. "Thank you," she said. "I don't know what to say."

"Nothing to say, except they look great on you. Clearly you're their rightful owner and it was just a mistake that they got separated from you."

"Is that your theory of property?" Morag asked. "Ownership based on aesthetics?"

Marcel frowned. "Aesthetics is certainly a place to start."

"Did you steal these?"

"Of course. Anyone can buy you a gift but I gamble six months of my life to give you pleasure." He made a small, mocking bow and passed the samosas.

Morag did not know whether to be disapproving or thrilled. She picked the plumpest samosa and said she must show the earrings to Yvonne; maybe she could copy them. Marcel told her how when he was little, he wanted to be a contortionist. "We had a book with a picture of a man, his arms and legs wrapped around each other so small he fit under a chair."

Morag sat looking at him. His eyes did diverge slightly; she was sure. When he paused she said, "Why do you have an answering machine? Is it for business?" Then she realized she had given away her call to him. She reached for her beer and his eyes fell into unison.

"No, pleasure," he said. "How old are you?"

"Twenty-nine," said Morag, dropping a year and a half.

At Poppies the next day she told Lucy about the evening. She wanted to bring Marcel into the realm of the familiar, and Lucy, happily married, keenly interested in the adventures of others, seemed the perfect confidante. But almost at once there were awkward questions. "How did you meet him?" asked Lucy.

"At the pub."

"And what does he do?"

"I'm not sure. Somehow that didn't come up."

The two of them were at the counter folding scarves. Now Lucy paused in her tidy gestures. "It sounds a bit weird to me, Morag. I mean you don't want to run around with a stranger."

"Well, in a way I do," said Morag. She shook out a piece of chiffon, the color of mist. "With James, I knew the street where he grew up, his passion for Earl Grey tea, how he folded his underwear. And he knew those things about me. I felt smothered by all that information, as if I no longer had a self."

"Of course you have a self," said Lucy. "You're a thirty-year-old woman." She held a paisley scarf across her face, like a veil, so that the fabric fluttered as she asked, "Did he kiss you good night?"

"Yes," mumbled Morag. It was another half lie. Marcel had kissed her, but on both cheeks in a disappointing, grown-up way. To hide her confusion, she carried the scarves to the display table. The shop door pinged, and a woman who had been looking through the window came in. "Do you have that in my size?" she asked, pointing to Morag's red skirt.

That evening Morag went to the cinema with James. She had suggested the outing, her contribution to the idea that they were still friends, and throughout she was determinedly nice, asking about his family and taking an intelligent interest in the latest crisis at the hospital. She had been home for ten minutes when the phone rang. "Your red skirt is great," said Marcel. "It makes you look like a skater."

Morag was too startled to speak. She gazed wildly around the room: the empty armchairs, the empty sofa, the dark windows whose curtains she seldom drew because of being on the fourth floor. Hearing her silence, Marcel laughed. "Did you like the film?" he asked.

"Oh, you were at the Odeon," Morag exclaimed. The evening bloomed with new radiance; it had not been merely another dull date with James. Marcel had been there watching her, wanting her. "That was James," she said. "We're just . . ."

"Friends?" Marcel interrupted, his voice curling around the word like a dry leaf.

At the pub the following night Marcel showed up during the ten o'clock rush. Morag was too busy to say more than hello, and he fell into conversation with one of the regulars, Grace, who after a lifetime working on the Leith docks had turned to poetry. From behind the bar Morag watched her perform a poem: the one about the fire, she guessed, from the way Grace flapped her arms. The next time she looked, Marcel had gone.

Soon eleven o'clock came. Roy shouted last call and ushered people out. He was a graduate student, normally soft-spoken, who was writing a dissertation on the Battle of Culloden. When business was slow he entertained Morag with accounts of skirmishes and disasters. Together they cleaned the tables. She did the washing up, while he dealt with the cash. The rule was that Morag waited for him to lock up and kept him company to the night deposit box. "Think of yourself as the bodyguard," the owner had told her.

Roy was setting the alarm and Morag was joking about their tips for the evening, a stunning total of one pound ninety pence, when a figure sauntered out of the darkness. Immediately Morag shifted from laughter to apprehension. Was this danger?

"Hi," said Marcel. "I came back to see if I could walk you home."

"You can jog beside my bicycle. Roy, this is Marcel. Marcel, Roy."

The three of them walked to the corner, Morag pushing

her bike. Then Roy insisted he was fine. "It's brightly lit and look at all the traffic." He gestured with the folded Tesco's bag that contained their takings for the night.

"Okay," said Morag. "If you're sure." At the prospect of Marcel seeing the deposit box a thought she did not care to examine had slid into her brain and flitted away. She and Marcel continued down Broughton Road. He praised Grace, saying she could be Irish, and recited highlights of her poem. Outside Morag's flat he handed her a package. "For you."

It was the novel *A High Wind from Jamaica.* "I thought you didn't believe in stealing anything useful," said Morag. He had by now explained his philosophy of shoplifting— always from chains and, ideally, something useless. "To steal for a purpose is explicable and forgivable. Like a hunter killing only what he needs to feed his family." Marcel did not steal every week, or even every month, but periodically the hunger would come over him again for that moment of total concentration and he would put on his raincoat and sally forth.

Now he expostulated that the author was dead and the mere giving an act of superfluity. "I have to believe you like me anyway," he said, "else I wouldn't go to this kind of trouble."

He kissed her and although his mouth was warm, his body maintained a careful distance; a Catholic distance, Morag thought. Briefly she wondered if she ought to ask him in, but it was late and he said nothing. She wished him good night and wheeled her bike inside.

Uneasiness settled in Morag, like a stingray on the ocean floor, present but not always visible. When she left James, it had been with a keen desire to expand her life. She did not want to leave Poppies, where she had worked for four years, or Edinburgh, where she had lived for ten, but within these confines, she wanted something different and, so far, Marcel seemed to offer her best chance. His carefully cultivated air of mystery fascinated her and made her feel more fascinating. Lucy and Yvonne, even Roy, asked, "Are you in love with him?" and tut-tutted instead of rejoicing at her negative answer.

Morag continued to meet Marcel in public places. They ate or went to films and once, on a clear, cold day, climbed Arthur's Seat. From the top they gazed across the city to the Firth of Forth. Marcel said the view reminded him of home. He told her that the autumn he was eleven he and the other boys had smashed the windows of the parish school. "The fathers refused to mend them until spring. Of course they were toasty in their habits but we had to wear our coats and do jumping jacks between lessons to keep warm." He laughed. "It was tragic."

"Tragic," repeated Morag, charmed by the odd use of the word.

"So what were you like at school?" he said, turning from the panorama to her.

"I was a good girl. My mother was the school secretary so it was hard to misbehave."

"That's too bad. There are some things one needs to do at a certain age. If I had shoplifted as a kid, I wouldn't be doing it now."

His hair moved in the breeze and Morag noticed that today the color was definitely brown. "But what about what you said, the hunger?" she asked.

"I think most people have that. I mean, don't you? Isn't that why you left James?"

"I suppose." She did not feel an immediate identification with Marcel's criminal activities, but yes, there had been a kind of hunger. "So what do most people do about it?"

"Men do sneaky things at work, or mess about with women. As for women"—he put his arm around her shoulders—"you'll have to tell me."

In mid-November Morag went to Perth to visit her parents. Marcel begged to come too, but she resisted. James was the only man she had taken home and she was not yet ready to take another, especially Marcel, one of whose virtues was that her parents were sure to disapprove of him. "Maybe when I know you better," she temporized. "Besides, we're going fishing."

"Fishing," pouted Marcel. "Listen, you know me now. You apprehend my essence in its totality. As time goes on, you'll know me less, not more. Already we're both being obscured by a cloud of facts."

A cloud of facts, Morag thought, and smiled. Her father met her at the Perth bus station and they went fishing in the River Tay. Morag used a new fly her father had tied, peacock blue, and caught nothing while he, with his favorite black widow, hooked two small trout. He released the first. The second he left to Morag. In her hand the fish panted hard, but when she slipped the hook free and reached down into the water, it swam away almost drowsily. A little later the rain started and she and her father went home for baths and tea.

Over supper her parents asked about James. "He's such a nice man," said her mother. "And utterly reliable."

"You don't seem specially happy these days," added her father.

"I wasn't happy before, either," protested Morag. That she had felt she was already living the life she'd be leading when she was sixty struck her parents as an argument for James, not against him. They took turns listing his good points. The conversation, familiar in every detail, exhausted Morag. As soon as she got home, she went to bed.

Next morning she climbed out of the shower and approached the basin. Something was different. In the condensation on the mirror there were marks. Letters. They spelled "Listen to me."

Morag stared. She was about to wipe them away but stopped. Instead she hurried to the bedroom and put on her clothes. When she came back, the words were still there. She stood, looking at them, her arms wrapped around herself. Then she fetched her camera and took a photograph before she wiped the mirror clean.

She ate a bowl of cereal standing at the kitchen sink. What else, what else had he seen and touched? The idea of her most innocent possessions falling prey to Marcel's scrutiny made her squirm, but there was no time to check. It was her turn to open Poppies. By an effort of will she gathered her things together and set out on her bike. Normally the hill up to the shop left her puffing, but today she pedaled with furious energy, oblivious to the incline. At Poppies she did not pause even to remove her helmet before dialing Marcel's number.

"Morag," he said warmly, "I'm listening to Benjamin Britten's *A Midsummer Night's Dream*. Can you hear it?"

The high sweet notes of Titania's love for Bottom almost broke Morag's resolution, but she steeled herself. "Marcel," she said, "did you visit my flat yesterday?"

There was the slightest pause. Titania fell silent. Marcel laughed. "Fair cop," he said. "You made me feel like a parcel you wanted to leave in left luggage. And when you only used the Yale lock. . . ." He trailed off, as if the depths of her stupidity and his temptation were too obvious to be spoken.

"Wait a minute," said Morag. "You can't break into someone's flat just because they don't do what you want. That's fascism. How would you feel if I did that to you?"

"You're absolutely right," said Marcel, seemingly struck by the novelty of this insight. "I won't do it again. Cross my heart." He explained how he had written on the mirror with soap; it was an old Halloween trick.

They made a date for Wednesday and Morag hung up feeling relieved. She put away her outdoor clothes, opened the shop, and made a cup of coffee. But as she was cleaning the display cases, she saw again the mirror with the neat letters rising out of the steam, and her equilibrium vanished like a speck of dust. What was the promise worth of a man who would break into her flat out of peevishness? And now it was not so much that she had forgiven Marcel but been turned by him into an accomplice. That was the third category—sins of complicity.

Mondays were quiet at both Poppies and the pub, and by the end of the day Morag had a plan. Next morning it was Lucy's turn to open the shop and soon after seven Morag set off to Marcel's address. It was near the university, a five-story building in a close with only one way out. Best of all there was a bakery opposite with a few tables where she could sit and read the papers.

An hour passed and she had moved from satisfaction with her scheme to thinking that this was the stupidest thing she had ever done. Three people had come out of the close, two older women and a boy. Morag was giving up hope when a fourth person appeared, a man who walked like Marcel but was wearing some kind of navy-blue uniform.

Morag stared. It was indeed Marcel and he was heading here. She seized the newspaper and feigned absorption. He pushed open the door and stepped inside. She heard his voice say, "Good morning." And then the woman behind the counter, "Good morning, Frank. What can I get you?"

Frank, wondered Morag. She remembered that the initials in the phone book had been F. M. He ordered a ham-and-cheese roll and a coffee to take away. Soon the transaction was complete. He left, bidding the woman a cheerful farewell, and Morag followed. It was surprisingly easy. The streets were busy; he never looked back. Within ten minutes the riddle of the uniform was solved. Marcel was heading toward the Museum of Art. Morag lingered in Princes Street gardens and watched him go inside. She sat down on a bench and began to laugh. Even his vegetarianism had been a lie.

Morag had thought that simply knowing some basic facts about Marcel would redress the balance; she had not reckoned upon the disruptive nature of those facts. On Wednesday when they went for pizza, she could scarcely contain herself as Marcel ordered the vegetarian alternative. While they waited, he presented her with the large box he had been carrying. It turned out to be a picnic basket. When Morag exclaimed, he said he felt terrible about the other day. He'd behaved tragically. She was quite right to be furious.

Morag lifted the basket onto her knee and opened it. Inside, neatly strapped in place, was a thermos, with place settings for four and two boxes for sandwiches. "I thought maybe for when you went fishing," offered Marcel.

"How did you . . . ?" Morag broke off.

"I bought a cheap laundry hamper and put the basket inside." He described, with obvious satisfaction, how his hands had shaken. "Do you like it?" he asked.

Morag nodded, oddly saddened. Marcel had been brought low, she thought; here he was stealing useful things for useful reasons. It was partly out of that sadness that she invited him to come round to Steve and Janet's on Friday. Partly out of the hope that the tangled skein they had woven might yet be unraveled. She imagined her friends asking the questions she no longer could and Marcel giving simple, truthful answers. He accepted the invitation enthusiastically, then stood her up. Morag left three messages on his answering machine. The fourth time she remained silent out of embarrassment.

Next day Morag claimed an errand at lunchtime and bicycled to the museum. She jogged through the crowded rooms past gaggles of schoolchildren and elderly guards. Then, in the seventeenth century, there he was, being questioned by a stout man. Morag slowed her pace to match the other visitors. She did not want to accost him, or to be noticed, simply to see him. At the last moment, however, the stout man stepped away and Marcel's wandering gaze fell upon her. Morag stopped, rooted in front of a large, gloomy landscape. As for Marcel, he blushed fiercely and retreated into the sixteenth century.

Back at the shop, Morag blurted yet another message onto the answering machine. "Marcel, I didn't mean to be standoffish. I was just so surprised to see you. And I needed to get back to the shop. Please phone me. I'd like to talk."

Now she felt tragic. By her spying she had stolen Marcel's air of mystery. She told the whole story—as much as she could stand—to Roy. "Morag," he said, "he sounds mad. You do too. Why would you want to go out with a pathological liar?"

"But he's also sweet and he tells wonderful stories. It wasn't all lies. And I lied too—about my age, some other stuff. I mean"—she saw Roy's expression—"maybe that's what people do, but it's still lying."

In between pulling pints they argued. Roy remarked that his first thought on meeting Marcel had been that he was gay.

"Gay," said Morag, spilling the beer she was holding.

"Of course," Roy said apologetically, "you would know."

He moved off to empty ashtrays, leaving Morag to grapple with this surprising notion. That would make sense of the cautious kisses but not of the heat she had sometimes felt rising between them. A woman asked for an orange juice and Morag plunged back into work. By the end of the evening she was convinced. She would not make any more overtures toward Marcel; she would stay away from the museum, his flat, the phone. "And be careful going home at night," Roy admonished.

He was locking the door of the pub as he spoke, and Morag had the sudden prickly sensation of being observed, like a knife scratching between her shoulder blades, but when she turned around there were only the usual teenagers and drunks straggling down the pavement. Nevertheless she left her bike and took a taxi home.

Over the next fortnight there was no sign of Marcel and the intervals between the prickly feeling grew longer. It had been a mistake, a glancing encounter with psychosis, but she had learned—one did have to be careful of strangers. She paid another visit to her parents and talked with James about Christmas presents for their families. The shop grew busier and they stayed open until eight during the week.

So it was one Wednesday, a cold, sleety evening that Morag was alone at Poppies. She had made Lucy leave at seven, claiming she could manage the cleaning and cash alone. "If there's no one here at quarter to eight, I'll sneak away," she promised.

She was hoovering when a man's brown shoes appeared in her field of vision. She raised her eyes to find Marcel standing before her in his raincoat. The noise of the hoover had masked his entrance. Morag was so flustered that she did not think to turn it off. After a moment Marcel moved to the wall and pulled the plug.

In the abrupt silence, Morag felt the sweat spring up on

her palms. She was alone in a shop, her shop, with a man to whom shoplifting was a form of self-expression. "Marcel," she gasped, "I haven't seen you for ages. How are you?"

"I'm fine." He smiled, his divergent eyes seeming to take in not only her, but the racks of merchandise. "Did you sell the black lace dress? The one that was hanging up by the mirror?"

"You've been here before."

He nodded. "Why don't you finish so we can leave?"

"I am finished. Really. Let's go for a drink." Everything might still be all right if only she could pretend it was.

"What about the cash?"

Morag stood there, the handle of the hoover falling out of her hands. "Lucy already took it," she whispered.

Marcel walked behind the counter to the cash register and pressed the no-sale button. The drawer sprang open; he studied the contents with a smile. Before the sleet started, the shop had been busy. "Lucy didn't do a very good job," he said in his soft Irish accent.

"Marcel, what are you doing?" Morag stepped to the counter. Anyone glancing in from the street would have seen a salesman in a raincoat assisting a doubtful customer but she did not think of that. Her face felt strangely heavy and porous.

His lips were moving as he counted out the notes. "A hundred and twenty," he said. "That'll leave you enough for a float tomorrow."

"But we're a small shop," said Morag. "Money is useful."

"I'm making an exception in your case." Marcel folded the notes and slid them into his pocket. "What did you think? I was some dumb mick you could use for adventure?"

His left cheek twitched. But what was all this nonsense about adventure, thought Morag, remembering his kisses. He came out from behind the counter and she realized he was leaving with a hundred and twenty pounds. She grabbed his arm. "Marcel," she said. "Listen to me."

He looked at her coldly. "You could have locked the door," he said. "You could have rung the police. Stupid. You wanted me to steal this."

He shook off her hand, opened the door, and stepped into the street. With final insolence, he paused to put on a pair of gloves and sauntered away.

As soon as he was out of sight, Morag locked the door and ran to the phone, but even as she reached toward the receiver, she imagined herself explaining the circumstances of her first meeting with Marcel, the gifts, the complicity. In some ways she *had* wanted this, not exactly this, but something close enough that a genie could be forgiven for mistaking the vague specifications of her wish. The handsome sergeant who had investigated their burglary last year would not flirt with her this time. And what could she say to Yvonne and Lucy, whose livelihood she had jeopardized along with her own?

In the middle of the empty, festive shop, Morag stood, shivering slightly, trying to knit her ragged thoughts into a course of action. How to wipe out the evidence of Marcel's visit? She put the hoover away. Then she went over to the cash register and hit the no-sale button. She would take everything that remained home and sort it there; the deposit could wait until morning. But there was one thing that could not wait. Although she was cold and it was suddenly late, Morag opened her bag and took out her checkbook.

"Pay Poppies," she wrote. As she filled in the amount, a movement caught her eye, someone passing in the street, but not Marcel, not James, just a young girl in boots, who stopped for a moment, her face full of yearning, to look at the dress in the window, and then walked on.

FRIED CHICKEN

•

Lee Smith

Here comes the murderer's mother, Mrs. Polly Pegram. She walks to Food City every other day, then carries her paper bag of groceries home. When the boy at Food City says "Paper or plastic, ma'am?" as if he doesn't know the answer, as if he doesn't know who she is, she always says "Paper, please," and she always walks the same way home, past the tanning salon, past Lil's Beauty, past the Baptist church with its rosebushes blooming out front and its green Astroturf entrance and hymns floating out its open windows. She used to be a Baptist, years back. She used to bring Leonard here for Sunday school. He could sing like an angel, as a boy. Now he is forty-one years old.

Leonard used to drive Mrs. Pegram everywhere, so she never bothered to get her driver's license, she never needed it. She doesn't need it now, though Miss Bright—this is the social worker who won't leave her alone—keeps suggesting

it. It's true that Leonard's red car is just sitting out there
in the driveway. Sometimes when she's working in her garden, she'll rinse it off with the hose. But if she did learn to
drive it, where in the world would she go? Miss Bright swears
that the driving instructor from the high school will drive
right up to Mrs. Pegram's door to pick her up for her lessons.
He will ring her doorbell, she'll come out, and off they'll go
in the special car together.

The thought of this sets Mrs. Pegram's heart aquiver.
For nobody comes to this little house, nobody ever came.
Her husband, Royal Pegram, did not like visitors, and Leonard did not like visitors, either. Oh, she knows what they
said about Leonard! *Loner. Lives with his mother.* As if it
were a crime. Anyway, Leonard had plenty of friends. This
is one thing that never came out in court, how popular he
was, though he would never invite them over to the house,
preferring to go out, as young people will. Sometimes Mrs.
Pegram pages through the magazines as she stands in the
checkout line at Food City, lingering over the cookouts.
She used to wish Leonard would have a cookout, but he
never did.

Mrs. Pegram unlocks her door and walks through the
front room where the TV is, past the closed door of Leonard's room, into the spotless little yellow kitchen where she
puts the milk in the refrigerator and the two packages of
cellophane-wrapped chicken out on the countertop. She buys
Pick o' the Chick, all breasts and legs and thighs; it's more
expensive, but it's worth it if you want to fix really good
fried chicken. Mrs. Pegram knows that the girls behind the
meat counter whisper to each other after she has gone, saying, "What do you reckon she's going to do with all that
chicken, now that he's in the pen?" Well, they would be real
surprised to find out, that's for sure!

Leonard just loved her fried chicken; she used to fix it
for him on Sundays and he would eat every bit up, except

for one piece, which is all she ever ate. Mrs. Pegram just pecks at her food like a bird. She's a tiny little thing anyway, hardly five feet tall, and shrinking.

Mrs. Pegram takes the cellophane off the packages and rinses the chicken under running water. But before she gets started cooking, she'd better take off these nice shoes and put on her house shoes, fuzzy old things, and put on her apron, too. Chicken spatters. She's got to save her good clothes. Now that she's not working for Mrs. Calhoun anymore, she won't be getting any of Mrs. Calhoun's old clothes, which were actually not old at all, just things that Mrs. Calhoun had grown tired of. Well, most of them were too big anyway.

The awful fact is that soon after the verdict, in spite of all their years together, Mrs. Calhoun let Mrs. Pegram go. Oh, Mrs. Pegram saw it coming. She saw Mrs. Calhoun grow more and more nervous as the trial went on, acting exactly like she had when she was going through the change of life, or when her daughter Alicia was getting her divorces, or when Mr. Calhoun had cancer of the prostate. Mrs. Calhoun got to where she wouldn't look Mrs. Pegram in the eye anymore, and she never, *ever* mentioned the trial.

Finally there came the morning when Mrs. Calhoun did not come downstairs at all. Instead, Mr. Johnny Calhoun sat waiting at the breakfast table, wearing his three-piece suit. "Natalie wants you to know how much she has valued her association with you over the years," he said in his courtroom voice, "but she feels that with the children grown, we need to economize, and she wants to do some of the housework herself, for the exercise, and have a cleaning service come in once a month, which is all we really need. Natalie knew you would understand." Then Johnny Calhoun handed Mrs. Pegram a check for a thousand dollars. During the years she'd been working for the Calhouns, his hair had turned from black to silver. Now he was a very distinguished man.

Mrs. Pegram looked at him until he looked away. "I understand," she said. Of course he was lying through his teeth, Natalie Calhoun would kill herself before she'd touch a can of Comet. She didn't even know where the dust rags were kept. But who could blame Mrs. Calhoun, after all? Who could blame her for firing the murderer's mother, for not wanting the murderer's mother to be the one who knew that she hid her Xanax in the false bottom of her jewelry box, who knew that Johnny Pegram required clean sheets every single day and wanted his underwear ironed, who knew that their daughter was an alcoholic? Who would want a murderer's mother to know these things? Mrs. Pegram can't blame her.

Of course she was disappointed, because she had thought Natalie Calhoun was her *friend,* too, though Leonard had snorted at this idea. "Mrs. Calhoun is a bitch, Ma," he'd said. "Don't kid yourself."

For years Leonard had been after her to get a better job, but this was what she knew how to do, wait on people, take good care of their things. At least she still has Mr. and Mrs. Joyner two days a week; they're so out of it, poor souls, it is possible they don't even know about Leonard's case.

Mrs. Pegram puts flour, salt, pepper, and paprika in a plastic bag and shakes it. She puts Wesson oil in the skillet. She used to try to get Leonard to eat baked chicken the way she fixed it for the Calhouns, but he wouldn't have it. He liked it fried. Mrs. Pegram knew this was bad for him because he was such a big boy; she was sure his cholesterol was real high, but he wouldn't even get it checked for free in the booth at the mall.

You couldn't do a thing with Leonard when it came to his habits. For instance he wore the same outfit to his job at Lowes warehouse winter and summer, a flannel shirt and army work pants, and he had to have the same thing in his lunch box every day, too—three bologna sandwiches with

Miracle Whip on the bread, two packages of Little Debbie Oatmeal Pies with cream filling. Then he'd buy himself some chocolate milk at the 7-Eleven to go with it. Mrs. Pegram wished that Leonard would reduce and dress better so he'd have more of a chance with the girls, but actually he never showed any interest in nice girls or in marriage, either one. She always acted like she didn't know about the pile of nasty magazines in his closet, but so what? Plenty of people buy those magazines—there's a stack of them under Mr. Johnny Calhoun's side of the bed right now. Plus, Leonard was interested in plenty of other magazines too, such as those military magazines. Mrs. Pegram has always felt it was a shame that the army wouldn't take Leonard; it might have been the making of him.

Mrs. Pegram shakes each piece of chicken up in the plastic bag, coating it with the flour mixture, then slips it into the sizzling pan. This is the part where you have to pay attention—you want to get a nice crispy coating on all sides, but you can't let it burn. Mrs. Pegram stands close to the stove, turning the chicken frequently in the big old iron skillet. Royal Pegram hit her once with this skillet, years ago; she can't even remember the circumstances.

Mrs. Pegram is still not sure how it happened that Royal turned so mean. She'd met him in the little church up on Piney Ridge when she was not but sixteen, and him the same. He'd come into the county with a logging operation run by his older brother. Maybe it was because he was a stranger that she took to him so, since she didn't know anybody in the world that she hadn't been knowing her whole life long. They fell on each other like they were meant to. Looking back, Mrs. Pegram thinks of the young Royal Pegram as a different person from the one she was married to for so long. That boy had black hair and black eyes and a sweet, dreamy way about him. He was from West Virginia and proposed to go back over there to work in the mines, and proposed to take her with him. "Go," her mama said. "Go on while you've got the chance," for there were seven more at home and this would be one less mouth to feed.

It was the first time she'd been out of the county, not to mention the state of Virginia, and at first it was fine; he mined for the company and she got a job keeping house for the company doctor's wife, a tall, sad woman from Alabama who taught her how to set the table and polish silver with a toothbrush and slice ham real thin.

During those days Royal used to sit on the front porch and pick his guitar while she was stringing beans of a Sunday. He used to wear a straw hat with a feather stuck in the brim. Sometimes they went fishing in the river, and once he took her to the West Virginia State Fair. Then she had the baby, Rose Eliza, who was sickly, and Royal didn't like her whining and crying so much because he was working the night shift and needed to get his sleep. But Rose Eliza cried and cried and did not grow. She had something wrong with her blood, and there was nothing they could do about it, and she died right before her third birthday. She was buried in a little pine box on a mountainside that was later strip-mined.

After Rose Eliza's death, Royal would not allow her name to be mentioned in his presence, and he burned her clothes and the two pictures they had of her, so that now Mrs. Pegram has none, and sometimes she wonders if she ever had that little baby girl at all, just as she wonders if those slow, sweet days over in West Virginia right after they got married were some kind of a dream. Because it all becomes a blur after that, her life a kind of a whirlwind. The mine fell in, and Royal got trapped for a day and a half next to a dead man, and so they left there, and went to another mining town, and she had the twin boys Roger and Royal Junior, and Royal got laid off and started drinking pretty bad, and then they moved again. And again. Finally she got to where she never unpacked the boxes, and she learned to stay away from him when he was drinking and never to answer him back. Leonard was born at a free clinic over in Kentucky.

Everywhere they ever lived, Mrs. Pegram had a job keeping house for somebody, because she had a nice genteel way about her and she was quiet, and she knew how to do things right. The homes where she worked were a comfort to her, the shining windows, the orderly flower beds, the pale expanses of wall-to-wall carpet. At her own place it was nothing but yelling and broken things, except for Leonard.

Leonard was the joy of his mother's life. And he was certainly *not* retarded, no matter what anybody says now. When he was not but five, he'd play Chinese checkers with his mother by the hour. He loved Chinese checkers. He always picked the blue marbles to be his, and to this day Mrs. Pegram cannot see the color blue without thinking of her little boy, fat and serious, with eyes as round and as blue as those marbles. Leonard knew the words to all the popular songs too; he'd sing right along with the radio. He especially liked "Kawliga was a wooden Indian," which they played on the radio a lot then. There was nothing retarded about him!

Now Mrs. Pegram puts a tablespoon of water right into the hot grease and turns the heat down and covers the pan quickly, to trap the steam inside. This is the real secret of good fried chicken; this is what most people don't know to do. This is what makes the meat tender, so it just melts in your mouth like it ought to. After ten minutes of steaming, Mrs. Pegram takes the lid off the chicken and turns the heat back up and fries it some more, turning it constantly, so the nice brown coating gets crispy again.

People who are so quick to judge ought to know that Leonard was the one who ran his daddy off finally, as soon as he got bigger than Royal Pegram. The other boys were long gone by then, and who could blame them? It was the day after Christmas and Royal had been on the wagon—

he'd bought her a new car coat for Christmas, and a Schwinn bike for Leonard, sometimes he could still be real sweet— but then he'd started up again and by the time Leonard came in the house from riding his bike, she was on the couch crying, too dizzy to get up. Leonard was thirteen years old then and they wanted her to sign the papers to send him to the special school but she wouldn't; she needed him at home too bad, though of course she couldn't explain this to his teacher.

"Ma?" Leonard called, coming in. Then he came over and looked at her and then he went in the kitchen and then he came back and sat down in the ladderback chair by the door. She kept falling in and out of sleep. When Royal came in, Leonard hit him in the face with a ballpeen hammer and then kicked him in the side when he fell. He kept kicking him. Leonard would have broken every bone in Royal's body if she had not gotten up and gotten in between them finally. By then the neighbors were there, and the police came.

The upshot of it was that a judge sent Leonard off to the special school, and when Royal got out of the hospital, he moved back over to West Virginia and died there several years later of cirrhosis of the liver. His sister wrote to Mrs. Pegram that Royal turned yellow at the end and spoke her name before he died.

After that, Mrs. Pegram kept to herself. She worked steadily and lived frugally and paid off her little house. When Leonard came back from the special school, she was glad for his company, though he didn't talk much. But it was a steady life, a good life, hers and Leonard's. Leonard was nothing if not dependable, regular as a clock. He kept things fixed around the house and watched *The Newlywed Game* every night after supper. You could set your watch by Leonard. This was such a comfort to Mrs. Pegram after all those years of uncertainty and constant moving. And though she was never one to put herself forward, Mrs.

Pegram made quiet little friendships all over town. Besides the people she worked for, such as the Calhouns, of course, and the Joyners and the Streets who moved away, she came to know Mr. Harris the pharmacist, Betty at the bank, Lil who did her hair, and the Banner sisters who ran the fabric shop and took her out to eat at the Western Sizzling on the bypass, though Leonard didn't really like for her to go.

Now, since the trial, Mrs. Pegram has been wishing she lived in a big city, so she could be anonymous. Here, everybody knows her. Everywhere she goes, they're whispering behind their hands, "Look! Here she comes! It's the murderer's mother!" They all think it is somehow her fault. Even when they pretend to be nice, such as when the Banner sisters asked her to go to the outlets with them or when Preacher Rose came by to invite her to prayer meeting or when Margie Niles from next door brought her a piece of red velvet cake, Mrs. Pegram did not respond. She heard what Hubert Liles, the manager at Lowes, said about him at the trial. She knows they are only acting out of pity, all of them. Or perhaps they are acting out of curiosity, perhaps they are all just dying to know what it's like to be the murderer's mother! Well, she will not give them the satisfaction; she will give them the cold shoulder instead. Completely alone now, the murderer's mother feels somehow exhilarated, exalted, singled out.

This chicken is perfect. Mrs. Pegram lifts it out of the frying pan and puts it on paper towels so it won't be greasy. Suddenly she recalls Royal Pegram telling somebody, years ago, that he married her for her fried chicken. She blushes hot all over for a minute, remembering this. Then Mrs. Pegram takes off her apron and her house shoes, and puts her good shoes back on. She goes in the bedroom to comb her hair, powder her face, and put on her little black hat. She looks nice. Anybody would know, just from looking at her, that she is a nice woman. That girl was *not nice*, this certainly came out in the trial, ditto those other girls who came up to testify against him, just look at the way they were dressed. Look at the way *she* was dressed, of course he didn't have to do what he did to her. Mrs. Pegram pushes these awful thoughts out of her mind. She never, *ever,* thinks about it. And today, she's got places to go! People to see!

She goes back in the kitchen and lines a basket with more paper towels, then carefully transfers the chicken to it, piece by piece. The phone rings, startling her, just as she finishes putting tinfoil over the top.

"It's Heidi Bright," the cheerful voice says on the other end of the phone. This is that pesky social worker. "It's such a beautiful Sunday afternoon, I thought you might like to go for a drive with me. Maybe we could drive out to the lake."

"Thank you so much," Mrs. Pegram says, adopting the tone Mrs. Calhoun always used when she wanted to get rid of visiting Mormons, "but I've already made plans."

"Oh, you *have!*" Miss Bright sounds encouraging. She'd really like to know, wouldn't she, just what kind of plans a murderer's mother makes!

"Yes," Mrs. Pegram says, "I've got an appointment. Thanks so much for asking, though." Then she hangs up, before Miss Bright can say another word. An appointment! She likes the sound of it.

Mrs. Pegram takes her basket and her purse and steps outside, turning to lock the door behind her. It *is* a beautiful day, Indian summer they call it, lovely warm sun and the leaves just beginning to turn. Leonard never appreciated nature at all. Still, he was the cutest little boy, hair so blond it was white. Mrs. Pegram walks past the Baptist church, Lil's Beauty and the tanning salon, past Food City, which is real busy now, on downtown past the bank and all the closed shops, past the Presbyterian church, which the Calhouns attend, past Hardees.

She goes into the big new Trailways bus station and sits

on a bench to wait for the bus from Charlotte, due in at 3:30.
It's 3:25. Mrs. Pegram peers around. She has never seen the
man behind the desk, a good-looking young man with a mus-
tache; she's sure he's not from around here. She doesn't know
him, he doesn't know her, and he would never suspect, of
course, that such a nice-looking little woman could possibly
be a murderer's mother. Not in a million years! Then the
bus from Charlotte comes in, a flood of strangers. The young
man calls out connections for Roanoke, for Atlanta. People
go this way, that way. It's exciting. Mrs. Pegram watches
the crowd.

Finally she moves over to take a seat beside a tired-
looking young blond mother and a squirmy little boy. Sometimes it's a mother with several children, sometimes it's a
child traveling alone, sometimes it's a whole family.

"Where are you going?" she'll ask pleasantly after a while,
and the young mother will say Atlanta or Norfolk or Rich-
mond or Washington, even L.A., it could be anyplace, and
then Mrs. Pegram will ask where they're from, and the young
mother will tell her, and then Mrs. Pegram will say, "My
goodness, that's quite a trip," and the young mother, warm-
ing to her, will tell all about it; why they're going and how
long they'll be there, and sometimes it will be a long story
and sometimes not. The little boy will be climbing all over
his mother, eyeing Mrs. Pegram's basket. Finally she will
say, "I'm just taking my son some fried chicken; it's real
good and I've got plenty, would you like a piece?" and when
she takes off the tinfoil, the heavenly smell of fried chicken
will be everywhere as she offers it to them. The mother will
eat a breast, then a thigh. "It's so good!" she'll cry. The little
boy will eat all the drumsticks. His eyes are as round as a
plate, he's so cute; he is the most important thing in the
world to his mother, he is her whole life. The good-looking
young man will call their bus. Mrs. Pegram will wrap up

two more pieces in tinfoil and insist upon giving them to the mother as they hurry to get in line. It's okay—she's got plenty of chicken left. Plenty! Mrs. Pegram clutches the basket to her beating heart and waits for the next bus to come.

ROCKETS ROUND

THE MOON

●

A. M. Homes

WE WERE THE BOYS of summer vacation, Henry Heffilfinger and me. It was my fifth summer at my father's house, six years after my parents divorced, three years after my mother remarried, the summer of seventy-nine, the summer I was twelve, the summer the world almost stopped spinning round.

Henry's mother picked me up at the airport. "Hello! Hello!" she called from the far end of the terminal, waving her arms through air, as if simultaneously fanning herself and guiding me in for landing.

"Oh, you look tall," she said, trying to wrestle away my carry-on bag. "Your father was busy; he asked me to come. So, that's why I'm here." She stopped for a minute, combed the hair out of my face with her fingernails. "We're so glad you've arrived; we're going to have a fine summer."

For that moment, while her pink frosted nails were tickling my skull, I believed her.

Luggage spun on a wide stainless-steel rack; suitcases slid up, down, sideways, crashing into each other with the painless thud of bumper cars. We stood watching until everything had come and gone, until there was nothing left except a couple of old bags that probably belonged to someone who'd died in a plane crash, who'd left their luggage forever going round and round.

"Where's Henry?" I asked.

Maybe Henry was my hero, maybe just my friend, I don't know. He had a mother, a father, and a little sister, all in together, on one street, in one city. He had no secrets.

"Guarding the car. I'm parked in a terrible place."

While I stood by the carousel, hoping my suitcases would home in and find me, Mrs. Henry took my luggage checks and went off in search of information.

If you're wondering what the point is calling Henry by his own name and then calling his mother Mrs. Henry, well what can I say, all the Heffilfingers were Henrys to me. Mr., Mrs., baby June, and Henry himself.

I rolled my eyes in a full circle counting the brown-and-yellow spots that made up the tortoiseshell rims of my glasses. They were new glasses, my first glasses. No one in Philly had seen them yet except Mrs. Henry, and she was sharp enough not to say anything.

A couple of months ago my school borrowed vision machines from the motor vehicle department and lined us all up. I looked into the viewfinder and said to the school nurse, "I can't see anything, it's pure blackness."

"Press your head to the bar, wise guy," she said.

I pressed my forehead against the machine and the screen lit up, but all that light still didn't do much good. The nurse sent me home with a note for my mother who simply said,

"You're not getting contacts; you're too young and too irresponsible."

I thought of not taking the glasses to Philly, of going through one more blind, blurry summer, but the fact was they made a real difference, so I wore them and kept the unbreakable case, and a thousand specially treated cleaning sheets jammed into my carry-on bag.

Four-eyed, but alone in the Philadelphia airport, I may as well have been a boy without a brain. Like a sugar donut, I was glazed. Stiff.

It was the day after school ended. My mother had put me on the plane with a list of instructions/directions for my father, written out longhand on three sheets of legal paper, stuffed into one of Dr. Frankle's embossed envelopes. I was to be returned on or by the twenty-first of August, in good time for the usual back-to-school alterations: haircut, fresh jeans, new sneakers, book bag. I was only just becoming aware of how much everything was the product of a negotiation or fight.

"Let's find Henry," Mrs. Henry suggested.

Let's not, I thought.

We were at the age where just showing up was frightening. You never knew who or what you might meet, a twelve-foot giant with a voice like a tuba, or Howdy Doody himself. Without warning, a body could go into spasm, it could stretch itself out to a railroad tie, it could take someone familiar and make them a stranger. A whole other person could claim the name, address, phone number, and fingerprints of a friend. There was the possibility that in those ten missing months a new life had been created, one that intentionally bore no relation to the past.

"Don't worry, they'll find your luggage," Mrs. Henry said. "They'll check the airport in Boston and the next plane coming in, and when they've got it, they'll deliver it out to the house. You'll have it by suppertime. Let's go," she said. "Makes no sense to wait here."

The automatic doors popped open. Henry stood there, arms open, exasperated.

"What the hell is going on?" He screamed, "They're about to tow our car. They asked me for my license!"

Mrs. Henry turned red. She tugged on the strap of my shoulder bag. We ran forward.

"I've never heard of anything taking so long," Henry said when we got outside.

There was no tow truck. There was nothing except a long line of cars dropping off people and men in red caps going back and forth from the cars to the terminal wheeling suitcases that weren't lost yet. There wasn't even a ticket on the Henrys' windshield.

And Henry wasn't a giant. He wasn't six feet tall, either. He was skinny with shoulders that stuck straight out of him like the top of a T square.

"What happened?" he asked.

"The airline has misplaced your friend's luggage."

He turned to me, finally noticing I was there, I existed. "Why'd you get glasses?"

"Blind," I said.

Five years ago, before I ever met him, Henry was offered to me by my father as a kind of bribe.

"Philadelphia will be fun," my father had said. "We bought this house especially for you. There's a boy your age living next door; you can be best friends."

My first day there I stood three foot and something, waiting smack in the middle of the treeless, flowerless, nearly grassless front yard as nonchalantly as a seven-year-old could. I knew no other way of announcing myself. When the sun had crossed well over its midday mark, when what seemed like years had passed, a station wagon pulled into the driveway just past me and the promised boy jumped out and without stopping ran toward the kitchen door of his house. The screen door opened, but instead of admitting him, a yellow rubber-gloved hand pushed the boy out again. The body attached to the hand followed and Mrs. led Henry to the edge of their yard and nodded in my direction.

"Henry, this is your new friend. He's here for the whole summer," she said.

"Bye," Henry said, taking off again in the direction of the kitchen door, whipping open the screen, and vanishing into the house.

"You can't stand outside all summer, you'll be a regular Raisinette, go on, after him," Mrs. Henry said, clapping her hands.

The geography of the Henrys' house was the exact same as my father's house, but theirs was more developed. The top floor had blue carpet; the middle level, yellow; and the lower level was green. The sky, the sun, the lawn. It made perfect sense. It was beautiful. Everywhere I'd ever lived the floors were wooden or carpeted a neat and dull beige or gray. Here I had the sensation of floating, skimming through the rooms like a hovercraft. I went through the house, stunned by the strangeness of being alone among the lives of others.

I found Henry on the lower level setting up a Parcheesi board.

"Do you know how to play or do I have to teach you?"

"I know how," I said.

"That's a relief. You don't look like you know anything."

I didn't answer.

"Can you swim?"

I nodded.

"Tomorrow we'll go to the pool."

He hurled a series of questions at me like rockets, little

hand grenades. I ducked and bobbed; I answered as best I could. It was a test, an application for friendship.

"I'm allowed to go off the diving board but I don't like it," he said. "But I don't tell anyone that. If someone is going, I go too, but it's nothing I'm in a rush to do. You first," he said, dropping the dice into my hand. I started to shake them. He immediately stopped me.

"We don't play that way," he said. "You go like this." Between his thumb and forefinger, he held one up in the air then dropped it with a whirling twist. Before the first one stopped spinning, he dropped the second one the same way. The dice splashed down onto the board, knocking over my marker, giving me a six and a four. "See," he said, moving my marker for me. "It's better that way."

"I should go home," I said when the game was over, when he'd played the whole thing for both of us, when I'd never touched the marker or the dice.

"Are you sure you wouldn't like to have a snack?" Mrs. asked me as I headed for the screen door. "I made cream-filled cupcakes."

"The ones with white stuff inside," Henry said.

"You can make cupcakes like that?"

"Yes." She smiled at me.

Every year just as I started to have a sense of how things were laid out, of where Philadelphia started and stopped, it was time for me to leave. The Henrys' car wound down the streets with me pressed to the window, wondering where the hell we were.

"Where's baby June?" I asked, my twelve-year-old voice cracking with what I thought was middle age or Parkinson's disease.

"Day camp," Mrs. June Henry said.

Baby June's real name was Susan, but since her mission

in life appeared to be a well-studied imitation of Mrs., everyone except Mrs. and Mr. called her baby June.

Henry and I were quiet. There was the familiar awk-
wardness of beginning again, of seeing a body once more
after months away. In between, we'd talked a couple of times,
signed our names to birthday cards picked out by mothers
in a hurry, we'd given the okay to a present we knew would
be perfect only because we wanted it so bad for ourselves.
But that was about it.

"You'd better check in," Mrs. said when we pulled into
the driveway. "Then come over for lunch. We'll be waiting."

"You'll be waiting," Henry said, slamming the car door.
"I'm eating now."

Except for the hum of the air conditioning which was
running even though it was only seventy-some degrees out,
my father's house was without signs of life.

I left my carry-on in the hall and called my mother. Dr.
Frankle answered the phone. I didn't tell him his luggage
was missing.

"Is my mother there?"

"She's on the Lifecycle," he said, and then there was
silence.

"Could I talk to her please?"

"I'll have to get the cordless."

"Thank you," I said. There was the longest silence, as
though Dr. F. thought if he waited long enough to get my
mother, I'd grow up and be gone.

"You're there," my mother said, out of breath.

"I'm here."

"That was fast."

"They can't find the suitcases."

"Don't worry, they will," she said. "They have to. Did
your father pick you up?"

"No. Mrs. Henry did it."

"What the hell's wrong with him. That's part of our agreement."

"I don't know," I said.

"Have you spoken to him?"

"I called you first."

"When you talk to him, tell him to call me right away. That's all. I'll deal with him. I don't want to drag you into this."

"What if my stuff doesn't show up?"

"Your father will take care of it," she said.

According to all reports—except my own—by marrying Dr. Frankle, my mother had done well for herself. On the other hand, my father seemed to have taken a small financial slide. Even though Dr. F. could more than cover the world with money, my father still sent my mother a check every month, supposedly for me.

"Did they leave you lunch?" my mother asked.

"I've been invited out."

"Well, have fun. I'll talk to you Saturday morning before my hair appointment. If you need anything just call." I could hear air rushing through the sprockets of the Lifecycle.

My father answered his own phone at the office. "Hi ya, sport. Get in okay?"

"My suitcase is temporarily dislocated."

"Happens all the time."

"Mom wants you to call her."

"Why?"

"I don't know," I said, lying.

"Well, I gotta get to work," he said. "There should be something there for lunch if you're hungry."

"I'm invited to the Henrys'."

"Oh, that's good. Well, run along. Don't keep people waiting. And don't forget, Cindy's making dinner tonight."

"Great."

Every year Cindy made dinner my first night in town. "A real dinner," she called it: sitting down, plates, glasses, a meatlike item, strange salad—one year with flower petals in it—doctored brown rice, and herbal iced tea. After that, for the rest of the summer, eating was pretty much something I took care of at the Henrys', where they seemed to have a firmer grasp of what was food and what was indigenous vegetation, animal habitat, something to be seen, perhaps cut and put in a vase, but certainly not eaten. Sometimes, I'd ride to the grocery store with Mrs. and buy real food, making sure to get enough for my father and Cindy, who ultimately ate more crap than anyone.

Cindy was ten years younger than my dad, and all they'd talked about when they bought this place was how great it was for kids. For these five years, I've felt the burden of making that seem true.

"He shops," I once overheard Cindy tell someone. "And he's such a pleasure to have around."

A pleasure because I was hardly around. Plus, I was household-oriented. I liked things clean and neat. I found comfort in order. I was also used to being around people I didn't know, living with people I wasn't related to. I kept my own secrets. I'd taught myself to be a little less than human. I'd taught myself to be a person who people like to have around, half boy, half butler: half—just half—no one wanted the whole thing, that was one of the tricks, if you wanna call it that.

I pulled the box of chocolate I'd brought for Mrs. H. out of my carry-on. I'd picked liquor-filled thinking it was safer than milk chocolate in terms of keeping it from Henry and baby June. Liquor-filled tasted so foul that only an adult would eat it. I washed my hands and face and set out for the Henrys'.

Lunch was like something out of a commercial or a dream, although I suppose there was nothing unusual about it.

Baloney-and-cheese sandwiches on white bread—mayo on one side, mustard on the other, and pale pink meat and yellow cheese in the middle. Heaven. In Dr. Frankle's house the only baloney was verbal and in my father's the only meat was a soy-based pseudohamburger mix called bean-burger.

"Chips?" Mrs. Henry asked.

"Yes, please." Real chips, not extra crispy, gourmet deep bake-fried, slightly, lightly not salted. Normal American chips out of a big old bag-o'-chips. I was glowing. Orange drink. Not orange juice, but drink. It may as well have been a birthday party. Henry didn't notice, he didn't care, he didn't appreciate anything.

Mrs. H. topped off my glass. My tongue would be orange all day; if I sucked on it hard, I'd be able to pull out little flashes of flavor for hours to come.

"I'm so glad to be here," I said, meaning it completely.

"We've missed you," Mrs. said.

"I haven't," Henry said. "I've been busy."

"Oh, Henry, you sit in the house, whining all the time, 'I'm bored. There's nothing to do.' "

"TV is your best friend," I said.

"No, yours," Henry said.

"No," I said. "Yours. We don't have a TV."

"God, how depressing," Henry said.

There was a moment of silence while everyone—even Mrs. H.—reflected on the idea of life without television.

"That was great, thank you," I said to Mrs. when we were finished.

"It was baloney," Henry said.

I carried the plates to the sink.

"You're so considerate," Mrs. said, staring Henry down.

I try, I thought to myself. I try so hard.

"Come on," Henry said. "Hurry up." He pushed me out the screen door.

From the edge of their backyard, if I listened hard, I

could hear the deceiving rush that five years ago I thought was water. From the end of this block that went nowhere—dead-ended three houses away into a thick wood—I'd heard a clean whooshing sound that I thought was a lot of water. A waterfall maybe. A paradise on the other side of something. An escape from the starkness of this street. Before I knew better, I went charging off into fifteen feet of thick woods, the kind of woods bogeymen come from, woods where little kids playing find a human hand poking through the leaves, the nails long from the inattentions of the not-so-recently dead, the kind of place where animals crawl off to die. I punched my way through only to find that what whooshed and roared was an eight-lane highway where a hundred thousand cars sliding by in both directions had the nerve to sound like a waterfall. Hearing it again on this first afternoon depressed me.

"Give me your glasses," Henry said, kneeling down.

I handed them over, imagining Henry slipping the frames under the ball of his foot, and then leaning full forward, laughing at the snap crackle pop sound of two hundred and fifty dollars shattering.

"They're very expensive," I said.

"I'm not buying them."

He used the glasses to catch the sun and burn holes through an old dead leaf.

"Handy," he said, giving them back to me. "I guess you can keep them." He stopped for a second, then looked at me. "So, what's wrong with you, how come you're not talking? Brain go blind, too?"

"Trip," I said. "I don't like to fly."

"Wouldn't know," Henry said. "Pool's open. We can go tomorrow."

In Philadelphia there was a community pool, long and wide. All you had to do was show up and sign in. Henry and I ruled it in the summer. We never took showers before entering. We stepped over the vat of milky green below the sign, All Bathers Must Immerse Feet Before Entering Water. Whatever disease we might have had, we thought it better than the lack of disease we saw around us, we wanted to infect everyone, anyone, we wanted everything about ourselves to be contagious, we were dying for someone to be just like us. We were the boys who only got out of the water when the guard blew his whistle fifteen minutes before the hour—every hour—and announced, "Adult swim. Eighteen and under out of the pool." Those words were mystical, almost magical. We'd crawl out and sit by the edge watching, as if adult swim meant that the pool would become pornographic for those fifteen very adult minutes just before the hour. But nothing ever happened. The only pornography were the old women with breasts big enough to feed a nation and old men with personal business hanging so far down that it sometimes fell out the end of their bathing suits.

Every day we stayed at the pool until Henry's mother called the office and had us paged and ordered home. Then waterlogged, bloody eyed, bellies bloated from the ingestion of too much chlorinated water, cheap snack-bar pizza, and too many Milky Ways, we walked home, wet towels around our necks, our little generals shriveled, clammy, and chafing under our cut-offs. We bore it all proudly as though it were the most modern medical treatment, the prescription guarantee for a better life, a bright manhood. Our flip-flops slippery wet, heels sliding off and into the dirt, strange evening bugs and twigs snapping at our ankles, we wound down the long hill onto the road, and then across the road, through some yards, through the short woods between developments toward the light in the Henrys' kitchen window.

As the days stretched out to full length, Mrs. Henry always started talking about where she wanted to spend her summer vacation, two golden weeks she'd suffered the year for. She'd talk about going to Rome to see the pope or to

Venice to ride in a gondola or even off to Australia to see koala bears, but in the end the Henrys always ended up going somewhere like the nearest beach, toting me along because it was easier to bring an extra kid to entertain Henry than to try and do it themselves.

In the evenings, after dinner, Mrs. Henry went out onto the new wooden deck that Mr. had spent the last summer building over the old slab-o'-concrete porch. While baby June played with her dolls, Mrs. Henry sat back on a lounger holding a tall glass of diet soda, filled with ice cubes melted down into hailstones. Every now and then, she'd shake the drink, mix it up, and say, "Brings the carbonation to life."

As soon as the weather got warm and everyone started running in and out of the new sliding glass door, Mrs. Henry went to the hardware, bought a roll of glow-in-the-dark orange tape and made a huge safety star on the glass door, top to bottom, to remind everyone not to go charging through.

"I don't want anyone ending up with a face full of glass, stitches, scars, and disfigurement. I'd feel terrible."

It worked. We all felt careful and safe. Mrs. H. sat out there resting with baby June while Henry and I played badminton in the yard. *Shuttlecock.* We loved that word. We said it loudly and brightly a thousand times a day for absolutely no reason. We'd go down to Woolworth's and loudly ask each other, "You don't think they'd have shuttlecocks here, do you?" The shuttlecock would go up high in the air, its red rubber end obscene, wonderful, and probably the only reason we played the game. The cock would rise into the last moment of light and then sink into the darkness of the Pennsylvania backyard, dropping softly onto the grass.

Deep at the farthest end of the yard, round, multicolored plastic lights bobbed up and down on the back fence. The lights had been up every one of my Philadelphia years, as though the Henrys' life was a never-ending tropical party,

as if they were the happiest people in the world. Sometimes
the lights were like buoys. Henry and I would lie out on the
deck pretending we were at sea. Depending on our mood,
the lights were beacons, telling us how to steer, how to avoid
dangerous straits and shipwrecks of summers past. Other
times they were other yachts filled with wonderful and famous people. We'd stand on the bow, waving. We'd look
through Henry's binoculars into the dead black of night and
pretend we were seeing all manner of decadent behavior. In
detail, we'd describe it to each other.

Late one afternoon, as the sky faded, Mrs. Henry started
gliding around the kitchen in a definite rhythm—one–two–
three: refrigerator–sink–stove—as though cooking were dancing, as though she could waltz with hamburgers.

Tiny grease balls spattered and popped in the frying
pan, shooting off into the gas flames where they exploded
into miniature blue-and-orange fireballs of fat, cheap summer sparklers. The hamburgers were almost done. I usually
didn't pay this much attention to the state of dinner, especially dinner that wasn't really my own, but I happened to
be in the middle of a growth spurt or something and was on
the verge of starvation. My stomach was puffing out, and I
was having difficulty concentrating on anything other than
the six hockey pucks of beef sizzling not a body's length
away, wondering how the six pucks would be divided among
four, hopefully five, people.

Voluntarily, I'd set the table, pretending not to be anything other than a good neighbor, a nice boy.

Mrs. turned from the stove to a dying head of lettuce.

"Where is he?" she said referring to Mr. Henry. "I hate
it when he does this. Dinner's almost ready. We're going to
have to eat."

She raised the frying pan up off the fire. The phone rang

and rang again. She answered it. "I'm sorry, what?" she said, using her chin to pull the phone closer to her ear. She held the pan above the stove, slightly tilted. The hamburgers stopped sizzling. "No," she said. "No, I don't think that's right."

Without realizing what she was doing, she pushed the frying pan forward, threw it down in the sink, which was more than six inches deep with dirty water, dead lettuce, and mixed vegetable scraps.

Henry screamed, "No."

The burgers landed with one great searing hiss, immediately sank, and neither Henry nor I could figure a rescue plan fast enough.

Six burgers a goner was all I could think. I could tell Henry was furious. His top lip had disappeared into a thin white line of pure Henry fury.

"I'm going to give you ten dollars to keep an eye on Susan for a couple of hours. Don't use the stove or the oven. You can microwave." She turned off the gas, picked up her purse, and went out the door.

Nothing about her voice or her actions gave the impression that true disaster had occurred, that the Henry family was being pulled a notch tighter.

"That's our dinner," Henry said, pointing to the handle of the frying pan poking up. A single burger had risen and was somehow skimming the surface of the muck looking less like food than the final result of eating. "It's gross, I'm not touching it."

We went through the cabinets, found a box of macaroni-and-cheese mix, bright orange and gooey. Later, it made my stomach turn.

"I'm hungry," Henry said after the neon glop was gone.

"Would you like me to make you something?" baby June said, dragging her Easy-Bake out of the kitchen closet.

"Oh, I wanna a cake baked by a lightbulb," Henry said. "That sounds wonderful, a gourmet treat."

"You do?" She lit up like she was the electricity that would power the bulb. "Isn't it wonderful," she said, patting the oven. "What kind do you want? Yellow or black."

"It's yellow or chocolate," I said.

Baby June shrugged. She didn't care. She baked us each a cake and then delivered them as though waiting on us was the greatest thing in the world. We thought she was nuts.

"You want a real toy?" Henry asked her. Baby June nodded. He went deep into his closet and pulled out an old machine gun. "It still works," he said.

Baby June took the gun, raised the barrel to her eye, looked inside, and simultaneously pulled the trigger, shooting herself in the face, no joke.

"I don't get it," she said. "It doesn't do anything except make noise."

"It kills people," Henry said.

"Oh."

Mrs. arrived home, hours later, white as rice. She locked the sliding glass door, the front door, and turned out the lights while Henry, baby June, and I sat silenced by her strangeness in the sudden dark of their living room. We watched her go wordlessly up the stairs and heard the bedroom door shut.

"The hamburgers are still in the sink," I said to Henry, who didn't get it. "Your mother has never gone to bed leaving the kitchen dirty. She doesn't do that. She always wipes a damp sponge across the counters, turns off the light over the stove, and wraps her dishrag through the refrigerator handle before going upstairs."

"What are you?" Henry asked. "A pervert?"

I didn't answer.

"Six burgers are drowned," I said, emphasizing the sinking sensation of the word *drowned.*

Henry went up the stairs, stood outside the door of his parents' room, and said in a loud, demanding voice, "When's Dad coming home?"

"Sometime tomorrow" was the muffled answer.

The fact that she'd answered at all compelled Henry to push the questioning further.

"Are you getting a divorce?" he asked in a loud booming word-by-word voice you'd use to speak in the face of a tidal wave.

From the bottom of the steps, I saw Mrs. open the door in her robe.

"This isn't about Daddy and me," she said. "Your father had a problem with the car. He's trying to straighten things out."

"There are dishes in the sink—it's gross."

Mrs. adjusted her hair, pulled her robe tighter, put one fuzzy pink slipper in front of the other, and marched into the kitchen. She snapped on her rubber gloves, reached deep into the muck, pulled out the macaroni dishes, the frying pan, and one by one, with the expression of a woman changing diapers, plucked hamburger after hamburger out of the water, held each up in the air for a few seconds to drain and then dropped the remains into a trash can. She brushed her hair back with her elbow, shook Comet over everything, and went to work under hot water. The steam and Comet mixed to form a delicious noxious cloud-o'-cleanliness that drifted through the house. Whatever had happened hours earlier, the moment that caused dinner to drown, had been a kind of lapse, a seizure of sorts, but now with the green cellulose sponge in hand, everything was all right.

Mrs. Henry turned on the floodlight by the kitchen door, so I could see my way home. A three-foot path of white light cut through the darkness and lit up the grass green and bright.

There was a hill, a gully between the houses. A five-foot bump of dirt that changed things. The adults in either house didn't know each other well; it was too much work. To say hello they had to go around the long way, out the front door, down the flagstone blocks to the sidewalk, up the next driveway, up the flagstone blocks to the three steps, to the front door, and ring the doorbell, ring, ring. Hi, just thought I'd stop over. It didn't happen. If the land had been flat, if geography had been on their side, everything would have been easier. But the way it was, the Henrys were trapped. On the right edge of their property was a high homemade fence and on the left was this grass-covered tumor-o'-land that may as well have been Mount Baldy.

"Good night," I said and ran up the mountain toward the house on top of the hill. Mrs. turned the floodlight out behind me.

Using my key I opened the door to the house that would never be my own. The clock in the front hall banged out ten chimes.

My father and Cindy were sitting at the dining-room table, gnawing on the remains of a huge salad like rabbits—my father's evening grazing as always supplemented by a microwaved Lean Eating entrée, parked by his plate like someone's morning vitamin pill. Every night after their evening meal my father and Cindy disappeared into the "master bedroom suite." I could hear the click of the door locking. Buried in the "suite" was a custom-crafted tub big enough for six people, a cross-country ski machine, an exercise bike, VCR, twenty-six-inch TV, king-size bed, and even a small fridge. In case of nuclear attack, close bedroom door and wait for the next generation to save you.

What annoyed me the most was the locking of the door. Who did it? Cindy or my father? And how could they think that me, Mr. Privacy himself, was going to come busting in on them? It was infuriating. The other possibility was that they were really doing something in there, something I couldn't even begin to imagine, although I did imagine.

Alone, I did the dishes, mine and theirs, flipped through the mail, pretended to read the paper and then, suffocating in boredom and frustration, turned on the eleven o'clock news.

"Early this afternoon, a Philadelphia boy was struck and killed by a car as he was crossing the street on his way home from a program for gifted-and-talented youth at Herbert Hoover Junior High. Thomas Stanton the Third, who had just turned thirteen earlier this week, was taken to University Hospital where he was pronounced dead. According to police reports the car was traveling at substantial speed. The driver, forty-three-year-old John Heffilfinger, also of Philadelphia, was arrested at the scene." A picture of Mr. Henry flashed on the screen—Heffilfinger, no wonder I called them all Henrys—I truly almost didn't know who it was. I'd never seen him as anything other than Mr. Henry, until that moment when he was plucked out, taken from the Henrys, and put in a whole new category, John "Henry" Heffilfinger, Killer.

When Mr. Henry seemed to be late getting home, I didn't even think twice about it. Sometimes when fathers are late it's a good thing. Sometimes they're buying things, surprises you'd asked for but never thought you'd get—snorkel mask, fins, a better bike.

At thirteen Thomas Stanton III had enough names and numbers behind his name to sound old enough and scary enough to run a bank. Poor Mr. H., was all I could think. Poor all the H's. Did Henry even know? After turning out the floodlight behind me, did Mrs. call him into the kitchen for a long sit-down? Or was he alone up in his room, discovering this for himself on his private thirteen-inch Sony?

"Early this afternoon," the newscaster had said. It hadn't even happened at night, or at twilight when darkness and light mix together like spit in a kiss. It didn't happen at some forgivable moment when Mr. Henry could claim the sun at the horizon line blotted out everything, and he and the boy had dipped into darkness. In the middle of a perfectly good afternoon in the end of June, with a breeze that tickled the air like fingertips, he'd become a killer.

News travels fast. "Stay home today," my father said, ducking his head into my room before he left for the office. "Mr. Heffilfinger has a problem and should be left alone."

I didn't say anything. After he and Cindy were gone, I got up, got dressed, ate breakfast, and sat looking out the front window at all the houses just like my father's, every single one pressed out of the same red brick Play-doh mold. The ones across the street didn't come face to face, eye to eye, with ours, they looked into a small half court of their own. I saw those neighbors only in profile, coming and going, carrying bags of groceries up the sidewalk, watering the lawn, pounding a rug, or tending a failing barbecue. They were all Flat Stanleys. Human color forms, flat slices of bright, shiny, plastic laid down on a pre-painted cardboard world—they could be peeled up and put down again and again, in any order or combination.

With nothing better to do and no options, I started putting wood-grain contact paper in all my dresser drawers. Halfway through, Henry rang the doorbell.

"Can I come in?"

I nodded and stepped back. Henry followed me upstairs to my room.

"I'm just gonna sit here," he said, patting the edge of my bed.

I didn't say anything. It was one of those times when clearly no one should talk. I finished cutting, peeling, laying the paper in the drawers, and then put my clean clothing back into the dresser much more slowly, more carefully than a normal person would. When I finished, and Henry still hadn't talked, I started cleaning, dusting, polishing, re-arranging. I was on the verge of remodeling the whole house before he said anything.

"I guess you found out why dinner got wrecked," he said.

"Yeah."

"My father killed a kid," he said and then stopped. "I guess you know that," he said.

I nodded.

"That's why dinner got wrecked."

I nodded again and thought I'd never be able to eat hamburger again, macaroni and cheese, either. I'd end up becoming a vegetarian like my father and Cindy, eating rabbit-food dinners at midnight, then locking myself in my room.

"He's coming home this afternoon," Henry said. "Why? Why are they letting him out?"

He looked up at me; I looked away.

I shrugged and shrugged and shrugged, and Henry shrugged, and then finally we went downstairs, ate all the decent things we could find, and sat looking out the front window, waiting for Mr. Henry to be brought back.

I can't say Mr. Henry came home from the police station a different man. He was exactly the same the day after as he was the day before. There were no signs of him having snapped out of himself for the instant it took to kill, no indication that all the badness, the frustration, the lifetime buildup of a man's anger, had risen up through his gut, through his blood like a whirling dervish, like the man out of the Mr. Clean bottle, and that all the swirling, whirling-ness had forced his foot to the floor and hurled the car forward over Thomas Stanton III. I looked for that but saw nothing except dull gray around the eyes from too little sleep, too much fear, and stubble from a day's missed shaving.

"I'm being used," Henry said, two days later as he was putting on the clothing his mother had laid out for him: gray pants, striped shirt, tie, blue jacket, hard shoes. The Henrys were going to court. A skinny lawyer with teeth so rotten they smelled bad had shown up the night before and explained to all the Henrys that they had to "dress up and put on a show, featuring Mr. Heffilfinger as father, provider, and protector."

In the hall all the Henrys went by, ducking in and out of the bedrooms, the bathroom. There was the hiss of aerosol spray, the dull whir of the hair dryer. All the running around and good clothes would have been festive if it wasn't ten A.M. on a weekday, liable to be the hottest day of the year so far, and if the destination weren't the county courthouse.

As soon as the lawyer pulled into the driveway, Mr. Henry went out, got into the backseat of his car and closed the door. The rest of the Henrys were all downstairs, ready to go, except for Henry himself.

Mrs. Henry came upstairs. "We're ready to leave," she said.

Henry was lying down on the bed. He didn't move.

"Henry, we can't be late. Come on now."

Still nothing. His mother took his arm and began to pull. Henry pulled in the opposite direction.

"I don't want to fight with you," she said, leaning back, using her weight and position to good advantage. "It's for your father. Do this for your father."

Henry stopped resisting and was pulled off the bed and onto the floor.

"Stand up or you'll get dusty."

The lawyer came into his room. "Get up. We have to go."

Henry lay flat on the floor in his coat and tie. The back of the blue blazer picking up lint balls like it was designed to do that.

"I'm not going," Henry finally said.

"Oh, yes, you are," the lawyer said.

Together, the lawyer and Henry's mother lifted him to standing. I was sitting in the corner, in the old green corduroy chair that used to be in the living room. For the first time ever I felt like I didn't belong there, I felt like I was seeing something I shouldn't, something too private.

"Unless you plan on dragging me the whole way, leave me alone," Henry said to the lawyer.

The lawyer pushed him back onto the bed. "Do you want me to tell you something?"

Henry shook his head.

"If you don't sit in that courtroom and act right and if your daddy gets sent to jail, I don't want you to ever forget that it might be your fault. Just because you felt like being a bogey little brat. Think on that," the lawyer said, checking his watch.

Henry looked at me, then stood and dusted himself off. Mrs. turned and went out of the room. Henry tipped his head toward the lawyer and said, "You're the biggest fucking asshole in the world."

The lawyer didn't respond except to look down at Henry like he wanted to kill him.

"And your fly is open, fuckwad," Henry said and then marched out of the room on his mother's heels, not staying to see the lawyer's face flush red, his hands grab at his crotch.

From Henry's bedroom window I watched the rest of them get into the lawyer's Lincoln. You could tell it was going to be the kind of day where the heat would raise people's tempers past the point of reconciliation. After they left, I left, pulling the door closed behind me and crossing the grass to wait in the air-conditioned silence of the house next door.

Later, that afternoon, when I was back at the Henrys', their phone began to ring. It started slowly and then rang more and more, faster and faster, until it seemed to be ringing nonstop. Strangers, reporters, maniacs, guys Mr. had gone to junior high school with, lawyers offering to consider the case for a fee, someone from a TV show in New York City.

"You really should call the TV people back," Henry said to his parents.

"Stay away from it," Mrs. Henry said, when the ringing started again. She held her arms down and out like airplane wings. "Don't touch."

"Are you going to work tomorrow?" Mrs. asked Mr.

"I don't know."

"Have you spoken to your office?"

"No," he said.

"You don't have to be afraid. Accidents happen," Mrs. said.

"You shouldn't say that," Mr. said.

Mrs. pointed her finger at Mr. "You have to stop acting like a guilty man," she said. "Did you wake up that morning and say to yourself, 'I'm going to kill a little boy today'?"

"I have blood on my shoes," Mr. shouted, "I feel like my feet are dripping in blood."

"It's your imagination," Mrs. said.

"I killed someone," he said, pushing his face close into Mrs.'s.

She pushed him away. "Stop acting insane."

Henry sat on baby June's swing set in the backyard, waiting for time to pass, for everything to return to normal, but Thomas Stanton III was ahead of Henry, six months ahead. He was already across the border of thirteen when he died and he stayed there like a roadblock, a ton-o'-bricks, like all the weight in the world. Without seeming to know what he was doing Henry started combing his hair that same certain way that Stanton's was in the newspaper photo. He started wearing clothes a gifted-and-talented type would wear: button-down shirts with a plastic pen protector in the pocket, pants a size too small. He started trying to look like a genius and ended up looking like a clown, like someone permanently dressed up for Halloween.

"Henry," I said, sitting facing him on the double horse swing. "It has to stop. You don't know what you're doing."

He brushed his hair back with a whole new gesture, just the way the dead kid would do it.

"Henry, you're making me hate you."

"Go home. Get your own life. Leave me alone," he said.

And so with nothing else to do, with no other options, I did exactly that. I went to the pool alone.

Without Henry I was too intimidated to step over the pool of muck by the door. I dipped my feet in and in a split second the milky white wash cauterized the summer's worth of cuts and scratches and I was sanitized for sure.

I unrolled my towel down on a lounger just at the edge of the tetherball court and next to a group of kids my own age. I watched a boy smack the ball so hard I could feel the stinging in my palms. The ball spun fast, its rope winding quick and high over the head of the other boy. I saw the smacker jump up and hit it again. The ball spun harder, faster, in tighter circles, until all the rope was wound and the stem of the ball itself smacked the pole, froze a second, and then slowly started to unwind.

"Thomas was my boyfriend," I overheard a skinny girl with blond hair hanging down the sides of her face like wet noodles say. "No one was supposed to know, but since he died, the secret came out. It was the single most horrifying experience of my life." She adjusted and readjusted the empty pink-and-white top of her bikini, pulling on the bottoms where they would have latched onto her butt if she'd had a butt. "The car stopped only after Thomas was sucked under and came out the other side, with grease smears down his body." She took a breath. "My mother tried to hold me back, but I touched him. 'Thomas,' I said. 'Thomas, can you hear me?' He lifted himself off the street and walked himself over to the grass, then crumpled like when you pull the middle out of a stack of things and it all falls down. He opened his mouth and a brown nutty thing, they said later was his tongue, fell out. 'Thomas,' my mother said. 'Thomas, everything is going to be all right. You've been in a little accident. These things can happen to anyone.'"

"What about the guy who did it?" the girl she was talking to asked.

"He sat in his car until the police came and then jumped out and started to run. They chased after him and dragged him back so we could identify him."

"I don't think so," I said, interrupting, without even knowing what I was doing.

"What does that mean?" the girl asked.

"It was on TV," I said. "I don't think he tried to get away."

"So what if he didn't, what do you care," she said. "He wasn't your boyfriend. And you're not even from around here anyway."

I shrugged and looked evenly at her. Without a word, I got up. As I walked, the rough cement around the pool sanded the soles of my feet. At the edge of the water, I threw myself forward, hoping that when the water caught me, it would not be hard, it would not be icy cold, it would be enveloping like Jell-O. I broke the surface for air and went under again. Without Henry, with nothing to do, I swam laps, back and forth a thousand times.

Henry and I made up. We didn't talk about anything.

He just came over to my house with new Ping-Pong paddles and said, "My mother bought me these, wanna play?" and I said, "Why not."

Two weeks to the day after the accident, while Mrs., Henry, and I were eating lunch—reheated tuna noodle casserole, with fresh chips crumbled on top, and green Gatorade— someone rang the doorbell and without waiting for an answer tried the knob.

Mrs. went to the kitchen door, cracked it open, and called, "Can I help you?" around the corner of the house.

"I've come about my son," the woman said. She stepped into the kitchen, opened her purse, pulled out a stack of papers, and with the palm of her hand spread them out into a messy fan on the kitchen table. Henry and I moved our plates back to give her more room. We held our napkins up to our mouths to hide our expressions.

"These are his report cards. He mostly got straight A's except in spelling and music; he wasn't very good at music, couldn't carry a tune. This is his first school picture," she said, digging out a photo with three rows of kids, twenty-six young scrubbed faces, one kid holding a black sign with white lettering, Hither Hills Elementary School, Kindergarten. "We didn't buy his school picture this year. He said he didn't like it. He thought his hair looked funny. Why didn't I just buy it anyway?" She was talking to herself. "Maybe if I'd taken the photo this wouldn't have happened. Why do I have these?" she asked, looking at Mrs. "What are they for? The insurance company wants me to calculate what he would have been worth if he'd had a life. I have to give them a figure. It's like playing *The Price Is Right*." She stopped for a minute, drew in a breath, and pressed the back of her hand against her eyes, blotting them. "You want to see how it feels, you want me to take one of yours?" She put her hand on Henry. "Christmas is coming," she said even though it was July. "What will I do?"

The dead boy's mother stood crying in the Henrys' kitchen and when Henry's mother tried again to touch her, to comfort her, she wailed. Then, without a word, without a sound other than the swallowing of great gulps of air, she turned and walked out the kitchen door.

Henry's mother scooped up all the dead boy's report cards, prize certificates, letters from the governor for being on the honor roll and handed them to me. "Go on, get her before she goes," she said.

I charged out the door, got to the lady before she got into her car, and said, "You forgot these."

"I didn't forget them," she said, again blotting her eyes with the back of her hand.

"Well, I'll put them in your car," I said. I went over to the passenger side, opened the door, and left them there on the seat.

"You're a good boy," she said.

I fought the urge to tell her, I'm not one of them. I'm not his son. I'm just the boy who lives next door, part-time. I'm no one, nothing. Instead I said, "I hope you feel better soon," and walked back toward the house.

Henry came out and on the ground where the lady's car had been, there was a photo, it must have fallen out of her purse, my hands, the car. It must have just slipped away and landed face up next to an oil stain.

"That's him," Henry said, picking up the photo, wiping it against his shirt, rubbing the boy's face over his heart.

"We should give it back to her."

"No," Henry said. "He's mine."

One afternoon while Mrs., baby June, and Henry were somewhere else, I watched Mr. digging a shallow trough through the yard. He was bent over a shovel, flipping clods of grass and dirt off to the side. He pulled a wilted piece of notebook paper from the back pocket of his shorts and consulted a diagram. Then, with his fingers as rulers, his feet as yardsticks, he began measuring his work. By the time I got from my bedroom window, across the tumor-o'-land and into the Henrys' backyard, Mr. was sprinkling the floor of the trough with lima beans.

"What are you doing?" I asked, as he opened a third bag of beans and dropped them one at a time into the trough. He didn't answer. "Planting?"

As soon as the beans were gone, he hauled over two large bags of charcoal briquets and started laying the charcoal out over the beans.

"It looks like something out of *Gourmet* magazine," I said. "A new kind of barbecue recipe."

When he finished laying out all the charcoal, he sat down on a deck chair, took off his shoes and socks, pulled his shirt over his head, wiped his face and chest, dropped it down in a ball, and sighed a big one.

"They're not home yet?" he asked.

"Not yet," I said.

Mr. got up off the deck chair, picked up a can of starter fluid and went down the length of the trough, holding the can at crotch level, squeezing it so the fluid arced up like piss then softly splashed down onto the coals. In seconds the coals went from matte black to shiny wet and then back to matte black, as the stuff soaked in. He put down the can and picked up a box of those long fireplace matches.

"What's this supposed to be?" I asked. I thought it was probably another one of those things some people did that I just didn't know anything about.

Mr. Henry stood at the end of his trough, his runway of coal, lit three matches at once, held them in a tight fist, bowed his head, then dropped them in one by one. A line of flame spread the length of the ditch, sometimes golden, sometimes blue, sometimes spitting on itself. The coals shifted. Mr. stood at the end of the line looking down at his feet. He stepped out off the grass into the fire. In a split second he had both feet in the fire and was doing his best not to run. You could see it in his legs, in the muscles twitching.

"Don't," I shouted, going toward him.

He put both arms up in front of him, like someone sleep-walking and the fluid that had splashed back on his hands ignited and his hands turned into ten fingers of flame, like a special effect, like something that would happen to a cartoon character. I stepped back and watched the flames jump three feet high, the hair on his arms and legs melt away, the edges of his shorts turn black, the flames at first just kissing him then starting to eat him alive. Mr. was silent until half-way down when he began to howl, to cry, and wail.

Mrs. came flying out the kitchen door, her purse over her arm, bag of groceries still in hand, screaming, "Don't just stand there, do something." She dropped the groceries and charged toward Mr. I ran into the Henrys' house and called the fire department. From the kitchen window, I could see Mrs. chasing Mr. around the yard, tackling him at the edge of the woods. The fire had reached out of the trough, chewed through the empty briquette bags and was gnawing on the porch. I saw Henry and baby June standing off to the side, watching their mother in her Bermuda shorts lying on top of their naked father.

I went to the front door and waited for help.

Two days later, while Mr., all red and black, charred, swollen, bandaged, blotchy, with his arms and legs tied down, was still in intensive care, two men came and took away the remains of the new deck.

"He wants to be punished," Mrs. told the men. "Even though this was an accident, he's convinced it was his fault."

When they were gone Mrs. took the garden hose, a ladder,

her trusty Playtex gloves and scrub brush, and with an industrial-sized bottle of lemon-lime Palmolive she washed the side of the house, the patio, and even the grass. "Go on down to the basement and bring up the beach things," she told Henry and me when she finished. "We're taking a few days off."

Henry and I plunged into the clammy cool of the basement, into the history packed away on deep wooden shelves Mr. had put up a few summers before. We took out all of Henry's old toys, played with them again and lived our lives over. We did the memory quiz—do you remember when?—testing to see if we agreed on history, making sure we'd gotten everything right. We pulled out the beach chairs, inflatable rafts and the Styrofoam cooler, and loaded them all into the back of Mrs.'s station wagon.

While Mrs. and baby June stayed at the foamy edge of the ocean, Henry and I danced in the waves, hurling ourselves toward them, daring the ocean to knock us out, to carry us away.

Despite our being coated with layers and layers of thick white sunblock, by the time the lifeguard pulled his station far back on the sand and walked off with the life preserver, we were red-hot like steamed lobsters.

We walked back to the motel dragging the beach chairs, the Styrofoam cooler, and all the extra sand our bathing suits would hold. To save time and hot water, Henry and I showered together and then turned the bathroom over to Mrs. and baby June. On our way out of the bathroom, Mrs. grabbed Henry by the head and recombed his hair the normal Henry way. He didn't stop her. He didn't rearrange it Stanton style.

Scrubbed and desalted we sat at the four stations of the dinette set eating two large and wonderful pizzas, drinking orange soda from cans, and simultaneously watching television. After dinner we all walked down the boardwalk watching seagulls plucking free food out of the sand and the sky and disappearing into darkness. Mrs. bought each of us a warm puffy ball of fried dough dipped in powdered sugar, and as we walked baby June fell asleep in her mother's arms.

It was eight-thirty when we got back to the room. Mrs. lay down on the bed with baby June. Henry and I writhed around pillow fighting, changing TV channels and generally spinning on the edge until finally Mrs. had enough, took a twenty-dollar bill out of the nightstand, and told us to put on sweatshirts and long pants, to go out and blow off some steam. "Be careful and have fun."

We raced out of the motel and back onto the boardwalk. Immediately, Henry bought a bucket of french fries and a Coke. We ate our way down the wooden planks, stopping to play darts and balloons, frog flip, and skee ball, stuffing our pockets with cheap plush prizes. We bought vanilla-and-chocolate soft swirl ice-cream cones and fresh-made caramel corn. We sat on a bench eating while a summer's night parade of all human possibility swept by: deformed people, big families, small families, orphans, kids on first dates, guys in sawed-off leather jackets, old people. My skin was so hot from the sunburn that it felt cold. Shivery goosebumps covered my arms, legs, and the back of my neck. I was sugar intoxicated. Music came out of every store, arcade, and refreshment stand, a thousand radios all tuned to a different station.

As we got closer to the amusement park at the end of the boardwalk, the music got louder, each little radio competing with the next, and all of them competing with the mechanical *oom pah pah* of the giant carousel that cut through the night. At the gates where the boardwalk met the park everything melted into a multicolored, multiflavored, sensomatic, dizzying, swirly whirl. We had to run one way or the other, but couldn't stay there in the black hole of sensation. We charged toward the amusement park, toward the ticket booth. Henry slammed down what was left of the twenty and got two fistfuls of tickets. We ran from ride to ride watching each one for a few seconds, deciding which were the best investments: Roller Coaster, Haunted House, Swiss Avalanche.

"That one definitely," Henry said, pointing across the park to spaceships taking off into the sky, trailing red-and-white afterglow. "Come on." We ran to the far edge of the park, to this last ride, sandwiched in the corner that touched the ocean. Rockets Round the Moon. There was a plot of grass, a metal chain-link fence and then barnacle-covered rocks, railroad tie shoring, and the water evenly slapping against the edge of the world.

Henry gave the man our tickets and we slid past him and ran toward the space octopus, climbing into our own personal rocket ship, pulling the chrome safety bar down in front of us. We took off smoothly, the giant mechanical arms swinging us high into the air, shifting, then throwing us out toward the sea, where we hung over the water for a second before being snapped back. We were pitching and swaying, more like a bucking bronco or something with transmission trouble than your typical flying machine. Henry threw himself to the left and then to the right, slamming against me, getting the ship rocking in a rhythm all its own. The huge groaning arms flew us up, down, round and round. When we landed Henry was absolutely sparkling. He pounded the side of our rocket, the hollow metal echoed. "Again, again," he shouted. The ride emptied and refilled. The ticket taker came by and Henry dropped too many tickets into his hand. The man counted them but didn't give any back. "More," Henry screamed. "More."

The ride started again and we were up, up, and away. Whirling, twirling. I closed my eyes and held on. I was being pulled in a thousand different directions. I was struggling to stay in one place. I could feel the force of being whipped through the air again and again starting to bend my face. I saw the picture from *Life* magazine of a man in a wind tunnel, his mouth, stretched out, blown back, teeth and gums exposed. I was that man.

We landed smooth and safe, two feet above the ground. All there was to do was push the safety bar forward and step down and out.

"Once more, just once more," Henry said, digging into his pockets, dropping the last of the tickets into the man's hands.

We were airborne, we were flying, Rockets Round the Moon. I focused on the taillights of the ship on front of us, up and down, it went before us, side to side. Looking at it, I knew what would come next, I had a second to prepare. Up and away. Pushing off my knee, Henry stood. He rose up, steadied himself, then raised his arms up and open. His legs pressed against the safety bar. All of his weight was there. I pulled back on the bar hoping it would hold. I pulled back hoping Henry wouldn't take flight, fall free, roll out over the nose and into the sea. He stood in a trance, face taut, hair blowing, arms extended, scarecrow of the universe. Then his face dissolved into a colorless puddle of flesh. His jaw fell open, raw sewage spilled out and was whipped into the wind behind us. I slid down under the safety bar, onto the floor. I wrapped my arms around his legs, pressed my cheek to his knee and pulled down. I looked up to see Henry still standing, his face covered with his own chunky blue. From the floor I could smell the noxiousness of its mixture, hot and rich, like some hearty soup a grandmother would serve on a winter night.

When we landed, the ticket man came running over with a bucket I thought was for Henry, but instead he flipped the safety bar back, pulled us out, and dumped a bucketful of sudsy water into the belly of our ship. "You fool," he yelled at Henry who was unsteady on his feet, searching his pockets for more ride tickets, wiping his mouth with the sleeve of his sweatshirt. "Go back where you belong. Go home."

BABY AT THE LAKE

•

Clyde Edgerton

WHILE HE SAT ON a towel, in his bathing suit, pulling on his big black frog feet, Billy looked around for the owner of the green canoe resting on the sand. Up toward the parking lot, he saw his daddy, mama, and the baby between them, walking slowly down a narrow sidewalk toward the small beach. His mama was carrying a lightweight pink raft—one that had blown off somewhere in the wind one time. A man dressed in khaki clothes, carrying a paddle, walked behind them.

Nobody else was around.

Billy watched the man hurry around his parents on the beach, push his canoe into the water, and hop in. Billy wondered if the man was going to say anything to his daddy. He was staring at him. He wasn't paddling. He was just kind of staring. People stared at his daddy because of the way he chewed tobacco. That had to be the reason. There was nothing else all that unusual about him as far as Billy could tell. Except for his tattoos.

His daddy tossed his tobacco plug quickly from cheek to cheek with his tongue. He didn't exactly chew it; he batted it around in his mouth very rapidly, hardly ever slowing down or stopping. And people were all the time staring at that. Or sometimes maybe they stared at the tattoos.

Billy liked to study his daddy's tattoos when they were driving somewhere together or watching television, a snake winding around some kind of pole with vines all around, and one that said Mother in the middle of some flowers.

After the man in the canoe stared for a few seconds, he paddled away, along the shore, and around a bend, out of sight. Billy's daddy, standing not so far from Billy, reached into the pocket of his unbuttoned plaid shirt—he wore only a bathing suit and the shirt—and pulled out a cigarillo, one of those small cigars, from a pack. He lit it, put the matchbook back into his shirt pocket, took off his shirt, and tossed it on the sand.

Billy's daddy never touched the cigarillo with his fingers after he got it out of the pack and hung it in his lips until he threw it away after it was smoked to a nub. He chewed and smoked at the same time—chewed, drew, exhaled, chewed. He shook off his flip-flops at the water's edge. He had big, wide feet. He walked slowly straight out into the lake.

Billy pushed himself up off his towel, lifted his feet high so as not to drag the toes of his frog feet, and headed across the sand and into the water for a swim, for deep water, way out. He liked the deep water. He knew what his daddy would do. He would walk out into the lake until he was shoulder deep. That was a long way out. Then he would stop and stand still, his back to shore, his arms crossed, chewing his tobacco and smoking the cigarillo, hanging in his mouth, touched only by his lips and the air above the water.

Billy swam to a spot far out. The water was over his head. Billy pretended to be a navy frogman during war. He could see his mama splashing water on the baby's legs way up there at the water's edge. The baby was laughing and squealing, lifting his feet one after the other. Billy decided to swim in toward them, quietly, underwater most of the time, until he was within poison-dart distance. Poison darts were top secret—effective antipersonnel weapons recently discovered in Australia.

Underwater, he could see only vague light above, a red muddy color, and darkness below. The silence seemed everlasting and from somewhere doomed. He tried to see his arms and hands in front of him as he swam underwater, but couldn't. He surfaced quietly, watched the enemy for a few seconds, then swam on, underwater, by his daddy, quietly kicking his legs behind him, heading in toward the unavoidable action.

He surfaced and eyed his mama on shore. She was wearing a bikini. She was small, but had a great big belly. She was an enemy sergeant. He would blow the dart into her stomach, an easy target. She was talking to a little bitty private first class—dark hair, white diaper. He would let this private live, maybe take him prisoner. A pink enemy destroyer rested on shore. He would capture it.

He finished killing everybody and was about to launch the enemy raft when his daddy, who'd walked back in, said, "We gone float the baby on that. Put it back."

Billy swam on his back toward deep water, watching his family over the splashes made by his frog feet. His daddy kicked the raft into the water, hauled the baby up by the arm, plopped him down onto the raft, and started walking out into the lake, pulling the raft behind him. His mama followed. They stopped, splashed water onto the baby, and talked to him. Billy's mama laughed and put the baby's fingers in her mouth.

Billy dropped his head back into the water. He was floating on his back and the water was cold on the back of his head, which had just been up and in the sunlight. He looked straight up at the white clouds. One was swirling along in a circle as if caught in a gentle tornado way up there in the blue sky.

He raised his head and looked in toward shore. His daddy waved him in and hollered, "Git back in here. You're too far out."

A while later, Billy's daddy was back out at his spot, smoking and chewing. His mama was out there with him. Billy, on shore to watch the baby, decided to put the baby on the raft again and give him a ride. Something fun.

First, he placed the baby in the middle of the raft and ran the raft in circles in very shallow water, then he decided to take the baby to deeper water. He started out, walking, pulling the raft behind him with one hand and with the other hand splashing water straight ahead, annoying enemy ships.

Billy turned to look at the baby. The raft was empty.

Panic burned his neck, face, and hands. He looked on shore. Nothing.

He quickly moved around to the side of the raft, looking this way and that, turning himself all the way around. He raised the raft, looked under it, and then dove underwater. The silence was solid and heavy and forever. His eyes were wide but he could see only orange muddy light. He reached in front of his face, out as far as he could, kicked as hard as he could, to cover a lot of ground.

He came up as the man in the canoe was paddling by. He dove again. Could that man help him? He found an ankle, arose from the water with the baby in both hands high over his head. He took long strides toward shore, suddenly stopped, held the baby upside down and shook it.

Water gurgled out of the baby's mouth. He gasped air, started coughing, then crying.

Billy's mama yelled, "What you *do*ing, Billy?"

Billy, holding the baby up by the foot, over the water, turned and looked out at his mama and daddy. For an instant he didn't know who they were. "Nothing," he said. "Teaching him to swim."

"Quit it. Put him up on the damn beach."

His daddy, chewing frantically, pushed his wife's head underwater. She came up, grabbed him around the neck, and bit his ear.

Billy took the baby onto shore and set him on a white towel. The baby tottered, then caught his balance. Besides being blue, he looked okay. Billy sat down beside him. His heart was still beating faster than it ever had.

In a minute, the man, a camera strapped over his shoulder, walked back from the parking lot and across the sand to his canoe. As he passed Billy, he said, "I forgot my camera." He stopped suddenly. "You think you might like to do some photography work?"

"Huh?"

"Some photography work. I'm a photographer. I might need some help on some photographs."

"I don't know. I got to take care of him now."

The baby looked at the man, then looked at his own hand as if he'd never seen it before.

"Well," the man said. "Maybe some other time." He got in his canoe and paddled off.

By the end of the summer, Billy had a new baby brother, and his mama and daddy brought the whole family to the little beach several times before the weather got too cool in the fall.

Billy and his brothers didn't move away after they grew up. They got married and had children and they all came with their families to swim, on summer Monday afternoons, at the same place at Camden Lake.

Over the years, Billy became more and more convinced that the man in the canoe had seen, had been a witness, and might show up there at the beach again some Monday. Billy thought about how he and the man could talk about what had happened, even laugh about it. But he decided to wait until then to tell anybody. It would be his secret—and maybe the man's.

And even when he was very old, Billy's daddy, bald-headed and shrunk-up some, still liked to chew tobacco and smoke and stand with his arms crossed—very still—out there where the water was pretty deep.

BEGINNING LESSONS

●

Molly Giles

It's their last day in Mexico and Harriet is *muy feliciando*. No. Wrong. What sort of word is *feliciando?* She ducks her head and studies the two iguana masks it is her turn to carry; balanced on top of the backpack on her lap, they gently scratch her sunburned arms as the minivan bounces from one pothole to another on its way out of the city toward the airport. *Feliciando* sounds like something she might have made up; she's been doing that lately: faking it. "Happy?" Ben asks. She looks across the aisle at him, startled. That's the word.

"How did you know?" she asks.

Ben grins and snaps her picture. Harriet sticks her tongue out, too late. Ben turns to the man beside him and opens his phrase book. He likes factual questions, ones that can be answered with numbers. What is the population of your city? What is the elevation? On and on. Yawn and yawn.

Harriet leans against the torn vinyl seat and tries to look out the window but the glass is so smudged it scarcely lets light through. It almost looks licked. She remembers the pilgrims Ben photographed kissing the glass case of saints' relics in the old stone cathedral. What were they praying for? She frowns, recalling their rush of quick, soft Spanish. In two weeks, she thinks, I have said only two words: *No comprendo.* And half the time I can't remember those.

"Hon?" She looks up as the van brakes to a stop and sees the man Ben was talking to leaning above her. "He's getting off here," Ben says, "and he wants to know your name before he leaves."

"I can't say my name," Harriet reminds him.

"Try." Ben's expression is as good-humored as ever, but his voice is tight. Drop the *H,* Harriet reminds herself, roll the *r*s, do a diphthong with the *ie:* try. Her name, made Spanish, is all air, shrill as a curse word. The man leans closer, his breath rich with breakfast and Chiclets.

"He wants you to ask his name now," Ben prompts.

Harriet looks at the man's face, sweating faintly, at the expectant glint of gold teeth. Her head crowds with inappropriate noises, then stills, utterly empty. She played the Spanish tapes Ben gave her for her birthday but she never really studied them and the nights she was supposed to go to the conversation class were the nights she was meeting her company's sales manager in a hotel room, downtown. She raises her eyes and opens her mouth. What comes out is not Spanish, nor English, but high-school French. "*Alors,*" she says to the man. "*Je regrette.*"

The man straightens, pleased, and waves as he leaves.

"Thanks a lot," Harriet says to Ben when he's gone. "You did that on purpose."

Ben looks genuinely hurt by this. "I'm just trying to help you out. You'll never learn unless you try." He waits. "Right?"

Harriet shrugs. She knows he'll say, "Right?" again—
and again—until she nods, and she knows too that she will
eventually nod. Because he is right. Ridiculous as he is, with
his camera and straw hat and bright tourist T-shirt, Ben is
right. He has been bold and curious and playful on this trip,
and she has been shy and fearful and wrong. She has mis-
pronounced everything, of course, but she's also misread
maps and lost luggage. She's eschewed the drinking water
but thirstily sucked the ice; she's been sick from insect bites
and coral cuts and diarrhea and sunburn; she's been pun-
ishing herself, she knows it; what she hasn't known is why.
She broke off with the sales manager weeks ago. I should be
rewarded, she thinks. I made the right choice. I saved his
marriage and I saved my own. I should be forgiven for . . .
sinning is the word she comes up with, but *sinning* seems
too strong for the weary erotic wrestling she and the sales
manager engaged in, week after week.

The van starts up with a lurch and she grabs for the
masks before they slide to the floor. They are papier-mâché;
Ben bought them at a street stand last night. Both are ugly;
the trick is to decide which is the ugliest. One is a blue iguana
with a hand sticking out of its forehead. The other is a yellow
frog with an iguana rolling out of its mouth. This one reminds Harriet of herself, of the way she's been feeling lately.
She holds the mask to her face, inhales its cheap resin scent,
and drops it back on her lap.

When she looks up she sees that a well-dressed young
woman with a briefcase has taken the seat next to Ben. The
woman flashes a blank, radiant smile at both of them, and
Ben, straightening, smiles back. Here goes, Harriet thinks.
He's about to make another "contact with the people." She
turns back to the window. She can see her own reflection,
pale and wavering. She looks young and drowned, like someone floating underwater. She feels as if she's underwater.
Feverish, remote, detached. She shakes her head and presses

her fingers to her tired ears. Someone behind her opens a newspaper; the rustle it makes reminds her again of water. She thinks of the little lake she and Ben hiked to a few days ago. On clear days, Ben had told her, you could actually look down through the lake and see an entire village below—it was all there, the church, the bank, the bare branches of the plane trees in the square. It had been flooded twenty years ago by a government dam and it still stood, intact. Harriet had tried to see through the water but it was a dull, overcast afternoon and the top of the lake was opaque with scum. Above them, buzzards had watched from the cliffs. "Everything in Mexico," she had complained, "looks good until you get up close," and Ben had said, calmly, "That's true of most things, don't you think?"

She wants to lean forward now and say, "What did you mean?" but Ben is chatting with the woman with the briefcase and anyway he'd deny he meant anything. She could have had five affairs and Ben wouldn't notice. No, that's not fair, she amends. Ben is a good man. He just doesn't see things. He is asking the same old questions about population and industry that he asks everyone and the woman is responding as everyone has, politely, and with pleasure. How nice these people are, Harriet thinks. Too nice. It's exhausting. She listens to Ben say he thinks Mexico is *"muy interesante"* and feels a rush of despair and affection and envy; he is, at least, talking.

The woman is unusual looking for a Mexican, with pale, dense, mushroom-colored skin and a large unlipsticked mouth. Her dark hair is chopped short and curls close to her head. Her ringless hands twist on the embossed leather lid of her briefcase as she listens to Ben, and her eyes still have that intense, expectant sparkle that Harriet saw when she first stepped into the van. "I notice you like to speak my language," the woman is saying, "but I speak English if you prefer."

Harriet leans back and closes her eyes. She hopes that whatever they speak they will not speak very loudly. She has been up since four and feels the full weight of her weariness now. The church bells this morning next to their hotel sounded off-key and jangled, as if they were being played by a tantrumming child, and then the roosters, with their hoarse, reckless, strangle-me-now screams in the dark. What will it be like at home? she wonders. Quiet, of course. She can see their bedroom, waiting: the white spread, the skylight beaded with drops of gray Seattle rain, the exercise bike and rowing machine gleaming like hospital equipment in the gloom. There will be no message from the sales manager on the answering machine, no little pornographic poems in the mailbox. She tries to feel sad about this, but the sad thing is that she feels nothing at all.

"Hon?"

Harriet looks up.

"She's speaking to you," Ben gestures to the woman beside him.

"Do you speak English?" the woman repeats.

"I used to," Harriet says. "I'm not sure I speak anything anymore."

Ben clucks his tongue: he wants Harriet to be what he calls her "real self" when she meets people, warm, natural—two things Harriet is touched he thinks she is or ever could be—but the woman leans forward and, breathless, says, "I know what it is like to be silent for too long. I know how that feels. You get all locked up inside. At first you want to talk then, no, you don't want to talk, then pretty soon you don't even want to try. You just want to be left alone in your cave! To suffer! But that isn't good for you, to stay locked up in silence. That can really hurt you. Because we are all people, right, brothers and sisters? And we need to talk to each other and say, 'Hey! I am here! You are too! Let's be happy together!' "

Harriet stares. Oh brother, she thinks. She glances at Ben, but Ben is in love. This woman—girl, really—is exactly who he'd like Harriet to be. Fresh, innocent, open. Harriet is surprised by the quick, deep bite of jealousy this stranger makes her feel.

"I notice you," the girl says, shaking a finger at Harriet, "living in a cave. But you will feel better as soon as you start to talk to other people."

"That's what I've been telling her," Ben says, radiant. "All she has to do is try."

"Just try," the girl agrees.

They beam at Harriet, and Harriet shrugs. It is quiet for a minute, and then the girl—who introduces herself as . . . Ariella? Gabriella? . . . something quick and soft— begins to tell Ben about her three years in the United States as a college student, the fun she had with her girlfriends, the American boys she dated. Harriet yawns and taps the masks in her lap. Used to drifting out of conversations in Spanish, she soon drifts out of this one as well. It is so easy not to listen. It is a little gift. The thought of gifts makes her remember the embroidered pouch of amber beads she bought herself last night, as a present for her new pure life. They had been in a display case, the price clearly marked, and she had not had to barter. What a relief it had been, to simply point and pay. Of course they might not be real amber. That is a possibility. They might be plastic or glass. She slips her hand into her purse, pulls out the pouch, and cautiously spills the contents into her palm. "Oh hell," she mouths to herself. The salesgirl in the shop made a mistake. Instead of the long rope of honey-colored beads, she must have taken out the pendant that was displayed in the case beside them. Oh ugh, Harriet thinks. She hates this pendant, a lump of Coca-Cola–colored stuff with an actual—she looks closer—dead bug of some sort inside it. She hates the pendant and she hates herself. Why didn't she pay attention?

Why did she look away when she should have been watching what the salesgirl was doing? Her disappointment in the pendant releases other hurts that have stung her recently and she darkens, remembering the old woman who cursed her from a doorway, the dead dog she bent to pet in the street, the baby with sores on its eyes lying sick in its mother's shawl. "I notice you are back in your cave," the young woman says.

Harriet has had it with picturesque speech. "I bought the wrong damn thing," she says.

"You did?" Ben, clear-eyed, peers at her. "What'd you buy, hon?" He takes the pendant she hands him, turns it over, and hands it to the young woman.

"But it's very beautiful," the young woman says. "It is a fossil. You know that? Many hundreds—thousands, millions!—of years ago this insect he was just traveling along, you know, like you and me, clump clump clump, eating his flowers and flying his wings and then he lands on this tree all covered with gold, he thinks it is blossoms, he thinks it is honey, and suddenly he can't move, he's stuck, and the sun it goes down and he gets more and more tired and pretty soon he says, 'Oh, well, I'll go to sleep' and here he is now." She hands the amber back to Ben, who fingers it respectfully and gives it back to Harriet with a pleased steady look.

"Are you a teacher?" Harriet asks, her voice as toneless as she can make it without sounding rude. "You sound like someone who spends a lot of time with children."

"No. I am too big a child myself. Don't you think? You think: a little. Well, you are right." The girl laughs and smooths out her skirt. "I would like to teach children, though, someday. I would like to do some good in the world. That is why we are here, don't you think? What do you do?"

"Ben's an engineer," Harriet says briefly, dropping the amber back in its pouch. "I work in publishing."

"Ah, yes, but what do you *do?* For the world?"

"Not as much as we'd like to," Ben says. "That's for sure." He clears his throat. "So. Where are you flying to today?"

"Oh I cannot afford to fly anymore," the girl says. "It is so expensive, it is only for rich people."

"We're not rich," Ben protests. "Even with both of us working, we don't have much money . . ."

"Oh, yes, money. I know about money! You know what I would do if I had money? I would give it away!"

"You have to have it to give it," Ben agrees.

"Yes. I used to have a great deal of money, when I worked. But now . . ." She lifts her hands and shrugs. Her skirt, Harriet notices, while well-cut, is thin from many washings, and the cuffs of her jacket are frayed.

"So you're between jobs?" Ben asks.

"I had a job, yes. But it was bad. My bosses were bad. You had to watch every word you said because if they didn't like it, or they didn't agree with you, out you would go, they would not let you stay even in the same building with them."

"And you're too independent for that," Ben says.

"Yes. I am too independent to make money! I am too independent to be rich! But I don't care. I just like to be happy! Don't you like to be happy?"

"It's hard to be happy," Ben says.

"Very hard," the girl agrees. "But when I am not happy, you know what I do? I go to bed! I sleep for three, maybe four days. And when I wake up, everything is normal again."

"Three or four days?" Ben repeats. "That's a long time."

"Yes." The girl nods brightly. "Sometimes it takes a long time to get normal."

Harriet stares. The girl is pale but strong-boned, and with a strong glow. She does not look like she has ever been sick.

"So you quit your job," Ben continues. "That takes a lot of courage, to just quit and walk out."

"Yes," says the girl. "Well I did not quit, no. They fired me."

"Because those crazy bosses didn't like you?"

"No," the girl says. "Because I was crazy myself." She laughs again and lifts her head. And suddenly Harriet sees something she has not seen before—a jagged white scar across the girl's throat. "I had many problems," the girl explains, "with my nerves."

"Nerves," Ben repeats. He glances at Harriet, who frowns at him, hard. The frown hasn't worked in the past when she has tried to pull him out of endless conversations with silver vendors and hammock salesmen, but it seems to work now. Ben doesn't say any more.

"I was sick with nerves for a long time," the girl continues. She touches her throat and Harriet watches her fingers tiptoe across the long line of the scar. "I saw things . . . terrible things . . . you cannot imagine the things I saw. Worse than those masks! Much worse than that! And I heard things too, voices, bad voices, saying to do . . . bad things to myself. It was as if I was inside"—she leans forward and presses her hand to the smudged glass of Harriet's window—"and outside too. I could not reach myself. I could not pull myself through. Do you know what I am saying?"

"Yes," says Harriet.

"Yes," says the girl. "And then Jesus came one day and helped me and that is why I love Jesus so much—you love Jesus don't you?"

Jesus? Harriet does not know what to say. She feels as if a door has just been shut in her face. She turns with familiar relief as Ben finally looks up from the camera he has been fiddling with and speaks for them both. "We respect him as a teacher," Ben says. His voice is flat, his eyes are far away.

"A teacher? Oh yes, a fine, a wonderful, a beautiful

teacher! But also . . . a savior! You must love Jesus as a savior?"

"We don't believe in God," Ben says, patting his pocket for a fresh roll of film.

"You don't . . ." the girl twists her hands and looks down at her lap, close to tears. "I am so sorry," she says. She starts to open her briefcase. "You must let me give you some books, you must let me help," she begins, but Ben interrupts, "No thanks. We're really not interested. And look. We're at the airport already."

Harriet looks up, as surprised as she's been by anything on this trip to see the terminal shimmering before them. She gathers her things and, with a weak wave to the girl, who is praying, actually praying, follows Ben across the parking lot.

"Whew," Ben says, as he opens the door of the airport. "Imagine coming all this way just to run into a Born Again. I guess people are crazy all over." Then his voice softens. "Poor kid," he says. "Did you see that scar?"

"I did. I kept wondering how she got it."

"Maybe she tried to cut her own throat."

"Can you do that?"

Ben is suddenly impatient. "How should I know?" he says. "You always think I know things I don't."

Harriet waits. What *do* you know? she wants to ask. And when will you tell me? But all she says is, "Did you catch her name?"

"No."

Harriet stands behind him as he checks in their baggage. He is talking to the man behind the desk about their flight—what gate they should go to, what time they will leave. She listens to his slow stumble through Spanish and hears nothing but the exhaustion and—what else? yes—the disappointment in his voice. He wants to believe, she thinks, like I do. He wants to believe that people can be sweet and funny without being crippled or crazy, he wants to believe that lovers can be faithful and that there truly is a way we can—what had the poor girl said?—do good in the world. Because that's what matters. Isn't that why I ended that stupid affair after all? To do good? To be good? To try?

She shivers and looks up. The ceiling is not yet finished in this new airport and there are squares of sky between the crossed steel beams. It could flood here, she thinks. It could flood anywhere. She feels the old kick of panic; my life, she thinks, what is happening to my life? She twists around to see the girl standing just outside the door with her briefcase open on the sidewalk before her. A flash of light from a passing cab's mirror sparks off the girl's head and for a moment she is impossibly framed in a halo. Harriet touches Ben's shoulder, says, "Be right back," and turns toward the door.

The girl does not look so young in the sunlight. There are a few strands of gray in her hair and olive-colored bruises beneath her bright eyes. She is not the sort of person I talk to, Harriet thinks. Ever. She is the sort of person I avoid.

"I would like to say good-bye," she says. "I enjoyed meeting you and I felt I understood some of the things you told us." The girl holds a placard neatly printed with Bible verses in four languages in her hand, and Harriet is careful not to look at it. "I would also like to learn to say your name."

The girl smiles her sudden luminous smile at this. "What will you do when you learn it?" she asks.

"I don't know," Harriet admits.

"Will you learn another name? And another? Will you learn the name of Our Father and Jesus and . . ."

"Come on," Harriet interrupts. She shields her eyes and squints as a jet roars off from the airfield behind them.

"Well," the girl says, her voice high and sweet and relentlessly happy, "we will have to start somewhere with you, I guess." She opens her mouth. And Harriet listens.

TINY LOVE

●

Larry Brown

TINY WAS TINY, BUT he had a wife and he loved her. The love he had for her was a lot bigger than he was. He did it all for her, ate the bologna sandwiches, changed the flats on the side of the road in the cold winter evenings when the rain was coming down, worked in the danger of the factory. Especially the factory, where gigantic presses could smash his hands and crush them, make nubs of his fingers. The machines crashed and pounded, and the huge wheels at the tops of the presses turned, and Tiny slid his little piece of metal under the die and hooked both hands on the buttons, and the presses turned over and came down with unbelievable force and stamped out one part at a time. He hooked the part with a little rubber suction cup on a rod, drew it safely out of the way, and inserted another piece, inhaling the exhaust of the Towmotors while standing on a skid to raise himself up to the level where other men stood.

He smoked constantly, not looking around, always watching his hands and where they were because he knew Sonny Jones and Duwayne Davis who worked in the stockroom with their nubbed and shortened hands, victims of the same machines he stood before. So he watched his hands to see where they were. The young boys drove the forklifts with cigarettes dangling from their lips and threaded the forks of the lifts into the pallets with insolent skill and roared away, blue fumes roaring from the grilled exhausts in the back.

Every afternoon Tiny spent his two dollars. Every day he drove by the liquor store, the last one on the way out of town, and picked up a half-pint of Four Roses or Heaven Hill or Old Grand-Dad or any of the other cheap and hangover-producing brands of whiskey, whichever one she had summoned from her bed that morning as he stood with his lunch sack in his hand at the bedroom door. All day he kept the name of that label in his head and that afternoon he fired up his rusty seventy-one Ford Fairlane with the busted muffler and drove out of town with a smoke hanging from his lip, winter and summer, good times and bad, and stopped by the little store on the outskirts of town where he was a regular but unknown customer, a place run by college boys whose faces always changed, and there he would shuffle in and pick what she wanted from the shelf and produce his two dollars and change and take his bottle once they'd sacked it and move once again through the coming darkness toward his small house in the country, where he had a little vegetable garden, a car shed, some rusted and warped pianos sitting in the yard in a muddy collection like a neglected group of behemoths.

He would stop the car in the driveway and get out and grab his jacket and go in, pulling on the screen door, and there she would sit on the couch in front of the gray television screen, in her robe and her nightgown, her nicotine-stained fingers trembling, her mouth moving in the first tremblings of a smile, and Tiny would think, Lord, I love her. She would reach for him and the bottle at the same time, and Tiny knew that the hug she had for him was at once a hug for him and a hug for him for bringing the bottle, and he would bend and kiss her quickly and go to the kitchen and fix her a glass of Coke with ice so she could mix her first drink, and then he would sit down and she would begin to tell him about her day.

Men lost their hands in the presses. The presses were thirty feet high and they had wheels that were twelve feet in diameter, and they were made of iron and they weighed hundreds of tons, and a man's hands were a small thing in the face of the quarter-inch thickness of metal parts the presses stamped out without stalling. A man had no power in the face of power like that. The press-department bosses looked sharply in the press department and watched where men put their hands and talked to them and measured small pieces of metal with micrometers and checked blueprints and eyed everything and ordered runs for the presses, and Tiny hooked both his hands on the buttons and watched the die come down and make another part. He hooked it with his little rubber-suction-cup rod and drew it out safely and inserted another piece. He leaned on his machine and thought, Lord, I love her, and the press came down and Tiny, locked in his lifetime's work, watched his hands and where they were and rehearsed the name of that afternoon's bottle in his mind.

He ate bologna sandwiches every day. It never changed. It was always bologna, and he bought a pound a week, seven slices, where Mr. Carlton Turner sliced it on his machine and where the people who lived in the community with Tiny and his wife knew him and knew that she drank. Tiny would always hang around the store for a while, looking lost, talking about the weather or whatever had just happened, and he would twist the neck of the paper sack that held the bologna tight around the small cold mound of meat inside there, and he would tell everybody to just come on and go home with him. But nobody ever did. It was just something to say, like people in the country often say.

He fixed the bologna sandwiches in the kitchen each morning while she was sleeping, quiet in the kitchen with only the radio playing, two pieces of bread and mayonnaise, wrap it in waxed paper, put it in the sack. She hardly ever went anywhere. Her day began when his ended. She was articulate to the point of wittiness once she'd had her first drink, but he couldn't sit up with her all night watching network television.

He ate the sandwich in the break room with one of those mixed soft drinks that came from machines that drop first the cup and then some ice and then several squirts of different liquids and finally fizz up the drink and click to signal when they are ready. He watched checkers games sometimes or just talked with other people about work or how the fish were biting or who had died, and he kept his eye on the phone booth and waited until almost everybody had headed back to punch in and then dashed to the booth to call her and speak to her for just a few moments. Sometimes she was up. Sometimes she wasn't. He needed to hear her voice always. Sometimes he did. But sometimes he didn't.

He'd try to get her out to go places with him, but she hardly ever would. She'd say she didn't look right, or her hair wasn't ready, or she hadn't had a bath. He was sometimes only asking for her to go buy groceries with him. They couldn't go dancing because she was semicrippled, from a car accident a long time ago. It wasn't that she couldn't actually walk. She actually could. She just preferred not to. Tiny had to help her bathe. He would roll her in her wheelchair with her

thin legs crossed under a robe and lovingly draw a tub of
warm water, testing it frequently with his hand, talking
softly to her, making sure the water wasn't too cold or too
hot, and then together they would work her out of her robe
and he would help her pull her arms out of the entrapments
of the sleeves until she sat naked and pale and defenseless
and semicrippled and slightly drunk in the chair, and he
would slide his hands under her legs, feeling the movement
of her loose skin under the slack muscles of her thighs, and
lift her, gently, careful not to bump her, and pick her up,
stand balanced with the precious weight of her in his arms,
his hands cradling the soft, withered flesh of her back and
legs, and lower her, gradually, slowly and carefully, almost
herniating himself sometimes, into the warm water and bring
her an ashtray and replenish her drink, and he would sit
there and bathe her back, her little sad and drooping breasts,
and she would talk about David Letterman and what he'd
said, and he would rinse her back slowly, lovingly, and try
to fix her eyes with his eyes, and she would prattle on, the
water cooling, her toes red and distorted and pruney.

It seemed to go on forever sometimes, the two of them
sitting in the bathroom, because she could lean forward and
turn on the faucet with her toes and let more hot water in,
and Tiny would keep replenishing her drink, because it was
a prelude to love. Once the bath was done and she was done
and she said that she was ready, he would let the water out
and dry her partially where she sat in the tub, because he
didn't want to pick her up while she was wet and risk dropping her, and she would lift her legs and let him dry her
under each one, and he would carefully run the towel under
and over everything involved, so that she would be dry, and
safe to hold, and he would, once he was sure of this, bend
once again and put his hands under her legs and behind her
back and lift her up, and reposition her in the wheelchair,

toss her little robe over her, and wheel her back to the bedroom.

He would kiss her and tell her how much he loved her before he took her out of the chair. There would be only a small lamp burning. She would nod and smile, holding out her empty glass, and he would hurry to make her another drink. He would bring it to her and sit beside her on the bed until she was ready, and then he would lift her out of the chair and put her on the bed and pull the covers up over her, so that she was not exposed, and undress quickly in one small dark corner of the room, and go to her, naked and fully engorged, and spread her thin withered thighs and get in between them and try to give her all the love he could feel.

It was dirty, dangerous work, and there was no way to get out of it, because once it started you were locked into a clock you had to punch into for forty hours a week, and that left no room for looking for other jobs, and Tiny never expected that his life would merit more than this anyway. He believed in Social Security and he believed that he would live a long and healthy life and he believed that his job was a form of security as solid as anything anybody could ever hope for. Sometimes he longed to drive the forklifts. Sometimes he longed to be the foreman over the assembly line where fifty people put stoves together and drilled holes with drills and inserted screws with air-driven screwdrivers and sent them on down the line, because the press department was too loud for talk and almost too loud for thought, but Tiny had only two thoughts anyway and they were, Lord, I love her, Kentucky Tavern.

He tried not to think about her too much when he was at work. He tried to think about his hands and where to

keep them as the huge wheels turned and the die came down
and shook the concrete floor where he stood on the skid with
his cotton gloves and his rubber-suction-cup rod. There was
two weeks' vacation a year, time he usually spent in his
garden, early in the spring when everything needed to be
tended to, when the pole beans needed poles and the tomatoes
needed staking and tying off, when the grass was coming
strong in the watermelons and they needed a good hoeing
out. If she was okay, or sleeping, sometimes he would fish,
settled against a tree on the riverbank, a small can of worms
beside him, the line lying slack in the slow muddy river
current, flotsam piled in the eddies, empty milk jugs and
beer cans and tiny sticks and trash. But he thought of her
even then, wondering if she was all right, if he should stop
fishing and go see if she needed anything. The two weeks
always overwhelmed him. Here were two whole weeks where
almost anything might be accomplished, where a man might
search out and find a better job, one that paid more money,
that was not so dangerous and depressing, one that might
allow him to buy a better car, new furniture, a motorized
wheelchair, any number of things that might improve their
lives. She had never been able to have any children and Tiny
had accepted it early, but he still grieved in his heart for
the loss of what might have been, children to come home to,
to help with their homework, to take fishing. And there never
seemed to be enough time in the two weeks to do all the
things that needed doing. Each year he told himself that he
was going to get ahold of a truck and some men to help him
move the pianos out of the yard, but there were always other
things to tend to, a coat of paint on the house, the reworking
of her little flower gardens, and every afternoon the trip to
town for the little half-pint bottle. She would not allow him
to buy a fifth. She would say that she was not alcoholic and
did not need a fifth. She would say that all she needed was

a little half-pint. And Tiny never even thought, for a long while, of arguing with her. He loved her too much.

Sometimes Tiny fried the fish he caught, when he caught some, rolling the headless lengths of pink catfish flesh in yellow cornmeal and dropping them into hot grease and turning them with a fork until they were a nice even brown. She would help him, sitting by the stove in her wheelchair, offering advice as to the doneness of each piece, chain-smoking and drinking her little drinks. Tiny knew that she didn't have anything else to do, that she was lonely, that the drinks helped her cope with her life and her reluctance to walk. He dreaded the end of his vacation and the return to the brutalizing noise of the factory, the danger of losing his hands, the same cold tired bologna sandwiches. He never complained, never regretted being saddled with her and his life, never asked the big Why? He enjoyed his two weeks off as best he could and when it was over went back to the thing that brought in his three dollars and sixty cents an hour.

Her liver was not in good shape and there were frequent trips to the doctor. There was no one else to take her and so Tiny would have to be excused from work for a few hours. The press-department foreman didn't like it because then he had to pull somebody out of spot welding and put him on Tiny's machine. Sometimes she would call the factory and ask for Tiny and somebody would have to come and get him, usually the press-department foreman, and he would never fail to tell Tiny that they weren't paying him to talk on the phone. Tiny would nod his head and agree and thank the foreman and go into the foreman's tiny office where the phone was lying on its side and he would listen to whatever his wife was telling him, nodding his head rapidly, trying to get off the phone as soon as possible, and it was always bad for him to have to go back out and tell the foreman that he needed a few hours off so he could take his wife to the doctor.

The foreman would more often than not get mad at him, and cuss, and then tell him to go on, but hurry up, goddamnit, and Tiny would rush to the time clock, punch out, rush home, load his wife up, rush to the doctor's office, see the doctor, then rush back home and unload her, and rush back to the factory, where the foreman would be so mad he wouldn't speak to him for the rest of the day. And anyway, after a trip to the doctor, there was never much left of the rest of the day. And after a trip to the doctor, Tiny could never stop thinking about what the doctor had said, because he always said the same things. He always told Tiny that her liver was in bad shape, that her drinking was going to kill her, and that Tiny had to stop buying it for her. After Tiny had pushed his wife back out to the waiting room, he and the doctor would have these small private conferences in the doctor's office, behind a closed door. The doctor would say that he understood she had a need, but her liver was getting worse, and if she didn't stop drinking, one day it was going to kill her. The doctor would say for Tiny to just stop buying it, but Tiny would shake his head and tell the doctor that he could hardly stand to do that, that she needed it, that she was lonely, that she would cry if he didn't buy it for her, and that there were a lot of things he could stand but seeing her cry wasn't one of them. Then the doctor would shake his own head and write a prescription and tear it off the little tablet and tell him a definite and somewhat huffy good-bye.

Her health had never been good and it continued to get worse. She seemed to get weaker each year. And neither one of them was a spring chicken. She coughed badly from the cigarettes, and at night Tiny would sit on the bed with her and pat her back while she coughed herself into strangling fits and wheezing spells that he tried to cure by slapping her gently on the back. He'd hold her close and think, Lord,

I love her, and then she'd ask for another drink and Tiny would get up and fix it. One time he told her that he wasn't going to fix it, and she cried and immediately Tiny relented and fixed it. He sat there watching her drink it and wondered if he could bring himself to be strong enough to do what was best for her. He knew it wouldn't be easy. He knew she'd cry. He didn't know if he could take that or not. But the doctor knew what he was talking about. He was a doctor. He'd been to college and had learned all those things. And if he said it was killing her, then, by God, it *was* killing her, and he, Tiny, was the one who was doing it by buying it for her, so in a way, *he* was killing her, and if he kept buying it, and it *did* kill her, then what would he do? What would he do for love?

Tiny tried to save a little money from time to time. It wasn't easy, because he didn't make much, and he spent a lot, but he managed to stick back a little here and there. One Saturday afternoon when things were pretty smooth, when she was happy in front of the television with a Tarzan movie on, Johnny Weissmuller in *Tarzan Finds a Son!,* and a drink in her hand, Tiny told her he was going to go look at another car. He asked her if she wanted to go. She didn't. She just happily waved him on out the door. Tiny thought, Lord, I love her, and drove eight miles to the driveway of a man with a seventy-eight Buick for sale, high mileage but clean, good floormats, the paint faded just a little. Tiny got in and cranked it up and revved it up. It was a smooth-running little engine. The man swore it wouldn't use a drop of oil. He said there wasn't any way you could get it to use a drop of oil. He said you could run the dog*shit* out of it and it wouldn't, it wouldn't *ever* register the *least* bit *low* on the *stick.* He said it was the best car he'd ever had. He said the only reason he was getting rid of it was because he'd bought a new one, and there it sat in the carport, all shiny and new.

Tiny cut it off and got out and kicked the tires. They didn't have a whole lot of tread left. But the man was only asking four hundred dollars for the whole thing.

Tiny asked the man if he could drive it. The man said he could. Tiny drove it and liked it. It handled well. It cruised like a Buick ought to. Tiny came back and parked the car and told the man he believed he'd take it. He pulled the money from his pocket, the carefully saved twenties and tens, a whole wad of them, and counted it into the man's hand. Then he asked the man if he'd mind following him home in the car, since he only lived eight miles away, and then Tiny could bring him back home, and the man said he'd be glad to. So that's what they did.

Tiny told his wife, "Come on, let's go riding around." He bundled her up in a robe and fixed her a big drink in a jelly glass, stirred it with a spoon, and they got in the car and took off. It was a warm summer evening that evening, and people were riding around, and they rode down some roads, and she drank, and Tiny smoked, and they talked. The air smelled good, and once in a while they'd meet somebody they knew, and Tiny would wave. He felt good, having her with him, in this new (to them) car. She told him how much she liked the Tarzan movie. They talked about what a good swimmer Johnny Weissmuller was and about what a good Tarzan yell he had. Tiny felt so good he let out a Tarzan yell himself, but it wasn't nearly as good as Johnny Weissmuller's. It didn't matter. The cotton fields were growing and it had rained earlier and the air smelled clean, wonderful, and Tiny had hopes that things would get better.

They stopped by a small store and bought some ice and some more Cokes. She had secreted the better half of a half-pint in her purse so there was no need, really, for them to stop riding and enjoying the scenery. But they happened

upon a bad wreck. Law officers were directing traffic in the
middle of the road. A bridge railing had been crashed
through, and as they crept past they could see a car upturned
in a creek, the muffler exposed, all the underparts showing.
People were standing in the road, watching. They crept past.
Cars were parked everywhere. An ambulance was waiting.
People with white coats were standing down on the bank of
the creek. There was a stretcher on wheels they were standing
beside. Somebody was being pulled out of the car, and he
looked dead, an old man, with gray hair, a bloody wound in
his chest. A man standing in the road wearing overalls told
Tiny they thought he was drunk. The lawmen waved to Tiny
to move on through. Tiny and his wife craned their necks
to see as they crept past. But other people were waiting
behind them, and they didn't get to see the dead man brought
all the way out and placed on the stretcher with a sheet over
him for his ride to the morgue.

In the winter it got dark early. Sometimes it would be almost
dark when Tiny got home. He cooked hamburgers sometimes,
smoking in the kitchen, drinking coffee, never touching a
drop of what she loved so much. Usually on Friday evenings
he bought groceries with part of his paycheck and in the
winter it was always dark when he got home with the groceries. That made him late with her bottle, and she was
always a little ill on Friday afternoons and would want her
bottle brought in before the groceries were brought in. Tiny
was used to that and did it and didn't mind it, although the
doctor's words kept nagging in his head. He could see the
doctor's head, and how he'd shake it, with that air of res-
ignation he had, and sometimes Tiny would actually think
about trying to do what the doctor had told him he should.
And one Friday afternoon, he tried it.

He didn't stop by the liquor store and get her bottle. He went straight to the grocery store, pushing his cart up and down the aisles, trying not to think about what she was going to say when he came in empty-handed. There was going to be some crying, and some arguing, he was sure, but he felt like he was doing the right thing. He knew she was sitting at home at that moment, anticipating her bottle, and he knew she was going to be disappointed. He knew she might pitch a fit. But he thought he could handle it. When he got home, it turned out he couldn't.

He took the groceries in—it was winter, dark—and set them on the table in the kitchen, two sacks, two armloads. There were all kinds of good things in the sacks, stuff like fresh catfish, some fatback, some cracklings for crackling bread, buttermilk, Jimmy Dean smoked sausage, some nice chicken legs, and candy. Tiny thought he might be able to get her off whiskey and on candy. He was hoping he could, anyway. But she seemed a little furious when she came rolling into the kitchen in her wheelchair.

He turned around to her while he was setting the groceries on the table and she demanded to know where her bottle was. She looked a little wild, and she looked a little shaky. She looked, Tiny thought, like she had revved herself up to do some real nasty talking. He tried to be calm. He tried to be as benevolent as he could. But it didn't work. She knew, right away, that he hadn't brought the bottle. She knew, right away, that he was stiffing her, trying to put her off, and she looked in the sacks and found the sacks wanting. And she went into a rage. She pulled out the chicken legs and started throwing them. She had a cigarette hung in the corner of her mouth and she threw the pack of cracklings against the wall where they slid down behind the stove. Tiny tried to reason with her, but it didn't do any good. She wanted her bottle, and she wanted her bottle right away.

Tiny tried to explain to her that it was killing her, tried to get her to remember all the things the doctor had said, but she wouldn't listen to any of that. She knocked the buttermilk off the table and it broke and ran all over the floor, and she took the Jimmy Dean smoked sausage and tried to hit Tiny with it, and then she backed him up into the corner where the heater was and beat him with the catfish until he finally agreed to drive her back to town and get her a bottle. She just wouldn't listen to reason. It was Friday night and the Grammy Awards were coming on.

But that night was a wonderful night. She always seemed to keep a little piece of a drink secreted somewhere, maybe for emergencies, and she had one when they went to town. She sipped on it and moved over in the seat close to Tiny and sort of rubbed on him while they were going to town. She whispered all kinds of wonderful things she was going to do to him once they got back home. Tiny stepped on the gas in the Buick and they went to the liquor store and he got the bottle and they went back home after stopping by Kentucky Fried Chicken for two dinner boxes with coupons they'd saved from the mail. They didn't watch the Grammy Awards, and the chicken got cold in the kitchen. Tiny's wife got him down on the bed and yanked his pants off and did things to him with her mouth that he'd never seen or even imagined before, and he didn't even question where she'd learned it or heard of it or seen it or imagined it, just enjoyed it and thought, Lord, I love her, and woke up the next morning with different thoughts in his head.

Now things seemed to take another turn. Now when Tiny was at the presses he had more things on his mind than Lord,

I love her, and Old Crow, and where to put his hands. He began to be trained to know that as long as he brought the bottle, she would do those wonderful things with her mouth. It was hard for him to think about where to put his hands when he thought about where she put her mouth. The presses were still just as big, still just as dangerous, but Tiny had more to live for now. He couldn't wait for the days to get over. He couldn't wait to get back home with that bottle and take it in to her where now she waited on him in the bedroom in her robe, smiling, her lips ready. For Tiny it was deep love, the deepest love, and he'd think, Lord, I love her, and Shit, and Damn, and that was about all the superlatives he knew. After he'd exhausted them, he just had to moan and groan.

That went on for a while. A long while. A long, slow, pleasurable, mesmerizing while. It went on through the whole two-week vacation the next year. The pianos didn't get moved, just kept moldering in the yard, but once in a while Tiny would go out there and tinkle the rain-swollen keys, rub his hands over the cracked and splintered veneers. He thought of hiring a bulldozer and having them just bulldozed over into the hollow behind his house. Tiny had to mow around those pianos.

She seemed to get weaker all the time. Tiny knew the cigarettes and the booze were killing her. She never ate anything, and her phone calls to the factory became more frequent, sometimes at lunch when he was trying to eat his bologna sandwiches. At night he cooked chili, fried chicken, tossed salads, baked potatoes, did roast beefs, but nothing seemed to interest her. All she wanted was her drink and smokes. He knew he was going to have to try it again. He didn't want to. He knew it would be tough. He knew she'd cry. But he hoped there wouldn't be any violence this time.

One day he made up his mind. He stood all day long at the press and thought about it. He decided to get tough. He knew it wouldn't be easy.

He didn't buy a bottle that evening. He just went home. He didn't even go in the house at first. He just went out in the backyard and started pulling up some weeds. But before long, she started calling to him. He could hear her in there. She was wanting her bottle. That was plain. He kept pulling up the weeds. He was trying to take his mind off it. He was trying to think about something else.

Before long he heard her crying. She was screaming and ranting and cussing and crying all at the same time, and he heard her say some things about why God let good men die and bad men live, and he didn't know what she was talking about, and didn't want to know, only wanted for her to hush and not keep on about all that. But she made it back to the kitchen in her wheelchair. She raised the window. She screamed at him out of that. She screamed some things that were pretty bad.

She screamed, *"You motherfucker! You little sawed-off midget asswipe! You cheap prick!"* It hurt Tiny pretty bad to hear all that. But he just kept pulling up his weeds. He thought he could weather the storm. He thought maybe she'd cool off if he just stayed out in the yard and minded his own business.

But she got to knocking over stuff in the house. There were all sorts of big crashy noises. She was screaming the whole time. It was a good thing Tiny didn't have any close neighbors because no telling what they'd have thought. Probably something like, Aw, hell, that's Tiny's drunk-ass wife again.

Then she got to yelling that she was going to set the house on fire. She screamed out the window that she'd *burn this goddamn house to the ground!* Tiny didn't think she meant it. But it turned out that she did.

Before long there was a big orange glow in the living room. Smoke started coming out of one of the windows she'd been screaming out of just a few minutes before. Tiny didn't think, Lord, I love her. He thought, *Oh shit!* and rushed inside. A whole wall of the living room was on fire. Burning embers were on the floor. Smoke was mushroomed near the ceiling like a small atomic bomb. And there was Tiny's wife, hacking and strangling, trying to get out on the front porch, her wheelchair hung in the doorway.

Tiny didn't know what to do first, rescue his wife or try to put out the fire. He ran over to his wife, grabbed her, pulled her wheelchair back. The smoke was terrible and it was burning his eyes. He could barely see. He couldn't breathe for it. They were both coughing and strangling. Tiny could feel his hair getting singed. He could see his wife's hair getting singed. He lifted her out of the wheelchair, kicked the chair out of the way, and carried her outside and put her on the porch swing. Then he jumped down in the yard and grabbed the garden hose and turned on the faucet. The fire was getting bigger in the living room. The heat was awful. Tiny had to go inside and face that with a garden hose.

The fire was licking at the ceiling. Tiny squeezed the nozzle and put his hand over his mouth. The water knocked the fire down quickly, but the smoke turned black and got about four feet thick near the ceiling. Tiny's eyes watered and he thought he might puke. He got down on his knees. Black water and charred debris covered the floor. He could hear his wife coughing out on the porch swing. He kept spraying the water and the fire finally went out. He saw that the house wasn't going to burn down after all. But it sure had made one hell of a mess.

Tiny could have done a lot of things. He could have cussed his wife out, slapped her around some, whipped her ass good for setting the house on fire. All he did was drop the hose on the floor and walk out on the front porch to look at her and think, Lord, she sure is a lot of trouble.

All of a sudden, Tiny didn't know what to do with his wife anymore. It looked like she was capable of nearly anything to keep on getting her drinks. He started worrying about her more at work and almost stepped into the path of a moving Towmotor a time or two. People had to yell at Tiny for him to get out of the way. If they hadn't, he might've just stepped on out into the aisle and gotten mashed.

And Tiny had to lie to his insurance company about the fire. They sent a man out to investigate and Tiny told him the heater caught the wall on fire. The man wanted to know why they were running the heater in such hot weather. Tiny told the man that his wife had gotten a chill, and then had pulled a chair over in front of the heater, and had gotten up to go to the kitchen for something, and the chair had caught on fire, and then caught the wall on fire, and the man said he thought Tiny's wife was in a wheelchair, and then looked over at her sitting there in her wheelchair. Tiny had to hem and haw, and finally admit that he didn't really know what had happened. He said it might have been an electrical short.

The man said *Ha!*, and then stood around for a while and acted like he was getting mad. He wanted to talk to Tiny's wife but Tiny didn't want him to talk to his wife. The investigator finally left, with nothing settled. About a week later Tiny got a notice in the mail saying that his house insurance had been canceled. Somebody, maybe the investigator who had come out, wrote a shitty little note in there that said, "You're lucky we didn't sue your lying little ass."

Tiny had to dig deep to find the money to fix his living room back up. Some Sheetrock had to be torn out, and new Sheetrock put in, and sanded, and painted, and new trim had to be put on, as well as new linoleum where those burning embers had melted holes in the floor. The ceiling was all screwed up and that had to be fixed, repatched, and painted. It cost Tiny a wad of money he couldn't really afford to spend. They had to buy new curtains and new venetian blinds, a new window shade. Tiny had to shake his head every time he thought about the whole thing being caused by a little two-dollar bottle of whiskey. He asked himself why he didn't just go on and buy the whiskey. He'd stand there at his press and not think too much about where to put his hands as the wheels turned over and came down and slammed out another part. Tiny got to be kind of like a machine, kind of like the machine he was running, something that moved when it had to, an automaton, kind of. He worked like a robot, doing the same things over and over and over and over and over and over and over.

He kept buying the whiskey for her. He didn't know what else to do. And sometimes, late in the evenings when he was headed home, all by himself, just cruising along in the Buick, with the little sack on the seat beside him, things would pile up on him and get to him, and he'd drop his head, a cigarette dangling from his lips, and he'd cry. It wouldn't be loud crying. He'd just shake his head and a little snot would run out of his nose. He'd wipe it off with the back of his hand. And after a while it would end. He'd be all dried up by the time he got home, and saw his wife sitting in the living room, smiling, holding out her arms, making little smoochy noises with her mouth, all ready for that Tiny love. But Tiny was about sick of love. He'd just hand her her bottle and head into the kitchen to see what was in the refrigerator to fix for supper. He still, after all, had to eat.

He worked all day five days a week and he didn't see anything but the press in front of him. He put the piece of metal under the die and leaned against the press and mashed a button with one hand and smoked a cigarette with the other hand and the press came down and stamped out the part and Tiny hooked it with his little rubber-suction-cup rod or just his hand sometimes and drew it safely out of the way and stuck in another piece of metal and leaned on the machine and pushed the button.

Sometimes somebody had to punch him when it was time to go to lunch because sometimes Tiny wouldn't even hear the whistle. If nobody punched him, sometimes he'd just stand there and work all the way through his lunch break. And when he did take lunch, he just sat there and chewed and stared at the table. People started looking at him and talking about how funny he was acting, but Tiny didn't pay any attention. He had too much other stuff on his mind.

Some evenings he'd go home and hand his wife her bottle and go out on the front porch and sit in the swing, swinging, swinging, staring out at the road. People would drive by and wave and blow the horn, but Tiny wouldn't wave back. He couldn't figure out what to do about her. She'd holler out for him to come inside and see what was on the television, but Tiny wouldn't do it. He'd sit there until it got dark and sometimes he'd sit there until after dark and beyond. But his wife never complained that supper wasn't ready. Sometimes it would be only the screaming hunger gnawing inside his stomach that would drive him back inside. And sometimes the cure for that would only be another bologna sandwich. Tiny just about lost his appetite over his wife. He'd go to bed by himself, lie in the dark bedroom while the television played in the living room, while his wife chuckled over Johnny Carson and Ed McMahon and coughed once in a while. Tiny didn't know what he was going to do. He didn't think he could keep on going the way he was. And it turned out that Tiny wasn't wrong.

There was a little fat woman who worked down on the assembly line, and she started coming into the break room and sitting down at the table with Tiny, across from Tiny, and looking at him. She had a hot-dog sandwich every day. It never changed, just like Tiny's bologna. She looked at Tiny and smiled at him, and every once in a while Tiny would look up and see her smiling at him, and he'd smile back. Nothing special, just a little grin once in a while. But it escalated.

Tiny would go to the bathroom, which was down by the assembly line, and he'd climb the stairs and the little fat woman would be looking up at him and smiling. And one evening, she asked Tiny if he'd give her a ride home from work. Tiny said, "Sure." He wasn't doing anything but going by the liquor store for a bottle for his wife. He told her he needed to do that first. She said that was fine, that she might just get a little bottle herself.

They went into the liquor store kind of like a couple, kind of like a date. It felt a little funny to Tiny, but it also felt a little good to Tiny, whose wife had never gone anywhere with him in ages.

Tiny didn't mean for it to happen, but one thing sort of led to another. They got back in the car, and the little fat woman started telling dirty jokes and telling him how cute he was, and Tiny laughed and lit a cigarette, and the little fat woman opened her bottle and took a drink. She offered him a drink and Tiny took it. It was the first one he'd had in a long time, seeing as how he'd seen what it had done to his wife.

It turned out the little fat woman lived about twenty miles away and she apologized for that, but Tiny told her that was all right, he didn't mind, that it had been a good while since he'd spent any time with anybody but his wife. The sun was going down and the evening was pretty, and the little fat woman had a few more drinks and got to flirting with him, and crossed her legs under her skirt. Her legs were a little hairy but Tiny didn't care. He thought they were pretty nicely shaped. He opened his wife's bottle and started drinking out of that. It was Ancient Age that evening.

The little fat woman had some nice fat little breasts and the thing she had on was sort of low cut, and whenever she leaned over in the seat toward Tiny, which she did a good bit, Tiny could sort of see right down that little valley. He didn't mean for it to happen, but his love muscle got inflated, and the little fat woman noticed it and giggled and pointed to it, and then told him maybe they ought to pull over and see if they couldn't let a little of the air out of it. Tiny had polished off about half his wife's whiskey, and it sounded like a good idea to him, so they did. It had gotten dark by then and they pulled up into an old cemetery and all of a sudden the little fat woman was all over Tiny, spilling her whiskey on him, smooching on him with her mouth, and she knew things to do with *her* mouth that Tiny's wife had never thought of or seen or even imagined, and they stayed there for about three hours, plenty long enough for Tiny's wife to be totally enraged when he staggered in drunk, whooping and laughing, and then falling like a tree down on the couch, hiccuping and grinning before he passed out.

The next morning, Tiny woke up on the couch and realized that things didn't have to be the way they were. He didn't have to put up with that bullshit from his wife. The little fat woman was a whole lot more fun than his wife had ever thought about being. Tiny had loved his wife a lot at one time, but now he didn't love her so much. As a matter of fact he'd sort of started hating her. All she did was complain and cough and drink and cost him money. There was no telling how much money she had cost him over the years. She didn't have any sense of humor at all, and the sex they had together was kind of like something she paid him just to bring the whiskey. Tiny stayed there on the couch awhile and thought about the little fat woman's fat little naked body and how nice and fat it had been. She really had some meat on her bones. He got all excited again thinking about it. He wondered if maybe she'd want him to give her another ride home sometime. He hoped she would. Tiny thought that maybe he might ought to put a quilt in the trunk and start carrying it around with him, just in case. Just keep it for emergencies, kind of like how his wife kept her little parts of bottles of whiskey hidden.

Tiny got up and walked into the bedroom and peeked in on his wife. She was in bed with the covers up over her head. He couldn't see her face. She wasn't moving at all. She looked dead but he knew she wasn't.

Tiny eased into the kitchen and fixed his bologna sandwich. He eased out the door and got in the Buick and cranked it.

He did some hard thinking on the way to work. He hadn't had anything but misery for a long time with his wife. He'd tried to do everything he could for her, had pampered her, had done what she asked all the time, and it looked like all she did was use him. Tiny wondered what he'd done to deserve all that. He'd always provided for her, and what had she given him in return? Nothing but trouble, that's what. All she wanted to do was watch television and drink. He was tired of it. He didn't know why he couldn't have a little fun in life. A man wasn't supposed to just work like a dog all the time, was he? Just be like a damn machine standing at a damn machine and drawing a damn paycheck that was always spent before the next paycheck came? Tiny started wishing he'd never married his wife. He started wishing he'd never even seen his wife. He started wishing he'd never started working in the factory. He'd done some carpenter work when he was young and he started wishing he'd just stayed with that. He might have been a contractor by now, making plenty of money, having a big crew working for him, being the boss, ordering everybody around. The more he thought about his life and how it was, the sicker he got. He was so sick of the factory that he didn't know if he could walk back in the door. He knew his wife was probably going to call the factory sometime during the day and say she was sick and needed to go to the doctor. Then the press-department foreman would get mad at him again. He felt trapped. He didn't know whether to shit or go blind. He didn't know how he was going to go on with his life. His life seemed so bad he could hardly stand to think about it.

He thought about not going in to work. He thought about just stopping by a pay phone and calling in sick. He didn't feel real good anyway. He had a bad hangover. He wished there was some way he could get the little fat woman off with him and just spend the day with her. But she was probably on her way to work just like he was.

Tiny didn't know what to do. He sure didn't want to go back home. His wife would raise hell with him all day if he did that. Tiny realized that people could get more problems on them than they could handle, and that they could talk themselves into doing away with themselves. He wasn't thinking about doing that, he was just seeing how it could happen.

He guessed he could divorce his wife. That was a possibility, but it sure would look bad on him. Her lawyer would be sure to get her in the courtroom in her wheelchair and create a lot of sympathy for her. She'd probably take his ass to the cleaners, and he knew his ass couldn't stand a trip to the cleaners. He was just barely making a living as it was. But one thing about it was he wouldn't have to buy her a damn bottle of whiskey every afternoon if he divorced her. He wouldn't have to go everywhere by himself. If he divorced her he could probably start going with the little fat woman, maybe steady. Or maybe they could even get married if they fell in love. Maybe that was what he needed to do, just trade in his old wife for a new one. The little fat woman might even want to go dancing on Friday and Saturday nights or something. Then they could go on picnics on Sunday afternoons, or go fishing. Tiny thought about the two of them sitting side by side on the riverbank, fishing. They'd have the quilt with them and the sun would be shining and if the fish weren't biting she could do those wonderful things with her mouth right there while the river flowed past. The more Tiny thought about it, the more it seemed like a good idea. What was the point of staying with his wife if he was unhappy? There wasn't any future in it.

But what would happen to her? Who would buy her whiskey for her? Where would she live? Who'd take her to the doctor? Who'd cook her meals? Who'd help her take a bath?

By the time Tiny got to work he was so confused and sick and sick at heart he hardly knew where he was. He punched in at one minute before seven and grabbed a fresh pair of cotton gloves and headed back to the press department. He wanted to walk down by the assembly line and see if he could see the little fat woman but he didn't have time. He went over and turned on his machine and the whistle blew. He decided he'd ask the little fat woman if she wanted to eat lunch in his car with him and maybe they could talk about some of his problems. Maybe he could talk to her and ask her advice. And maybe he could give her another ride home that evening. Maybe his life could work out all right after all. He hoped it could. Things had been bad for a long time, and he was ready for them to get better. Maybe this new relationship with this little fat woman was the light at the end of the tunnel, where happiness was possible, and life didn't have to be something you merely had to endure until the day you died.

Thinking about these things, Tiny put a piece of metal in, leaned on his button, and then noticed that he had not been careful where he placed his hand.

OVERTIME

•

Stephen Dixon

I DO EVERYTHING HE TOLD me to. Then there's nothing more to do. I check over what I did and it seems good as I can get it. I wait. I get up, sit down, look at the clock, walk around. Where is he? She? Where are they? How long do they expect me to sit, stand, look, walk around, wait for them like this with nothing to do? They say they'll be back in an hour, why does it have to be four? If I could go to sleep or take a walk outside and step in for coffee, it wouldn't be too bad. But if one of them caught me sleeping or not here when they got back, it would. They'd think I always slept or went out when they weren't here. Hell, I've waited long enough. I'm taking a walk and will live with the consequences if they find out.

Going down the stairs, I see them. "Where you been?"

"And where you going?" he says.

"I waited so long I decided to take a walk. Waiting tired

me out and I need some exercise like walking to undo that."

"Now you don't have to wait any longer and you'll get plenty of exercise working, so come on back up. We still got lots to do, which you could've started doing before us."

"Like what? I finished what you told me to do and checked it to make sure it was right. And you didn't leave instructions for anything else to do because you said you'd be back before I was through."

"You could've cleaned up the place."

"Cleaning's not what I was hired for. I left that sort of unskilled stuff for better pay and more demanding work like what you hired me to do."

"But that's how you could've spent your time. You should've thought of that. Anything can be cleaned. Ten minutes after you clean something it can be cleaned. Soap can even be cleaned. And cleaning or anything like that would've been more productive than getting bored and irritable waiting for us or going out for a walk."

"It might've been more productive for you but for my mind it would've been very unproductive. It would've been going backward from something I worked myself up to be, which might've ended up with my being even less productive than before for you."

"Come on, you're wasting our time talking. Let's get to work."

"I'm still so restless from waiting that I've got to take a walk."

"Walking's not what I'm paying you for except when you're doing it for me. You want to keep your job, you come upstairs now and work."

I think it over and go upstairs. They've already started working and I pitch in. Later he tells me what else I should do. Later she does too, tells me, and I do it. At times we're working on the same thing together. Other times we're working on separate things or the same thing but in different parts of the room. Sometimes two of us are working on the same thing and one on another thing. Other times one of us is in the restroom or on the phone or making coffee for us all and two are working on the same thing or separate things in the same or different parts of the room, and so on. Then it's all done. I even worked an hour longer than I'm being paid for and there's more to come. We put what we worked on into boxes, wrap and address the boxes and bring them to the post office and ship them off.

"That didn't take too long," he says.

"Long enough."

"About as long as I expected it to," she says.

"But we did it much quicker than I thought we would is what I'm saying," he says.

"It might not have been quicker but would've been sooner if both of you had come back earlier."

"Anyway, we got it done, and we'll see you tomorrow," she says.

"About tomorrow," I say to him, "if you're both not there or don't plan to be by the time I get to work, could you leave instructions for me if you're going back now or just give them to me or phone or send them in early tomorrow so I can get right to work rather than waiting for you?"

"If we're late and I haven't left instructions or sent or phoned them in or she hasn't phoned them to you for me, then just clean the floor a little, wash the windows. They're all dirty and the floor especially. Tidy up the place is what I'm suggesting, scrub down the restroom and all its parts. If we're really late and neither of us phone and I don't send in your instructions and you've cleaned the entire place to where it really shines, give a little paint job to the ceiling and walls. The paint, brushes, and turpentine are in the closet. One coat. If we're really very late and no instructions were left or got to you in any of those other ways and the paint's dried, give it two coats, but no more than two."

"I don't see how I could do more than two coats in one workday. You said turpentine, which means the paint has an oil base. Oil paint takes a long time to dry. I don't even think I can put on a second coat in the time I'm scheduled to work tomorrow if you have me do all those cleaning chores besides."

"So put in a couple hours extra."

"For money?"

"Do it because you like the job. Show me that. And that you want to keep it. Because you too often complain. You ever hear her complain?"

"I've complained," she says. "Plenty of times."

"About me you've complained. That I'm not nice enough to you after work. That I don't take you out enough, show you enough attention and make nice enough talk and give you enough good things. About those you complain a lot, almost all the time, but I'm talking about at work."

"About work you're right. I have no complaints. Pay's good and hours aren't too long and work's not too hard."

"So if neither of us is here tomorrow when you get in and we don't phone or I don't leave instructions or send them to you, clean up the room, scrub everything down, don't just sweep the floor but mop and wax it. And the windows and every shelf—really get this place into top-notch shape. Two coats of paint. And if you later have nothing better to do, put in a few extra hours painting the doors and windows and all the furniture and shelves."

"I'll have to get overtime pay for that."

"I don't pay overtime."

"Then I can't give you any more free overtime. I did it today and almost every day for months when you promised you wouldn't keep me beyond my normal workday, but no more."

"You only worked nine hours today."

184 • Stephen Dixon

"But I was here for thirteen and a half—that half for lunch and four of those hours waiting for you."

"You rest at home; you rest here. No big difference and for all I know, the office might be a nicer place to rest in than your home, and even more so after you clean and paint it."

"But it isn't my home. No overtime pay, no more extra work."

"Then I'll have to let you go," and he asks for my keys to the office, I give them, she waves good-bye, and they go toward the park and I head the other way. I turn around when they're a block away and about to enter the park and yell, "You bastard." Neither of them turn around. People walking past do. They look at me and seem to wonder what I'm yelling about and to whom.

"That bastard," I say to people who pass. "That one over there. The man. Well, now he's gone into the park or got in a cab or run one way or the other along the street, for he's not where he was or anywhere near there when I yelled at him. But he is a bastard. A slave driver. Wants me to work overtime almost every day for nothing. I wouldn't. Why should I? Man's got to get paid for his work. That slave driver. I hate him. Bastard," I yell toward the park. "Get another sucker to work any number of hours overtime for nothing, but not me again."

"These days you're lucky just to have a job," a woman says. "He fired you?"

"Just now. For not working overtime for free."

"I know. You said. Can you give me his name and phone? I might like to apply for the job now that it's open."

"You wouldn't like it."

"Why? I like steady work and money. Right now I'm jobless and broke. Let me speak to him and decide, unless you're planning to get your job back."

"Not a chance."

I give her his name and phone number. She says, "This is the best hope for a job I've had in weeks. Because if you just lost it then I'll probably be the first one to apply for it." She goes into a phone booth.

"You calling him now? Because I'm sure he won't be there till tomorrow. I just left him."

"What do I have to lose? He's not in, I've lost a dime. Big deal—I'm not that broke."

"Nobody will be in, so you won't lose your dime."

"Good, then I'm losing nothing by calling him."

"Time. You'll be losing some time."

"What else do I have to lose now?"

"Also your common sense. You'll be losing some of that too, because I just said he definitely won't be in and yet you still want to call him. You'd think you'd take my advice because you'd think I'd know."

"You lost your job, so who are you to talk that you know anything? If you still had the job, then I'd say they're keeping you because you know something."

"No, that common-sense loss gives you away. I don't think he'll hire you. Or maybe he will. Maybe you're just the person he needs."

"If you're saying all this to stop me from phoning or my applying for the job or even just to insult me, it didn't work."

She dials and I go home. By the next day I've thought about it a lot and call him and keep calling him till I get him in at eleven and say, "Look, I apologize. And if you give me the job back and still want me to, I'll work a couple hours overtime for nothing today and with no complaints."

"I already hired someone you told about the job but who said she wasn't using you as a reference because you insulted her when she started to call me."

"All I told her was that she wasn't showing common sense in trying to call you minutes after you fired me when I knew you wouldn't be back at the office till today."

"I did go back a few minutes after I left you. I forgot something and she got me when I was coming in the door. She said she heard you got fired and that she's exactly the opposite of you and is willing to work overtime for no pay every day this week."

"But I know how to do the job. And I'm willing to work as many free hours overtime as she is and all weekend if necessary and the following week, too. And me you won't have to teach how to do the job. Think of all the time you'll be saving—the jobholder's when he doesn't have to be learning what he already knows and yours when you don't have to teach him."

"What time? A few minutes? Half hour at the most? For what's so complicated about your job? I'll miss a lunch, that's all, and what do I do at lunch anyway but sit around and get fat and maybe take a nap."

"You sonofabitch."

"You know, that's the second time you cursed me in less than a day. You called me a bastard yesterday. I didn't answer or turn around so I don't know if you knew I heard. I know it wasn't meant for your former coworker as you've no reason for calling her one. And today a son of a bitch. How do you expect to be rehired cursing me like that?"

"You weren't going to rehire me."

"You don't know that for sure, and I won't tell you. I'll make you sweat, except to say I told that new woman to call me at noon today to confirm if I still wanted her to come in at one."

"You're just trying to make me feel as if I really lost something in not working for you, and I'm telling you that I didn't lose anything because there are always just as good jobs around and for you to go to hell."

"Three times in less than a day. Now I'll tell you what was in my mind before you cursed me the second time, and still in my mind, but only by a little, before you told me to go to hell. I was going to rehire you."

"Bull."

"Nothing you say will make it any worse or better for you. So if you only want to stay on the line to hear what was in my mind before, I'll tell you, and every word the truth, which I can afford to do with you now. I was going to rehire you if you agreed to working overtime for no pay whenever I needed it, but which I wouldn't be so excessive at, if I have. I thought I'd maybe been a little unfair to us both in so quickly firing you, because as workers went you were okay and why should I expect anyone better or more reliable or less complaining in that kind of job for the pay it gets? If you agreed to my terms, then when she called at noon I was going to tell her I rehired you but would keep her in mind in case you didn't work out again. But when you called only a few minutes before I was going to call you, I thought I'd let you shoot off your mouth and agree to all my terms without my even asking them, which would give me an advantage for asking more things out of you in the future. Now with your curses you're not going to get any work reference from me but the worst." He hangs up.

I start looking for work in the type of job I just had. All the interviewers ask for the name and phone number of my last boss. I give them. They call and later say he said such bad things about me that there's no chance they can give or recommend me for any sort of work. So I tell the next interviewers I see that I left my last job six months ago—though not because I got a better one, which was what I told the last interviewers—but because I felt I could do much better and make more money and also wanted to take a vacation for six months after working steadily for fifteen years before I looked for work again, and I give the name and phone number of the boss I had before the last one. It seems what she says about me isn't as bad as what the boss who just fired me said, but still isn't good enough to get the job I think I'm qualified for. "Maybe several months ago," one of the interviewers says, "you would've got the job we have with the kind of weak work references your last boss gave, but not with the way the job market is today."

So I go even further back to the job before the one I left six months ago, where I know the boss thought I was a good enough worker for the one after him to hire me. But because they think I've now been out of work for two years and his reference or memory isn't that great, whatever he tells the interviewers isn't enough to get me a job.

Finally I just tell the next interviewers that I haven't worked for seven years. When they ask why, I say I've been living off a series of women all that time or traveling around the world on my savings or an inheritance or have been on a bender for more than six years, but I'm okay now, have decided that living off women is unethical and traveling for so long doesn't get you anywhere but broke and I haven't had a drink for a year and am willing to work hard for little money in whatever kind of work they want to give me.

I land a really rotten job with about ten hours more work a week than the last one and for half the pay. My new boss wants me to work overtime for nothing, and I say I will and don't complain about it and after a year of this work and more free overtime than I did in any job I had over the last twenty years, I get a small raise. It takes me a few more years before I'm making as much, for almost twice as many hours, as I did in the job I was last fired from. Of course, the cost of living has gone way up since then, so in what I can buy for my wages, I'm actually making a lot less than I did several years ago. But like the woman who replaced me then might still say, I feel lucky to have a job.

THERESA

•

David Kranes

Aₙgₑₗₒ ₕₐₛ ₘₑₑₙ...

ANGELO HAS BEEN STARING at Theresa for two months now in Mr. Sykes's fourth-period history. He can't help himself, though it makes him feel weird. She sits two rows away, just a little in front, and so it's easy to stare. Sometimes she feels him staring and turns so that he has to look away. He can feel the blood rushing to the back of his neck when that happens, and he tells himself he's going to stop staring because he doesn't want to get caught. But he can't help it; he stares again. Something about Theresa—something about the way she looks and about the way she sits there—makes him do it.

Mr. Sykes could care less. He's a typical teacher; he's out of it. He flips maps and makes lists of names on the board. He draws lines with chalk between the different names. And then he calls on people. Whenever he calls on Theresa, she always waits about a minute and it looks like she's going to cry. Then she answers his question, and it's always right, and Mr. Sykes always says, "Very good, Theresa," and goes on. Any time he calls on Angelo, Angelo wants to hit him. Instead Angelo says, "I left my book in my locker," to which Mr. Sykes always says something like: "Angelo—you weren't listening. I was asking you your name." And the class laughs. Most of the time, Mr. Sykes is harmless—but when he makes smart-ass comments, Angelo thinks he's a dickhead.

Angelo feels, sometimes, like two people. It's because he's big—fourteen, six-foot-three, two hundred and eighteen pounds. It feels like he's supposed to be two people and not just one fourteen-year-old kid. Most of the time, during the days in school, he doesn't know what to do with himself— how to sit, how to fit who he feels he is into his own body. People make jokes. The coach begs him to go out for football. He wants to hide. He wants to go off someplace and split the two people who he feels he is apart, trash the dumb one, bring the better one back: surprise everybody.

Still, he can't keep himself from staring at Theresa. And it just gets worse.

Theresa doesn't seem to have any friends. It's not that she has enemies; what it is is Angelo never sees her with *any*body—either in a fight or hanging out. She's there first period in the morning; she leaves right after the last bell; there's never anybody with her. It occurs to Angelo that that's one of the things that makes him stare. A couple of times, he's tried saying hi to her: "Hi" or "Hey." Each time, Theresa lowers her head and says, "Hello."

Theresa's Mexican. Angelo guesses that; he's Italian. His father calls him *Angelo Mangelo* because he eats so much and guzzles beer. "He's a growing boy," his father says. Then laughs. Theresa's hair is very black, very shiny, and very long. Sometimes she has a flower in it; sometimes she has a comb. Most times it's just her hair, plain. Angelo thinks what it would be like to hold her hair in his hand. But then he

feels weird thinking that; he feels embarrassed. Theresa looks
like he could hurt her without doing much. But she looks
strong, too. So it's confusing. Angelo wonders if, like him,
she has brothers.

Thursday, he decides to follow her after school to see
where she lives. It's early November. The sun's pretty bright;
still it's cool; there's a chill. Angelo wears a Raiders' jacket
that was his brother, Roberto's. And an Oly cap. Theresa
has a coat that looks like a blanket: it's made out of the same
stuff and hangs that way. She wears it over the gray sweatshirt and Levi's she always wears. Angelo stays about a half
block behind.

First Theresa walks north, then she walks east. Sometimes she seems in a hurry; other times she slows down.
Angelo lives in just the opposite direction, and he wonders
how far he's going to have to walk to get home. A dog runs
out of a yard and up to Theresa. Angelo thinks, This is it!
THIS is where she lives! She sinks down, sets her books on
the sidewalk, and pets the dog. The dog is small and has
ratty hair. Angelo thinks he must stink. But Theresa's kneeling on the sidewalk, playing with him, until a woman opens
the door of the house and calls the dog, and the dog runs in.
Theresa scoops her books up, stands, brushes her knees off,
and starts walking again.

Angelo's crouching behind a Dodge pickup, watching.
Suddenly Theresa stops and turns back, looking, and it's like
history class. Angelo sees her big eyes. He sees her lips, full
and red even though she never wears lipstick. Except Theresa doesn't see him. She couldn't. He's out of sight; the
pickup hides him, and he's glad he didn't start out after her
right away. Now he lets there be a whole block between them.

Theresa walks east again. She crosses Fourth West and
then Third and then Second. At Second, she heads north
again. She goes into a Circle K. Just her going in makes
Angelo hungry. It makes him feel like a pull tab in an empty

drink can—a small thing rattling in a thing that's big. He fishes in his pocket. He's got a dollar and a half. He'd like some nachos or something. He'd like a beer. He drinks too much beer now. He knows. He's only fourteen. But he's started, and it's one of the few things that fills him, and he likes the taste. And it doesn't make him drunk either. Not like the assholes he sees at Thompson's Billiards. He doesn't walk weird or argue; he just gets mellow and then tired and then sort of half-thirsty, half-hungry again. His mouth gets dry. Right now—with Theresa inside the Circle K—it feels very, *very* dry. Like cotton. And he could kill for a beer.

But then Theresa comes out. She isn't carrying anything—just her books. She walks north. She crosses Twenty-third South, then Twenty-second. Angelo sees two guys wearing blue-and-brown jackets walking toward her from the opposite direction. They look maybe sixteen, tops, and have shit-eating grins on their faces. And Angelo can see the scenario, just exactly what's coming down. And it does. The two guys—even though, actually, they're pretty small—make themselves wide but leave no space between them, either. Theresa can't get around and she can't get through. The guys are laughing. One guy's face looks like cottage cheese; the other guy has greasy, long red hair.

Theresa just stands still and waits; she hugs her books, puts her head down. The guys' hands are on her ass and in her hair. There's an old, half-rotted piece of two-by-four in the empty lot beside where Angelo stands. It's worthless, worthless lumber, but—with both his hands on it and resting on his shoulder—it looks mean, and Angelo hefts it like a huge baseball bat and starts in toward Theresa and the two guys. He hears one guy say, "Oh, no—shit!" then sees them both seeing him. The other guy says, "Jesus—fucking monster!" They let Theresa go, turn and run. Angelo ducks behind a Dumpster. The word "monster" beats like an oil drum in his head. Who put him in this body, anyway?! He hates it.

He peeks out. Theresa's looking—one at a time—in each of the four directions. She seems confused. She seems sad. She seems relieved. She stands looking, again and again, for a very long time. Angelo sees her put her books down. He sees her reach into the pocket of her coat and take something out. He sees a blade flip out of the something that's in her hand, and the knife frightens him; it scares him. It's big. It's not that Angelo's afraid of knives; it's not that he's not seen a *lot* of them. It's just that he can't imagine Theresa with one in her hand. It changes her. It makes her into a different person. He feels pissed in a way. He doesn't want to have followed a girl who would have a knife. Theresa folds the blade over and puts the knife back into her pocket.

She wouldn't ever have cut the guys, Angelo thinks. She wouldn't ever have really. She just carries a knife like that to make herself safe, to *feel* safe. Angelo understands.

Theresa pulls something from her other pocket. It's a plastic Smith's Food King sack. She puts her books into it. Angelo can't see exactly, but he can see she's done something to the handles of the sack to make them bigger and so she can slip them over her shoulders, sort of like a backpack. And she does that—so that the books are riding just below her shoulders and her hands are free. She checks the block ahead. Then looks back. She begins to walk—but slower now, cautiously.

Angelo keeps the piece of two-by-four with him and starts off after her. He stays close to anything he might duck behind. He doesn't want Theresa seeing him. It would be worse than her catching him in Sykes's history class; it would be all over then; it would be the end. She would have caught him being interested. He wouldn't be able to explain his way out of it. It would be wicked. It would be brutal. Angelo imagines a conversation:

"Why are you following me?"
"Who says I am?"
"You don't live anywhere near here."
"Yeah? Well, maybe I do."
"So—what? You're after my bones? What is this?"
"I'm just walking."
"Touch my hair."

That stops him—his imagination imagining her saying, "Touch my hair." He can't make the conversation go beyond that. The back of his neck gets all funny and like pins. His breath feels like he's breathing through wet rags. Angelo wants a beer. He wants a beer pretty bad. He wants to fill up the spaces between himself and the rest of his body.

Theresa crosses block after block. She picks her pace up, moves fast. Angelo's about four miles from his own house now. He's going to have to take the bus back; he can see that. She crosses Ninth, Eighth, cuts through the parking lot at Sears, keeps walking. Pretty soon she's by the viaduct at Fourth. She crosses and moves under it. She's almost running now, her walk's that fast. She moves to a car without wheels. Actually, it's the cab of a truck without the truck *or* wheels—just the cab. She opens the door, slips the Smith's bag from her shoulders, leans in, puts the bag and the books inside, seems to be arranging them. Angelo is looking on. He's looking on uncertainly from the corner.

Then Theresa backs out of the cab and shuts the door and starts walking again. Again north. When she gets to the Third South block, she shifts directions. Now, Angelo's really thirsty. He thinks he's got to find a 7-Eleven or something and slip a beer into his Raiders jacket. Then he sees Theresa getting into a line. It's a line of people waiting on the sidewalk, and Angelo knows what the line is. He's seen it; he's heard about it; he and his friends have passed and made jokes on their way to concerts at the Salt Palace. It's the

Kitchen. It's the food line. It's for any of the people who don't have other places and are on the street.

Angelo's having trouble now. He's having trouble swallowing. He's afraid he'll cry. He doesn't want Theresa to be standing in that line. It pisses him off. He doesn't want her to know the people who she seems to know and be talking with. His family doesn't have a lot; they're Westside just like his friends. But they have a house; they have food. Between Angelo's father and his four brothers, they have three cars. They have a refrigerator full of beer. Suddenly Angelo can't help himself; he's crying. He turns back; he turns away; he turns into a building. He's thinking, *Fuck!;* he's thinking, *Fuckfuck!;* he's thinking, *Jesus, Theresa!*

He walks the block and a half back to where the viaduct and Theresa's truck cab are. He walks near. He wants to see how she has it inside, how she has it arranged. If she has a pillow for when she sleeps, at least. And a blanket. And where does she keep her clothes? He thinks. It seems she wears pretty much the same stuff all the time—gray sweatshirt, torn Levi's. Sometimes there's a flower in her hair. Sometimes a comb.

Angelo feels very, very weird. He feels cut in half. He feels small. He feels he'll maybe never drink beer again. He feels he may be in love with Theresa. He feels angry because he doesn't know what to do with what he feels. It makes him dizzy. It makes him weak. It makes him crazy yet, at the same time, glad. He wants to just go home. But he wants to (crazy as it seems) sleep—spend the night—with Theresa in her cab, too. He walks up to it.

As he approaches, a torn brown bag blows by him on the stippled avenue. He catches it with his Nike, bends, lifts it. He stares at it—blank—not knowing why he's done what he's done. And then it occurs—he wants to leave Theresa a note. He wants to say something. Not a thing that's dumb or stupid but something real. Something true. Something worth having followed her all this way for.

But he doesn't have a pencil or a pen. He never carries one. If he carried one, then maybe he'd feel he had to write down the stuff that Sykes said. Still, maybe Theresa has one. She's a good student. She does her work. He moves up to the edge of the cab and puts his hand on the door handle.

"So—What do you think you're doing?" a voice asks.

Angelo turns around. There are two men. They both look at least as old as his father. One's black; the other's white.

"So—what did you think you were going to do with that truck cab, Babyfat?" the same voice asks. It's the black man's.

"I . . ." Angelo can't talk. It feels like history class. Only worse.

"This is not your property," the white man says.

"I know . . . but I know Theresa," Angelo tries.

The two men stare. They're not sure. They just wait. And Angelo knows what their waiting, what their look is. It says: Okay . . . okay, Babyfat—prove it.

"I'm a . . . I'm a . . . I'm a . . . ." Angelo can't finish his sentence.

"ImaImaIma!" the black man mocks.

"I'm a friend of hers," Angelo says. "I'm a friend of Theresa's." He feels angry.

"She's not here," the white man says.

"I know. I was going to leave her a note."

"Okay, then leave her a note."

"And we'll make sure that's all you leave, too."

"Or take," the black man says.

"We look after each other here," the white man says.

"So go ahead," the black man says. "Go ahead. Leave your note. Do it."

Angelo swallows. Hard. He touches the handle of the cab, opens the door. He can see Theresa has a little pencil box on the shelf by the windshield. It has ballpoint pens, pencils, erasers. He takes a pen and can feel the men's eyes behind him. He backs out, sets the brown paper on the roof, holds the pen between his fingers, thinks a minute, writes: "Theresa: I followed you. I need a friend. Do you? I drink too much." He signs it "Angelo (who keeps looking at you in history)" and sets it on the seat by her books. He sees a flashlight, the one she must study by.

He sets the pen back and closes the door. He stares at the men. They don't move. They just watch. Neither one could be Theresa's father. Neither looks at all like her.

"Okay," the black man says, "okay, you've left your note."

"Move on," the white man says.

So Angelo nods and does. And he can feel their eyes. He can feel their attention—weird. Weird—someone looking, someone watching your back, watching your moves, as if they mattered. It makes Angelo nervous. It makes him tense. Still, it makes him wonder, too, wonder if he might ever fit into the size of himself in another way, do something—move in some way—that would make a difference.

MARKET DAY

•

W. D. Wetherell

HOLD ME, SHE TELLS him because it's like a little motor when he does. Out from the car they go, out across the hot, boggy macadam, out past the abandoned shopping carts that on lucky days have food caught in the mesh, yogurt drip, mashed-up pastries, the red ooze of jam—out past the surveillance cameras angled down from the lampposts to make sure no one takes one and runs. She's tempted anyhow, tempted just to look, and it's only the continued pressure of Cameron on her wrist that makes her keep on. There in the closest, most convenient spaces are the cars of the prime shoppers, a year newer than hers but noticeably shinier, with larger, more commodious trunks. By detouring through them, by making your face superior and hard, you can make it seem like you have just emerged from one and coax the cameras onto someone else. But Cameron won't have any of this trick, either, and he pulls her straight across the lane to the spot where, intercepting the sunlight, the store's shadow bends it crooked into bars.

How big does something have to be before it exerts gravity? She wonders about this every time she comes. All across the parking lot she felt herself struggling up a mountain too steep for her hollowness to accomplish, but close by the windows—the immaculate black windows through which nothing can be seen—she feels sucked in and captured by the store's rectangular extent.

Don't leave me even for a second, she tells Cameron, kneeling down to arrange his hair. You stick beside me and help me push the cart. You help Mommy push the cart; I'll get a treat for you. Mommy's weak and can't push the cart by herself and needs a strong little boy to push it for her. You stay near me; I'll get a treat for you when we check out—maybe a candy this time only don't leave me, not even once. You leave me, you're going to get spanked. You hear me, my Cameron my munchkin, my little tiger boy, my little man?

He nods, but it's only to fool her, and the moment she stands up again he's away from her, racing madly for the entrance. Cameron! she wants to shout, but checks herself just in time. There by the glass, joking easily with the big-breasted woman who collects the carts, is the doorman, tall and frilly in his high hat and gold braid. Thanks to the care she'd taken in dressing Cameron, the doorman hardly glances up—the boy shoots past him through the sliding doors inside.

Her turn next. She leans toward the black windows for what reflection they offer, fluffing back her hair until it looks bouncy and fresh. It's blond now—the checkers are said to favor blonds. Below it she can see the flash of the necklace she'd put on, and below the necklace the top of the white jersey she wore to show off her tan, and below the jersey's straps the spindly, hateful lines of her ribs. When she was younger, she had gone around sucking her breath in to make herself slender, but now she wants to do just the opposite— to draw in as much air as she can and puff it down her chest so she won't look so emaciated and worn.

She squints again toward the black, indulges herself in a last moment of despair, then with a graceful, girlish movement, pirouettes around and makes right for the doorman at the entrance.

He's left off chatting with the shopping-cart woman— instead, he's fanning a newspaper toward a pair of checkers who lounge with their backs against the glass, taking their breaks in the sun. One of them is slight and professorial, hardly like a checker at all. The other is more in the mold. Stout, fleshy, his smock open on his chest like a prizefighter's robe, he leans his head back with an oddly feline smile, as if he's doing the sun a favor in permitting it to caress him.

She makes a mistake here, small but inexcusable: she crosses in front of him so his sun is interrupted. Opening his eyes, seeing her, he leers with a lazy stretching and wets his lips—they're so puffed and carmine they seem rouged. She knows what she's supposed to do—answer his leer with a flirty pout—but there's something stubborn in her that refuses, and she walks past him without changing her expression at all.

Oh, ma'am? Excuse me there . . . ma'am?

The doorman leans backward and takes her arm. Coming so close to the door it almost shatters her, and she has to bite down on her tongue not to sob.

Yes? she manages.

He's smiling, pointing. It's only that you forgot to take a cart.

Oh, yes, thank you very much, she says. That's very kind of you, and a moment later she has it in front of her and the wheels are breaking the laser beam and the doors are opening like the entrance to a magic cave. There's a rush of air against her legs that in her weakness passes for exhilaration, and the cold shiver of it sends her safely through.

Not quite believing her luck, she glances back out the window, half expecting to see her shadow being tugged off by the doorman. There *is* a woman there, a slender woman not much older than herself, but dressed with less care, her hair duller and grayer, her chest more shrunken, her arms burdened with twins. The doorman is pushing her back toward the parking lot with his arms wide about the three of them, doing it so smoothly it seems he's dancing them back rather than pushing, until all four of them disappear in the purple immensity of the pavement, and there's no trace of any disturbance at all.

I'm in, she says to herself. I'm in and she's out, and superiority gives her another rush as intoxicating as the first one, and for a moment she has the illusion the entire supermarket is hers.

It doesn't last. The entrance is up high so the entire store is briefly visible, and looking at it all at once tips her exhilaration over toward vertigo. It's ridiculous in its way. The shelves, endless as they stretch, take up only a fraction of the store's space, and the rest seems designed merely to humiliate her, convince her she shouldn't even begin. There's music, soft and narcotic. Over everything, metallic and sugary, hangs an aerosol of fresh-baked bread.

At least she can't see the registers from that distance, not exactly. There's a chirping noise from that end of the store, a chewing more than a chirping, and above it—reflecting off the silver foil that drapes from the ceiling in a graceful balloon—are the lights of the checkout. Aisle Number One. Aisle Number Two. Aisle Number Three. This time of morning all thirty numbers are lit, all except one toward the right, Aisle Number Seven, where the light, flickering softly, seems to be saving its voltage for a later flash.

But she can't worry about that now—one careful step at

a time. From the entrance, the ramp plunges down to the produce section, launching her toward the shelves much faster than she wants to go. There in the first bin is a huge display of broccoli, open in the old way, the green coated with a spray that makes it glitter. Though she hates broccoli, there's a crazy moment when she's tempted to reach in and break off a stalk, wedge the umbrella shape of it down her throat so the florets would widen her, fill her up.

She doesn't. Instead, she pushes the cart behind the bin where its shadow hides her from the camera mounted on the wall. Opening her pocketbook, she pulls out an envelope and quickly counts what's inside. A hundred, a hundred and fifty, two hundred . . . The bills are all fifties, new and crisp. The clerks were impressed with clean money, and she's heard stories about them refusing to accept any bills that were soiled.

Three hundred dollars. She puts the bills back in the envelope, rummages in the bottom of the pocketbook for her calculator, presses the button that clears the figures from last time, presses it again, then, letting her breath out to release the tension, proceeds past the broccoli toward the potatoes. By keeping her hand around the calculator—by keeping her hand deep inside her pocketbook—she can punch in the prices without being observed.

The potatoes are green and puffy looking, injected with air—she walks past them without stopping. Peaches come next, but peaches are for prime shoppers—she walks past them without stopping. This deep in the store it becomes apparent the displays are different than they were last time, the bins smaller, the fruit and vegetables set up on little cardboard mounts as if they are samples, not to be purchased at all. The tomatoes, for instance. They're set in cases behind magnifying glass that swells them to twice their normal size. Beside them, a spotlight shines down on the lemons, exaggerating their yellow; behind the lemons, a black light shades the zucchini, making them look rigid and hard. There by the melons is paper to wrap them in, but it's not tissue anymore, but expensive-looking giftwrap she doesn't dare touch.

Beside the broccoli, only the apple bins are full, and this is where she finally stops. Cameron likes apples, so she reaches over, takes one off the top, squeezes it to force out the air, then lays it carefully down against the wire mesh of the cart. Once there it looks much smaller, and yet when she thinks of the price it makes the cart seem incredibly heavy, and she has to struggle to start it rolling.

She longs for Cameron to help, but there's no sign of him. It's hard to say what he will do on his own. Sometimes he goes to the lobster tank and makes faces at them or plays with the boxes the stackers left in the aisles, but other times he goes into a kind of fit where he tears wrappers off things and begins shoving food in his mouth. He had choked once on wrapping—she'd had to reach down his throat to pull it out.

No security guards had come that time—there was a gang of shoplifters in another part of the store. The guards are surprisingly indulgent toward children in any case, even ones who lose control of themselves and eat. There are stories about kids getting lost in the immensity of the store—how the guards find them and rather then restore them to their parents, give them to the bakery women or the butchers to be brought up as apprentices. She herself doesn't believe these stories, but the possibility, set against the heaviness of the cart, is dreamy and oddly soothing.

There are so many worries, so many things that can trip you up. Bananas, she had always been able to buy one, but now they've done something to the price and when she clicks it into the calculator—when she finally figures out the bars and digits of the incomprehensible code—the figure is monstrous. The same is true of the green beans. She picks out a dozen, making sure they're thin ones, but when she puts them on the scale the numbers keep flashing for minutes before they stop.

An apple, a banana, a dozen beans. They look lonely by themselves, so she goes over to the display of raisins and takes the largest box. Beside the raisins is a package of figs with Arabic lettering across the side—the wrapping is transparent, so she can see the fruit nestled against a prong with a clever gnarled end. She loves figs, though it's been ages since she'd eaten one. When she was small her mother would buy her figs as a treat for helping her shop, and she remembers the delicate creaminess, the surprising sweetness as the rind gave way beneath her teeth. How many years ago had that been? Twenty? Thirty? She would love to try a fig again, let Cameron share one, but the temptation frightens her and she moves quickly on.

There's a commotion up ahead—a group of produce men huddled over a head of lettuce, arranging it on its bed of excelsior as carefully as a diamond. They poke and prod, step back for appraisal, scratch their foreheads, lean forward, and tilt it again. Their suits, cut tight to show off their figures, bulge over their shoulders like the plastic of balloons. They aren't as huge as the checkers, but still have enough fat for prestige, and are always finding excuses to unbutton their jackets to let the mass of it unroll.

She hurries around them, trying not to stare, and then she's past the strawberries and pears and the other luxury fruits out of the produce section coming into the chocolates, then the wines. The floor slants uphill here, forcing her to linger, but it's a good idea pretending to look in any case—there are more cameras here than anywhere else in the store. She stops, leans down to stare at one of the bottles, makes a face she hopes is disdainful, then moves on again, as if the wine's not good enough for her and she's searching for a finer brand.

The bakery is next. It runs along the rear of the store, separated from the rest by a high glass partition. None of the baked goods can actually be touched—you have to tap on the window and hope one of the bakery women deigns to notice you. They're even plumper than the produce men, aproned in chiffon, and spend their time lounging about on divanlike benches, gossiping and primping and passing each other fresh trays of buns. Supposedly they have all been recruited through Aisle Number Seven, installed in the bakery so the clerks can have them close at hand. She finds this easy to believe; there's a sated, sleepy look to these women, a sensuous kind of negligence that makes it easy for them to continue munching while she taps.

One of them finally stirs herself long enough to wedge a loaf of bread through the slot. It's hard and crusty and the woman shoves it so fast the end breaks off, but she takes it anyway, presses the price into her calculator, then pushes the cart along the glass, staring enviously down at the jelly rolls and muffins magnified by the window's reflection.

Cans are next. She takes her usual—tuna imitation, macaroni paste, small tins of ravioli—then walks past the frozen foods in their padlocked freezers to the cereal section, the bewildering assortment of them with their flashy colors and contradictory labels. Big boxes sometimes hold less than small boxes, small boxes are sometimes more expensive than big boxes, the weight sometimes comes from prizes, the cheapest are less filling so it makes sense to buy premium except premium is air-filled so they aren't as filling as they seem.

It exhausts her—the constant figuring, the tentative reaching, the need to keep a smile on her face at all times, as if shopping is a recreation for her, a relaxed, inconsequential interval in her morning. There is two-thirds of the store left to go and she's sure now she can't make it. It's not just weakness, but the feeling she's crossing a tightrope over a chasm filled with cash registers—that there are checkers waiting to total up every move she makes, not only in the store, but everywhere in life. She closes her eyes trying to banish the illusion, but it only increases, so she even hears the beeping sound as the keys press down. If only I could have a bite of something, she decides. A snack, a quick rush of sugar. If only Cameron would appear and help me push the cart.

There are more prime shoppers in this part of the store. They push their carts with lazy extensions of their fingertips, as if they aren't pushing at all but merely following carts that are self-propelled, making packages drop into them with the briefest of affirmative nods. They're all fashionably fat, the women wearing halter tops that show off their fleshy rolls, the men in tight suits that imitate the produce men's, but without the same panache. As stuffed and stretched as they are, it seems to her she can see the outline of what they have last eaten. A long cruller down one man's leg; square lumps of candy down another woman's spine.

At first she envies them for their casual, easy progression, their reserves of flesh, the way food seems to drop of its own accord into their carts, then not a second later she's furious at them for exactly these things, mad with injustice, ready to ram her cart into theirs with all her force. How dare they be so casual. How dare they! But even to think this tires her and she ends up feeling what she always feels: a cringing kind of respect that makes her push her cart to the side of the aisle so she won't disturb them, get in their way.

She moves past the soda display, hesitates, puts three of the blackest, most syrupy-looking bottles in the cart. Past the soda are the crackers and she takes some of these, too, pressing the price into the calculator with quick nervous tappings. Past the crackers are the cookies, and past the cookies is the freezer with the poultry and meat, but rather than make for it directly, she stops in the shadow of a cookware display, opens her purse, puts on some fresh lipstick, and pats back her hair.

Careful now, she tells herself. Slow and lazy and nonchalant.

One of the older butchers comes out to serve her. Instead of the suits the others wear, he has on an old-fashioned apron caked with blood—it makes her feel absurdly grateful to him even before he speaks. He's fat like the others, but in a portly kind of way, and his puffy gray cheeks look kindly and soft.

Good day to you ma'am, he says pleasantly. And what will it be this morning, ma'am?

What's your best cut of steak today, butcher?

London broil is certainly nice today. We have some fine porterhouse if that's what you prefer.

Porterhouse? . . . No I don't think so. And your lamb?

Lamb is fresh. Some nice chops? Certainly. How many shall I cut you?

I'm so sick of lamb. Have you chicken?

Some fresh boneless breasts? Yes, ma'am, certainly. I can wrap some with your steak.

I enjoy breasts, but my son prefers wings. Just three wings please.

Wings? A chicken's wings? Excuse me, ma'am, we don't sell wings. What makes you think the store would sell wings?

Oh, well, breasts then. Whatever.

Why are you asking all these questions? You're just pretending aren't you? You're just wasting my time here. You're one of those people who likes to come to the store to window-shop and waste our time without any intention of buying. You get your kicks out of teasing don't you?

No, of course not. I asked for steak, didn't I? Yes one of your largest sirloins please.

He wraps it up and hands it to her politely enough, but when she turns and starts toward the dairy section, he's watching her and when she glances back again he's gone to the end of the counter and picked up a copper-colored phone.

Damn! She's furious at herself—it was madness to think she could outwit them. She turns the meat over looking for the price, then presses the numbers into the calculator, feeling the plastic jerk and spasm as it totals up the new amount. She can't put it back—the security guard summoned by the butcher would check for that first—so it's something else she'll have to do without, the crackers or the fruit.

There ahead of her is the dairy section. Usually she saves it for last, but she makes right for it now, slides open the ice-cream freezer, pretends to look, then with a motion so quick it's undetectable, pushes the raisin box down into the frosty cavern between the vanilla and black cherry. She does the same with the tuna imitation. She reaches into the cart, tucks it in close to her wrist like a magician, checks to make sure no one is watching, then slips it behind the sherbet containers where it will stay hidden until she's out of the store.

And it's funny, but while she does this she looks down the dairy section and sees a dozen other women doing exactly the same thing—pruning and ballasting in a last attempt to keep within budget. What's more, they look like her, too—look hard and shriveled and forced, as if what beauty they have left, what hope, is being dumped from their carts along with the food.

They all pretend not to see each other. There are informers and shoplifters and there is never any knowing who you can trust.

She finishes hiding what she can, but it isn't much, and before she reaches the end of the dairy section she makes impulsive grabs for cheese, eggs, and milk, so that her subtotal isn't any smaller than it was before she began. Two aisles left to go, she whispers, forcing herself to concentrate. Two aisles left to go!

She passes the potato chips and pretzels without taking any, goes by the canned juices with her eyes half-closed, and is just turning down the last aisle to the checkout—the last, longest, hardest aisle—when she catches a glimpse of denim-colored fabric scurrying behind a pyramid of salad croutons and dressing.

Cameron!

It's no use—her yell only accelerates his disappearance, and there's no hope of catching him without abandoning the cart. She thinks again of the rumor about how children are adopted and brought up in the store. Maybe it would be better in the end if something like that happened. At least there would be none of this reaching for him, this endless reaching and putting back. At least he wouldn't know the shame of seeing his mother have to sneak.

She's turning into the last aisle, trying to stop herself from worrying about him, when she notices a man step away from his shopping cart and start past the dog food in her direction. He's young and expensively dressed, with a brown Santa Claus belly and a crust on his chin that looks like paste for his missing whiskers. She had passed him near the ice cream, but he hadn't noticed her there. It was her yell, coming against the store's hush, that had attracted his attention.

Too late she remembers another rumor—that most of the store's security guards aren't in uniform at all, but go undercover disguised as shoppers. The man makes a half-hearted attempt to keep up the pretense, but it's obvious he's following her now, slowing when she does, stopping when she does, speeding up whenever she tries to outrace him.

She's gone too far on the tightrope to fall off now, even with the pressure of him pushing. There in front of her stretches the last, longest aisle, filled with delicacies and samples from the rest of the store, displayed in bins that aren't remote and unreachable, but open and generous and full. Truffles from the chocolate section, cheesecakes from the bakery, brownies with nuts on them, sardines in silver-blue tins, squabs stuffed with oysters, strawberries, salmon, and pâté. She knows women who make it safely around the entire store, taking only what is necessary, exercising enormous self-restraint, only to have something snap here, and they reach and grab shamelessly, filling their carts with all the temptations they have managed until now to resist.

She can understand their weakness; even now, halfway down it, smelling the aerosols, seeing the free samples, it's all she can do not to start grabbing herself, and not just put food in her cart, but tear the wrappers off and stuff the delicacies directly into her mouth. And it isn't just the taste or the nourishment that tempts her, but the possibility of stepping off the tightrope for a moment—of indulging herself in the sheer nostalgic pleasure of the fall.

She doesn't fall. She pushes the cart straight down the aisle, taking only the few small things Cameron likes best. She doesn't dare press the prices into the calculator—the guard follows her too close—and even if she could, there are no prices on anything in this aisle, no markings of any kind. Our New Pricing Policy reads the sign—it's up to the shoppers to guess on their own.

But she hardly cares anymore—it's as if care has been drained out a hole drilled in her spine. There near the ramp that leads down to the checkouts is a final small display—a rickety cardboard display that looks as if it has been thrown together in the last few minutes. Figs, whole boxes of them, the wrapping cellophane so the fruit lays revealed in its tapered, nestled perfection. They're luscious looking, dusted with sugar, and seeing them reminds her again of being a child when anything in the store was hers for the asking.

I've been so good, she tells herself. I've been so careful.

She takes the smallest box off the bottom, sniffs at it for

a moment, then adds it to the small mound of groceries already in the cart. Done, she whispers. She glances quickly at the lights above each counter, pushes the cart into Aisle Number Twelve and takes out her purse.

Ahead of her a prime shopper is just pocketing his change. She reaches for the wooden separator, puts it down on the mat, then starts taking out the milk, eggs, and bread. In between reaching, she glances back toward the shelves. The security guard, seeing her at the checkout, shrugs and goes off to follow someone else.

Good day to you, ma'am. Have you any coupons?

Asking for coupons is the oldest trick in the world. She shakes her head emphatically, as if she's outraged even to be asked. The checker smiles at her to show he means no harm. He's fat like they all are, the folds of it draped down from his stool like a woman's skirt. She's afraid to meet his eyes, but the skin below them looks varnished and smooth. With a dignified lazy stretching motion, he leans toward the register and starts pressing in the keys.

It's like the calculator, only on a bigger scale. There above the keys is a screen where the numbers appear as they click through, and there above the aisle is a larger screen where the numbers are visible for all to see. The digits themselves are green and they flash by with amazing speed as the checker works into his rhythm . . . $75, $85, $123, $147 . . . and then he's pressing a button and the meat is sliding toward him and all at once there's a two where the first one had been, and she feels her skin flush and bites her lip and prays to the decimal point to stop moving, and yet the numbers only flash faster and the apple and beans and banana are rolling toward his hand.

$285.00 . . . $285.78 . . . $286.00 . . . $286.56.

Thank you, ma'am. That will be two hundred and eighty-six dollars and fifty-six cents.

She feels a surge of energy so sudden it's like sugar has

been crammed down her throat, so that she wants to sob in victory and triumph. She takes out the bills, flourishing them at him to show how clean they are, but before he can take them there's a plastic crinkling noise, and there on the far end of the counter falling free of the separator that's hidden them are the figs.

Whoops, he says, pressing another key. Correction. That will be . . . Three hundred and thirty-three dollars on the nose.

He has his hand out, but she won't give up the bills; she turns through them frantically, counting and counting again.

Could you retotal please?

A retotal request? Certainly . . . Three hundred and thirty-three dollars on the nose.

There must be some mistake, she says.

Three hundred and thirty-three dollars on the nose, the checker says, pursing his lips as if he's pleased by the sibilance.

I tell you, there's a mistake!

A mistake claim?

No. No, but . . . I haven't gotten paid yet this week. I mean, someone must have taken it from my purse. I'm sure I had four hundred when I started. I could put the figs back, couldn't I? We've always paid our food bills before—always! I've been coming to this store for thirty years. I used to come here with my mother. I remember there was a gumball machine you put nickels in. There was a deli man who gave out free pieces of cheese. There was . . . I do have some coupons. Here, I'd forgotten but here they are.

There is no change in the checker's expression. Stretching as lazily as he had before, he reaches for a lever above the cash register. Instantly, though she hadn't seen it until now, a striped gate swings down across the aisle, barring her way.

At the same time, or maybe a second earlier, there's a liquid ringing noise from speakers at her feet.

This way please, ma'am.

Behind her is the young security guard who had followed her and a taller man with the funny round hat of a senior supervisor. They put their hands on her arms and pull her back with great gentleness.

My other purse—she begins.

There is just enough pressure in their grip that she can tell it's considered wrong to struggle. Part of her wants to anyway, but the other part—the tired hollow part—feels only a calm, anesthetized acceptance so that it hardly seems like it's her being dragged off at all.

They lead her past the other aisles. Aisle Number Eleven, Aisle Number Ten, pulling her so smoothly it's clear they've had long practice in this kind of synchronization. There are shoppers waiting on line at the other counters. Some of them turn to stare, but most keep their eyes on their carts pretending she and her escort don't exist.

When they stop it's at the one aisle whose light is off. The supervisor reaches forward and pushes a button. She looks up and isn't particularly surprised to see a large crimson seven flash on above her head. It's like the other counters, only there's a screen around it, a tentlike wall of plush, heavy fabric strung up on rods. The guard, with a little patting motion, pushes her past it, then disappears.

She stands alone beside the counter. It's wider than the other counters, with a softer-looking mat. There is no cash register. In its place is a wedge-shaped pillow and a large bottle of some kind of oil.

She waits a long time. There's the smell of onions and cinnamon—coming after all the artificial smells it makes her knees go weak with desire. At last there's a sliding noise and from the other side of the tent enters the checker she had seen lounging outside in the sunshine, the one with the car-mine lips and robelike smock. He nods toward her in con-firmation, then with a shrugging motion lets fall the smock from his shoulders so the buns and rolls of his skin shimmy down into place. He strokes himself for a moment, watching her. He holds up his fingers so she can see how fat they are, wets them with his lips until the knuckles glisten, then crooks them for her to come.

She pulls her blouse up on her own. Scrawny, he sneers, bringing his thumbs to her ribs, Scrawny. And then he digs them in.

THE KING OF

FLAPJACKS

●

Jim Humes

THE TROUBLE STARTED BACK in March, during the first week of real heat. I was on the tennis courts with a seventeen-year-old named Sarah Dilley. This was at Eisenhower High School. This was where I worked. During the day I taught juniors that Gregor Samsa was a black sheep, that specific examples make a good essay, and that there is a *rat* in *separate*. In the afternoons I coached the tennis team. The girls had the late practice that day, and everyone had left except Sarah and me. I'd told her to stay after practice to work on her passing shots. I said she'd win more matches if she could hit her backhand down the line. We were the only two people on the courts when she pulled up lame running for a wide ball.

Her body made wet angels on the court as she rolled back and forth, holding onto her hamstring. I knelt down and told her to concentrate on breathing deeply and evenly. Then

I put one hand under her calf and the other on top of her thigh. I slowly raised the leg. She didn't say anything. She was blowing air out of this little O her lips made, then breathing in some more like she was getting ready to birth a child.

The head coach of the football team, Tad Dimmit, was bringing his boys in from their spring-training activities, marching them back to the gym. The tennis courts are built on a little hill above the track, and in the stripe of fence below the windscreen I could see them walking by, talking, goofing. A few of the boys whooped as they passed, one whistled as I took Sarah through a series of stretches. She put her hand on top of mine, pushing it harder into the muscle above her knee. She kept her eyes closed, kept breathing. Tad yelled, "Red line!" and the team trotted to the red painted sidewalk that led to the gym. Sarah and I stayed there another five minutes, stretching her leg, working the knot out of the muscle.

Tad Dimmit is well-known in the area. He is a tall, balding man who addresses the student body at pep rallies in a calm, deep-throated drawl, but during games he throws clipboards and kicks coolers as he paces the sidelines. He has won two 5A championships in his twenty years of coaching, and almost every November his team prepares for the playoffs. I once saw him grab a boy's hair and tug him to the ground during practice. He held the boy's face in the grass and yelled in his ear while the other players, who had kept their helmets on, watched with their arms folded across their chests. Tad Dimmit, good ol' T. D.

That afternoon, as I was getting changed in the coaches' locker room after stowing the hoppers of balls, Tad asked me to step down to his office.

"She had a cramp," I told him. "I was helping her stretch it out."

He shook his head. "It didn't look good. No sirree, not at all."

"Christ, Tad, you were there."

"My men were there, too. What if one of them saw you putting your hands where they'd like to put theirs. Then we got a problem." He leaned back in his chair and folded his hands on top of his head. I could see the dark caves of his nostrils and a scab under his chin from the nick of a razor.

He spoke to the ceiling. "The next time you decide a girl needs a massage, I want you to run and get a girls' coach."

I'll tell you now that I have a girlfriend. Vicki (petite, blond, twenty-seven years old, hardworking, busty, and smart) and I live together in a one-story house that we rent in Bluff Oaks. I don't consider myself single, although as I think about it I realize that's my official designation—taxes, insurance, every form I fill out. But while I sat in Tad's office, I felt my fingers opening and closing, forming hard balls at my side. He didn't acknowledge my commitment to Vicki. He was implying crimes. My shoulders tightened up, and I felt a strong urge to hit him or at least to grab the wispy hair on the side of his head and scream something in his ear, something about love, something profound and in-structional that would change the way he looked at himself and at the world. But the words didn't come. I just sat in the chair and bobbed my head seriously to let him know I understood.

I didn't say a thing to Vicki about the incident. I might have mentioned from time to time that Dimmit was an ass-hole, but that was more of a general observation. I didn't worry about it. Up until May, I was in good shape. Then I found my name missing from the list of teachers who would be rehired for the next year. It was a yearly contract written under the eye of the teachers' union so I couldn't complain to anyone. It happens every year, I'm told. Not every teacher comes back.

It's not the first time my stars have crossed, and it won't be the last. My second semester of college, for example, I was walking to class and a guy running the opposite direction collided with me, somehow making solid contact with my right forearm. There I was, in the academic quad in the middle of my walk-on trial with the tennis team, lying on the sidewalk with a dislocated elbow. Other things: Grand Bahama, where I worked as a club pro after I finished school—I started a side business renting jet skis on the beach with a girl, an American, who looked good in a bathing suit. Tanya and I bought the skis, hired a man to collect twenty dollars for a twenty-minute ride, and were well on the way to having everything paid for when a group of men, our competition I assume, came after me one evening on the beach. I could see the dull gleam of a machete by one man's legs. I outran them to the water and started swimming. They didn't follow me in, but I could see them waiting on the beach so I treaded water until it was almost dark. Then I remembered the sharks and barracuda beneath me. So again, I started swimming, trying to angle away from the small mob that had gathered on the beach. It was dark when I reached shore and found out the men who had been waiting were actually trees.

All of this has taught me to keep my head up. Water flows downhill, things have a way of working themselves out. It's a matter of imaging life as a river and knowing you'll get bounced off a few boulders. Now, after making it through the latest section of rapids, I've eddied out for a while. School ended two months ago and I've filled in my farmer's tan. Vicki goes through the Employment Opportunities for me, making checks and stars next to jobs I might want to investigate. I talked about building a deck in our backyard, and the next day she brought home a book called *The Deck,* the cover depicting a man dressed in flannel hammering on some planks, flowers blossoming on the trellis behind him, a tape measure clipped to his belt, and a power saw resting on the finished part of the deck behind him. I got a check in the mail—a lump-sum payment for unused vacation and salary normally paid in increments throughout the summer. I bought lumber for the deck and new tennis shoes. I ran the air conditioner even when I wasn't home.

Then the utility bill came. The landlord revised his approval of the deck's construction to say that he'd reimburse me for the lumber only after I finished the job and he could be sure the structure was solid. My credit card was carrying four digits. I didn't let Vicki know about any of this. When it comes to worrying, one head is better than two.

"You'd look good in blue," she said one evening when I was thumbing through a glossy newspaper insert that pictured men's suits starting at $499. Add tax, tailoring, a new shirt and a couple of ties to complete the ensemble and it would exceed the blue book value of my car.

"You think?" I asked her. I threw the advertisement on the floor and I pulled her close. I kissed her neck and her ear, which always makes her squirm, but this time instead she pushed me away.

"You're going to need something for interviews," she said. "Maybe we can go shopping this weekend."

"Sure," I said. "That sounds like a plan." But at that very moment I decided I needed to resod the backyard or change the oil in Vicki's car or go through my T-shirts and throw out the ones I was no longer attached to.

I can feel Vicki nudging me back toward the current. She wants me to finish the deck. She worries about the fact I don't have any letters in the mail for a new job. But this last month I've found some work here and there—cutting firewood, trimming trees, teaching tennis lessons a couple days a week. I cook and I clean, and the deck is coming along. I've got the posts in solid. They're rooted deep in the earth, surrounded by concrete, strong as trees.

This morning I cooked pancakes. I put apples, cinnamon, pecans in the batter. I threw away the first few I cooked because they weren't perfect. As I waited for her to get out of the shower, I sampled a short stack. They were delicious—smothered with syrup I heated on the stove, a pat of butter, a cup of coffee to wash it all down. I rinsed my plate and put it back on the table, flanked by a knife and fork and a brand new napkin, just like hers. Vicki was mad because I turned off the alarm instead of hitting the snooze button, and she was running late. She appeared from the bedroom wearing the white cotton blouse that I ironed for her. She also had on her plum skirt, black belt and shoes, and a gold thing pinned near her shoulder. When I asked her if she had time for breakfast, she showed her teeth in what could have been mistaken for a smile, and if I were an animal I'd have been slinking off to a corner.

Vicki shoved folders into her briefcase like I wasn't there. I told her again that I was sorry, and to have a good day. She said, "Bye," and marched out the front door. I waited until I heard her car whining out of the driveway in reverse, then I went to the stove and got out the rest of the pancakes. I drenched them in syrup so they'd slide right down.

Luck can change, and what first seemed like good luck might turn out to be bad. I met Vicki at a couple of parties thrown by mutual friends, but the first night she noticed me I was in a bookstore. My legs were tired—I played basketball at lunch with the other coaches, then worked out with the boys late into the afternoon. In one part of the bookstore, rows of folding chairs had been put out. I sat down and started thumbing through a novel I had picked off a shelf. After a while, other people sat down in the chairs around me, and before long a poet came up to the pedestal. He was wearing red boots and his bifocals hung from a red cord. He read long, wandering poems I couldn't really follow, but sounded nice because of the slow words he had put side-by-side. I sat through to the end, and when I got up to leave, Vicki saw me. She looked surprised for a second, then she said, "That's right. You're an English teacher."

Before I could think, I was acting like an English teacher. "How'd you like it?"

She knitted her brows together, measuring, weighing. After a minute she said, "I liked it."

"Me, too."

We went out for a beer afterward. I called her up the next week for a movie, a foreign one. She liked that, too. I decided not to tell her that the great thing about teaching, the best thing, was getting summers off.

After the surfeit of flapjacks, I sat on the couch with the last cup of coffee from the pot. Coffee didn't really taste good in this weather. It had been raining lately. Every other day the sky turned charcoal and then opened up, thunder and lightning, rain so thick you could only drive in second gear. Then the sun reappeared and heated the water out of the ground, and when you tried to breathe it felt like you were suffocating. When building the deck in the backyard, I could smell the coffee coming through my skin.

Just thinking about work made me tired. I finished the cup and leaned back. I tried not to lift my feet onto the couch. I resisted putting my head down on a cushion. It was so easy, though, with the air conditioner blowing arctic, to lie down for a while, the pancakes battling the coffee, making me almost drowsy enough to fall asleep.

Here's where I stood: The posts were in and I had tacked two-by-fours onto them to form the frame. I was going to drill holes and bolt everything together. Then I needed to cut the joists, nail them to the frame, and put the floor on top. Some beautiful redwood planks I had paid too much for were yellowing a strip of grass in the backyard. I would nail them down, and sand the rough edges, and brush on a couple coats of sealant, and I'd be done.

I filed the steps away in my head. Then I made a mental list of friends to contact about finding a job. I'd make the calls after the deck was finished because I couldn't hear the phone ringing when I was outside. The couch was good for these decisions—action items, low-stress choices. It was only when I tried to plot out the trajectory with me and Vicki that I got sleepy.

I closed my eyes to think better. I could picture the wedding and the friends we would invite, and my dance with Vicki and the look in her eyes—happy, surprisingly happy. Then my best man (a roommate from college) gave a drunken toast that gave way to more drunken toasts, and soon the grannies were shaking their heads and I was laughing and Vicki and her father were dancing together and he was looking dreamily at the low-scooped back of one of her bridesmaids. So I had another drink and stood around with my buddies and pretty soon Vicki was crying about something and I wanted to wake up and be off that couch but I couldn't, so I stayed there and tried to calm her down, told her I was sorry for whatever was wrong. It didn't do any good because somehow in this dream I acquired the knowledge that my very person didn't fit with her image of the man she had married. She looked at me like I'd fooled her all along, which I protested by saying loudly and determinedly to all the people who remained, "This is who I am."

It was the wrong thing to say. It started to rain, and the water leaked through the tent that floated above the reception, and everyone ran inside except for me and Vicki. I grabbed her, held her, pulled her to me and hugged her, and said it again. "This is who I am." I felt her shaking inside my arms and I tried to squeeze it out of her, tried to hold her so tight that she'd never doubt for a second my arms or my chest, or the chin I rested on top of her head. Only that I felt her tears gliding along my throat. I smoothed her hair and put my hand on her back, on the bare skin that her dress offered me, and I swayed back and forth in a dry patch of grass, trying to keep time with the rain, sure that this would make everything all right. When I opened my eyes I saw through the sliding glass door that it was raining outside—a short cloudburst that darkened the planks lying by the fence and turned the earth around the posts soft and black.

Lies, lies, what's in a lie? Is a lie something you don't say? If it is, then I've got plenty. I don't tell Vicki things that could erode the foundation of our togetherness, like the fact that I really don't like poetry. I think that people who work long hours do so to cover up a lack of imagination, and I still remember a dark-haired girl from high school, who I think about sometimes when I lie next to Vicki. I don't share every thought that runs through my head. To begin a dialogue that circled even one of our fundamental differences would be to begin a conversation that never ended. I keep some things to myself. I don't know a couple who shares everything.

What I can talk about is how when the sun came out, I jumped off the couch and got to work a little after noon. By four o'clock I had drilled the holes and bolted in the frame. I drove down to the icehouse and bought a six-pack, and by five o'clock I had completed drinking half of them. I doubled up during the news and ate a cheese sandwich while I took in the important events of the day. In the shower I shaved (ten minutes total), straightened up the kitchen and living room, taking special care to fluff the headprints off the couch pillows, and promptly recycled my empty beer cans. Then I drove to the store and bought an eggplant, a giant eggplant. Its color called out to me, and when I touched it, it was cold. I researched methods for preparing it in my cookbook: soak, salt, pat dry, dip in egg whites, roll in bread crumbs, cover with marinara and mozzarella, then bake. I put it in the oven by seven.

Vicki got home a little before eight. I was sitting on the couch reading a book. Half moons of sweat under her arms darkened her blue leotard. She takes aerobics after work. She's laying this attrition upon herself, nickel and diming away at the thighs and butt that make her Levi's a thing of beauty. She said she was tired and didn't have an appetite.

"There's too much cheese on it."

"You can scrape it off," I said.

"I'm not hungry."

I asked her if she was still mad about this morning, and she shook her head while she held a glass and ran the tap water to get it cold. I started to get angry because I had been so excited about the goddamn eggplant.

"Come on, Vicki," I said as I stabbed a piece on a fork.

She backed away. "I said I'm not hungry."

She walked out of the kitchen and scurried to the bedroom, me following her with the fork in the air, one hand underneath to keep it from dripping. I heard the bathroom door shut and then the hum of the pipes as she turned on the shower. I stood in the living room and put the eggplant in my mouth. I looked around the room, at the books I had alphabetized on the shelf and the fan of magazines on the coffee table. I felt something rising in me. Disgust is what I think it was. Disgust at what I'd become: a cooking, cleaning, out-of-work teacher, tree-trimmer, tennis pro who gets mad when honey doesn't appreciate dinner. I stopped chewing and opened the back door. I walked outside and spit out the eggplant.

There was still a little light, and so I wandered around the deck, feeling the different boards, surveying how the corners felt when I pushed on them. It all looked pretty solid. It was a house of cards, though—one post shifting would affect how the stress was distributed. I imagined at best that the structure would appear rough-hewn and rustic, embodying a handmade charm; at worst the frame would slowly loosen as we walked on it until one day, the day that Vicki's parents were in town sipping iced tea around the umbrella table, the deck would collapse.

I picked up one of the redwood planks and carried it over to the frame. This was premature, but I just wanted to see how it'd look. They'd cut the boards to size at the lumberyard, and when I slid it onto the frame it fit just right. I carried another plank over and put it next to the first. Then another and another, until they were all on top of the frame. I turned the porch light on because it was getting dark, then I stood back and whistled. I thought it looked good. Pretty darn good. But the longer I studied the deck, the more I noticed that something was wrong. Maybe it was the ground that I was standing on was uneven, or the porch light was casting a strange shadow, but the deck looked crooked.

"Shit!" I yelled out. "Shit shit shit shit shit."

Vicki slid open the glass door. "What's the matter?" She walked out onto the deck.

"Wait! Those boards aren't nailed in." The wood creaked under her feet. She kept walking out toward me, the light behind her making her face hard to see.

"Hey," she said. "This looks great. What's the trouble?"

She walked up and down the deck, looking at it, then looking at me. I could have told her a hundred things.

Like how I heard about making mountains of money on

a fishing boat in Alaska. Or about the tightness I sometimes felt in my back and my lack of health insurance. I could have told her that when I was on the tennis courts with Sarah, how my stomach jumped when she put her hand on mine, and for a moment I closed my eyes, too. For a second I forgot who I was, and then the words "Red line!" shot through the air, more, it seemed, for my benefit than the football players'. I could have told Vicki that when Sarah finally stood up, I saw dust and sweat on her thigh, all in the shape of my hand.

Vicki stopped walking. "What's the trouble?" she asked again.

I really wanted to tell her everything, from the beginning, but I couldn't bring myself to start talking. I shook my head. "The frame's not right. Something's not even."

I walked up to the deck and took a board off and put it back by the fence. "I'm going to take a look at it tomorrow and see if I can figure out what's wrong."

"Okay," Vicki said. She walked back inside and sat on the couch. I think she was watching as I carried the planks one by one back to the fence. Every once in a while I looked up at her and she was reading a magazine. I hoped she glanced over, though, as I put my foot against the post in the front right corner. I pushed on it as hard as I could. Then I kicked at it with my heel, but I couldn't feel it budge. So I got down and leaned my shoulder into it, like the kids do on the blocking sled, and pushed as hard as I could. My tennis shoes slipped in the grass, so I turned my body to make it parallel with the front edge of the deck. The posts stood five feet apart, and with my feet against the one behind me, I started to push again. I locked my knees out and bulled my shoulder hard against the wood. Maybe Vicki heard me groan. Maybe she heard something moving, something breaking. Somewhere down deep, I could feel it through my whole body, the posts were loosening in the earth.

SAFETY SPEECH

•

Cynthia Baughman

I'M IN ONE OF my celibate phases," Lewis had protested in July. His friend Arliss was calling to invite him to a party given by the director of the Women's Studies Program. "Calm, sublimating, productive."

Arliss replied that she felt obligated to her straight friends to force even a broken-down old type like himself into circulation.

"If I go to this thing," Lewis warned her, "I'm just going to make you sit in the corner with me and talk about the masculine voice versus the feminine." He was writing an article on voice-over narration in *nouvelle vague* cinema, and there was a sexual politics angle on which he felt a little shaky. "You can stop me from saying something that will get me in trouble."

"But I like to see you get in trouble," Arliss said sweetly. "It's been one of my chief and regular amusements, lo these many years." Their friendship went back more than two decades, to Berkeley, where she had been a smart young graduate student who spoke with careful wit in his classes and in the same political meetings and reading groups where Lewis and his then-wife, Catherine, had argued about non-violence and struggled with Marcuse. Now they both had teaching jobs in Cambridge where they had developed a surprisingly intense attachment, alternately sparring and tender. They read each other's manuscripts, went to the movies now and then, and met for lunch almost weekly to gossip about their colleagues, bemoan the latest retrenchments in civil liberties, and haul each other back from the brink of various forms of self-destructive behavior.

"No," said Arliss. "No. You will have rich and rewarding conversations with legions of wonderful women. You will ask them about their work and compliment their outfits; you will compare vacations. You will be generous and charming and warm. For one brief night, you will be very, very nice."

The night of the party was a hot, hot night, and the subdivided Victorian mansion was clotted with vaporous people. Within five minutes Lewis was trying to cajole Arliss out onto a small balcony for a confidential chat. He steered resolutely through the crowd in the living room, squeezed through a sticky porch door, collapsed against the banister, and breathlessly turned only to realize that his friend had been snagged—or had escaped—at the last moment. As the heavy night air cooled him ever so slightly, he leaned against a rail and watched her back there in the lighted room, smiling at the guest of honor, an enormous woman who'd just published a highly praised social history of makeup. Small, lithe Arliss thrust her hands in the back pockets of her jeans and rocked back and forth in her tiny boots, nodding intensely. Lewis recalled the aftermath of a long-ago dinner party at his house in California. Arliss had stayed to help him and Catherine with the dishes, and Catherine had remarked chattily that one of the women, a rather dramatic painter whom Lewis would eventually sleep with (though none of them knew that then), "looked particularly *made up* this evening." Arliss had replied, "Charlotte has always strained my credibility, but I've never actually considered her a *fictional* character."

Eventually Lewis's eyes wandered away from Arliss and the historian and over the other gabbing guests—there were dozens and dozens of women in that room. He scanned their sculptural earrings and short skirts and breezy summer haircuts. A slim one in a silky tank top, laughing at her own story, feigned a small collapse against another, and both women staggered a little, clutching at each other in a delightful pantomime of feminine camaraderie. He saw someone else rummage around in her bag for her appointment book and avidly write something down. An address? A bibliographical citation? Her interlocutor reached for the book and appended a few more lines. Just behind them was the hors d'oeuvres table, and a long-fingered woman dipped one blanched broccoli spear after another into a yellow sauce, and then made her way to a cluster of friends, where she gingerly passed out the dripping things. The room was revealing itself, Lewis realized—as he struggled to hang onto his grumpy mood—as a sea of reception and exchange among highly evolved creatures, rich in appetite and sensibility. For a moment, it seemed that he had never seen such a confabulation of interior and exterior vitality: kindness, talents, plumage. They really did look wonderful, these women. And, of course, he was capable of being very, very nice.

———

Now it was a Monday night in October, and Lewis sat on his sofa in front of his VCR, reluctantly turning down the sound on Jean Vigo's *L'Atalante,* an old French film he was teaching that week. He had just made himself a nifty little supper; he had paper topics to write and seminar notes to polish and three letters of recommendation to compose. And one of those terrific women was on the phone.

"I just want to know what happened," said Phoebe Dean.

"I'm not sure what you mean."

"Well, it's been a while since I heard from you. I left a few messages. I don't get it. Are we seeing each other or what?"

"Phoebe," the hostess had announced that night, "is writing this fascinating dissertation on Hollywood films about Vietnam. And she works at the Media Arts Center." Lewis had left the balcony and wound his way into the kitchen looking for something to drink, and that was where the hostess had grabbed him. This Phoebe was tall—more gawky than elegant—with a thrown-together, graduate-student look about her, standing awkwardly, wedged between the refrigerator and a Formica counter piled with empties.

"Great topic," said Lewis.

"Lewis does European," said the hostess.

Phoebe claimed to know an article of his on music in Riefenstahl films. "I found it really helpful at a difficult juncture," she said. She punctuated the compliment with a pat on his upper arm, which he thought she held one interesting beat too long. They swapped academic gossip for a while, and then Phoebe suggested that they check out the dancing in the next room. After a few minutes in the cramped space, she declared it impossible. Lewis followed her back into the bright kitchen.

"Hollywood is a late interest for me," she informed him, extracting a couple of beers from the refrigerator. "In college

I was totally European." And as she prattled on about her intellectual development, Lewis realized that they were alumni of the same institution. "I'm class of," and he lowered his voice and smiled sheepishly, "fifty-five."

The reigning expert on Hollywood films about Vietnam took this coolly, but Lewis was tickled—she was the first Dartmouth woman he had ever met, and he had always wondered what it was like for a girl to go there. She had been an undergraduate in the seventies, she told him, "in the ice age of coeducation." She launched into shocking anecdotes about the hostility and sexism of the male undergraduates. "And half the administration was right in there with them." She described a dean chiming in with a fraternity songfest's adaptation of a fast-food chain's jingle: "Fur Burger." And "that meant us."

These salacious, sadistic stories had aroused him slightly. Lewis was attracted by the notion of a woman who belonged in a category that had not existed when he was twenty. Plus she had an animated, intelligent face, if not a particularly pretty one. He suggested that they give the dance floor one more try and was disappointed when he lost her there to a group of buoyant women dancing in a sort of free-form cluster.

He had been astonished two weeks later—"O brave new world!" he actually said to himself—to come home from the library and find on his answering machine a message from "Phoebe Dean, Dartmouth eighty," recounting their meeting and describing a dance band she'd like to check out with him, all in a voice whose self-assurance was charmingly belied by a final rattle and clatter at the end of the message when she had dropped the phone. "And then you dropped the phone," he said to her some days later. She pulled the covers over her head in burlesque mortification.

"You *heard* that? That re*cor*ded?"

"I thought it was marvelous. I laughed and laughed. I

played it three times." He did not tell her that he had called up Arliss and played the message for her. "Go for it," Arliss had commanded him.

"I deserve some kind of explanation," Phoebe's reproachful voice was saying on the other end of the line.

Lewis punched off the movie on his VCR and it was soundlessly replaced by football. He recalled the fretful look on her face when she had asked, after their first evening out—they had gone dancing—"What do I have to do to get you to kiss me?" At the time he had been charmed by the urgency, the directness of her appeal, and replied, "At this point, not much." He had crossed the room to the ratty armchair where she crouched like a miraculous incarnation of both Miss Muffet and the spider, her long legs sheathed in something skintight and black. Tonight he poked wistfully at his cooling omelette with his free hand and said, "I'm not exactly sure what you mean."

"I've heard so many of your stories. Now I want to hear the one about me."

"No," he said and tried, unhappily, to recall what stories he might have told her. He saw her folded into a corner of this very sofa. Wearing a sleeveless green dress sprigged with cartoonish black wristwatches. "It's a pun," she had explained, fanning out the skirt. "Black watch." She had kicked off her sandals, and it looked like her dusty feet were smudging his upholstery, and that had been okay with him. He was splayed across the other end of the sofa, with his shirt half unbuttoned and a drink in his hand, in a goofy, erotic, expansive mood. Talk talk talk. About Julia's illegal abortion. That had fascinated her in a grisly kind of way. He had recapped his and Catherine's disastrous experiments with open marriage in the late sixties when he was still at Berkeley. He remembered the bemused expression on Phoe-

be's face when he recounted buying a "marriage manual"
sometime during the Eisenhower years and learning oral
sex. "We felt very daring," he'd confided. "Very avant-
garde." She had said, "This certainly is educational—oral
history," and they had laughed at her bad joke. She had
sharp, crooked teeth, and her gums showed when she
laughed. He had thought how much prettier Catherine had
been at that age, awkward and unexpectedly pregnant, self-
consciously arranging herself into the diagrammed positions
and gently adjusting his limbs.

"You seeing somebody else?" the telephone Phoebe
prompted him tonight.

A sweatshirt of Gillian's lay puddled on his coffee table.
Lewis placed one socked foot on it and felt mildly consoled,
connected with a sensible, optimistic person who always had
several cheerful orgasms before she had to go home and pay
her baby sitter. Tonight Gillian and her daughter were shopping for a Halloween costume. "She wants to be Madonna,"
Gillian had said tolerantly. "We are looking for a black lace
bra in a size twenty-three quadruple A." When Gillian held
him in her freckled, exercised arms he felt collected, sal-
vaged. "You look like this great beached whale that I want
to drag back into open water," she had told him, standing
by his bed, fastening her bracelets. "In the few hours granted
the working mother for that kind of endeavor." Gillian was
a fund-raiser for the Aquarium and frequently spoke in
terms of fish and projects. She and her daughter were handsome redheads who called each other "Ginger," though no
one else was allowed to.

Lewis said to Phoebe, "I'm sorry things didn't work out
between us. But honestly, it was just one of those things.
Most things are." The phone felt very heavy, and his dinner
was looking congealed.

After a few more rounds, Phoebe finally said, "I left my
Motown tape in your car."

"I'll get it back to you."

"Well then. I suppose I ought to bid you good-bye. I wish you well."

Bid you good-bye! Wish you well! Who the hell was this? Bette Davis?

But Lewis was not a callous person—he had not embarked on the affair casually, knowing that it would end badly, or even that it would end at all. He was not the kind of guy who deliberately indulged in brief, shallow liaisons. He had, in fact, prepared himself to be dropped by Phoebe—she'd struck him as practiced and impulsive, and she seemed to have asked him out on a whim, in some kind of wild mood. She had certainly not seemed poised to fall in love or whatever it was that had happened to her. Some pathetic father thing, probably. If he were being perfectly honest.

Tonight she had demanded that he account for the waning of his interest. But Lewis assumed that waning was the sad rule. Waxing was the blessed exception. "I've told you how things stand," he had said. "What more could you possibly want to know?"

"I am interested in my effect on people."

"This makes me very uncomfortable." It was embarrassing and painful. He didn't see how her effect on him was any of her business.

"Maybe it's a generational thing," she had said. "We like to talk about our experience now. We pay attention to our emotional lives. The personal is not only the political, it's also the intellectual."

"Don't talk to me like you're the representative of some sexual/emotional avant-garde."

"I just want to be someone on whom nothing is lost."

"I don't like being handed a subpoena."

The guilt she induced stuck with him all evening. It was unfair.

As he lay in bed that night, with five essay questions on early European film tucked into his briefcase alongside several misleading accounts of the mediocre accomplishments of talentless, tin-eared graduate students, this unfair person rose up, clamorous and insinuating. Her scrawny, imperfect form thrust aside Vigo's ghostly long shot of a bride on the deck of a canal barge and light-drenched images of strong-limbed young men in numbered jerseys, chugging across enameled grass, tumbling and rolling resiliently, springing up undamaged.

"You," she had said to him, with reluctant admiration, ruffling the hair on his shins, "you are my Dartmouth karma." She had knelt beside him on this bed, passing her hand lightly over his flesh, like someone idly brushing the sand on a beach.

"Explain." He had plumped up a pillow and settled back to watch her playful, reflecting face.

"I hated it there. I hated the Winter Carnival, the fraternities, the big noisy boys, and the plastic cups all over the place on Sunday morning. I *really* hated seeing the big bruiser football team boys trotting into their private dining room to devour their scholarship steaks and testosterone sauce. I lived near the stadium and could never study at home on Saturdays in the fall, they made so much noise. Their horns, their stupid cheers. The big alumni cars and their useless wives mixing cocktails." She had shrugged and smiled. "Lucky for me, I managed to find these delicate, sweet, articulate, sensitive boys. These really nice literary boys. Boys studying philosophy and making sculpture. I never so much as ate dinner with one of those dreadful jock boys. You know the only time I ever was in a fraternity?"

"When?" he asked. Her hand had fallen still on his calf. One of her nipples seemed slightly walleyed.

"My freshman year, this girl I was in love with all through high school, who had gone to Yale, drove up with some friends for the Yale game. We went to this fraternity party together with these idiots who gave her a ride."

"You went as a couple?" The idea intrigued him. Two studious, artistic girls standing entwined, drinking rank beer, and making disgusted, discerning remarks in bold voices, in a parlor where he might have felt up Catherine twenty years earlier.

"Yeah, sure," she said. Her countenance was unreadable, but her tone was superior and slightly contemptuous. "And then, ten years later, what do I do, but start messing around with a fucking Dartmouth football player." She lightly slapped his thigh. "This enormous, hairy, manly, Dartmouth football player. Plus he's from the fucking *fifties*. This class of nineteen fifty-five football player. God knows what you did to women back then." She shuddered deliberately and looked like someone had pulled the plug on her face. He remembered squatting outside the bathroom of Alpha Phi, listening to retching, whimpers, and running water, as his friend Dougie Fugate murmured, "Come on baby, it'll be okay. Come on now. Let's go get some breakfast. Nobody's coming near you."

He had held out his hand to Phoebe. "I trust you don't find the experience as loathsome as you expected."

"The jury," she had said, flopping onto her stomach beside him and nuzzling his neck, "is still out."

Lewis woke to the cool October morning feeling pestered and apologetic. It took him a moment to remember that he was fully prepared for class and that his paper topics and letters were in his briefcase. His mood was courtesy of Phoebe. Oh, it was depressing, it was costly, to reject someone's affection. As he angled his jaw to give his sagging skin a framework over which he could shave, he felt vain and foolish. He was on his way to becoming an old man; his curly hair had grown thin and wiry; he fluffed it up to hide a bald spot. And he had hurt a vulnerable young woman. Who did he think he was?

He smiled at himself in the mirror and rubbed his bare chest. Its solidity comforted him.

He lived in a turn-of-the-century Gothic high-school building, which had been transformed into a mall of trendy specialty shops topped by three floors of offices and apartments. The two main entrances were ornate granite archways capped by keystones, one carved Boys and the other, Girls. When he passed in or out (usually under Boys), especially on crisp, back-to-school autumn days like this one, he imagined the two segregated lines of befrocked and knickered adolescents, eyeing or ignoring each other. On his long, pleasant walk to campus he passed a couple of students from his lecture course—a rangy boy wearing a dead man's coat and carrying a lush leather bag, and a girl tidily contained in a buttery aviator jacket and crested with an expensive explosion of hair. "Hi," the girl said. "Professor," nodded the boy. So many college students looked so rich these days. Such perfectly confident, complete little beings.

He had never slept with a student. He was proud of that, at least.

His department secretary liked him. She waved from the phone as he entered the office, and he flapped his paper topics and mimed gratitude as he dropped them in the duplication basket. He gathered his mail for reading between office-hour customers and settled at his desk with his door cracked cordially open. Outside his first-floor window, a bicycle rack attracted a noisy crew. Tomorrow's leaders clattered in and out of it all day, banging their locks and chains and hailing the mutts that loafed and skirmished around the door of the building, while their negligent owners improved themselves inside. He could hear a girl yelling, "I'm psyched, I'm psyched," while another one boomed, "All *right.*"

A pink While-You-Were-Out slip informed him that Catherine had called at nine and would call back at eleven. Even though their divorce had been Catherine's idea, she preferred calling him at the office to calling him at home because she dreaded finding another woman there—sometimes this unresolved jealousy made Lewis wonder how competent a therapist Catherine could be. Catherine still lived in Berkeley. Her genial, flaky husband, Paul, who was also a therapist, called Lewis "my main man," wore dashikis on holidays, and greeted Lewis and Catherine's son, Luther, with soul handshakes, even though they were both white people. Luther played drums for an insolvent punk band called Milk Carton Kids and lived in a warehouse, doing all the worst drugs. Lewis and Catherine spent a lot of time on the phone wondering what to try next.

His mail yielded university press advertisements, a divestment rally announcement, a memo on campus recycling, a packet of offprints of an article he'd written on paranoic films from the cold war period—with his photographs and captions maddeningly scrambled—and a blank envelope enclosing a copy of *Steal This Book,* which Lewis had forgotten lending to Phoebe after she'd unearthed it in his study. "I considered it" was written on a piece of computer scrap wrapped around the book. The girl must have delivered it personally, on her way to her office that morning. He wondered if she had hoped to run into him or if she had figured that the prompt return hot on the heels of last night's valedictory phone call would sting him, or if ridding herself of the book was a relatively healthy act of closure, which he should greet with relief. He imagined her gangly, disheveled form darting into the mailroom and snooping around, poking through the letters in his box.

He was flipping through Abbie Hoffman's book, chuckling, relishing it anew, when an engineering major from his survey course showed up to talk about her paper. She wanted to compare Murnau's *Sunrise,* which he had screened two weeks ago, with this week's film, *L'Atalante.* "In both of them this couple almost splits up but then they get back together," she said eagerly.

"Yes, that's true. There's a plot similarity." He watched her write down "PLOT" and underline it twice. "And where do you want to go after that observation?"

"Well, I think it's interesting." She seemed genuinely excited. It was nice when science students were touched by a humanities course. Except when you pictured them ten years from now, better able—thanks to you—to relax at the movies after spending the day designing the weapons system that would vaporize your grandchildren.

"It *is* interesting. Have you noted any other interesting similarities?"

The girl thought for a moment. "Water. Boats."

"True. Could you generalize about the function of water and boats in these two films?"

She smiled sheepishly and absently dotted her cheek with her pen.

"Well, do they lead anyplace in particular?"

"It's a canal barge in *L'Atalante.* In the other one it's just this little rowboat."

"Right," he said. "But where do the characters end up when they ride these boats?"

"In the city!" She wrote that down.

Lewis talked patiently with the future engineer about what she might do with her material. In high school it was okay to just analyze two things and show how they were different or similar, but in college the comparison had to lead to evidence for some larger argument. That seemed to come as bad news, and despite his best efforts to be encouraging and instructive, the girl got up to leave deflated and confused. Then she stopped at the door and kicked cautiously against the jamb with one sneaker. "I have a question."

"Yes."

"You know the scene where the guy's in bed, after his wife's gone?"

"Mm-hmm."

"What do the spots mean?"

"That's a very good question. It is a famous shot." It was an amazing sequence. The separated newlyweds rest fitfully in lonely beds—the man in the hold of his barge and the woman in an urban flophouse. Images of water and the face of the other—the face of the beloved—are superimposed on the faces of each of the lovers. Leopard-spot shadows play over the two estranged bodies, giving their skin an astonishing tactile quality. It is as if they are breaking out into a rash, dappled with their own desire for each other. The man, tossing and turning, rubs the hair of his armpit, and it is clear that he is dreaming of his wife, imagining that he is caressing her hair. Perhaps her pubic hair.

"I love your body," Phoebe had said. She lay propped on one elbow, wrapped in a sheet, trailing her fingers up and down his arm, lightly tickling his armpit, while he dozed naked on his back.

"My body likes you" was his customary response.

Lewis asked his student what she thought about those spots.

She tugged on the zipper pull of her jacket. "I didn't get it. Are they supposed to be real? Were those guys dreaming them?"

"That's an excellent question," he said. "Maybe you could

kick off class tomorrow by asking it." He would rather not get into that rash, that hair, here and now.

"Sure," said the student. *"Mañana."* She executed a pleased little salute. One skimpy compliment could turn a baffled, sneaker-scuffing backpack-toter into a raffish cosmopolitan.

A "C" student from the same class, who had missed the last two quizzes, ambled in. He was there to fish for makeups with a story about a suicidal roommate. "It's been, like, you can't leave him alone," the kid said dramatically. "I go out to the library and I come back and he's in the bathtub trying to get the razor blades out of a Trac II cartridge." Lewis noted the Frisbee sticking out of the kid's knapsack, suspected that he was a con artist, and told him to come back after talking with psychological services and the dean. "They should know what's happening with your roommate. And you need support," he said with his kindliest air.

The kid said "Right," and left sulking.

At ten of eleven Catherine called. "Between patients," she said, and she had some rough news. One of the Milk Carton Kids had taken Luther to the emergency room the night before, after he had lain comatose for six hours in the freight elevator of the warehouse. Now he was ambulatory and seemed fine. But maybe the time had come for some kind of residential treatment program? She and Paul were looking into it. They might need Lewis to sign something.

"Jesus," said Lewis. "You should have called me last night."

"I tried," Catherine said with a hint of reproach. "Your line was busy."

Lewis's son, Luther, had been one of those babies who cried a lot. The doctor said there was nothing the matter— some kids just were criers. "It's probably a kind of exercise they need." But it had been wrenching to listen to his howls

and extrapolate from the terrible sounds all manner of an-
guish and fear and be helpless to comfort or explain. On top
of that, Luther had also been a baby who wouldn't take a
bottle. Catherine would stock the refrigerator with slippery
little bags of breast milk, and when she went out on her
own—to one of her umpteen groups or a class—Lewis would
empty the flopping pouch into the bottle, warm it, and hold
the nipple over his child's yowling mouth. He would squeeze
a few drops onto the bright tongue; he would sprinkle his
own finger and rub it over the slick ridge of baby gums. But
Luther would never close his little lips and suck. Sometimes
he would fall asleep, tears in the creases around his eyes, the
folds of his neck damp with the sweat of his exhaustion. Lewis
would just watch him then, grateful, and afraid to move,
afraid to reach for a book or bend over the paper. He would
talk to him, quietly, asking questions about his mysterious
infant world. "Are you dreaming now? Do you like sleeping
in your daddy's arms? Does my boy feel secure?" Sometimes
Luther did look as if he felt secure; the tears would dry, and
the tired little face would begin to look peaceful and blessed.
But the minute Catherine waltzed in—with some jolly,
knowing friend of hers, perhaps—the child would stir to
alertness and whimper for his mother. "Is my baby hungry?"
Catherine would say. "My baby is so hungry," she would
sing as Luther settled at her breast. "Your day will come,
Dad," the friend would promise Lewis in that tone of indulgent consolation with which women tease ego-wounded
men. And Catherine would stroke Luther's cheek and coo,
"Yes, yes. Mother will be all forgotten."

Lewis protested to her now, "I called him last week and
he sounded fine. All excited about some van they were buying. I sent him a check."

"The singer drove that van into a parked car while Luther
was at the hospital."

"Jesus. Maybe I should try to get him to move out here."

"I really think he needs something local."

"It might be good for him—" Lewis floundered a little, "getting away."

"Sweetheart," Catherine said firmly, "he has a life going on here. The Kids are beginning to get some work—a little bit of a reputation. Whatever happens, he should stay in touch with that." She promised to keep Lewis posted, and then asked what was going on with him. Lewis expressed general grumpy exhaustion and complained about his flubbed offprints. He resisted an impulse to unburden himself about last night's phone call and his disturbed sleep. Catherine relished hearing about any sexual relationship of his that went badly, but confessions of guilt or anxiety always launched her into therapist lingo, and it made him feel lonely and estranged when she talked to him that way. He hadn't told her about Gillian yet: he wasn't ready to be pumped for details, to receive Catherine's strained and cautious felicitations.

After Catherine hung up, Lewis dialed the Milk Carton Kids' warehouse and an answering machine clicked on and began playing some discordant, undisciplined music, which he figured was probably theirs. A voice he didn't recognize broke in, saying in an aggressive staccato, "Are *you* talking to *me?* Are *you* talking to *me?*" Lewis left a message asking his son to call him collect, at home or at work, whenever he got in. He looked up the number of the student with the probably fake suicidal roommate and called him. A different boy answered the phone, with a vigorous "Yo." Lewis left a message for his student asking him to call.

As Lewis hung up the phone, a pallid graduate student appeared at his door, toting a nifty laptop computer. He was there to weasel out of one of the languages required for the Ph.D. He cited extensive undergraduate work in FORTRAN. "Certainly it's a language," he insisted. "There are natural languages and there are artificial languages.

Programming languages employ a sophisticated grammar and vocabulary." He unfolded his laptop and typed out a mess of numbers, bars, asterisks, brackets, and stunted quasi-words in capital letters. He planted the computer on Lewis's desk and turned the screen toward him with a flourish. "I can read this," he said. "Fluently." He rested his sparsely bristled chin on the top edge of the screen and asked eagerly, "Shall I?"

"Later," Lewis said.

"Philosophy and Math accept programming languages," the student said. "Would you like to see their procedural guides?" After making a few obvious points about the relevance of particular languages to particular disciplines, Lewis told him that he would take the matter up with other members of the department. After the kid left, he found himself dialing Luther's number again and listening, with more appreciation this time, to the music on his machine. He hung up and called once more, and this time he felt himself anticipating a particular crash which sounded, gratifyingly, just where he expected it. Thank god *his* son was not an officious prig or a lying little weasel. No. His son was bold and wild, and he stood in the winds of the world and took them in the face. Luther was a musician. An artist. Lewis longed to see his bulky, handsome boy standing before him in all his tattered gear—his leather wristbands, his menacing boots, his tinkling chains.

Lewis was meeting Arliss for lunch, just off campus, in an Indian restaurant where the mournful, deep-eyed waiters and the whiny sitar music matched his mood. Gillian was not available at lunchtime—she went swimming in a hotel pool near the Aquarium—but if she were, she would have been the wrong person for Lewis today. It took a lot out of you, all the self-revelation and self-protection at the beginning of a relationship: unveiling your talents and taking your bows; keeping your bad habits, your chronic meannesses, your characteristic ways of being a disappointment a secret for as long as you possibly could. Lewis was in the mood for a friend who had no illusions, but who liked him anyway, who got from him exactly what she wanted. Arliss had said just that to him once when she was nursing a broken heart: "I was thinking this morning," she had said, "that I have with you exactly the relationship I want to have with you. You give me just what I want you to give me, and I think you feel the same: you don't make me feel like I'm disappointing you—holding out—not giving enough. Neither one of us wants more or less. How often in life can you say that?"

She was there when he arrived, dressed entirely in the gray-to-black spectrum which she favored, sipping a yogurt concoction, and making marginal notes in a journal of Marxist art criticism. He bumbled into the chair opposite her, jarring the table so that her water splashed on the purple binding of her journal. She dabbed it with a napkin, looked up, and regarded him inscrutably from behind her red plastic glasses. Something about her smallness, her lesbian self-containment—her physical imperviousness to him—often made Lewis feel gross and self-revealing around her —a bearer of too much body, a welter of sexual symptoms. He wondered what it would be like to be her rival for some woman's affections.

"A bad morning?" she ventured.

Arliss talked sympathetically with him about Luther, even offering to cover a few classes if Lewis wanted to fly out west. She reminisced about the godawful things she had done as a kid, and noted that she didn't regret any of them: "Did I ever tell you about my weekend with the fashion designer and her husband, when I was seventeen?"

"A glamorous alumna of your high school or something?"

"I should dig out the profile I wrote for the school paper. 'On the Cutting Edge.' And then she came to speak in assembly and I introduced her. God I was cool."

Arliss rippled her shoulders gracefully, reached across the table, and lightly stroked his wrist with her tiny fingers. They were cold and wet from holding her drink, and he flinched a little. She withdrew her hand. "No matter what, you are always a little defended around me, aren't you?"

"Just worn to a nub. I had this awful, sleepless night."

"Do you want to talk to your friend? Your very best pal." In less tender moods she referred to herself as "the only woman you've never fucked over."

Lewis recounted last night's phone call. "This was almost two months ago. And she's hounding me."

"You're being melodramatic," Arliss said. "You fancy yourself stuck in *Fatal Attraction*." She rummaged in a basket of exotic stuffed and fried breads.

"You know I'd never have the nerve to say this to anyone but you, but I think that movie was on to something."

"I'm all ears." Arliss relished his willingness to incriminate himself around her. "Your endearing yen for reproval and absolution," she called it. She pushed the bread basket toward him, and he fingered its splintery rim.

"It seems to me that—in an insidious, distorted way, of course—*Fatal Attraction* captured a real moment in our socio-sexual history. Women have learned to be sexually aggressive—it's great, okay, no arguments here—they call people up, they make the first move. But then they can't follow through. The thing flops, and they start acting all hurt, like they were seduced. Misled. Betrayed. Suddenly we're in radio song land, and yours truly is a brute and a cad who willfully picked out Little Miss I've-Been-Cheated-Been-Mistreated as his personal victim."

"Hmm." Arliss nibbled at a puffy biscuit with tiny smiling lips.

Lewis probed his ground lamb. "Maybe I should teach it next year. You always give me ideas. I'm doing *Virus* this afternoon." *A Virus Has No Morals.* It was a funny, complicated, German film about AIDS, which Arliss had taken him to in August.

"I wish I could be there," Arliss said, bemusement puckering her lips.

The film's basic narrative line concerned the unsympathetic response of a cherubic classical musician to the illness of his bathhouse-owner lover. It was intercut with a confusing subplot about a predatory woman with a penchant for bisexual men, and with lurid, disturbing vaudevillian sequences: a transvestite nurse quintet sang an instructional safe-sex anthem. A monstrously self-absorbed mother chatted superficially with her stricken son, oblivious to his lesions and pallor. A smug research scientist dumped test tubes containing four different body fluids into a small tank and dipped two dildoes, one sheathed in a condom and one bare, into the brew. Gloating, she watched the unprotected dildo bubble and steam, and then triumphantly exhibited it to the audience, a half-dissolved, drooping stump.

A student filmmaker, who was clearly out of his element in Lewis's seminar room full of critics, presented an enthusiastic and touching assessment of the contribution this film made to "our struggle."

Then a sophisticated theorist wittily analyzed the misogyny pervading the film: "He scapegoats women. He displaces blame from culpable institutions onto a female sexuality that is presented as resentful and voracious." She threw in a few ad lib remarks about who counted as "us" in "our struggle."

The filmmaker obviously felt outshone and personally attacked but lacked the rhetorical wherewithal to respond effectively. A few students attempted to diffuse the tension with neutral, off-the-track comments about the *mise-en-scène* and the cast.

Lewis felt compelled to refocus discussion on the question of misogyny, while reviving the filmmaker's best points about the political efficacy of the film. "Ben," he said to the intimidated young man, "do you think it's possible to bracket Helen's criticisms and preserve your sense of the film's usefulness? Or might you incorporate her points into a more global reading?" Lewis smiled conspiratorily: he was passing on trade secrets and wanted his students to realize that. "Of course you can always try arguing that a film doesn't just instantiate its fantasies—it critiques them. You know: 'It's not *violent*—it's *about* violence.'"

"I'd like to look at the first heterosexual seduction scene," the theory student said, "okay?"

Lewis turned on the video monitor and slipped in the cassette while someone dimmed the lights. He fast-forwarded to a scene where a woman in black satin underwear, garters, and heels sits on the stomach of a bisexual man.

"He is clearly presented as her victim," said the theorist. "She's a vampire."

While the scene played, Lewis stole glances at the rapt, discomfited faces of his students. Some of them took notes. Others nodded, or signaled each other at key moments. One face was squinched into a sustained wince. Lewis shifted uneasily in the dinky, unyielding classroom chair. The movie conjured up unpleasant scenes from his brief affair with Phoebe. That first night, after they had kissed for a while (she had drawn him into her armchair with twining limbs), he had gently disentangled himself and asked "What do we do now?" He had meant it as a nice way of acknowledging his ardor, while gallantly leaving the choice up to her. But when she replied knowingly, "We discuss our body fluids," all desire drained from him instantly. He took a few unnerved steps around the stranger's cluttered living room, noting an arrangement of peculiar tin toys, which she obviously considered evidence of an idiosyncratic eye. They struck him as childish.

"We what?" he had said.

"You read the papers." She rose and plucked a small biplane from her collection and twirled the propeller with one finger. He almost expected her to draw blood with the corroded blade and present it for his inspection. "Mine check out," she said, glancing up at him. She smiled. "I'm a responsible person." Her speech seemed cold and scripted. He wanted to bolt, but before he found an exit line she had tucked the toy in his jacket pocket and was kissing him again, slipping her hands under his shirt. "You aren't interested in my antibody status?" she asked.

"No," he said, tangling his fingers in the curly hair around her neck, matted with dance-floor sweat. He kissed her throat. "You're so nice and tall."

"I'm interested in yours."

He disengaged himself, crossed the room, and inspected her bookshelf: a predictable assortment of fashionable titles.

"It's not exactly the Summer of Love, anymore," she had said. And he found himself being catechized and lectured about sero-conversion and population profiles and epidemiology by a woman who had thrown herself at him only moments earlier.

When he recalled the tense sex that they had eventually negotiated, he mainly remembered her wounded reaction to his frank report on latex and pleasure. And he saw her crouching over his penis with a revolting air of self-sacrifice, as if she were about to sip poison. He remembered the rational, confident tone in which she had patiently explained the simple solution of voluntary testing and full disclosure, and the baleful look on her face when he pointed out that such a scheme presumed monogamy and commitment.

Since then he had felt a bit contrite—his behavior, he decided, had been somewhat retrograde. "You shouldn't have complained about the condom," Arliss had informed him. "And you shouldn't have suggested she was working out some other issue through this. Hysterical sexuality. Jesus."

"I never said hysteria."

"Bisexual ambivalence? Adult heterosexuality as contamination? You had your little theory."

But the fact that it was his theory didn't mean it wasn't true. He remembered her Dartmouth boy stories and her nasty anecdotes about predatory professors and other assorted jerks. He felt like she was dusting off a spot for him in her gallery of pathogenic agents and beasts. Plus she had been impatient. She had treated him like an irresponsible dope. She had acted like a sleek, *au courant* denizen of the fast lane, while he was an out-of-it square, a yahoo, a geezer. Gillian had not thrown up these roadblocks. "I assume you consort with neither drug addicts nor other boys," she had said, working a womanly hand under the waistband of his underwear. "And I have led a blameless life."

Lewis scanned the dimly lit faces of his students, many of whose lives were probably heaped with blame. How did they handle these things? Did they have suave rituals? Code words? Implicit understandings?

"You see," said the theory student. She punched the remote control and froze the picture. "Look at her mouth."

Lewis ended the class with what he thought were lame, canned remarks about the contradictions inherent to radical art in a repressive culture. With a familiar mixture of relief and contempt he watched his students ardently write down some version of his words. A few nodded intensely as they bore down on their felt-tips. They seemed satisfied as they stuffed their notebooks into their bags and shuffled out into the dusk. After they had gone, he read a page of scattered notes that someone had abandoned on the seminar table—

a disconnected list of phrases: "Figure of woman/state apparatus," "Politically effective <u>and</u> compromised?" and "Radical art + Repression = Contradiction. Adorno?" This didn't mean, Lewis told himself firmly, that nobody had learned anything. He had done a credible job in one of those difficult moments that tested a teacher's mettle. The filmmaker and the theorist had exited together, trying to agree on something, saying, "Exactly," and "That's what's crucial."

It was dark when Lewis passed under Boys and into his building and climbed the several flights to his apartment. When he switched on a lamp and put down his briefcase, he was suffused with a delicious sense of solitude. His rooms were in the high school's old gymnasium—he had high windows, skylights in the distant ceiling, and sprung floors, built to give under the impact of basketball players. A perfect place for a dance party, and he had meant to give one ever since he moved in.

Lewis drew the curtains over all but the skylights and punched on his answering machine. There was a message from a student asking if his letter of recommendation was done. Gillian wanted to know if they could make it eight instead of seven on Friday. She and the sitter had got their wires crossed, but the girl had promised to stay until two. Then Luther's voice: "This is your only son, here to inform you that you can't call an answering machine collect." And Phoebe's resolute voice announced that she had a few follow-up questions to last night's phone call. He could reach her at home all evening; she'd appreciate it. "You owe me this."

Lewis had a can of clams and a box of spaghetti in his cupboard and a few inches of leftover white wine in the refrigerator—all the ingredients for one of his specialties.

He rifled through his box of cassettes for Phoebe's Motown tape, to give it one last listen. As he moved competently around his kitchen, he found himself dancing in spurts to the familiar music. An impossibly young Michael Jackson started to sing and, at a favorite refrain, Lewis put down the bottle of wine and the wooden spoon, and raised his hands, thrusting them lightly into the air, while he bent at the knee.

On their first date, Phoebe had led him to a converted fire station with a kitchen and bar at one end and an all-female rock-and-roll band at the other—the Neo-Boys, it said on their drum, in jagged pink letters. The place was filled with energetic people in their teens, their twenties, and their thirties, and it had pleased and excited him to be there. He had not felt out of place, and that realization had pleased him, too.

They ate Mexican food and talked about movies they'd seen recently. She moaned about procrastinating referee readers for the journal the Media Arts Center put out—she seemed proud to be doing a little editing—and she fumed grandly about lousy academic writers who were overinvested in their own convoluted prose. He inquired about her lingering dissertation, and she said, "My dissertation is a mess," and miserably dragged a tortilla chip across some guacamole.

"Hollywood does Vietnam. Such an interesting topic," he had said, encouragingly. "Are you focusing on any particular movies?"

"I've got sort of a chapter on rock-music soundtracks. Some stuff on voice-over narration. The good black soldier who gets killed in the first act. A few pages on helicopters and credit sequences. So far it doesn't add up to squat. I don't have a coherent take on the genre or the period."

"Are you going to write about what they do—or don't do—with the antiwar movement back home?"

"Good question," she said, nodding. She squirmed a bit and sat up straighter. "Did you see *Born on the Fourth of July?*" As she gave him her line on that movie he saw that she had one of those changeable faces that could be opaque as lard or expressive as Garbo. He wanted to ruffle her dark, shiny curls. Touch her chin. Tell her to lighten up. Not be so hard on herself.

He told her how two of the Weatherpeople had spent a few underground days with him and Catherine at their place in Berkeley once. But Luther had been little, and it had seemed risky to put them up for very long.

"Wow," she said, impressed, and asked a lot of questions.

She told him that she lived alone. She had recently broken up with a guy that she had lived with since college. They had tried to put things back together, but they hadn't pulled it off. They were still friends, though.

Lewis described his exemplary divorce and encouraged her to maintain a connection with her old boyfriend, if that was what she wanted to do. It had been difficult for him and Catherine, but they were very glad, after all these years, that they had made the effort. Catherine was his best friend, and he was hers. Phoebe brightened at this. "That's how I want it to be with me and Sam," she said, fiddling with the little plastic bull that dangled from the neck of their bottle of Spanish wine. "You haven't gotten married again?" The bull slipped from its satiny tether and Phoebe brought it to her mouth and bit one white horn.

"No," said Lewis.

"You were married such a long time." She carefully balanced the bull on all fours next to the guacamole. It cast a romantic shadow across the greasy table. "It must be hard." She started looking glum again and he refilled both their glasses. "I can't imagine ever loving anybody the way I love Sam. When I allow myself to think that this is really the end of all that, that I am going to live my life without him,

I feel like a boat person. I feel like I've lost my culture and my language. That there was this little village someplace where I grew up, and now it's blown to smithereens and I'm the only person left to remember it. That wherever I go, whatever I do, whoever else I'm with, I'm some kind of refugee." She plucked at her shirt. Hawaiian, splashed with ukuleles and orchids and coconuts. "Does that make any sense? Do you know what I mean?"

"Yes," Lewis had said, thinking it made plenty of sense. "I do."

"You know what it's like when you feel like you grew up with someone? When you learned whole vocabularies with that person? Painting, for instance. I took maybe one art history class in college. Same for him. But painting is something that Sam and I learned to look at together. It's what we would do when we traveled. We read the same books and articles; we went to the same shows. And so there's a whole history of responses there, and when I think of going though my life looking at painting without him, it just seems too unbearably sad." She threw herself back against the high bench and smiled crookedly. "Am I being too self-absorbed? Depressing?"

"No," Lewis said. "I'm interested." In fact, he had been moved.

"It's a bad attitude to have, I know. I mean if I don't stop mythologizing what we had I'll never move on." She reached out and lightly tapped the hand with which he held his wine glass.

"What went wrong between you two?"

She had looked around the room in an agitated fashion. "Believe me, you don't want to know."

The Neo-Boys were tuning up, checking plugs and mikes, and joshing with some fans. "You're still very much in this, aren't you?" Lewis had said to her. "It's going to take you a long time to get out of it. And that's as it should be."

She'd seemed alarmed. "It's been a long time already. A friend of mine, someone who cares about us both, said to me last week, 'Face it, honey, it is time to clear out. It's Saigon. 1975. And the helicopters are on the embassy roof.'"

One of the Neo-Boys, dressed in a black tutu, with stiff, sparkling red hair, approached the microphone and began to sing in a raspy, high-pitched, voice. "'Lip-Synch,'" Phoebe said. "One of their hits." And she excused herself for a moment.

The drummer began to whale away, and Lewis wondered if Luther was better. The two guitarists, wearing matching mod, silver-sequined tunic-and-pants outfits, executed neat dance duets while they thrashed their instruments. "Boat person," Lewis repeated to himself. It wasn't a bad metaphor, really. He had felt that way for three, four years after Catherine had moved out, taking Luther and his pint-sized clothes and all his primary-colored clutter. All through his complicated affair with Abby. He remembered the stricken look on her face whenever he whispered, "Cath," or when he would lapse into one of his distant, morose moods. It had been a terrible thing for Abby. It had damaged her. It was years—until he moved back east, really—before Catherine really seemed part of his past. Before he began feeling complete.

The floor filled with dancers. As Lewis wondered if he would be able to do anything but make a fool of himself to this music, two drunk, hearty young women, wearing layers of gauzy shifts and bangles, trooped over to his table and asked him to dance. He hesitated for a moment, and then joined them. When Phoebe returned she looked momentarily abandoned, then simply quizzical and amused. She sat down sportingly and reached for her glass, but the two girls drew her onto the floor. "Come *on*," they said, and the four of them danced together for one raucous song. One of the women said, "You guys are great." She put her arm around her friend's shoulders. "She just moved here. From San Diego. This week."

The drunk woman from California said, "Jeez you two are tall. Are you married?"

Lewis and Phoebe looked at each other and laughed. "Only the first time we've gone out," he said to Phoebe.

"Cali*for*nia," Phoebe said, turning to him, rolling her eyes and shimmying her hands helplessly around her ears.

During the last years of the Truman presidency, Lewis had trudged grimly off to a high-school gymnasium every other Friday night to study the waltz, the cha-cha, the jitterbug, and the lindy. He had learned how to ask a girl to dance, how to lead, how to cut in, and the zones of a girl's body where it was permissible to place one's hands. And then, after he was cut loose from all instruction, dancers stopped touching each other. He learned to twist. He held his arms crooked in a jogger's position at his waist, his hands in fists. After the welcome eclipse of the twist, which had been hard on a knee he had wrenched in a Cornell game in fifty-four, dancers started moving their legs any which way. Lewis had reintroduced into his repertoire staccato versions of his old waltz and lindy steps, but he never figured out what to do with his hands. They seemed eternally stranded in that waist-level jogging position where the twist had beached them. For variation, he occasionally raised one arm above his head. Then, in one of those moments of gratuitous marital cruelty for which there is no forgiveness, Catherine had mocked his dancing to friends. They sat in a seafood restaurant next door to a disco in L.A. She said, "Lewis does his own patented dance. It's called 'The A Train.'" Lewis and the friends had looked uncomprehending. "You know," Catherine said, actually rising from her seat at the laden table, dragging in her wake a corner of the tablecloth, which clung to her skirt, forcing Lewis to reach out and save the whole meal from being whisked to the floor. She raised one hand as if she were grasping a subway commuter strap, bent her knees, and vibrated. "I'm taking the A Train," she sang out. Ever since that night Lewis had kept his hands in his jogging position.

Phoebe was a marvelous dancer. Her long slim arms snaked and syncopated in mysterious choreography. With unabashed admiration Lewis mirrored her movements. She put her hands on his shoulders and drew him close. "You know what's the best advice I ever got about dancing?" she yelled over the music. "A friend told me this. He said, 'You know those gestures the stewardesses make during the safety speech? They point out the emergency exits.'" Phoebe extended her arms in a wide funnel and her hands became blades, slicing toward the far corners of the room. "'They show you where the life preservers are.'" She stretched her arms directly over her head and pointed at the life preservers with pulsing index fingers. "My friend said to me, 'We have to take our culture's eloquent gestures where we find them.'" She dipped, and her hands cut through the air like fins. "He's dead now." She crossed her wrists in front of her face, in what was perhaps a stylized gesture of mourning, embracing the memory of her dead friend.

As his clams sizzled in the wine, and Michael Jackson lamented that it was too late, Lewis dropped his knees and raised his hands and sliced the air. Could that possibly be the best advice about dancing anyone would ever give him? He pointed his index fingers at the life preservers. He reached up and jerked down hard on the emergency oxygen supply. He cupped one hand loosely over his mouth and passed the other behind his head, as if adjusting the elastic strap, and he breathed in deeply. He kept dancing like that for a few bars, with his eyes shut, and his arms cradling his skull.

THREE MOTHERS

●

Elizabeth Graver

Aᴿᴼᵁᴺᴰ ᴰᴬᵂᴺ ᵀᴴᴵˢ ᴹᴼᴿᴺᴵᴺᴳ as I lie sleeping, I am visited by my grandmother Rebecca, who died two years ago this week. I see her in a room, reach past someone toward her. Who is it I reach past? I don't quite remember, except that she is a big-bosomed woman, wide and German-looking, someone I feel I once knew well. In fact, I think now that she might have been Molly, the elderly German nanny who used to baby-sit our neighbor's daughter Mara. When I was a girl and Mara a baby, I would follow them on their walks, Molly in her stout shoes pushing the big stroller, me walking barefoot over the pebbles and the soft, hot tar. I remember loving both Molly and the baby, loving them more than it seemed I should, really, since they were only a tiny, tangential sliver of my life. In my skinny, nervous, ten-year-old body, already poised for loss, I loved them for their solidness—the baby, blond and firm, her bare heels hanging out of her stroller like breakfast rolls.

We walked distances, the three of us. Sometimes I pretended the baby was my baby. In fall and winter I tucked her beneath her afghan, pulled her hat down, touched snow to her hot cheek. Other times she was my sister, Molly my mother. I had, at home, a mother and sister who loved me, but in the space between my skin and theirs, there was always room for more.

In my dream, perhaps it is this Molly I reach past, Molly who is probably dead by now, for she was an old woman even then. Perhaps she is caring for my grandmother. If so, they are a strange pair, the unmarried German nanny and the Spanish Jew, mother of six. Still, they are in a room together, and though my grandmother only had one leg when she died, she is whole and standing. She smiles at my confusion at seeing her, and then, in the way dreams buckle time, we are going for a walk, I am pushing her on a long stretcher, and she is all wrapped up in many cottony, tangled blankets, the whole heap soft and old and a bit complicated the way she was, and we are going past gardens, up hills, by fences, through some town I do not know. It is a good, calm, lovely walk, not painful even though she is on a stretcher. Only one thought jars a little with the rhythm: my entire vision of this world as I know it should be shifting because I am walking with a ghost.

And then my grandmother is sitting up, flipping through the blankets, and reeling off the names of her children: Albert David Frank Jack Suzanne—who is my mother. And leaving out only one, her stepdaughter, Luna, the name I love most, Luna like moon, like luna moth, lunatic, loon— the aunt who has always hovered, uncomfortable, on the edges of the scene. My grandmother names the names, then sings them in a kind of chant, folding back the layers as if she might find her children burrowed down inside this nest. And afterward, the grandchildren: Lisa Rachel Pam Jen Sam Matthew Helaine Jonathan Ruth. Luna's son Carl and I are the only ones she does not name.

Me, I want to say to her, me, me somewhere in the blankets, and then she says it, laughing—*Eee-leesa-bet*—and I feel, for an instant, what it is like to be quite newborn and swaddled. Wrap the baby womb-tight, the doctor says, or she'll panic at the way her limbs fall through the air.

And then I am grown, a woman with breasts, calm in my stomach and strong as I push the stretcher up steep hills. We talk about the flowers we pass; each time we stop she grips my arm the way she used to, picks up my hand and exclaims over its beauty, my beauty. As I look down, my hand becomes a thing outside myself, the bones like slight green twigs when I arch my fingers back. She is almost giddy with something, some delight that seems to be mixed up with my reaction to her being there. She is thrilled, I think, at the shock she is creating in me, even as I am not exactly acting shocked. Instead I feel relieved at the return of the familiar, her tangle of white hair, her accent when she says the word *look*—like *luke* almost, and the way she must, really, have been speaking the truth when she used to say she could read minds and pass over oceans, for here, without fanfare, she is.

And then I am leaning over the stretcher and fumbling for my grandmother, and I think she has hunched down beneath the covers, gotten tangled up, tricky as always, dodging me, but as I go through layer after layer, I realize she is gone.

I am woken early this same morning by an argument taking place in the yard that meets my backyard. A son and a mother, thirty-seven years of his unspoken rage. As I lie

alone in bed among my heap of sheets, he explodes. The words
are so pointed, so condensed that I feel as if I am listening
to a play by Tennessee Williams and have to remind myself,
lying there half asleep, that what I hear is real.

"Three sons," he says, "you didn't have three sons, you
had two sons and a punching bag! You never loved me—
you never ever loved me. Tell me you ever loved me."

A silence, at least from where I am.

"What did I tell you? You never loved me and you hated
me because I loved Dad, I did love Dad, but from you it
was only *Willy Willy Willy!*" His voice is shrill here, fake-
womanly.

She laughs, a staccato, hard laugh, and says something
too soft for me to hear.

"I don't care!" he yells. "You were my mother, for Chris-
sake!"

"Stop yelling," she says, and across the distance I can
feel what is goading him—the control in her voice, the cool
sharpness of her laugh, can picture him throwing himself
up against her as if she were a steel door, trying to get a
dent to show itself, a tiny shudder even, some kind of
mumbled answer to his pain. I think: this man is *bruised*—
that is the only word I can think of—and although when I
rouse myself enough to peer out my window I cannot see
these people through the trees, I picture him middle-aged
and a little portly, his skin blotched and mottled, a heart of
sweat showing through the back of his shirt. A man with a
Boston accent, a balding man who grinds his teeth in his
sleep. And she, the mother, must be small and tight-featured,
her hair the color and curl of pencil shavings; she must be
wearing a clean and stingy apron, sitting on the back porch
as he stands below her on the grass, flailing his arms.

Only maybe because he has the loudest voice I am missing
a whole half of it, maybe it is unfair, his story, the child
always the one who gets to throw the blame. Still, I do not

like her; he has won me to his side though he does not know
I am listening. As I lie there, all I can think is *Yield a little
for him, yield. Step closer, one foot toward him, down those
steps he probably climbed on as a child.*

"Let them," he yells. "Let them hear, I don't give a fuck,
I've waited thirty-seven years for this—God how you used
to humiliate me, every single day, in front of everyone. Listen!" Now he is calling out to us, the leafy neighborhood.
"Hello?!"

In my mind I see him as a baby in the lurching, toddling
stage, all possibility—to himself, to her—and how, when he
walked, at first, it was always toward her outstretched arms.

"Don't you see I don't give a *shit* who hears me—I've
waited my whole life for this!"

And the mother, her voice finally rising a little, "You're
rotten! A rotten egg! Get away from my house, you get out
of here, you're no good."

And he, still yelling, a jubilation to his voice now. "Well,
too bad, because you made me how I am!"

Then the words get softer, and though I strain to hear
and raise my head to squint through the leaves, it is a green
blur between me and them. Finally she must begin to cry,
because he says "Ha, it's a miracle, look at that, water from
a fucking stone, I've waited my whole life to see that."

After that, a silence, and I picture him getting into his
car and the way she sits there, her face set as he drives away.
Picture, actually, my grandmother in her worst moments,
how her mouth could get set in a thin line and her gaze level
out into something resolutely blank, for there was hatred,
too, in our family, between my grandmother and her stepdaughter Luna, the one she feared her husband loved more
than life itself. And as I lie there listening for more, another
sign from the yard that touches mine, I wonder how many
other neighbors have been witnesses, lying, like me, alone in
bed, or next to people they love or do not love, their children

sleeping in the rooms down the hall or waiting, all hunched halves of potential, in their testicles or ovaries.

Again I must fall asleep, because I wake to the phone ringing loud beside my bed, and a voice in lilting, non-Parisian French—"*Allo, allo?*" When she says she is the mother of François, I say "*Ah oui, bonjour,*" in false recognition, though I have no idea who she is. My recent trip to France flips like flash cards through my sleepy head—all the mothers I met there: the mother with the son about to take the English exam; the one with twin baby boys; the mother of the bride, of the groom, of the child I used to baby-sit when I lived there; the mother—

"On the plane," she says. "We sat together."

And now I am awake, now I remember. A flock of them on the plane from Paris to Boston, fifty or so women from Zaire, all dressed in bright, lush dresses sewn in different styles but from the same fabric, a deep blue background, curled flowers, and printed on the cloth, a kind of scroll covered with lettering: *L'Association Internationale des Amis de Dieu.* Or something like that, something religious, and one of these women sat next to me, twice my size in her blue dress, taking up her seat and half of mine. For the first part of the trip we did not speak, but then I asked her where she was going, and she said to a religious conference in Boston, where her son lived (François, yes, that was his name, twenty-four years old, an engineering student; he lived with her sort-of other son—here she hesitated—the son of her husband, *tu vois,* but not her son).

She was informal with me, called me "*tu,*" reached deep into my lap to take a magazine, flipped up the armrest between us so that her hip could sink into my seat. And I wanted to talk to her and did not want to, wanted to ask her did she have a daughter and did her daughter have a daughter, and yet was not sure what to make of how she took the roll off my plate as if we had known each other forever and pressed me far into the corner of my seat.

As we neared Boston and she began to peer into a compact mirror at her eyes and lips, I said, "It must be nice to get to see your sons. How long has it been?"

"My *son*," she corrected, and sighed a sigh that pressed against me where we touched. "I made this all"—she gestured down at her dress—"so he wouldn't think his mother had turned into nothing with him gone. Zaire is a beautiful country. You should come visit, I'll show you things."

In the end, after I had translated her customs form and shared my bag of candy with her, she asked for my phone number—to meet for coffee in Boston, she said. The same way, when I was on the train from Paris to Strasbourg two weeks earlier, the widow next to me showed me photos of her dead husband and grown children and said if I were ever in Nancy, here—her address, scrawled on a chocolate wrapper and pressed into my hand. Lonely women, all of us, I could feel it from one seat to the next, not terribly lonely, for we all had photos in our wallets as we sped down tracks or through air, but I could tell, still, that they wanted something from me, could feel a thin line of longing, just enough to make me a little nervous. And yet I wrote my address out, each time, gave it to these women, these mothers.

This morning, on the phone, she says she has a gift for me. No, I say, that's not necessary, but she says, Yes, just a little something she brought from Zaire, a *tout petit cadeau*.

"Thank you," I say. "Really I don't need a gift, but maybe we can meet for coffee?"

And behind my voice, my two selves—the adventurous, lonely one: yes, coffee with a woman in bright blue whose son lives across oceans; and the other self, leery of strangers: she will try to convert me, ask me for something, press me far into the corner of my seat.

No, she says, her voice urgent; no she can't, she's going home tomorrow, but she will leave the gift with her son; they will call me back at exactly six tonight, will I be there? He will give me directions to his house.

I want to say, but wait, what does this gift mean? Does she want me to meet her son, to become his wife, for she asked me on the plane (both of them asked me, she and the widow from Nancy) if I had children, if I were married yet, and when I said no, she frowned a little frown. Or perhaps she wants to convert me to Christ. Or maybe this is a simple gesture, a glance toward the fact that in a world with fewer distances, I might have been her daughter and she my mother; her son might have stayed close to her; my grandmother might have loved all her children equally and then not died, leaving my bones aching for her hand to transform them into new, green twigs.

I picture, then, a swatch of bright fabric from Zaire, the kind of cloth my grandmother would have held to her cheek and pressed against her mouth, deep cotton fiber and colors so bright they seem to be multiplying, still, on the cells of a leaf just about to open.

I say, yes, I think I can be home.

IRONWOOD

•

Rick Bass

IF I DIE, YOU will take care of Tricia and Kirby
Nichole?" Kirby asks.

"I will," I tell him. That's the job of the godfather.

"I have a hundred thousand dollar life insurance policy,"
he says."

"I don't think that's enough," I tell him. "If it runs out,
I'll take care of them."

We're down in Mexico, shooting pool in a bar, as always.
What's unusual is that Kirby and Tricia are getting divorced
after eleven years. Kirby Nichole is four.

"She can marry again," Kirby says, making the shot.
"You'll watch after both of them, right?"

We've come to Mexico to get a *nalgai,* yet again.

———

When we started out—me, Kirby, and Tricia—was in our first year of college, seventeen years ago. That first year, I was Tricia's boyfriend. I had only started the weightlifting, and we'd go to the meets all over the state on weekends. Tricia would shave my thighs and powder them before each lift so the weight would slide up. I skipped all around in weight classes—165, 181, even the 198s.

Kirby would sit up in the bleachers and cheer for me. I made quick gains. It was a small world, the world of powerlifting, and it was an easy one to set on fire. There's always been this *something* inside me—I don't have any idea what it is, only that it's still in there and feels as big as an apple—some kind of glowing *source,* and it wasn't even really fair to all the other lifters for them to be in the same meet with me. Lifting heavy weights was what this glowing source demanded I do, and the others never had a chance.

(Later, of course, in the national meets—and the internationals—everyone else I went up against, I found out, had that same glowing white-hot lump within them, and it was no longer easy to win, in fact, was often impossible. But that was later. . . .)

What I think it was like for Tricia, after that first year—when I started to win so much and so easily—was like when you are at the eye doctor and he or she clicks those lenses into place and says, "Better this way? Or this?" It was just a shift, is all, when Tricia realized I was a weightlifter and would never be anything more, whereas Kirby—well, there was really no choice, once she stopped to analyze it. And they fell hard in love. It was done honorably. Tricia came to me and told me what she was thinking and feeling; and then she went to Kirby. And he took her—she let herself be taken—though I think now that part of the problem, some natural fissure along which Kirby's and Tricia's current split might have unraveled, had to do with the idea that maybe

Kirby thought there was something slightly damaged about Tricia for me to have "let her go."

Whatever went through Kirby's young mind back then, it was all wrong; Tricia was neither damaged nor stolen goods. It was not that way at all, but I feel like Kirby thought that she was, that I did not want her enough, and therefore perhaps Tricia *wasn't* enough: that she had that seam of weakness curled and twisted, tiny within her, like the split in a tree trunk, ready to fracture under either sudden or prolonged stress.

My lifts just kept going up, getting stronger and stronger. Kirby was making C's and D's in Ag Science. Tricia was making A's in pre-law. I was already on my way out of college, bored out of my mind with the kinesiology classes. If I had it to do over again, I'd have studied muscles and ligaments a little harder. But there wasn't time for it. All I wanted to do was bend over the weight and pull it up, again and again. Nothing else.

We went to the big lakes in east Texas. Old trucks and cheap gas were the language of our raw youth. We drove through the hot summers, past the drying hay fields and into the cool pines, and then saw the sparkling blue waters through the forests. Tricia wore a huge hat to protect her fair skin. We would drive right down to the water's edge and onto the beach. We'd build a driftwood fire in the crackling heat and listen to the radio and fish and sweat.

We'd ride home, then, after dark, smelling like fish, and stop at some raggedy-ass little diner in the woods and order whatever was good. Old people in the restaurant would study us in a way that reminded me of great hunger.

———

We moved to Houston after college. That was where the best gyms were, and it was where Tricia's job was. Kirby and Tricia tried a long time to have a baby, but Kirby said the doctors said Tricia was too nervous; Kirby thinking again, I think, of that seam, that twist in the heartwood. Kirby got a job appraising real estate and learned it well in a gung-ho way. And there his story pauses, if not falters. He is now the junior partner, the senior-most young person, just below his supervisor, his manager, his boss, his lord—Tom.

TLB, Kirby calls him, which is how Tom signs his office documents.

Tricia worked in a bank as some kind of trust accounts attorney and rose quickly, in a way that reminded me of those early years of my powerlifting. The suits she wore all the time fit her in a way that we had never seen; she moved, when she was in those suits, with a kind of fierce, free, angry happiness, as if she might have her own kind of joyous source balled up within her.

And then came Kirby Nichole.

So while Kirby and Tricia were doing all this *stuff*, laying the framework for their lives, all I was doing was working out in basements. Most of my gains were behind me—by the time Tricia had Kirby Nichole, a good year for me was one where I increased my totals by 2 or 3 percent—but that was what I did.

I almost went to the Olympics the year of the boycott— 1984. I did not make the team, but I almost did, and if the rest of the country had gone, I almost would have, too. It was real close. I *almost* went. I even took those drugs— Winstrol, Anavar, Deca-Durabolin—for a couple of weeks, but then people started telling me how they'd give you cancer, so I quit and went back to tuna sandwiches and was relieved not to become dependent upon the drugs.

Powerlifting is different from other sports. You don't reach your peak until your late thirties or early forties. Fred Hatfield, down in New Orleans, forty-five years old—"Dr. Squat." Alexyev in seventy-six, gray-haired, a grandfather, taking the gold medal, belly and all. In this sport, you get stronger as you get older.

"Do you want her to leave?" I ask him, on one of our trips south, heading down after the *nalgai*—an impala-like animal of whose meat Kirby's boss, TLB, is fond. Her leaving is a long process: lots of papers, lawyers, and counseling. We're a bit like ironwood, the three of us; they've even had me come to some of their counseling sessions, since it's going to affect all three of us so strongly.

Kirby can't answer me. He just shakes his head, says, "I don't know."

The way he's determined to ride through this and remain Tricia's friend, it's not just for Kirby Nichole's benefit. He truly loves Tricia. And so why is she leaving? Isn't that all that's needed—to feel loved? To feel utmost, to feel unrivaled?

Sometimes I think Kirby's getting a little old and a little slow, that he's selling out a bit—hanging around with TLB so much. But this stuff with Tricia—it's like Kirby's found some kind of white-hot source within him, which is going to get him through this. He is not going to stop loving her.

Where will she go? How can she possibly go out on her own, separating from the three of us?

There was this trick she would do, with her fingernail: lighting a match on it. She'd pin the matchstick upright between her thumbnail and her fuck-you finger, and then bear down, letting the match quiver as it got tenser and tenser—the tip of the match pressing against the nail of her middle finger.

Tricia would be watching that match with a barely contained joy, her tongue between her teeth, the tension building as she pressed harder, and finally—she'd open her mouth right before this happened—the match would light, would jump a sixteenth of an inch to one side, and the sulfur tip would flare, and Tricia would drop the match and laugh, and it was a wonderful thing to see her so happy.

Except one time, the sulfur on the match tip lodged there in a gob on Tricia's fingernail; it stuck there when it ignited and burned a hole in her fingernail. It didn't burn all the way through, but it scared the hell out of her, because we couldn't put it out.

We were out at the lake, sitting around a campfire at night on a sandy beach, and she jumped up and tried to *flap* the fire out, waving her hand like it was caught in a trap, while all the time, that sulfur blazed and burrowed deeper and deeper into her fingernail. I jumped up and tried to cover the flesh-flame with my hand, but she screamed that it was still burning, and I could feel it still burning, so I picked her up and ran with her down to the lake and carried her out into the cool night water—and still, with her hand underwater, the sulfur kept blazing, stuck way up under that fingernail—but then it was finally out.

There was a terrible smell in the woods and in the tent. Tricia cried all night. It left a harsh little crater, and I still see her rubbing it with her thumb whenever she's distracted.

She has always had her own source within her, this fire, which Kirby and I are only now understanding: as much as that source can ever be understood.

Is Tricia disappointed in me? Sometimes I think that she is. And it shouldn't matter to me—but it does. I can't help but feel that by leaving Kirby, she's leaving me again, and that Kirby and I are the ones with those seams of weakness inside, as when a tree gets hit by lightning and doesn't die, but has that hollowed-out spiral within its trunk, smoldering—sometimes for years.

Is she disappointed in Kirby?

He just goes on steadfastly about his way, his job, his life, with no raging, no howls.

Perhaps he *has* gotten a little weak.

About those *nalgais* that we go get: they're rare. They're scary looking, like something that might have come from hell—some kind of weird mutant impala that some crazy rancher in the brush country came up with a hundred or so years ago, a Scottish cattle baron, as one story has it. This baron sold the *nalgais* to traveling circuses, but a few got away from the circus and established a small population in the area—just that fierce, ugly scrub brush and salt flats all around, no towns of any size for a hundred miles.

Nalgai meat is what Tom—TLB—wants, though. It's as if TLB is some kind of vampire—he must have that rich rare red-purple meat—and Kirby, the eternal number-two man, is the one who goes down into Mexico and gets it for him.

Has Kirby sold his soul? Not yet. But what if there is a fissure within? Might someday all fall apart?

We were like ironwood.

Kirby and I shoot the *nalgais* at night. For some time, the Mexican farmworkers and migrant families had been claiming occasionally to have seen a *nalgai*—almost always at night, never in the daytime—and though the Parks and Wildlife Department did helicopter surveys and set live traps, they had never seen a single *nalgai,* never where people said they had been seeing them, and so it was thought they did not really exist.

But Kirby and I found them, with an inside tip gotten from a cowboy in a bar in Crystal City one night. There's a herd we can always count on finding, down in this one salt wash, up an old uranium mining company's gravel road. (The first time we went there, we followed a map drawn for us on the back of a napkin.)

We take Kirby's big Suburban out into the scrub, the mesquite and huisache, with a Q-beam spotlight, and surprise the *nalgai* herd—it usually numbers between twenty and thirty animals—and I'll hold the light on the biggest one.

In the bright blaze of that light, their eyes are red, and they have enormous, noble horns and white zags of lightning on their faces, like war paint.

In the glare of the light, caught like that—the herd rising in a cloud of dust and beginning to bolt—the *nalgais'* eyes are *burning,* and the males have beards, like devils.

Kirby shoots whichever one I'm following with the Q-beam. He's always been a good shot, and he always drops one.

Then it's my job. We go out into the brush and clean the big animal—gut it, pull the stomach out, and leave the entrails for the coyotes. Then I hoist the animal over my back, carry it up out of the gorge, and load it into the back of the Suburban on a plastic tarp.

We will have brought a gallon of warm soapy water with us, and Kirby will pour the water over my hands, holding the flashlight in his teeth, while I scrub away the blood and then dry off with a towel, and then I will hold the flashlight and pour water over Kirby's hands. It's always amazing to me, looking at the *nalgai* in the back of the truck, to think of that fine and immediate line between being alive or dead.

We take the *nalgai* back to the States. There's a spot where Kirby lets me out, right on the Rio Grande; again, at night. I carry the *nalgai* on my back and wade the river—swim it if the water's high. I've got to watch for the border guards.

Then I climb the steep cliffs, dragging the great beast behind me like a leopard. It's hard, but the glow-ball burns bright. It's a thing to do.

I'll stay there in the moonless night, looking at the stars, sitting on top of the dead *nalgai* as if it's a couch, and I'll wait for Kirby's headlights. It's usually a two-hour wait. I'll just watch the stars. I'll think about Kirby Nichole. There will be shooting stars out there in the desert. Sometimes they pass so close you can hear them crackling, like lightning.

In Houston, then, there's a place that processes the meat; we don't have to do that work.

TLB saves the *nalgai*'s head each time; keeps them in a pile in his garage, like second-rate trophies. It's a big pile.

It becomes clear to me in the quiet times—alone at night, looking up at the ceiling just before falling asleep—that to judge Kirby would be to endanger my own hope for the future. We are still too much like ironwood, in spirit if not body. To view him or Tricia as weakening would be to grow weaker myself.

I know he's doing it—everything—for Kirby Nichole, his daughter. That he's getting stronger, not weaker.

It just looks like he's getting weaker.

Tricia won't tell us what she's got in mind. And she may not have anything specific—maybe she truly does just have to get out. And in the way that I "let" her go, seventeen years ago, Kirby is also "letting" her go. But it's different, now, and it bothers me; I have to work hard to keep it out of my mind, to keep it from distracting me and affecting my lifts.

I would still like to be a champion. I am still as good as any of the other lifters I go against. But I can't seem to get any better.

Some nights, with the separation in effect and the divorce imminent, Kirby and I get in the car and drive. We go to a place that we like to think of as having lower atmospheric pressure and the feel of calm, like a harbor, or a grove of old trees.

Sometimes that calming place is a bar and sometimes it is a movie or a basketball game, and sometimes we go on a road trip, but other nights we just go to TLB's house.

We park a block or two away. We get out and walk down the dark sidewalks, past all the warm lit colonial homes.

We walk up TLB's driveway, having parked a block or two away, and pause at the windows. We rarely see anyone. There is always the blue light of the television throbbing, rolling across the walls in the den, and we assume that's where the family unit is located, but we never see anyone moving around inside. Kirby has the theory that TLB is like a vampire and that his body ceases to exist after he gets off work.

Sometimes, though, it feels to me like TLB knows we're out there, that his whole family does, and that they're *hiding* from us.

Kirby goes into the garage and begins picking up all of TLB's tools—brooms, rakes, and shovels—hefting them, turning them over and studying them like an archaeologist. Then he puts the tools back in their places carefully.

I would like to mess with TLB's mind and hide them in strange places, as if leaving our wild scent, but Kirby is oddly protective of his boss and doesn't want me to disturb things. Sometimes Kirby gets in TLB's car, or in the station wagon that TLB's wife drives, and closes the door and just sits there.

He's drawing something from the air, from TLB's *place,* but I don't know what, and I don't want to know. I don't ever ask what it is we are after. I just accompany Kirby and watch.

Kirby looks tired, sitting in that car, and whatever it is he's trying to gain by sitting there, I don't want to know about.

Then Kirby will get out of TLB's car and go to the back of the garage and stare at all the bleached *nalgai* skulls; a dozen of them, maybe more, a nest of tall sharp horns, old history, old bounty, old sell-out. Kirby will have a soft smile on his face, and I know he'll be thinking of Kirby Nichole.

Wait, Tricia, I want to say. You don't know what you're leaving. You don't really have any idea.

But then I realize that in Tricia's mind, it's not an act of leaving one thing, but an act of moving toward another—moving toward the future.

Spirals running down through all of us, coiled, just waiting to be tapped.

"I'm going to stay friends with her," Kirby tells me. He's angry and anguished.

"She's changed," he says, with a little shrug. "I have to let her change," he says. "She's right. I can't *own* her."

"But my little *girl,*" Kirby says and begins to cry, which is a thing I have never seen before.

"At the divorce court," Kirby says, "I had to go down there alone and sign the papers. I went up to the sixth floor of the courthouse on the elevator. All the women were in pairs—with their friends. They were so angry and happy *both,*" Kirby says. "It was like all this *rage,* all this anger, was finally being lifted. And it was like those powerlifting meets we used to go to: it was like they'd won some huge victory whenever they got a great settlement. They were giving each other high-fives and hugging each other," he says. "Happy and angry both. And *mean*," Kirby says. "All of them looking at me with all this hate." Kirby shakes his head. He's speaking quietly now.

"I'm not going to be that way," he says. "I still love Tricia and don't want her to *die,* or anything. And I don't want to upset Kirby Nichole. I don't want to stretch her all thin and twisted, all nervous and neurotic, the way I've seen too many other divorced kids get."

There's just the sound of his breathing. There's just the sound of his heart.

He has lost what was treasured. And I will too, someday. All my life, all I've ever treasured is my great dumb strength. But to lose a *family?* To lose a complex, woven strength, rather than a simple brute strength?

I study my friend to learn from him, to see what happens when the glow-source, the white-hot lump, tries to fade.

What takes its place, when that glow-source is gone? Empty air? Regret?

I could have been a champion, back in eighty-four. And I might still be.

I watch films of the other older lifters, such as Alexyev, watch to see if I can pick up when and why they begin to lose it. At first, it's a certain dulling of their fury, in the snap and the rip of their initial jerks. In the beginning it's hard to spot, because that dulling can be masked by an increase in the older lifters' concentration—a good thing, as they bend over the bar and pause for a second. But I've been studying the films, all their old films, and I can spot it— I can point it out, almost to the day—when they begin to lose it.

A thing we weightlifters do sometimes is judge other

people. We look at them and decide, just by looking, how strong we think they are—though we have no right, of course, and we can't ever really tell.

A game that Kirby and I play sometimes, on road trips, involves our being out on the back roads, just driving—as we do with the *nalgais,* just out driving in the country— only this time where we can do no harm, and where there is, always and again, the chance of running across something rare.

Kirby looks around for heavy objects sometimes, trying to find one too heavy for me to lift, but only just barely. He wants it to be a challenge, but it's a game, too. After all these years, he still doesn't know exactly how strong I am: what I can and can't lift.

He looks for big buried objects, boulders up in the hill country or stumps in the sand.

It's just a game. We're best friends. There's only the tiniest bit of edge to it.

Kirby stops the truck when he finds the boulder he wants to test me with, and gets out and points to it and asks if I think I can lift it.

If I think I can, then I'll crouch beside it and wrap my arms around it, shifting my feet, looking for a good hold. And then I'll wrench and wrestle with it, rocking and pulling, and rip with everything I've got. And sometimes I will pull it out of the ground and lift it.

But other times it does not even budge.

We get back in the truck and drive on.

"Try that one, hot rod," Kirby says, pointing to a boulder. "Or that one," he'll say, waving the bottle toward an even larger one.

I'm lifting it for all of us, it seems—for Kirby and Tricia and Kirby Nichole and myself—and each time, it seems to me that if I can lift that boulder, then nothing's going to be lost, and nothing's being taken from us. *Nothing.*

"That one," Kirby says. "Lift that one." He watches me with curiosity, and then when I lift it, he points to a larger one. "That one," he says, "and then that one."

When you're out in the field like that, and you lift one of those big boulders, the white-glow fluttering and then spreading warmth throughout you—call it youth, or love, and call it never selling out—what you do is look straight out ahead at the horizon, shuddering: just looking straight ahead, with the boulder in your arms.

You ignore the coiled tiny quiver that's vibrating within, the seam of weakness that twists down through your heart's trunk: the one you always knew you had.

Instead, you just shut your eyes and pull hard, with everything you've got.

"Try that one," Kirby says, pointing to yet another boulder, searching for the biggest one.

I've got my arms wrapped around it, and I'm straining to pull it free, I'm shuddering and threatening yet again to fracture from within; and finally, as I start to move up with the boulder, as it breaks its grip with the earth, I hear the sound I have not been hearing, but the sound I need to hear.

The sound I hear is like a flaming, crackling roar: a sound that has been there all along, but which I am only just now hearing.

It is the sound of Kirby's heart, and he is not lifting anything, but instead is just standing there calmly beside me, *surviving.*

It is the sound of a maelstrom.

He will be the last among us to fracture. He will hold the rest of us up, the likes of Tricia and me, long after we've crumbled beneath our fierce and rigid notions of what we're after.

I stand there with the giant boulder against my chest, trembling to hold it up, and listen to Kirby's heart.

The sound of it is like a volcano. It roars louder, with more fury, each day.

Unlike everything else, it is not a thing that will diminish with time.

I've got to get my shit together. I've got to stop lifting heavy things and trying to hold on. I've got to let go and catch fire, like the rest of the world.

I am not yet in the real world. I haven't even started to get strong.

C O M M U N I O N

•

John L'Heureux

SNOW HAD FALLEN ALL through the night
and it continued to fall through the short bleak morning of
the day before Christmas. Though the sky remained overcast,
the snow stopped falling about noon, and the plowing crews
were able to clear the main highways and some of the side
roads. Conor was glad of this because it meant he would be
able to get through to his weekend call.

Conor had been ordained a priest the previous June and
so this would be his first Christmas mass. He was still studying at Shadowbrook, completing the fourth and final year
of theological studies required by the Jesuits, and though
he offered mass privately each morning, he was eager to be
out in a parish, hearing confessions and saying mass for real
people facing real problems in the real world. It would mean
missing the mulled wine after midnight services at Shadowbrook, but they'd probably give him a drink at the parish

anyhow. And it was good to get away. Life at Shadowbrook was fine; it was all that a young priest could hope for; but, in fact, it was a hothouse of spirituality, and Conor saw little point in preaching God's love and Christian forgiveness to the already saved.

And so on the morning of Christmas Eve, Conor packed his overnight case and went out to the back step of the theologate to wait for the car that would pick him up, along with five other newly ordained Jesuit priests who would all be dropped off at parishes around the city. They were a somewhat suspect group in the parishes, filled as they were with radical new ideas about scripture and the sacraments, but at Christmas all the local pastors were shorthanded and so these young Jesuits were welcomed for the work they could do, even though three of them sported beards.

Conor felt happy, he felt fortunate, as he charged out into the snow to do good, to bring a little peace into this world, to make people feel loved and valued and saved. How lucky I am, he thought.

He arrived at Our Lady of Victories parish with an hour to spare before afternoon confessions. The parking lot at the side of the church was still not plowed, and no path had been cleared to the front door of the rectory, so Conor, with only rubbers on his feet, plunged into the snow and waded, knee-deep, up the nonexistent path to the stoop. He shivered as the snow seeped down inside his shoes; he would get a cold out of this, for sure.

A snow shovel was propped up against the wall next to the door. Conor was just about to ring the bell when he thought, Oh, hell, it's Christmas, and he put down his overnight bag and began to shovel the stoop. When he finished, he cleared the stairs. He had made a good start on the cement walk when suddenly the front door opened and somebody yelled at him.

"What the hell do you think you're doing?"

Conor turned around and saw, standing in the doorway, an elderly priest with a red face and glasses. He was wearing a white T-shirt and black trousers, and his belly hung over his belt. He had his right hand curled around a coffee mug as if it were a grenade.

"You deaf?"

"Oh, sorry, Father," Conor said, all innocence and charm. "I saw that the walk hadn't been shoveled and I thought I'd just give you a hand."

"Get in here; it's freezing out there."

"Why don't I just finish this walk?" Conor said. "It'll only take me a few minutes and I'm almost . . . " But the door slammed before he could complete the sentence. Conor stared at the closed door for a moment, blushed, and said, feeling like a fool, ". . . done."

Snow had begun to fall again in heavy wet flakes and Conor pulled his scarf tighter around his neck. Yes, he'd get a cold from this; with any luck, he'd get pneumonia. God damn.

He finished shoveling the walk and then stamped his feet several times to shake off the snow. He stood on the stoop and examined his overnight case. He blew his nose. He took off his rubbers and placed them next to the door. Then he picked them up; they should go inside the door or they'd freeze. This was awful. Should he ring the bell? Should he just walk in as if nothing had happened? He waited there, in dread. Finally he pushed the door open and went inside.

"Out here," someone called, and Conor pulled off his rubbers and followed the voice into the kitchen where the priest sat at a table hunched over the sports page of the newspaper while the cook stirred something on the stove.

"Happy Christmas!" Conor said.

The cook turned and looked at him for a moment and then went back to her stirring. The priest said, "Have some coffee," and kept on reading his newspaper.

Conor took off his coat. "Good afternoon, Father. I'm from Shadowbrook? I'm here to help with confessions and mass. Gosh, that's some snow. I was afraid I wouldn't be able to get through." He looked around for some place to hang up his coat. "You're Father . . . ?"

"Just toss it anywhere," the priest said, folding his paper and scooting back his chair, all action suddenly. "Have some coffee. What's the matter with you anyway, shoveling the walk. You're a Jesuit, right? Beard and all. What are you, New Breed or something?"

"I don't know what you mean, Father. New Breed."

Conor knew exactly what he meant. Any priest this old and this fat used the term "New Breed" to mean all those things that menaced his existence: antiwar activists like the Berrigans; folk masses with guitars; the usual threats—the threat of English in the liturgy, the threat of birth control, the threat of every single thing they were now talking about at Vatican II, a council already in its second year and bound to turn out disastrous. That's what he meant.

The priest merely stared at Conor and Conor stared back.

"Have some coffee," the priest said, and this time he pointed to a little sidetable with a coffeepot and some cups. "How long have you been ordained, Father?"

"Six months; almost six months to the day."

"Six months. That's not long, even for a Jesuit. You burn draft cards and that sort of thing? You want to stop the war?" He waited for an answer, but there was none. "What kind of last name is that you've got, anyway? French? You French?"

"I'm half French. Half Irish. Hence Conor for a first name."

"Hence," the priest said, with a laugh. And in a prissy voice, "Hence."

Conor stared into his coffee cup. "And your name, Father?"

"Pure Irish. Mahoney. And this is Mrs. Carberry; she's Irish too." Mrs. Carberry turned and frowned at them both just as another priest entered the kitchen, this one also in a T-shirt and black trousers. He was thin, scrawny even, with a pointy face and the smell of alcohol on him. He could have been any age between forty and sixty. "And Father Riley is my assistant. He's Irish too. This is the Jesuit, Riley. Father here is a French Jesuit. With a beard. Shovels walks, he does."

Father Riley rubbed his eyes and yawned. "Can't wake up," he said. He walked to the refrigerator and stuck his head inside. "Nothing here but a load of castiron crap," he said.

"Now, listen up, sonny," Father Mahoney said to Conor. "Everything around here is done by the rules. In liturgy, we follow the rules of the Church. And around the house, we follow *my* rules. Got it?"

Conor smiled. "But of course."

"But of course," Father Mahoney said, in that voice again. "But of course. So, here are some rules. Confessions this afternoon from three-thirty to five-thirty. Dinner at six. Not six-fifteen. Six. Confessions again from seven-thirty to nine. Midnight mass at midnight. Get there at a quarter to. It'll be a High Mass, but don't panic; I do most of the singing. One thing Jesuits can never do is sing. I'll be celebrant; Riley here will be deacon; you'll be subdeacon. There's a rubrics chart in the sacristy, so study it sometime before mass tonight. One thing Jesuits never know is rubrics. Got that?"

"Got it. And I do happen to know the rubrics."

"You happen to. Good. Now do you happen to know why I don't want you doing any more shoveling?"

"Father, it's Christmas," Conor said, the peacemaker.

"I don't want you shoveling because we pay a man, pay him very well, to do exactly that. But he's out today . . . on a bender. And when he comes in tomorrow or the next day or whenever he finally makes it, I want him to see just how much trouble he's caused us. See?"

"See," Conor said.

Father Mahoney took one last sip from his coffee cup and left the kitchen.

Conor turned from him to Mrs. Carberry who was now busying herself at the sink. He turned to Father Riley who still stood with his head in the refrigerator.

"I wonder if someone could tell me where my room is?" Conor asked.

Without a word, Mrs. Carberry pointed to a door at the far end of the kitchen.

"Happy Christmas," Conor said.

"It's *merry* Christmas," Mrs. Carberry said.

Above the door to the confessional was a slot for the visiting priest's name. Conor was just inserting the strip of white cardboard printed with his name, and the S.J., when Father Mahoney came up behind him and said, "I see you're advertising the S.J. That should bring the customers in."

Conor could tell some answer was expected, but he refused and offered the old priest only a hard smile.

Father Mahoney took a step backward and said, almost apologetically, "It was only a joke," and when Conor continued the hard smile, Father Mahoney turned and made his way slowly down the aisle and across the church to his own confessional.

Conor sat in the darkness and thought of his wet feet.

He caught cold every year, and once he'd caught it, it would stay around till spring. He'd dried his hair and changed his socks before coming out to hear confessions, but he had only the one pair of shoes and, of course, they were wet all through. It's that damned Mahoney, he thought, and then asked God's forgiveness because Mahoney was probably a good priest according to his own lights, dim though they were, and who could guess what private suffering Mahoney had to endure, etc., etc.

There was no room for emotion, hot or cold, in Jesuit piety, Conor liked to say. No room for hate or even resentment, and certainly no room for sentimentality. And so, who was he to judge the Mahoneys of this world? The long course of Jesuit training—indeed, fifteen years long—was intended to produce men with a naked and ruthless knowledge of self; it went without saying that that knowledge presupposed the desire and commitment to reform the self in the likeness of Jesus Christ. And he himself was as far from the likeness as you could get, Conor knew. So leave poor Mahoney alone. And at once he found himself thinking, Yes, leave the dead to bury the dead. But at just that moment someone entered the confessional on his right, and Conor immediately forgot his failure of charity, his head cold, the unspeakable Father Mahoney.

"Bless me, Father, for I have sinned. It is two weeks since my last confession, and these are my sins."

"Mm-hmm," Conor murmured, an encouraging sound.

"What?"

"Nothing. That's fine. Go right ahead."

"Oh, okay. Bless me, Father, for I have sinned. It is two weeks since my last confession, and these are my sins." Pause. "I was mean to my little brother twice; I told a lie once; I sassed my mother seven times; I masturbated six times; I forgot my evening prayers twice; and I took the Lord's name in vain nineteen times."

Ah, Conor thought, the sin sandwich. They all did this, dropped the big sin in the middle of all the little ones, hoping it wouldn't get too much notice.

"I see," Conor said. "Well that's fine. It sounds as if you're trying hard to be a good guy. How old are you anyway?"

There was silence. None of them were used to being spoken to as if they were people. After a while, the boy said, "How old?" And then, "Fourteen."

"Fourteen!" Conor said, as if he were astounded that anybody could be fourteen. "Well, that's a really rough age. I had a terrible time when I was fourteen. Let me ask you something about your confession, okay? You said you were mean to your little brother; how old is he?"

"Six, Father."

"Oh, six. Well, they can be an awful pain in the neck at six, right? But of course, you're so much older—you're practically a man now—you can be patient with him. I mean, you want to be, don't you."

"Yes, Father."

"Sure, of course you do. I know you do. Now, the other thing. Taking the Lord's name in vain. What do you think about that anyhow?"

"It's a sin, Father."

"Well, I don't know how much of a sin it is, but it *sounds* lousy. Don't you think? I think so. Oh sure, all the other guys say it and we figure we sound like one of the guys, you know, we really fit in if we say it too. But it sounds like hell. It's a bad habit."

"Yes, Father."

"Now I guess that's all. Oh, wait, you mentioned something else; masturbation, was it? Well, a lot of fuss is made about that. I don't know. Just do your best and try to help around the house. And be nice to your little brother, especially tomorrow, because it's Christmas and he's gonna be very excited and will probably drive you crazy. But just try to make it a nice day for him and for your folks, your mom and dad, all right?"

"Yes, Father." Relief in the voice.

"You're a good kid, don't forget that. Now, for your penance say one Our Father and thank God you've got such a good family."

Conor gave the boy absolution, sketched a large sign of the cross in the air, and slid the little window closed. He sighed once, happy, and tilting his head to the other side, slid open the little window on his left.

Let me help, he prayed silently, let me just help.

"Bless me, Father, . . . " It was a woman's voice—birth control, of course—and Conor's long afternoon of confessions began in earnest.

The same old sins. There were no new ones. Fornication, adultery, masturbation. Birth control. Drunkenness. Theft. Wife-beating. And then the nice category nobody minded confessing: sins against charity. Uncharitable thoughts, uncharitable conversations, uncharitable actions. No murderers and no rapists: apparently murderers and rapists made their confessions only after they'd landed on death row. And so he sat there for two hours and heard the endless catalog of small failures. Of good people. Because only good people came to confession in the first place.

"God bless you, you're a fine woman," Conor said and gave her as a penance that she do some nice thing for herself—nothing big, necessarily—just buy herself a magazine she wanted or take a morning off and watch television or something, just to thank God that life is good. He gave her absolution then, and as he slid the window shut, he prayed—a little self-conscious about the words—Oh You whom I love, please let me help.

During the final hour he had begun to sneeze and his handkerchief was already soaked through, but he didn't mind; this was wonderful; this was the priesthood at its most intimate and effective. He could sit here frozen and sneezing forever.

As it happened, Conor sat there long beyond Father Mahoney's five-thirty curfew and as a result arrived at the dinner table ten minutes late. He noticed at once there was no wine in sight. Water, water everywhere.

Father Mahoney gave Conor a suspicious look, as if he had come late to table because of some criminal activity, and then he explained that they had to serve themselves tonight because Mrs. Carberry had the evening off, that Conor had already missed the soup course that was Mrs. Carberry's masterpiece, that out of respect for Mrs. Carberry's troubles—she had buried her husband earlier in the week—they would eat their small meal in silence.

Conor was surprised that the laconic Mrs. Carberry—it's *merry* Christmas—featured so largely in the life of the rectory, but he was grateful for the silence because he had come to dinner fearing another inquisition. Beard, birth control, New Breed. He shot a quick glance at Father Riley, who, very clearly, was drunk. Conor gave his complete attention to chewing the stringy meat. Veal?

When Father Mahoney got up to clear the table, Conor started to get up too, but Father Mahoney gestured him back to his chair.

"But I'd like to help," Conor said.

Father Mahoney repeated the gesture and then gathered the plates and took them to the kitchen.

"Well, that was delicious," Conor said, half to Father Riley and half to his plate. He looked up and saw Father Riley staring at him, curious.

"What was it?" Father Riley said.

"The dinner," Conor said. "It was delicious."

"But what was it?" Father Riley repeated.

Conor looked at him blankly.

"I'll tell you what it was," Father Riley said. "It was a goddamn rubber boot, that's what it was."

Conor laughed at what he presumed was a joke, but Father Riley merely continued to stare at him with that same curious look.

Father Mahoney returned with a pot of coffee and two wedges of chocolate cake. "Devil's food," he said, smiling, and told them to leave their plates on the table; he would get them later. "Fathers," he said, bemused, and left the dining room.

They were silent for a moment and then Father Riley lifted the coffeepot and said, "Some?" He filled Conor's cup but poured only a splash or two into his own. From deep inside his cassock pocket he pulled out a half-pint of scotch and poured at least half of it into his coffee. Conor stared at him, astonished, and Father Riley said, "I'm not hearing confessions tonight." And then, when Conor continued to stare, he added, "It's all right. It helps me relax."

Desperate, Conor asked, "Does Father Mahoney always serve at table? That's very impressive."

"Once a week. It's a thing with him." For a moment he assumed Father Mahoney's mocking voice: "*So he'll never forget that he's a servant of God, and therefore a servant of man.* Or so he says. I think he just likes to do it."

"Well, it's very impressive."

"There's something I want to ask you." He stared at Conor with his curious stare, and then took a long swallow of his drink.

"Yes?"

" 'Yes?' 'Very impressive!' 'Quite delicious!' You *are* the proper little priest, aren't you." He raised the cup to his mouth. "Well, you're young."

"I think I'll go take a look at the rubrics for tonight's mass," Conor said and started to get up.

"No, please. I'm sorry. I do want to ask you something and I am sincere about it. Okay? Okay. So keep your seat. What I want to know is how you Jesuits get away with preaching birth control. And why do you want to? I mean, the Pope has said we can't. Period. And that's that."

"Well, I'm afraid I see it as a little bit more complicated than that, Father. Maybe some time we could talk about it. Right now . . . well."

"Right now I'm too drunk to understand, you mean. Right? Try me. Go ahead, explain."

As soon as he saw he had Conor hooked, Father Riley pulled the bottle from his pocket and refilled his cup. "It helps me concentrate," he said.

And so, doubting he should do this but unable to stop himself, Conor explained the complicated process of reasoning by which he—and indeed most of the other young Jesuits from Shadowbrook—concluded that he was not preaching birth control but only helping concerned Catholics to form their own consciences in an intelligent and responsible way. "Do you see the difference?" he said.

"But how do you actually do it?" Father Riley asked him. "What do you actually say?"

"You just help them see where *they* feel their duty lies. It's *their* conscience, after all."

"But how do you get them to see? What do you tell them?"

Conor gave Father Riley a long hard look. Was he, in fact, drunk? Was he sincere? Was Riley just getting the goods on him so that he could stagger off to old Mahoney, or even to the Bishop, and cause all kinds of trouble?

"You could help me," Father Riley said. "Sincerely."

Conor blew his nose and thought about it. This could be very dumb. Everybody knew that parishes were the last outposts of the scalping conservatives and here he was about to tell a drunk how he advised penitents in confession. There would be trouble with the pastor. There would be trouble

with the Bishop. There would be trouble out at Shadowbrook.
And eventually Conor himself would have his ass handed to
him. No, he should simply refuse.

"I'm coming down with a terrible cold," he said.

"Help me" Father Riley said.

Oh, God, Conor said to himself, help *me*. And to Father
Riley he said, "Well, I do this. First off, I talk to them about
the other things they've mentioned—you know, the usual
stuff, impatience with their kids, missing mass, sins against
charity, stuff like that. And after I've talked for a while, I
say something like—let's see—'I think you mentioned that
you've been practicing birth control? Is that right?' And
they'll say they use the pill, or they've been trying to stop,
or they know it's a sin. But the thing is to ask them, right
away, why they think it's a sin, and invariably they'll say:
'because the Church says it is.' "

Conor paused to see how Father Riley was taking this.
He was hunched over his coffee cup, but not drinking.

"And then?"

"And then I try to explain that it isn't just a question of
what the Church says; the birth control issue is far more
complicated than that."

"But what do you *say?*"

"Oh, God. I *say* that, yes, the Church sets down as a
general rule—and I underline those words for them: *as a
general rule*—that Catholics shouldn't use birth control. But
the issue, I tell them, is essentially a personal one, involving
private rather than general norms of morality, and so it's
the responsibility of each of us to *in*form our minds on the
matter so that we can properly *form* our own *consciences.*
You see, I've got it down to a rote speech, practically."

"And then you help them inform their minds."

"I tell them they should ask themselves three questions.
Like this. I say: 'First, you should ask yourself if you are
shirking your Christian responsibilities; that is to say, do I

just want the pleasures of sex without the responsibility of children? Now, you've already got three children, you said, so obviously you're not out just for pleasure.' Or, if they don't have any children, I say that 'probably you'll want to have children later, someday.' Anyway, I take away their worry about the sex part. 'Second, you ask yourself if there is some real *need* for you to use birth control. But you've already indicated financial reasons—or psychological, or physical, or whatever.' I just fit the answer to the case, you see. 'Third, you should ask yourself if this is going to help you and your spouse to lead a fuller, happier, more responsible Christian life. Now only you and your spouse together can answer that, so you should have a discussion with him or her, and then once you've made up your mind to use or not to use birth control, then just go ahead and live comfortably with your decision. And whatever you do, don't mention it in confession again, because eventually you're sure to run into some crazy priest who'll scream and yell and say you're committing mortal sin.' "

"Fantastic."

"Wait. I'm not done. Then—because by now they're usually so excited they're liable to forget—I give them a quick run-through once again. I say, 'Now I'll repeat those questions just to make sure you've got them right. One: Do I just want sex without the responsibility of children? Two: Do I have a genuine need to practice birth control? Three: Is this going to help me and my spouse live a better, fuller Christian life? Got it?' And then I send them on their way. Rejoicing."

"Fantastic."

"Well, it's sound morality, I think. And it helps people to assume responsibility for their own lives." Conor paused a moment and then added, "I try to get them past fear, past blind obedience." He paused once more. "I try to help them see it's only love that matters."

Father Riley, saying nothing, looked past Conor at something or other. At once Conor felt trapped, terrified; he turned to see what Father Riley was looking at, expecting to see Father Mahoney, expecting to be denounced for hypocrisy, for New Breedism, for God knows what. But no one was there; Father Riley was merely looking into a new world of possibilities.

Conor let out a long breath and turned back to Father Riley. "Well, I hope that helps," he said, thinking, I've done it now; I'm gonna pay for this.

"I always wanted to be a priest," Father Riley said, and a boozy tear slid crookedly down his cheek.

Conor excused himself to go get ready for evening confessions.

There had been a number of people lined up at his confessional by the time Conor arrived, but now he had heard them all and was free to think about himself for a moment. He blew his nose, too hard, and got a terrible pain in the ear. His feet were wet all over again and his cassock was soaking from the knees down.

On the walk over to the church he had helped push a stalled car, and when the wheels suddenly caught traction, they sprayed snow and slush all over him. His overcoat was soaking wet too. And he was sweating. Pneumonia, just watch.

He wanted a drink. Maybe Father Riley would still be in the kitchen after confessions, maybe with a new bottle, and Conor could have a good belt, and then lie down until midnight. But of course he couldn't lie down; he'd have to study rubrics for the midnight mass. Because of course that damned Mahoney was right; Jesuits *never* knew what to do or where to go during a High Mass. Still, as subdeacon, he'd have very little to do; it would take only a few minutes to go over the rubrics.

Conor thought of Father Riley. He was supposed to be the deacon. Could he do it? With all that booze in him? Worse yet, with all that booze in him, would he blab to Mahoney about the birth control stuff? And, oh God, this filthy cold coming on.

I've got to learn prudence, Conor told himself. Prudence in speech. Prudence in action. What a boring virtue. "Prudence, the ugly step-sister of Incapacity." Blake? Yeats?

There was a rattle and a clunk in the confessional on his left, so Conor closed one window and opened the other. He would have to think of prudence later. After a moment of waiting for the penitent to start, Conor said, "Fine. You can begin anytime."

"I can't see you." It was a woman's voice.

"That's okay. So long as we can hear."

A long pause.

"*Can* you hear me?"

"Do you have a beard?"

"Um, well, yes. But what is the point?" Conor began to feel very uneasy. This is not how confessions were supposed to go. There was no room for the personal here, no room for chats. If there was any chatting to be done, the priest would do it. "What is the point of asking if I have a beard?"

"A friend who came to confession this afternoon told me about you. She said to be sure to go to the one with the beard, but I can't see through this screen."

"Well, perhaps we can begin," Conor said, a little icy, and the woman, picking up his tone, began at once. Birth control again.

It was like that for the next hour: a succession of women and men who had not been to confession in months, a year, in several years. Conor was moved and sympathetic, but he had been rattled by that first woman, chummy and chatty, and so he was careful to remain a little distant, a little formal, a little . . . he searched for the word . . . a little priestly.

His head ached and his throat felt raw. Between the penitents he checked his watch; it was eight-thirty. Good. He wanted to lie down.

And then, just as he was about to slide the screen open, he heard the voice of Father Mahoney booming from the other side of the church. "You people kneeling over there. Yes, you. Come over to this side and I'll hear your confessions."

My God, Conor thought, talk about bringing in customers! What a scandal that Mahoney was. What a woebegone wreck of the priesthood. What a commentary . . . but there was no point in going on about how hopeless priests were. The point was to do something about it.

Conor slid the window open and yet again the non-sin was birth control. And yet again he launched into his three-point speech. Love is what matters.

"You three over there." It was Mahoney's voice, booming. "Two of you come over here. It's nine o'clock and we're closing now. So you two come over here."

God, I hate that man, Conor thought.

He refused to be rushed with this last confession. He was saying the words of absolution and had just raised his hand to begin making the sign of the cross when someone knocked hard and long at the door to his confessional. Mahoney, of course. "Father? You! Father! We're locking up now, so finish up here and leave by the left rear door. The left. Rear. No more confessions after this."

Conor repeated the words of absolution, apologized to the penitent, and then sat silently for a moment, blushing, furious. That utter fool!

As Conor went out by the left rear door, he was startled to find Father Mahoney there, shouting at three young men who were standing at a little distance, up to their knees in snow.

"This isn't a supermarket, you know," Father Mahoney

was saying. "If you want to go to confession, you get here on time. You can't just come in here any old time you want. This is no supermarket."

The three young men continued to stand there listening, uncertain what to do. Finally, one of them turned and started making his way out to the street. The others followed him.

Father Mahoney cleared his throat noisily and said to Conor, "I know that type. Confession once a year and then three hundred and sixty-four days of sin."

Conor had watched the scene in disbelief, his annoyance at Father Mahoney giving way to embarrassment and then to rage. Suddenly he came to himself. He jumped down from the steps and took off after the young men. "Wait," he shouted as he plunged through the deep snow. "Please wait."

He caught up with them at the street, out of breath and soaking wet all over again. He apologized for Father Mahoney; he grimaced and shook his head conspiratorially so they would know he was on their side; and then he led them off one by one to hear their confessions. He stood on top of the church steps, his back turned, his head lowered. It was just as Father Mahoney had said; none of the three had been to confession in a year. All the more reason, Conor thought, for hearing them. It was like the Middle Ages, really: priest and penitent huddled at the church door, the once-a-year reconciliation on the feast of Christ's birth, the snow falling. It was romantic, beautiful. It was an act of love.

Conor absolved the last of the three, shook his hand, and waited as he went down the steps to rejoin his friends. They turned and waved to him. "Happy Christmas," Conor called after them. He watched as they made their way down the snowy street. One of them jumped in the air suddenly and let out a war whoop; the others laughed, and one of them scooped up a snowball and threw it at the one who had whooped.

"I have done a *good thing*," Conor said aloud to the empty air, and then he descended the steps and walked slowly through the snow to the rectory and to the inevitable encounter with that fool Mahoney.

Conor paused inside the front door, listening. There were loud voices in the kitchen; Father Riley, thoroughly drunk by now, was trying to explain something to Father Mahoney, and Father Mahoney was trying to convince him to go to bed. Conor was shucking off his rubbers when suddenly the voices grew louder and he heard Father Riley say, in his muzzy voice, "Listen to me. I'm serious. We just have to tell them to ask themselves three questions, and then it's all right and they can practice birth control." And he heard Father Mahoney say, "Go to bed, Father. Now." Father Riley protested further, and again Father Mahoney said, "Now," and then Father Riley broke off in the middle of a sentence, walked unsteadily into the living room and, without a word to Conor, went up the stairs to bed.

So, this is it, Conor said to himself and squared his shoulders, ready for the fight. But when he entered the kitchen, expecting to find Father Mahoney red-faced and righteous, he was astonished to find him instead with his eyes shut and his hands knotted in prayer. Conor stood there waiting for Mahoney to open his eyes and get on with it, but the old priest continued to pray for what seemed like minutes.

Conor stood silent all this time, waiting.

"Ah, it's you," Father Mahoney said finally. "I didn't hear you come in."

"Little cat feet," Conor said, his voice cold, his wits ready for a fight.

But Father Mahoney did not seem to hear him. He took a deep breath and Conor, watching him, realized suddenly that Father Mahoney was a very old and very tired man.

"My son," he began. He ignored Conor's smile, which might have been genuine or merely ironic, and continued in a tired voice, "You are a very, very young priest. What you say in confessions is between you and God, and therefore between you and the Bishop as well, but it's God finally that you're going to have to answer to. But since you're preaching birth control—in the confessional of all places—and here in my parish, I feel it is *my* duty to say this to you."

Conor's smile now was certainly not genuine.

"I want you to ask yourself one question. Not three. Only one. You make a lot of people happy by what you say in confession. They wait outside your confessional. They stand on the church steps in the snow. And they think you're wonderful. Of course they do. Of course they do. But I want you to ask yourself this question. Whom are you serving? Who is your God?"

Conor had been ready for a direct attack, for bombast. By the time he was able to take in just what Father Mahoney had said, the old priest had turned and walked slowly from the kitchen. Conor stood there in silence, listening to the slow soft footfalls as Father Mahoney ascended the stairs.

I'm getting pneumonia, Conor thought; I'm going to die of this. There is a large wet cat asleep in my head.

His mind was racing back and forth through the day; his cold, confessions, Father Mahoney, poor old drunken Riley, the three guys whose confessions he heard on the church steps. But always he came back to Father Mahoney asking him, "Whom are you serving? Who is your God?"

Conor was sitting with his hands folded in his lap, his eyes lowered, the model of religious propriety. Father Riley was sitting next to him, he too a model of religious propriety. Father Mahoney was—forgive the expression, Conor said to himself—preaching. They were halfway through midnight mass and everything was going smoothly. Except for the cold. Conor's throat was raw and his nose was stuffed and he wanted a drink. Surely old Mahoney would loosen up after mass and give them all a Christmas belt of Irish whiskey.

Conor shot a glance at Father Riley. Amazing. He was sitting there, hands folded, eyes straight ahead, as if he had never had a drink in his life. How had he done this? Evidently his powers of recuperation were mammoth. Two hours earlier he had scarcely been able to walk and talk and now here he was, clean-shaven and clear-eyed, the perfect little Irish priesty-poo.

Priests. They made him sick. Always so right, so righteous, so complacent. Look at that old fool Mahoney up there, mouthing platitudes about the stable, the shepherds, the wise men. The *wise* men—my God!

Conor forced himself not to listen. He had spent the past two hours going over and over tomorrow's homily and now he launched into it one more time. He had written it a week earlier and had timed it with a stopwatch. Seven minutes exactly. Theologically sound. And to the point. "Love shows itself in deeds, not words. The Word of God is love."

Father Mahoney had stopped preaching, finally, and now the dreadful choir was beginning the Credo, and Conor had to give his attention to the mass itself. If only his mind would stop racing. And at that instant he decided he would say tomorrow's mass in English. He had done the translation himself and, though he had never yet used it publicly, he always carried it with him on weekend calls. Just in case. It was only a matter of time anyhow until Rome authorized the mass in the vernacular, so no one would care. Except Mahoney. But he'd never find out.

In no time at all they were at the Consecration, and then they were distributing Communion, and finally—Conor's mind was still on tomorrow's mass in English—Father Mahoney was giving the last blessing and the choir was bleating out "Joy to the World" and it was all done.

They took off their vestments in silence. Conor kept hoping Mahoney would propose a nightcap or two, but perhaps this wasn't the right moment. Father Riley disappeared almost immediately, in pursuit of his own nightcap no doubt, and then Father Mahoney got involved in a long conversation with the head usher, so Conor had no choice but to walk back to the rectory alone. Could it possibly be that Mahoney had no intention of offering drinks at all?

Snow was still falling, and it was very wet now, so the street was deep in slush. Cars were stuck in the snow and horns were honking, but everybody was calling out happily to everybody else as if—Conor found himself thinking—as if it were Christmas. He was suddenly very depressed.

"Father? Have you got a second, Father?" A bald man in a red-and-black mackinaw thrust a package—unmistakably booze—into Conor's hands. "It's for Father Mahoney, could you give it to him for me? It's a little Christmas cheer. And, Father, no sampling, right?" He let out a loud laugh and punched Conor on the arm. "Get it? Just a joke. Merry Christmas, Father." And he was gone.

Conor sat in his bed, comfy, propped up against the pillows. "Fate and free will," he said, filling his glass with scotch. "Here's to Father Mahoney, who alone has made this possible."

Now that he had opened it, he would have to take the bottle back to Shadowbrook. The card too. Imagine becoming a thief for a bottle of booze.

"Here's to you, Father Riley."

Conor refilled his glass and put the light out. The last thing he wanted now was for Father Mahoney to stop by and invite him to have a drink.

"And to you, Mrs. Carberry."

He sat in the dark, drinking and toasting penitents everywhere.

"Happy Christmas to all," he said. "God bless us, every one."

Conor woke at six, his eyes on fire, his throat raw. At first he could not remember where he was, but then he saw the half-empty bottle beside his bed and he remembered: Our Lady of Victories parish. And he had the seven o'clock mass to say. And then the ten o'clock mass.

And he was sick. The cold had settled in all right, but the hangover was the worst part of it. He knew how it would be: dull pain for a few hours, and then nausea for a while, and then—after the entire day had been ruined—recovery. The important thing was to get through mass before the nausea set in. Oh God, how did these things happen?

He blew his nose until it began to bleed, and then he dragged himself to the shower. A shave, a clean shirt, a forced fleeting smile; he began to feel a little better. But when he came through the passage into the kitchen, the smell of cooking made his stomach turn and he thought he was going to be sick. He put his hand to his mouth and concentrated on keeping a calm stomach.

"Good morning, Father, and a merry Christmas to you!" Father Mahoney was full of high spirits this morning.

Conor mumbled a good morning and made his way to the little table with the coffee cups.

"I'm making French toast especially for you," Mrs. Carberry said. "So you'll have your own merry Christmas. Right after your seven o'clock holy mass."

The thought of French toast made Conor's stomach turn once more.

"You're very kind," he said.

"Sure, it's only the start. There'll be ham and eggs and coffee cake and my own biscuits . . ."

Mrs. Carberry went on listing the things they would have for breakfast, but Conor interrupted her. "I never have more than coffee," he said. "But it's nice of you to go to all that trouble."

"Trouble! It's no trouble. It's all the pleasure I get in life, baking this and that, a little peach cobbler, a little . . ."

"Merry Christmas. Merry Christmas. A Christmas kiss for you, my dear," and Father Riley, fresh from his five-thirty mass, planted a kiss on Mrs. Carberry's cheek. "Merry Christmas, Father," he said to Father Mahoney. "And to you, Father."

They're all mad, Conor thought; they're all possessed. Yesterday nobody would speak a civil word and this morning nothing can shut them up. He took a long drink of coffee and immediately choked. "Excuse me," he said and made for his bedroom.

Only twenty minutes until mass and his head would not stop pounding. Just so that I don't get nauseous, he said to himself. Anything but that.

He got out his English version of the canon—yes, that will make them a wonderful Christmas present—and folded it into his breast pocket. He glanced at the opening paragraph of his homily. Yes, even hungover, he had that by heart. If he could just pull himself together a little more, everything would be perfect.

Walking over to the church he was dazzled by the sun. The snow had stopped and it was a beautiful winter morning, the air bright and clear. Conor slitted his eyes against all the light.

Mass started out well. The altar boys knew their Latin responses and the organist was on key and—proving the existence of a merciful God, Conor thought—the choir did not sing at the early morning masses. But everything began to go wrong at the Gloria. Conor suddenly went cold and his forehead broke out in sweat. He couldn't concentrate. Reading the Epistle and then the Gospel, he couldn't get any genuine feeling in his voice, in his heart. And now it was time for his homily.

"Love shows itself in deeds, not words. The Word of God is love." But everything he said sounded flat, rehearsed. It was all words. Only words.

Desperately, Conor tried to feel something. Anything. And so, while the words fell from his lips in perfect order, the sentences balanced, the images sharp, Conor's mind raced through this weekend for something to draw meaning from: the confessions, the good advice given, the sincerity and warmth of the people he had counseled. He thought of these things, but he felt nothing.

And then after the homily, while he was pouring the wine into the chalice, the smell of it went straight to his head and from there straight to his stomach. His eyes burned and his head swam. He *was* going to be sick. But by an act of the will, he choked back the nausea and went on. The important thing now was just to get through this.

But then all at once, as he was about to say the words of consecration over the bread, he realized that he had completely forgotten to say the canon in English. He should be saying "This is my body," instead of "*Hoc est enim corpus meum.*" He forgot his nausea for a moment in the sheer annoyance of it all. He had brought the canon with him; this was the perfect opportunity to use it; if any parish ever needed to be brought into the twentieth century, this was it. And now he had forgotten to use it.

Illogically, Conor found himself thinking, It's all that damned Mahoney's fault. And immediately, as if by thinking of him he had made the man come alive at the altar, he heard Father Mahoney's sad little question, "Whom are you serving? Who is your God?"

Conor bent low over the chalice for the consecration of the wine. He spoke the words simply, feelingly, in English. "For this is the chalice of my blood, of the new and everlasting covenant; the mystery of faith; which shall be shed for you and for many others unto the forgiveness of sins."

He could feel a stir in the church as the people, probably for the first time in their lives, heard the actual words of consecration in language they could understand.

Conor spoke the last of the words: "As often as you shall do these things, you shall do them in memory of me."

He paused then and gazed into the amber wine, this sacred drink, which is the true blood of Christ, and saw mirrored there only his own hard eyes, swollen, scorched. And for a second that would last forever, Conor knew who it was he served.

AUGGIE WREN'S CHRISTMAS STORY

●

Paul Auster

I HEARD THIS STORY FROM Auggie Wren. Since Auggie doesn't come off too well in it, at least not as well as he'd like to, he's asked me not to use his real name. Other than that, the whole business about the lost wallet and the blind woman and the Christmas dinner is just as he told it to me.

Auggie and I have known each other for close to eleven years now. He works behind the counter of a cigar store on Court Street in downtown Brooklyn, and since it's the only store that carries the little Dutch cigars I like to smoke, I go in there fairly often. For a long time, I didn't give much thought to Auggie Wren. He was the strange little man who wore a hooded blue sweatshirt and sold me cigars and magazines, the impish, wisecracking character who always had something funny to say about the weather or the Mets or the politicians in Washington, and that was the extent of it.

But then one day several years ago he happened to be looking through a magazine in the store, and he stumbled across a review of one of my books. He knew it was me because a photograph accompanied the review, and after that things changed between us. I was no longer just another customer to Auggie, I had become a distinguished person. Most people couldn't care less about books and writers, but it turned out that Auggie considered himself an artist. Now that he had cracked the secret of who I was, he embraced me as an ally, a confidant, a brother-in-arms. To tell the truth, I found it rather embarrassing. Then, almost inevitably, a moment came when he asked if I would be willing to look at his photographs. Given his enthusiasm and goodwill, there didn't seem to be any way I could turn him down.

God knows what I was expecting. At the very least, it wasn't what Auggie showed me the next day. In a small, windowless room at the back of the store, he opened a cardboard box and pulled out twelve identical black photo albums. This was his life's work, he said, and it didn't take him more than five minutes a day to do it. Every morning for the past twelve years, he had stood at the corner of Atlantic Avenue and Clinton Street at precisely seven o'clock and had taken a single color photograph of precisely the same view. The project now ran to more than four thousand photographs. Each album represented a different year, and all the pictures were laid out in sequence, from January 1 to December 31, with the dates carefully recorded under each one.

As I flipped through the albums and began to study Auggie's work, I didn't know what to think. My first impression was that it was the oddest, most bewildering thing I had ever seen. All the pictures were the same. The whole project was a numbing onslaught of repetition, the same street and the same buildings over and over again, an unrelenting delirium of redundant images. I couldn't think of anything to say to Auggie, so I continued turning pages, nodding my head in feigned appreciation. Auggie himself seemed unperturbed, watching me with a broad smile on his face, but after I'd been at it for several minutes, he suddenly interrupted me and said, "You're going too fast. You'll never get it if you don't slow down."

He was right, of course. If you don't take the time to look, you'll never manage to see anything. I picked up another album and forced myself to go more deliberately. I paid closer attention to details, took note of shifts in the weather, watched for the changing angles of light as the seasons advanced. Eventually, I was able to detect subtle differences in the traffic flow, to anticipate the rhythm of the different days (the commotion of workday mornings, the relative stillness of weekends, the contrast between Saturdays and Sundays). And then, little by little, I began to recognize the faces of the people in the background, the passersby on their way to work, the same people in the same spot every morning, living an instant of their lives in the field of Auggie's camera.

Once I got to know them, I began to study their postures, the way they carried themselves from one morning to the next, trying to discover their moods from these surface indications, as if I could imagine stories for them, as if I could penetrate the invisible dramas locked inside their bodies. I picked up another album. I was no longer bored, no longer puzzled as I had been at first. Auggie was photographing time, I realized, both natural time and human time, and he was doing it by planting himself in one tiny corner of the world and willing it to be his own, by standing guard in the space he had chosen for himself. As he watched me pore over his work, Auggie continued to smile with pleasure. Then, almost as if he had been reading my thoughts, he began to recite a line from Shakespeare. "Tomorrow and tomorrow and tomorrow," he muttered under his breath, "time creeps on its petty pace." I understood then that he knew exactly what he was doing.

That was more than two thousand pictures ago. Since that day, Auggie and I have discussed his work many times, but it was only last week that I learned how he acquired his camera and started taking pictures in the first place. That was the subject of the story he told me, and I'm still struggling to make sense of it.

Earlier that same week, a man from the *New York Times* called me and asked if I would be willing to write a short story that would appear in the paper on Christmas morning. My first impulse was to say no, but the man was very charming and persistent, and by the end of the conversation I told him I would give it a try. The moment I hung up the phone, however, I fell into a deep panic. What did I know about Christmas? I asked myself. What did I know about writing short stories on commission?

I spent the next several days in despair, warring with the ghosts of Dickens, O. Henry and other masters of the Yuletide spirit. The very phrase "Christmas story" had unpleasant associations for me, evoking dreadful outpourings of hypocritical mush and treacle. Even at their best, Christmas stories were no more than wish-fulfillment dreams, fairy tales for adults, and I'd be damned if I'd ever allowed myself to write something like that. And yet, how could anyone propose to write an unsentimental Christmas story? It was a contradiction in terms, an impossibility, an out-and-out conundrum. One might just as well try to imagine a racehorse without legs, or a sparrow without wings.

I got nowhere. On Thursday I went out for a long walk, hoping the air would clear my head. Just past noon, I stopped in at the cigar store to replenish my supply, and there was Auggie, standing behind the counter as always. He asked me how I was. Without really meaning to, I found myself unburdening my troubles to him. "A Christmas story?" he said after I had finished. "Is that all? If you buy me lunch, my friend, I'll tell you the best Christmas story you ever heard. And I guarantee that every word of it is true."

We walked down the block to Jack's, a cramped and boisterous delicatessen with good pastrami sandwiches and photographs of old Dodgers teams hanging on the walls. We found a table at the back, ordered our food, and then Auggie launched into his story.

"It was the summer of seventy-two," he said. "A kid came in one morning and started stealing things from the store. He must have been about nineteen or twenty, and I don't think I've ever seen a more pathetic shoplifter in my life. He's standing by the rack of paperbacks along the far wall and stuffing books into the pockets of his raincoat. It was crowded around the counter just then, so I didn't see him at first. But once I noticed what he was up to, I started to shout. He took off like a jackrabbit, and by the time I managed to get out from behind the counter, he was already tearing down Atlantic Avenue. I chased after him for about half a block, and then I gave up. He'd dropped something along the way, and since I didn't feel like running anymore, I bent down to see what it was.

"It turned out to be his wallet. There wasn't any money inside, but his driver's license was there along with three or four snapshots. I suppose I could have called the cops and had him arrested. I had his name and address from the license, but I felt kind of sorry for him. He was just a measly little punk, and once I looked at those pictures in his wallet, I couldn't bring myself to feel very angry at him. Robert Goodwin. That was his name. In one of the pictures, I remember, he was standing with his arm around his mother or grandmother. In another one, he was sitting there at age nine or ten dressed in a baseball uniform with a big smile on his face. I just didn't have the heart. He was probably on dope now, I figured. A poor kid from Brooklyn without much going for him, and who cared about a couple of trashy paperbacks anyway?

"So I held onto the wallet. Every once in a while I'd get a little urge to send it back to him, but I kept delaying and never did anything about it. Then Christmas rolls around and I'm stuck with nothing to do. The boss usually invites me over to his house to spend the day, but that year he and his family were down in Florida visiting relatives. So I'm sitting in my apartment that morning feeling a little sorry for myself, and then I see Robert Goodwin's wallet lying on a shelf in the kitchen. I figure what the hell, why not do something nice for once, and I put on my coat and go out to return the wallet in person.

"The address was over in Boerum Hill, somewhere in the projects. It was freezing out that day, and I remember getting lost a few times trying to find the right building. Everything looks the same in that place, and you keep going over the same ground thinking you're somewhere else. Anyway, I finally get to the apartment I'm looking for and ring the bell. Nothing happens. I assume no one's there, but I try again just to make sure. I wait a little longer, and just when I'm about to give up, I hear someone shuffling to the door. An old woman's voice asks who's there, and I say I'm looking for Robert Goodwin. 'Is that you, Robert?' the old woman says, and then she undoes about fifteen locks and opens the door.

"She has to be at least eighty, maybe ninety years old, and the first thing I notice about her is that she's blind. 'I knew you'd come, Robert,' she says. 'I knew you wouldn't forget your Granny Ethel on Christmas.' And then she opens her arms as if she's about to hug me.

"I didn't have much time to think, you understand. I had to say something real fast, and before I knew what was happening, I could hear the words coming out of my mouth. 'That's right, Granny Ethel,' I said. 'I came back to see you on Christmas.' Don't ask me why I did it. I don't have any idea. Maybe I didn't want to disappoint her or something, I don't know. It just came out that way, and then this old woman was suddenly hugging me there in front of the door, and I was hugging her back.

"I didn't exactly say that I was her grandson. Not in so many words, at least, but that was the implication. I wasn't trying to trick her, though. It was like a game we'd both decided to play—without having to discuss the rules. I mean, that woman *knew* I wasn't her grandson Robert. She was old and dotty, but she wasn't so far gone that she couldn't tell the difference between a stranger and her own flesh and blood. But it made her happy to pretend, and since I had nothing better to do anyway, I was happy to go along with her.

"So we went into the apartment and spent the day together. The place was a real dump, I might add, but what else can you expect from a blind woman who does her own housekeeping? Every time she asked me a question about how I was, I would lie to her. I told her I'd found a good job working in a cigar store, I told her I was about to get married, I told her a hundred pretty stories, and she made like she believed every one of them. 'That's fine, Robert,' she would say, nodding her head and smiling. 'I always knew things would work out for you.'

"After a while, I started getting pretty hungry. There didn't seem to be much food in the house, so I went out to a store in the neighborhood and brought back a mess of stuff. A precooked chicken, vegetable soup, a bucket of potato salad, a chocolate cake, all kinds of things. Ethel had a couple of bottles of wine stashed in her bedroom, and so between us we managed to put together a fairly decent Christmas dinner. We both got a little tipsy from the wine, I remember, and after the meal was over we went out to sit in the living room, where the chairs were more comfortable. I had to take a pee, so I excused myself and went to the bathroom down the hall. That's where things took yet another turn. It was ditsy enough doing my little jig as Ethel's grandson, but what I did next was positively crazy, and I've never forgiven myself for it.

"I go into the bathroom, and stacked up against the wall next to the shower, I see a pile of six or seven cameras. Brand-new thirty-five millimeter cameras, still in their boxes, top-quality merchandise. I figure this is the work of the real Robert, a storage place for one of his recent hauls. I've never taken a picture in my life, and I've certainly never stolen anything, but the moment I see those cameras sitting in the bathroom, I decide I want one of them for myself. Just like that. And without even stopping to think about it, I tuck one of the boxes under my arm and go back to the living room.

"I couldn't have been gone for more than a few minutes, but in that time Granny Ethel had fallen asleep in her chair. Too much Chianti, I suppose. I went into the kitchen to wash the dishes, and she slept on through the whole racket, snoring like a baby. There didn't seem to be any point in disturbing her, so I decided to leave. I couldn't even write a note to say good-bye, seeing that she was blind and all, and so I just left. I put her grandson's wallet on the table, picked up the camera again, and walked out of the apartment. And that's the end of the story."

"Did you ever go back to see her?" I asked.

"Once," he said. "About three or four months later. I felt so bad about stealing the camera, I hadn't even used it yet. I finally made up my mind to return it, but Ethel wasn't there anymore. I don't know what happened to her, but someone else had moved into the apartment, and he couldn't tell me where she was."

"She probably died."

"Yeah, probably."

"Which means that she spent her last Christmas with you."

"I guess so. I never thought of it that way."

"It was a good deed, Auggie. It was a nice thing you did for her."

"I lied to her, and then I stole from her. I don't see how you can call that a good deed."

"You made her happy. And the camera was stolen anyway. It's not as if the person you took it from really owned it."

"Anything for art, eh, Paul?"

"I wouldn't say that. But at least you've put the camera to good use."

"And now you've got your Christmas story, don't you?"

"Yes," I said. "I suppose I do."

I paused for a moment, studying Auggie as a wicked grin spread across his face. I couldn't be sure, but the look in his eyes at that moment was so mysterious, so fraught with the glow of some inner delight, that it suddenly occurred to me that he had made the whole thing up. I was about to ask him if he'd been putting me on, but then I realized he would never tell. I had been tricked into believing him, and that was the only thing that mattered. As long as there's one person to believe it, there's no story that can't be true.

"You're an ace, Auggie," I said. "Thanks for being so helpful."

"Any time," he answered, still looking at me with that maniacal light in his eyes. "After all, if you can't share your secrets with your friends, what kind of a friend are you?"

"I guess I owe you one."

"No you don't. Just put it down the way I told it to you, and you don't owe me a thing."

"Except the lunch."

"That's right. Except the lunch."

I returned Auggie's smile with a smile of my own, and then I called out to the waiter and asked for the check.

CONTRIBUTORS

P A U L   A U S T E R is the author of *Mr. Vertigo, Leviathan, The Music of Chance, Moon Palace, In the Country of Last Things,* and the three novels known as "The New York Trilogy." He has won literary fellowships from the National Endowment for the Arts in both poetry and prose, and in 1990 received the Morton Dauwen Zabel Award from the American Academy and Institute of Arts and Letters. He lives in Brooklyn with his wife and two children.

R I C K   B A S S is the author of *Platte River,* a collection of novellas, and a forthcoming story collection, *In the Loyal Mountains.* He is also the author of five books of natural history. He is working on a novel, *Where the Sea Used to Be.* His stories have been anthologized in *Best American Short Stories, 1988, 1991, 1992; Prize Stories 1989: The O. Henry Awards; The Pushcart Prize, XIII, XV,* and *XVIII.* He lives on a remote ranch in northern Montana with his wife and daughter.

C Y N T H I A   B A U G H M A N received her M.F.A. in Creative Writing from Cornell University and teaches screenwriting at Ithaca College in upstate New York. She has published film criticism and is currently at work on a novel, *What You Pay For.*

A M Y   B L O O M is the author of the collection *Come to Me,* which was a finalist for the National Book Award. Her stories have appeared in *Antaeus, Story, Best American Short Stories, 1991* and *1992,* and *Prize Stories 1993: The O. Henry Awards.* She has also published fiction and non-fiction in the *New Yorker.* She lives in Durham, Connecticut.

L A R R Y   B R O W N   is the author of *Facing the Music, Big Bad Love,* and *Joe.* He lives and writes in Mississippi.

R I C H A R D   C U R R E Y   is the author of a novel, *Fatal Light,* and a short-story collection, *The Wars of Heaven.* His stories have won both O. Henry and Pushcart prizes, and appeared in *Best American Short Stories, 1988* and *New American Short Stories.* He is a two-time National Endowment for the Arts Fellowship recipient in both poetry and fiction.

S T E P H E N   D I X O N 's tenth story collection was published in January 1994. *The Stories of Stephen Dixon,* compiled from twelve of his books, was published in April 1994. *Interstate,* his sixth novel, was published in December, 1994. His novel *Frog* was a National Book Award Finalist in 1991 and a PEN/Faulkner Fiction Finalist in 1992.

C L Y D E   E D G E R T O N   is the author of five novels, *Raney, Walking across Egypt, The Floatplane Notebooks, Killer Diller,* and *In Memory of Junior.* He was recently awarded a Guggenheim Fellowship and a Lyndhurst Prize. He is also chief pilot for Dusty's Air Taxi, based in Durham, North Carolina, where he lives with his wife and daughter.

M O L L Y   G I L E S 's collection of stories, *Rough Translations,* won the Flannery O'Connor Award for Short Fiction and the Boston Globe Award. Recent stories have appeared in *The Pushcart Prize, XVII* and *XVIII, Witness,* and *The Tampa Review.* She is an NEA grant recipient and recent PEN Syndicated Fiction Contest winner. She teaches Creative Writing at San Francisco State University.

E L I Z A B E T H   G R A V E R   is the author of a collection of stories, *Have You Seen Me?,* which was awarded the 1991 Drue Heinz Prize. Her stories have appeared in *Best American Short Stories, 1991,* and *Prize Stories 1994: The O. Henry Awards,* as well as in *Antaeus, Story, Southern Review, Southwest Review,* and elsewhere. Currently she is a visiting assistant professor of English at Boston College.

A. M. H O M E S is the author of the novels *Jack* and *In a Country of Mothers* and the story collection *The Safety of Objects*. The recipient of numerous awards, she teaches writing at Columbia University and lives in New York City.

J I M H U M E S grew up in San Antonio, Texas. He has received the Henfield *Transatlantic Review* Award, the Katherine Anne Porter Award, and the Wilner Award for his short stories. He lives in San Francisco and is currently at work on a novel.

D A V I D M I C H A E L K A P L A N is the author of a novel, *Skating in the Dark,* and a collection of stories entitled *Comfort.* His short stories have been anthologized in *Best American Short Stories, 1986* and *Prize Stories 1990: The O. Henry Awards,* and have appeared in the *Atlantic Monthly, Redbook, Playboy, Triquarterly,* the *Ohio Review,* and other publications. He lives in Chicago.

R A N D A L L K E N A N was raised in North Carolina. He is the author of *A Visitation of Spirits* and *Let the Dead Bury Their Dead.* He teaches writing at Sarah Lawrence College and Columbia University. He lives in New York City.

B A R B A R A K I N G S O L V E R is a writer of fiction, nonfiction, and poetry. Her best-selling works of fiction include *The Bean Trees, Homeland, Animal Dreams,* and *Pigs in Heaven.* She lives in Tucson, Arizona.

D A V I D K R A N E S 's recent fiction has appeared in *Esquire* and *Story.* His plays have been produced at Manhattan Theater Club, Mark Taper Forum, Actors' Theater of Louisville, and Long Wharf Theater.

J O H N L ' H E U R E U X 's most recent books are *The Shrine at Altamira, A Woman Run Mad, Comedians,* and *An Honorable Profession.* He was twice awarded fellowships by the National Endowment for the Arts. He is the Lane Professor of Humanities and teaches English at Stanford University.

M A R G O T L I V E S E Y has taught at Tufts University, Carnegie Mellon, Williams College, and Boston University, and has recently been in residence at the Iowa Writers' Workshop. She is the author of a novel, *Homework,* and a collection of short fiction, *Learning by Heart.* She lives in Boston and London.

R E Y N O L D S P R I C E has written many novels, short stories, plays, poems, essays, and screenplays. His nine novels include *A Long and Happy Life,* National Book Critics Circle Award winner *Kate Vaiden,* and the recent *Blue Calhoun.* He is James B. Duke Professor of English at Duke University and a member of the American Academy of Arts and Letters.

W I L L I A M H. S H O R E is founder and executive director of Share Our Strength, one of the nation's largest nonprofit hunger relief organizations, based in Washington, D.C. He is the editor of several anthologies of short fiction and science essays whose proceeds benefit Share Our Strength's hunger relief programs.

L E E S M I T H is the author of eight novels, including *Fair and Tender Ladies, Oral History,* and *Family Linen,* as well as two collections of short stories, *Cakewalk* and *Me and My Baby View the Eclipse.* She has twice been winner of the O. Henry Award and has also won the John Dos Passos Prize for Literature. She lives in Chapel Hill, North Carolina.

W. D. W E T H E R E L L is the author of eight books, including a short-story collection, *The Man Who Loved Levittown,* and the novel *Chekhov's Sister.* His new novel, *The Wisest Man in America,* is due out in 1995, and he is currently at work on a new collection of stories. He lives in rural New Hampshire.

T O B I A S W O L F F is the author of *This Boy's Life* and other books. His short stories appear frequently in *Harper's,* the *Atlantic Monthly, Esquire,* and other publications. He teaches at Syracuse University and lives in Syracuse, New York, with his wife and their three children.